ule

Katie Flynn has lived for many years in the north-west. A compulsive writer, she started with short stories and articles and many of her early stories were broadcast on Radio Merseyside. She decided to write her Liverpool series after hearing the reminiscences of family members about life in the city in the early years of the twentieth century. She also writes as Judith Saxton. For the past few years, she has had to cope with ME but has continued to write.

Also available by Katie Flynn

KATIE FLYNN

A Christmas Candle

arrow books

1 3 5 7 9 10 8 6 4 2

Arrow Books
20 Vauxhall Bridge Road
London SW1V 2SA

Arrow Books is part of the Penguin Random House group of companies
whose addresses can be found at global.penguinrandomhouse.com.

Penguin
Random House
UK

First published in Great Britain by Century in 2017
First published in paperback by Arrow Books in 2017

www.penguin.co.uk

A CIP catalogue record for this book is available from the British Library.

ISBN 9781784755232

Typeset in 13/16.5pt Palatino LT Std by Jouve (UK), Milton Keynes
Printed and bound in Great Britain by Clays Ltd, St Ives Plc

MIX
Paper from
responsible sources
FSC
www.fsc.org
FSC® C018179

Penguin Random House is committed to a
sustainable future for our business, our readers
and our planet. This book is made from Forest
Stewardship Council® certified paper.

For Geoff and Dorothy Chetwynd and their
feathered friends, not forgetting the bees!

Acknowledgements

I have had a dreadful year healthwise, and am still suffering from shingles, which scrambles one's brain in a very nasty way, and which has meant both friends and colleagues have had to work twice as hard as usual to keep my work on track. If I acknowledged everyone personally I should need half a book, but my editor Nancy Webber, my agent Caroline Sheldon, and my new in-house editor Viola Hayden, along with my daughter Holly Pemberton and my secretary Jo Prince deserve a special mention as they have all worked uncomplainingly to right the wrongs and check every word.

Still, I have great hopes that 2017 will be a better year since my Australian grandchildren hope to come over to Britain to help us celebrate our Diamond Wedding!

Prologue

The woman sitting in the back seat of the taxi cab was old; very old. Bert, who had been driving his taxi now for the best part of thirty years, was a connoisseur of the old. They used his cab to take them shopping, or for a weekly trip to the cinema, or a visit to relatives. They liked to chat as he drove, often preferring to sit in the front seat beside him, for most of them were a trifle deaf and found it easier to converse when their heads were more or less on the same level. By now Bert knew most of their names and could have recited those of their children and grandchildren, about whom he had heard a great deal. His passengers liked to discuss their problems with someone not involved and sometimes asked for advice, though he guessed it was seldom taken. Not that Bert minded the gossip; in fact it made his job more interesting. He quite pitied drivers who knew nothing about their fares and cared less.

But this old woman was different. She was a stranger, for a start, and her voice betrayed no hint of the warm burr of a Devonshire accent. He had picked her up at the railway station and had agreed to take her to a farm out on the Moorfield Road, although it was not an area with which he was particularly familiar. At first he had tried to inaugurate some sort of conversation, but he supposed this was one passenger who did not want to talk, for she had climbed into the back and now sat on the worn leather seat gazing absorbedly through the window as they left the suburbs of the small town and reached the countryside.

Bert hummed a tune beneath his breath and drove slowly. It was a glorious day and the breeze coming in through his window carried the scents of summer. Presently, he knew, the Moorfield Road would meet the main Neot road, so if the farm she wanted really was on the Moorfield Road her journey would soon be over. He slowed still further and twisted round in his seat to glance at his fare.

'This here junction ahead of us is where Moorfield comes to an end,' he said loudly. 'Have we passed Drake's Farm? It was a Drake's Farm you was wantin', wasn't it?'

The old lady nodded. 'Drake's Farm,' she confirmed. 'It's back off the road a way. Perhaps I missed the turning, but . . . ah, no, here it is. Stop here, please.'

Obediently, Bert drew his cab to a halt. He climbed out to give his passenger a hand, but she was staring past him and he turned to follow her gaze. He could see a rough – very rough – track, rutted and overhung by trees which arched overhead, but no sign of any sort of dwelling. He looked doubtfully back at the woman but she was already standing by the car, unclipping her purse. She had asked him about his charges when she had first got into his cab and Bert had guessed an amount which would cover the twelve miles. Now he glanced at the clock on the dashboard and named a sum which was slightly less than he had quoted. She took the money from her purse, plus a generous tip, and placed it in his hand. He thanked her, then cleared his throat.

'I see there's a lane which must lead to the farm you're looking for,' he said rather hesitantly, 'but I'm afraid I can't take the car up there. Is it far to walk?' He was struck by a sudden recollection. 'This must be the back way. I remember it was used many, many years ago, but I can take you round to the front if you like. It won't cost no more – it's just a matter of turning left at the junction and then left again. Here, I'll show you; I keep a map in the glove compartment. I doubt if this lane's shown, but the main road certainly is. Hang on a mo . . .'

She shook her head and gave him a charming smile, making it plain without words that she appreciated his feeling that she should not be left standing at the road-side. 'I've got a mobile phone, and anyway they're meeting me here,' she said, crossing her fingers behind her back as she did so. 'Well, a little bit further up the lane – only I'm earlier than I should have been. No point in going round to the front.'

'Oh, I see,' Bert said, feeling relieved. Today was his day for the school run and though taking his fare to the other end of the lane would only take a few moments he had never been late for the kids yet. He slipped back into the car and wound down his window, about to lean out and remind her that he had given her his card and if she wanted him to return for her she only had to ring the number. He opened his mouth and then realised he would be speaking to himself; the old lady had disappeared. He looked round wildly. The purple and pink of foxgloves and dog roses and tall grasses swaying gently in the breeze met his eyes, but of his passenger there was no sign. Bert turned on the engine and selected first gear, telling himself ruefully that she was pretty nippy for an old 'un. He drove a short way to the nearest point at which he could perform a three point turn, glancing up the rutted lane as he passed, but there was no sign of her. She had disappeared as completely as though she had never been. Bert fished in his side pocket and produced a tin of curiously strong mints. He wondered how she knew the folk from Drake's Farm, then decided it was none of his business. Doubtless they were friends or relatives and she would be well looked after, for Devon folk were hospitable by nature, and since she was being met she must have warned them of her coming before setting out. Satisfied, he popped a peppermint into his mouth, then speeded up a little. After all, though the kids were often late for him, he had no intention of ever being late for them.

The old woman sat on the bank above the limpid waters of the stream and thought about the past. She could almost hear the splashes as young feet jumped into the water. She closed her eyes, willing memory to come to her aid. Where should she start? She could still remember her first sight of the stream, the day Mummy had brought her to the farm for the first time; and later, the glimpse of Johnny Durrell's usually dirty face framed by the leaves of the tallest apple tree in the orchard . . .

But it hadn't really started with that. She had often dreamed of the farm and the happy band of evacuees who lived there, but dreams and memory are two separate things and today was for remembering. Go back, she told herself. Right back, to the moment when we got on the train meaning to join Daddy in Plymouth.

Chapter One

September 1939

Eve had been gazing through the window with lack-lustre eyes as the train on which she was travelling with her mother and her little brother Chrissie chugged slowly through the great city of London, but when it arrived at New Cross station she sat up straight and jerked her mother's sleeve.

'Mummy! Have you ever seen so many children? There are some grown-ups, but only one or two, and they look like workmen of some sort.' Eve shook her mother's arm again. 'Do look, Mummy. If Nanny Burton were here she'd say all those boys and girls were the great unwashed, only Daddy said that was rude and I should never repeat it.'

Eleanor Armstrong shook her daughter's hand off her sleeve and frowned pettishly. She adored her son, of course she did, but he was quite a weight and for the hundredth time she wished she had managed to retain the services of Nanny Burton. She ought to have been the one carrying Chrissie and answering Eve's questions. However, Nanny Burton was not present, having left the previous week to keep house for her niece, who had taken a job in a munitions factory, and Eleanor was having to cope alone.

'Mummy? What are the children doing? Are they going to get on our train? I hope they don't want to come in here – they'll wake Chrissie and he'll start to cry again.'

Eleanor heaved a sigh. A guard was pressing his way amongst the children, opening carriage doors as he went, and she had a horrid feeling that the compartment she had bribed a porter to reserve for them would soon be invaded. But the train could not possibly hold the great mass of children on the platform and she said as much, adding that she hoped Eve would behave herself like a little lady and sit quietly in her corner seat.

'And you needn't imagine that I intend to allow that rabble to squeeze in with us,' she added. 'They are what are being called "evacuees", you know, getting out of London before the war gets into its stride.'

'Like us!' Eve said chirpily. 'We're getting out of London before the war starts properly, Daddy said so.' She gazed into her mother's beautiful, carefully made-up face. 'Isn't that right, Mummy? Aren't we evacuees as well?'

Eleanor sighed. 'No we are not,' she said decidedly. 'Daddy wants us to be safe, but near him as well. He's found nice lodgings for us not far from Plymouth, so that's where we're going, and whenever his ship docks he'll join us there. And now will you kindly stop asking questions? If you watch you can see that only a small number of the evacuees are getting aboard our train. The rest will go on another one later, I suppose.'

But Eve was no longer attending to her mother. The guard was returning along the length of the train, slamming the doors shut, and Eve was about to sit back in her seat when a boy in long trousers and a blazer stopped directly outside their open window. He had fair hair which flopped across his forehead, and when he saw her looking at him he pulled the rudest face Eve had ever seen, banged on the glass and said loudly enough for her to hear: 'We're gettin' on a better train than this one. This one's for kids. Us older ones is goin' to the country, so yah boo and sucks to you!'

Eve drew in an indignant breath, then glanced towards her mother. Eleanor was not looking in her direction so Eve stuck her tongue out and whispered clearly, 'Sucks to you as well then. It's a good thing my mummy didn't hear you, or you'd be in trouble.' She hoped to wipe the grin off the boy's face, but even as the last words left her lips his grin merely widened.

'Stupid girl!' he said. 'Just as well I'm not getting aboard your train, or I'd come along to your compartment and give you a bloody nose.'

Eve gasped. She knew 'bloody' was a very rude word indeed, but before she could retaliate her mother grabbed her by one long fair plait and almost flung her back into her seat.

'What do you think you're doing?' Eleanor Armstrong said as the door to the compartment opened and four or five children filed in and began to take their places on the empty row of seats. 'If that's how Nanny

Burton allowed you to behave I'm glad she's left us. And now you've gone and woken Chrissie as well as upsetting your mummy. I'm ashamed of you; I never thought you would be so naughty.'

Eve opened her mouth to apologise as the train began to move forward, but the words 'I'm sorry' refused to come. 'He started it, Mummy,' she said defensively, pointing at the window. 'And anyway, Chrissie isn't taking any notice, he's too busy watching the evacuees.'

Eleanor frowned. 'Don't answer me back, miss, just you sit tight until we change trains. Daddy thought you would be a help to me on our journey, but I mean to tell him you've been nothing of the sort. No, don't say anything. I dare say Chrissie will be more assistance to his mummy than you've been.'

Eve leaned back in her seat, biting her lip. She *had* been a great help to her mother when they had boarded the train, but of course that would all be forgotten. Daddy would be told that it was Mummy who had held the tickets and hailed the porter, not to mention persuading Chrissie to get up whilst it was still dark and eat a breakfast of soggy cornflakes with a glass of milk, and thanking Mr Rogers, the caretaker of the block of flats in which the Armstrongs had lived ever since Eve could remember, before they left the building. Then there had been the wait for the taxi to the station, which Eve had enlivened for Chrissie by singing him songs and nursery rhymes. Mummy would be so keen to tell Daddy that Chrissie had been a positive angel that she would not give a thought to her daughter. I'm only nine; lots of girls of nine would not have helped half as much as I have, Eve thought indignantly. But perhaps Daddy would give her a hug and say he knew she must have been a great help because she was Daddy's girl, his favourite person next to Mummy, and he knew she would have done everything in her power to see that they reached his side as soon as possible. But at this point Chrissie, who had been staring at the other children in round-eyed amazement, began to jabber and point at the small satchel which he knew held chocolate bars. With a resigned sigh, Eleanor reached for the bag where it lay on the string rack above their heads.

'You may have one small bar,' she told him firmly. 'They have to last us until we reach Daddy, and that may be some time. And you mustn't get chocolate all over your face and hands; Daddy would be angry if I turned up with a chocolatey son.'

Eve watched with watering mouth as her brother snatched a chocolate bar from the satchel, tore the wrapper from the chocolate and cast it on to the floor. Looking around her, she saw that hers was not the only mouth that watered; if the evacuees had food with them she supposed it would be something boring like sandwiches. She remembered Daddy telling Mummy quite severely that she should not give Chrissie chocolate on the journey.

'If it doesn't make him sick, which it probably will, then he'll get covered in it,' he had said. 'Do you hear me, Ellie? He mustn't have chocolate. It would only make him thirsty anyway.'

'No chocolate,' Eleanor had agreed, dimpling at her husband. 'You are cruel, Bill! Waking him up and giving him his breakfast at five in the morning is going to be next to impossible unless I can bribe him with chocolate, and kindly do not call me Ellie,' she had added, fluttering her lashes. 'I wish you were able to come with us. You say that's impossible, though why you can't ask for leave . . .'

Eve remembered how for one moment the look of indulgent affection on her father's face had been replaced by a sort of weary annoyance. 'Darling heart, you must try to understand that war changes everything. No one will be able to get leave whenever they feel inclined. By the time you have arranged for the flat to be shut up and so on and are ready to come down to Plymouth, I may well be at sea. And you know I've had to sell the car now I've nowhere to keep it, so even if I'd got shore leave for some reason I wouldn't be able to pack you and the kids into the car and simply drive off into the wide blue yonder, the way we did on that last holiday.'

Just the memory of that wonderful holiday brought a smile to Eve's lips and made her forget that Mummy was showing, once more, how she regarded her daughter. Eve was quite as fond of chocolate as Chrissie, yet it had not occurred to her mother to offer her one of the bars with which the satchel was crammed. I could ask, of course, Eve told herself, watching enviously as Chrissie clutched the satchel closer to his chest and made the sort of growling noise that a dog makes when he thinks you mean to steal his bone. But asking would only make Mummy cross and besides, if I tried to take even the tiniest bar Chrissie would scream the place down, and I'd probably get into trouble all over again. But the train was slowing as it approached Waterloo station and Mummy seemed to have forgotten about the satchel and its contents. They had a big cabin trunk and two suitcases stowed away in the guard's van, and Eve imagined it would be her job to find a porter, discover from which platform the next train left, and go with the luggage to the new train, though it would be Mummy who handed out money when they got there. Better not to mention chocolate bars, then, or Chrissie's clutch on the satchel. She offered to sling it round her shoulders for ease of carrying, but apparently he suspected that such an innocent move might end in his losing it altogether, so she said nothing more, not even when Eleanor pulled her white velvet vanity case down from the rack and thrust it quite painfully into her daughter's arms.

'Stay with Chrissie and take good care of him,' she commanded. 'Show the tickets to any official who asks to see them but never give them up.' And then, as the train jerked to a halt, 'Ah, we've arrived. Stay as close to me as you can, children, and keep your eyes peeled for Auntie Ruby. She promised to come to the station if she possibly could, to help us with the luggage and so on. Oh, Chrissie love, you've got chocolate all over your face! What *would* Daddy say? And I promised him I'd not bring chocolate. Will you let me carry it for you – just as far as the cloakroom, you know? Then Eve can clean you up whilst I check our bags.'

Eve sighed, but knew it was no good complaining. Mummy had loved her once, Daddy said so, so it must be true; and according to Daddy she loves me still, Eve told herself rather dubiously, seizing Chrissie's hand. Oh, I do hope Auntie Ruby comes in time to help us get aboard the next train. What if we should miss it? And then there'll be a taxi at the other end, and the driver won't want a boy covered in chocolate in his nice clean cab. How I wish Daddy was here and not somewhere out at sea, because Mummy will expect me to look after Chrissie on my own and he's so obstinate and difficult.

Trying to look back, Eve wondered whether she had been as self-willed as Chrissie when she was his age, but she thought not. Why should she be difficult when her beloved daddy understood her so well? But that had been before Chrissie, when, according to Nanny Burton, Eve's mother had spoiled her too, just as Daddy did now.

It had been nice to be the favoured child and she supposed she should not grumble because Chrissie had taken her place. She sighed. One ought to love one's baby brother and take pains to help him in any way one could, but in her secret heart Eve did not even like Chrissie, far less love him. Oh, she pretended like anything, put on a good face, praised his golden-haired prettiness, but in her heart, deeply buried, she hated the little beast.

But now Mummy was ushering her out of the compartment to join the queue of people in the corridor heading for the nearest door.

'There's Auntie Ruby,' Eve said suddenly, stopping dead as she spotted her aunt's bush of tangled hair through the window. 'Oh, thank goodness. Chrissie

14

will let Auntie Ruby wash his face, because he's frightened of her.' She picked her little brother up, satchel and all, and made him wave to Auntie Ruby as the queue of disembarking passengers shuffled past behind them.

When at last they descended on to the platform their aunt whisked Chrissie up and sat him on her hip, ignoring his grizzling and smiling cheerfully at Eve. 'Your mum has given this child chocolate,' she announced needlessly, for one glance at Chrissie's face proved the truth of the statement. 'You're a good little lass; I see you've got your mum's vanity case. Well, you hang on to that whilst I clean the young master up. You'd better come with me, because we don't want to get separated. Your mother's gone to find a porter – we're meeting her in the buffet so you can get yourselves something to drink before you board the Exeter train.'

'The Exeter train?' Eve said. 'But we're going to Plymouth.'

Auntie Ruby looked surprised. 'Don't say your mother didn't tell you? You're spending one night, or possibly two, in Exeter before going on to your lodgings. Your father's decided that Plymouth, being a very important port, is no place for his family in wartime.'

'Where *are* we going, then? After Exeter, I mean?' Eve asked, thinking that it was typical of her mother not to admit that their destination had changed. 'Oh, Auntie Ruby, I wish you were coming with us.'

Auntie Ruby chuckled as she ushered the two children into the ladies' cloakroom. 'I have work to do here,' she said. 'As for where you're going, you wouldn't know where it was even if I told you.' She took the satchel from Chrissie, and when he wailed a protest and tried to snatch it back she gave him what Eve considered to be a well-deserved slap. 'Behave yourself!' she said sharply. 'Your train leaves in twenty minutes and if I have to spend all that time cleaning you up, young man, spend it I will.'

Despite Eve's fears, the transfer from the train to a small boarding house in Exeter had been far simpler than she had imagined. Mummy had been at her most charming, praising the town, the lodgings and their landlady, who was clearly fond of children and thought Chrissie adorable, admiring his curls, his big blue eyes and his delightful manners; for like his mother, Eve thought resentfully, he could turn his charm on and off to suit every occasion.

And there had been no difficulty in finding a taxi driver who would pick them up the next morning and take them to Drake's Farm, where Daddy had arranged for them to stay. Chrissie had pouted but Eve had felt a lift of the heart. So they were to stay on a farm, a real farm, one with pigs and chickens, and cows and horses – all the things she had read about, in short, but had never seen.

'Farms is the best place for children in wartime,' Mrs Edge, the Exeter landlady, had told Eleanor wisely. 'I don't know this Drake's Farm, but then I wouldn't, would I, if it's closer to Plymouth than here? But all farms is alike when you come down to it, and probably just what your children need, I don't doubt. You say your husband chose it? Well there you are then.'

Eve had opened her mouth to say the original plan had been to go all the way to Plymouth, then closed it again. Mummy hated it when she showed she had been listening to a conversation. Best play safe; Eve grinned to herself. 'Lay low and say nuffin',' as Uncle Remus had put it, 'and you won't go far wrong.'

But Mrs Edge and her comfortable little house were already part of the past, and right now Eve was seated beside her mother, with Chrissie on Eleanor's lap, watching the green and gold countryside pass by. She had entered the taxi whilst Mummy had been discussing the fare and so had missed any mention of how long this journey would take, which was unfortunate since it seemed to her to be a very long time indeed. She jerked her mother's sleeve, wanting to remind Eleanor that she was not a good traveller, but her mother was staring out of the window, a frown creasing her brow. Then she leaned forward and tapped the driver on the shoulder.

'How much further is it?' she said, making it plain from her tone that she had not realised how far they would have to go. 'I know you said it was a fair way but surely we must be almost there?'

The driver slowed and swivelled in his seat to give his passengers an amused look. He was a young man with bright ginger hair and a face full of freckles. When he smiled Eve saw that he had a front tooth missing.

'Another couple of miles, I dare say; mebbe three,'

he said jovially. 'But these country roads aren't kept up the way the main roads are, which makes it seem longer.'

Eleanor sank back in her seat. 'Well, I suppose we can put up with three more miles so long as it's not any further,' she said grudgingly.

Eve sighed. One of her many faults, according to Mummy, was her inability to travel by car without at some stage having to abandon ship or be sick. The journey had not been so bad whilst the taxi pootled along the smooth main road, but they had left that some time ago and Eve was beginning to feel distinctly queasy. Three more miles of this! There were potholes and bends, puddles and other obstacles, and though the countryside was beautiful it was also growing wilder by the minute. Eve cast a despairing glance at her mother; Eleanor knew her daughter's weakness and would surely take pity on her. If they could stop for a few minutes she could be sick in the ditch which she had noticed running alongside the road, but if she said nothing . . .

'Almost there now,' the taxi driver said cheerfully. 'We turn left here and the farm's about a mile up the lane. Oh . . .' He braked sharply, surveying in some dismay the deep ruts and untrimmed hedges that lined the track he had been about to turn in to. 'Well, I can't take the taxi up there. 'Twasn't meant for anything but horse-drawn traffic, clearly, and very little of that.' He grinned at them. ''Tis only a mile. 'Twon't take you above fifteen minutes if you step out.'

He drew the car to a halt, got out of his seat and went

round to the rear passenger door. 'I'll knock a bob or two off the fare, seeing as how you'll have to walk the last bit,' he said.

But her mother shook her head firmly. 'How can you be so foolish?' she said scornfully. 'We've two large cases and the cabin trunk and we only hired you because you had a trailer for our bags. You can't expect me to tackle that lane with two children and all that luggage. Kindly get back in the car so that we may all continue our journey.'

Eve was fighting her own particular battle – she could feel her breakfast heaving around inside her tummy – but she had heard the annoyance in her mother's voice; clearly Eleanor had decided that this man would respond better to bullying than to charm. But the taxi driver only grinned more broadly.

'It's all right, missus, I was only having a bit of a joke with you,' he said. 'This is the back way, seemingly. I'll drive you round to the front.' But even as Eleanor relaxed and began to smile the driver, who had ignored the children until now, suddenly pointed an accusing finger at Eve. 'You're car sick, aren't you?' he said, his tone so matter of fact that it did not occur to Eve or her mother to deny it, though Eve tried her best to hide the churning. 'Come you out of that.'

He seized her shoulder in a not unfriendly grip and pulled her out of the taxi. 'Oh aye, I can see all the signs and I won't have no kid throwing up in my cab, no matter how much you pay me.' He gave Eve an admonitory little shake, then addressed her. 'I can't say as I blame you for feeling a bit off, 'cos these roads are pretty rough, but you look like a healthy young woman. What are you – ten, twelve? If I take your mum, your baby brother and the luggage round to the front of this here Drake's Farm you can walk up the back way. You'll be there in no time and you won't have to put up with being shut in the taxi.'

'I'm nine,' Eve said, but she felt a glow of pride. Mummy might not value her or think her capable of finding her way up the steep lane without adult assistance, but the taxi driver had actually thought she was ten or twelve and therefore almost an adult herself.

Right now she was gazing at the lane, delighted to be out of the car and in the open air, yet secretly worried in case she should get lost between here and Drake's Farm. She said as much and the taxi driver patted her shoulder before climbing back into the driver's seat, winding down his window so that he might answer her.

'The only buildin', apart from Drake's Farm itself, is an ancient barn. If you just keep on walkin' you'll see the farm'ouse quick enough. Want to take your little brother along for company?'

Eve laughed. Her stomach was settling down and all of a sudden she felt excited rather than apprehensive, though the thought of being accompanied by Chrissie almost spoiled her pleasure in the sunny day. She shook her head decidedly.

'No thank you. I'd have to carry him, you see, as soon as he got tired or bored.' She lowered her voice. 'He hardly ever walks if he can help it. My daddy says he's terribly spoiled.' She would have gone on to explain that her mother never corrected Chrissie no matter how naughty he was, but Eleanor had opened her door and was clearly listening to every word her daughter uttered.

'Chrissie wants to come with you, Eve,' she announced firmly. 'It's only a mile; if you have to carry him for a bit, it won't hurt you. In fact it will probably be good for you to put yourself out for your little brother.'

Eve gathered all her courage and shook her head firmly. 'No, I won't take Chrissie. There are puddles and he isn't wearing wellies. Besides, I'm sure he'd rather go by car.'

Here she was proved wrong. Chrissie pointed at Eve and then at the lane, chuckling with anticipation and preparing to scramble off his mother's knee and into the warm September sunlight. Eve might have given in, but just in time the taxi driver gave her a friendly nudge.

'Off with you,' he said in a low voice. 'I bet that kid weighs a ton. Go on or your mum will nab you.'

Eve did not need telling twice. She hurried away from the taxi, pushing through the neglected verges and trying to ignore the screams with which Chrissie greeted the thwarting of his wishes. Within moments she was out of sight of the car, and alone. Above her, birds darted from one side of the lane to the other, somewhere in the distance a cow mooed, and presently she heard the taxi driver start his engine, its noise growing fainter as he continued on his way.

Eve gazed around her and thought she had never

21

seen anything so beautiful. A huge tree spread protective branches over her head, and telling herself that she
would be all the better for a bit of a sit-down she chose
a mossy log and perched on it to look around her. This
was a magic place, she thought, for in the roots of the
great tree there was dark mysterious water; she could
imagine a tiny person only a couple of inches high
sculling a small boat across the mirror stillness of the
pool. She wished she knew what the tree was called
and presently a name popped into her mind: it was a
beech, and the stuff that littered the ground around her
feet was beech mast. Eve frowned; how had she known
that? She supposed that at some stage or other they
had been taught the names of trees at school. She hoped
that whichever school she would now attend had
nature lessons.

She slid off the log, gave one last glance around her
and set off once again. With every step she took she felt
her surroundings becoming more familiar. Had she
been here before? If so, Daddy must have brought her,
because Mummy would never risk sullying her beautiful clothing or scratching the patent leather court shoes
with their narrow heels and cute little bows – cream
bows on black shoes – which were her present favourite footwear.

She heard the stream before she saw it and when she
did see it she felt she knew it as well as she knew the
great River Thames, beside which she had frequently
walked with Nanny Burton, pushing the baby Chrissie
in his pram.

But this river was nothing like the Thames, of course.

In fact Eve supposed it was not really a river at all, but what Daddy would have called a stream. But river or stream, it was as beautiful in its way as the great beeches. At this particular point it ran across the lane, gurgling over big flat stones, and it was easy to see that this was what Daddy would have called a ford, a place where cattle, people in wellington boots and even, she supposed, cars could cross. Eve leaned over the water and saw movement; she had hoped for mermaids but the little silver-gilt fish darting to and fro over the varied coloured stones were the next best thing, and anyway mermaids were sea creatures, not to be found in freshwater streams. She had peered into the depths of the Thames often enough and had never seen so much as a flicker of a fin, let alone a mermaid. But here in this enchanted place anything was possible.

Eve looked a little further upstream and saw the bridge. It was a wooden structure and not very wide, but she supposed that when the stream was swollen by winter rains anyone walking up this lane would have to use it. She hesitated. If she took her shoes and socks off she could cross by the ford, but that would mean replacing her socks on wet feet and she guessed how her mother would scold. Better to go by the bridge. She was halfway over when she remembered something else, and hesitated again. Daddy had told her the story of the three billy goats gruff, who had to cross the river in order to eat the sweet green grass which grew on the further bank. But the troll who lived under the bridge bounded out the moment he heard a footfall and announced his intention of eating the trespasser for supper.

Eve giggled, then leaned over the low parapet and glanced carefully at the tumbling water beneath. What a place for games! If she had to come this way to school she would make up a magic charm to keep the troll in his place, but though she might believe in mermaids – or half believe, rather – she knew that the troll was really just a fairy tale and would never pop out from his hiding place below the bridge to challenge all comers.

Sometimes I wonder if Mummy's right and I'm dreaming my life away, Eve told herself as she left the stream behind her and continued up the lane. Here it climbed between steep banks, banks so beautiful that Eve could not resist slowing her pace once more. She saw tiny flowers and cushions of moss, and in one particular spot a small plant which had a single red fruit dangling from it. One of Nanny Burton's stories popped into her mind, for Nanny had been a country girl and one day at nursery tea, when they had had delicious strawberries and cream, she had told Eve how she and her brother had once picked wild strawberries for their mother's birthday and how thrilled old Mrs Burton had been. Even the city-bred Eve had known that strawberries came in June and were well over by September, and she felt privileged that the little plant had saved one small fruit especially for her. Of course Mummy would say that the wild strawberry had not been saved for anyone, certainly not for her daughter, but so far as Eve was concerned the strawberry was for her alone and she agreed with Nanny Burton that its flavour far surpassed that of the larger cultivated sort.

Naturally enough she scanned the bank closely for several moments, but though she saw plenty of the small green leaves which belonged to the plant she saw no more fruit and presently, remembering how her mother hated being kept waiting, she abandoned the hunt and quickened her pace. She was aware that she must be nearing her destination, and when the lane took a turn to the left and the banks began to dwindle she saw Drake's Farm for the first time.

Eve stopped dead in her tracks, staring at the house which loomed before her. It was a long low building with a thatched roof, and was surrounded on three sides by what she took to be outbuildings. There were several windows set deep into the whitewashed walls of the house, and before it was a cobbled yard in which hens and other birds she did not recognise clucked and pecked. A wide farm gate separated the lane from the farmyard, and this was wide open. It was old and mossy, and even in one swift glance Eve saw enough to convince her that it was rarely closed. Since the lane appeared to lead nowhere but to Drake's Farm, she guessed that shutting the gate would be a mere formality.

And there was Mummy, holding Chrissie's hand in order, Eve realised, to stop him chasing the chickens, because when they went to Trafalgar Square to feed the pigeons his first action was always to rush amongst the feeding birds, trying to catch them and shouting with glee. He could get away with such behaviour in London because the pigeons did not belong to anybody in particular, but here, she guessed, the farmer and his wife would not appreciate a child who disturbed their flock. Next to her mother stood a large, rosy-cheeked woman in a print dress and a white apron. She had a mass of greying fair hair, shrewd brown eyes and a welcoming smile. Just behind her stood a young girl whom Eve judged to be about three or four years older than herself. She was a pretty girl, fair-haired and fragile. She wore a faded cotton dress and she gave Eve a conspiratorial grin. But Chrissie gave a delighted crow as soon as his eyes alighted on his sister, and he let out his well-known imitation of a train whistle.

'Evie!' he shouted. 'You was a long time. Mummy said you needed a smack to speed you up. We've been here hours and hours, just waiting for you. Oh, you are a naughty girl.'

'Don't be so silly, Chrissie; I came as fast as I could,' Eve said coldly. She turned to her mother. 'You said to keep my shoes clean and some parts of the lane are really muddy, so that's why it took me a bit longer.' But before Eleanor could deliver the scold Eve was sure was coming, the large rosy-cheeked woman who had been talking to her turned her head and spoke directly to Eve.

'Well, dearie? I'm Mrs Faversham, and you'll be young Eve. Your mum explained you're not a good traveller, and that's why you wanted to walk up the back way.' She chuckled. 'I dare say the exercise has made you hungry, so there's lunch set out in the dining

26

room, though as a rule we eats in the kitchen.' She gave Eve a broad smile. 'There's milk fresh from the cow to drink for you little 'uns, and when you've finished I'll get Mabel here to show you round the house.'

The lunch was glorious and the room allocated to the Armstrongs bright and airy. In fact the only incident to mar the afternoon occurred just as they were leaving the house to be shown round the farm, when Eleanor clapped a hand to her forehead and announced that she had forgotten where the bathroom was situated. Mrs Faversham raised her brows.

'Bathroom?' she echoed. 'We bain't on mains water, Mrs Armstrong; we uses the galvanised bath which hangs on the wall of the scullery. Very few farmhouses this way have bathrooms.'

'Oh,' Eleanor said faintly. 'And – and the lavatory?'

'Down the end of the garden,' Mabel butted in before the older woman could speak. 'And there are jerries in all the rooms – for night time, you know. We manage fine, don't we, Auntie Bess?'

'That's right, my handsome,' Mrs Faversham said. She turned to Eleanor and patted the other woman's slender shoulder. 'Mabel's staying here whilst this dratted war lasts, 'cos her pa's been sent to Plymouth and he reckons it'll be a dangerous place once them dratted Nazis start these here bombing raids we've heard tell of. He wanted her mother to come with her, but she chose to stay with him, and now she's gone and got herself a job of her own.' She smiled kindly at Eleanor, who was clearly still trying to come to terms with the lavatory at the bottom of the garden and the non-existent bathroom. 'I'll introduce you to everyone else when they comes in from the fields, but I can see you're a trifle shocked 'cos we don't run to mains water nor electric. Come back to the dining room and we'll have a cup of tea and a chat while our Mabel takes your youngsters round the farm.'

Eleanor made a little bleating sound which Mrs Faversham clearly took for agreement, for she turned back into the house, first informing the older girl that she must keep an eye on the little lad.

'Mabel's good with youngsters,' she told Eleanor. 'Go you off, Mabel dear. No need to take young Eve here back down the lane, nor Chrissie neither; just you concentrate on Drake's Farm itself. Time enough to see the village and the school and that, time enough.'

Mabel murmured an agreement, then took Chrissie's hand and led her companions across to what she informed them was the milking shed.

'We bring the cows in morning and evening and Uncle Reg or one or other of the land girls does the milking before they let the cows back out into one of the pastures.'

Eve looked round the dark and dusty interior. 'How many cows have you got?' she asked curiously. She looked at the stalls and the mangers. 'There's room here for six.'

Mabel laughed. 'The cows have to take it in turns to be milked,' she explained. 'Uncle Reg and the land girls take it in turns as well; if someone's on early milking they'll do mornings for a whole week, and if they're on evenings they'll do that for a week as well. I'm learning to milk too but I'm still very slow, though Uncle says I'll get faster the more I practise.' She giggled. 'Uncle Reg is slow in all sorts of ways. It's all very well for Auntie Bess; farming's in her blood, but Uncle Reg only came to the farm when her first husband died and she married him, and that was only ten years ago.'

'Oh,' Eve said rather inadequately. 'I sort of imagined that he'd been here all his life.'

Mabel laughed again. 'Why did you think it were called Drake's Farm?' she asked. 'Auntie Bess's first husband was a Drake, and you don't go changin' the name of a farm. Everyone for miles around knows it's the Favershams who own Drake's Farm, but they'd never dream of calling it Faversham's Farm.' She led them out of the milking shed and into the next building, which proved to contain a number of enormous farm vehicles. Mabel pointed out hay wains, a neat little carriage she called a trap and a large though ancient tractor. 'Cart shed; some of the stuff's old, but it all works . . .' she was beginning when Chrissie, whose hand she had still been holding, escaped from her grasp and headed for the farmyard.

'Come here, you naughty boy,' Mabel shouted, but Eve, knowing her little brother, did not waste breath on calling him but set off at once in pursuit, grabbing him just as he would have turned into the lane. She led him back to Mabel and began to apologise, but Mabel shook her head and gave Chrissie an admonitory slap. ''Twas none of your doing,' she said to Eve. 'We'll have to get your mother to keep her eye on this 'un.'

Chrissie opened his mouth to bawl but Mabel bent

down and addressed him directly. 'You're a big boy. You must be three or four – a good deal older than my little cousin Patrick, anyhow – and I'm telling you now that you'll get more slaps than kisses if you're naughty, because farmyards are dangerous places. Now, are you going to behave and come with your sister and me, or shall I take you back to the house where your mummy can deal with you?'

Eve gazed at Chrissie with awe. Two slaps in two days, administered by two different people who had made it plain that they would stand no nonsense from her little brother! Yesterday Auntie Ruby had smacked his trousered bottom, and now this girl had handed out another well-deserved reproof. But it appeared that despite the slap Chrissie for once preferred his sister's company to that of his mother.

'I'll come with you,' he said decidedly. 'Can I milk a cow?' As he spoke he grabbed Mabel's hand again, and though she laughed and told him it would be a few years yet before he was able to do anything really useful Chrissie appeared satisfied. 'I *will* be good,' he announced firmly. 'I will be *very* good. One day I will milk the cows and feed the pigeons and them other birds what have nice coloured feathers.'

Mabel laughed again, but shook her head. 'Time enough for all that,' she said cheerfully. 'Just you be a good boy and don't touch any of the animals or birds unless you're told you may. Even my little cousin Patrick knows better than to run about loose, disturbing the hens – they're hens, not pigeons – because the cockerel will attack if you upset his ladies. And if you're a good boy, a *really* good boy, I'll show you where the hens lay their eggs in the barn and you shall choose one of the eggs and have it for your breakfast tomorrow morning.'

Chrissie gave a little crow of glee. 'I shall have an egg, and soldier boy fingers,' he announced proudly. He looked up at Eve. '*You* shan't have an egg, 'cos you aren't a good boy.'

Eve giggled but Mabel did not seem to be amused. 'Don't you love your sister?' she asked incredulously. 'If you don't love her, then *you* aren't a good boy.'

Chrissie had been holding tightly to Mabel but had pushed Eve impatiently away when she had tried to take his other hand. Now, however, he snatched Eve's fingers and to her considerable surprise planted a moist kiss on her palm, then looked up at Mabel.

'Can Evie have an egg as well?' he asked anxiously. 'Must I share my egg with Evie, or can she have one of her own if I say I love her?'

He looked so enchantingly pretty as he raised worried eyes to Mabel's face that Eve was not surprised when the older girl laughed and nodded her head.

'We will *all* have an egg for our breakfasts if you go on being good,' she promised. 'And now we're going to meet the pigs in the sties, the two calves in their pen, the sheep in the fields and the new foal, Conker. I named her that because she's the colour of a ripe chestnut just out of its prickly shell,' she added proudly. 'Uncle Reg says I can break her in when she's old enough. She knows me already and comes to the gate the moment I appear because she knows I'll bring her a lump of sugar or a piece of apple.'

Chrissie was fascinated by the two pigs, both of whom had ten or twelve piglets and came snorting to the trough in the hopes of an early supper. For once in her life Eve was glad of Chrissie's company, since she was as ignorant as he and did not want Mabel to guess that the animals were as much a novelty to her as to her small brother. She had never realised that mother pigs – sows, Mabel called them – were so huge, nor their babies so small. The sows were not at all careful about where they planted their feet, but Mabel explained that the piglets were several weeks old and had learned to keep well clear of their mothers' careless tread. Chrissie had to be lifted up to see into the sties and chuckled and crowed when the sows looked hopefully up, eager for the apples with which Mabel had stuffed her pockets, guessing that she would be asked to conduct the Armstrongs around the premises.

But when they left the pigs behind and approached the long sloping pasture, and the mare and her foal came galloping towards the gate, Chrissie shrieked with fright and insisted that either Mabel or Eve should take him to a place of safety. Eve snatched him up, for in her secret heart she understood and sympathised with his fear, but one glance at Mabel's face convinced her that they were perfectly safe. And indeed, the wooden fence looked strong and the horses came to a halt several feet short of it. Mabel leaned over the gate and held out an enticing hand, and after no more than a whickering whinny the mare led her foal over to where they stood. Chrissie, however, still resisted any attempt to detach his tight grasp from round his sister's neck, and perhaps he was right, for as soon as the apple was finished the horses moved away and their place was taken by an enormous flock of large birds heading purposefully towards them. Chrissie twisted in Eve's arms.

'Swans!' he exclaimed. 'Does we have some bread for them? I threw bread to the swans when Nanny Burton took us to the park.'

Eve stared. They were certainly large enough to be swans, and yet . . . and yet . . .

Mabel turned and grabbed Eve's hand. 'They're geese, not swans,' she explained briefly. 'We don't want to mix with them; they really are spiteful. They're usually in the orchard or round the pond. Something must have disturbed them, but I don't think we'll linger here. Those big orange beaks can deal you a nasty blow. Come on!'

She led Eve at a smart pace down the hill towards a cluster of trees spangled with fruit of various types and colours, and presently the geese, who had chased them a short way, abandoned the pursuit so that the girls and Chrissie could enter the orchard unmolested.

'We're allowed to eat the windfalls,' Mabel said. 'We don't pick the fruit off the trees, of course, though some of it's ready, but the windfalls are just as good. There are earlies from a variety called Beauty of Bath which are really sweet. This way – the garden comes down to the edge of the trees and you'll want to see the lavvy so you can tell your mother that it's perfectly respectable and easy to access. You just have to cross the farmyard and take the path between the Michaelmas daisies, and bob's your uncle. It has to be quite near the lane because Lavender Bob comes up with his lorry and empties the sewage once a fortnight.'

'Lavender Bob?' Eve said faintly. 'That's a funny name!'

Mabel laughed. 'I think it's his nickname because what he smells of is definitely *not* lavender. Come on.'

When they reached the stout wooden hut which stood at the end of the garden she raised her eyebrows at Eve. 'Go on, take a peek. I promise you, it's perfectly civilised; there's even a bolt on the door so no one can walk in on you once you're inside. It *is* a bit dark in there – and a bit smelly towards the end of the fortnight – but perfectly respectable, as I said.'

Eve laughed. She had noticed that there were heart-shaped holes cut in the top of the door and guessed that this would be the only source of light during the day. But what about at night? Mabel had said something about jerries, whatever they might be . . . was it the Devon word for candles, perhaps, or even a lamp? But Mabel was turning away.

'We'll go back through the orchard; pick up some windfalls as you go,' she advised Eve. 'Then young Christopher here can drop them into the pigs' trough and we shall be just in time for your mother to meet the land girls and Uncle Reg before she puts him to bed.' She lowered her voice, glancing significantly at Chrissie, but he was collecting fallen apples and paying them no attention. 'There's something you ought to know if you're going to live here,' she said softly. 'But little pitchers have big ears and we don't want what I'm going to tell you to get about. So we'll hand your brother over to your mum and I'll take you up to my bedroom where we can talk without being overheard.'

This sounded exciting, like a Nancy Drew story.

They were retracing their steps through the long grass of the orchard when Eve got the feeling that she was being watched. She drew a little closer to Mabel and at that moment happened to glance up. Perched on a high branch of the biggest apple tree in sight was a fair-haired boy in a grey shirt and trousers. Eve was about to ask Mabel who he was when he caught her eye and winked at her, placing a dirty forefinger across his lips in the time-honoured gesture requesting silence. And even as he did so, Eve recognised him. It was that dreadful rude boy who had threatened to give her a bloody nose on New Cross station.

For one moment she hesitated; already she felt Mabel was her friend and the boy was most definitely not. However, she felt sure that if she drew attention to his presence she would earn his dislike, and she could do without that. So she gave the slightest of small nods in his direction and headed, with Mabel and Chrissie, towards the comfortable bulk of the farmhouse.

Chapter Two

In the farmhouse kitchen, Mabel explained to Mrs
Armstrong that Chrissie was tired and wanted his tea,
whilst Eve took the opportunity to look around her.
It was a large yet cosy room furnished simply with a
well-scrubbed wooden table, a number of ladder-backed
chairs, a low sink and a perfectly enormous dresser
upon which were displayed a great many homely-
looking plates, cups and bowls. She opened her mouth
to ask Mabel why there were so many chairs, but
Eleanor was speaking and Eve knew better than to
interrupt, so she listened instead.

'I can see my boy has had a wonderful time and is
tired out,' Eleanor said gaily, picking Chrissie up and
giving him a hug before turning to her daughter. 'Are
you going to give me a hand with bathing and bedtime? Or would you rather help Mrs Faversham – Auntie
Bess, I mean – with any little jobs she might need
doing?' She turned to the farmer's wife. 'He usually has
a light meal at about five o'clock and I put him to bed
at six.' She smiled winningly. 'A boiled egg would be
nice.'

Chrissie, Eve saw, really was tired, for he had cuddled into his mother's arms, nuzzling into her neck, but at the mention of a boiled egg he gave his train-whistle shriek and tried to struggle free of Eleanor's grip.

'Mabel said I might pick out an egg myself,' he said crossly. 'She said I could go into that barn place and choose any egg I liked.'

Mabel sighed and looked guilty. 'I forgot,' she said, holding out her hand to the small and now tear-streaked Chrissie. 'But you were going to have the egg for breakfast, not for tea, remember?'

To Eve's considerable surprise, Chrissie calmed down at once.

'Eggy for breakfast,' he agreed, nodding vigorously. 'Now Chrissie would like bread and jam and jelly.'

The farmer's wife laughed and held out a hand, then led Chrissie into a large pantry. 'Which jam would you like?' she said, pointing to row after row of jars, each with the name of its contents written neatly on a small white label. 'We haven't any jelly, but you can have a piece of plum pie instead.'

Eve wondered how Chrissie would take the suggestion, but was not given time to find out. Mabel seized her hand and tugged her across the kitchen and the small dark hall and up a great many stairs. At the top of the second flight she flung open a door and pulled Eve into a long attic room with a sloping ceiling and tiny windows set deeply in the thatch. Eve stared around her. There were four beds in the long room, three of them made up with bright coverlets and clean starched sheets. She turned a puzzled face to Mabel.

'If this is your bedroom, why are there so many beds?'
she enquired. 'At home I have a room of my own and
Chrissie sleeps in a cot in Nanny Burton's room. The
maids don't live in; they come each morning and go
home each evening.'

Mabel's eyes rounded. 'Maids?' she echoed, then
shrugged. 'Oh well, it takes all sorts. The beds that are
made up are where me and the land girls sleep, and
the other's for my mum if ever she has time to visit.'
She sat herself down on the end of one of the beds and
patted the space beside her. 'Look, Eve, what I'm going
to tell you is a secret, get it? I'm trusting you not to say
a word to anyone. How old are you? Nearly ten? Well,
I reckon that's old enough to understand how important it is not to repeat a word. Am I right?'

'Yes,' Eve breathed, tremendously proud that Mabel
was going to confide in her. 'How old are you, Mabel?'

'Twelve, going on thirteen,' Mabel said briefly, and
Eve tucked away in the corner of her mind the phrase
'going on thirteen', because it made Mabel sound older
than her actual years. But Mabel was speaking again
and Eve listened intently. Whatever it was this wonderful new friend was about to tell her she would keep
the secret as long as she lived, and she could scarcely
do so if she didn't listen with all her might and main.

'Auntie Bess is a really nice woman, but my mum
says it's clear that she and Uncle Reg are short of
money,' Mabel began. 'When they heard a rumour that
children from the cities were being evacuated to the
countryside they knew that because they have so much
room they would be expected to take some in and not

be paid to do so, or not very much at any rate. So Auntie Bess placed an advertisement saying she had a beautiful farmhouse deep in the country and would take paying guests. Do you see?'

'Well, not entirely,' Eve confessed. 'What's the difference between advertising for lodgers and taking in evacuees?'

Mabel heaved a sigh. 'She wanted people like you and me, children whose parents would pay a fair price for their meals and so on. Well, apart from the two land girls, who work on the farm and sleep in here with me. So you see? We're not really evacuees, but we have to pretend to be like everyone else, or people might say Auntie Bess was cheating, and that wouldn't be fair.' She looked enquiringly at Eve. 'Will your mum be staying here with you and Chrissie or does she have a job somewhere else?'

Eve shrugged. 'I think she had a job once, because that was where she met my daddy,' she said, having given the matter some thought. 'And once, when we visited Daddy in his office in London and his secretary had left early, he asked Mummy to type a letter for him. She sat down and did so and honestly, Mabel, her fingers just flew across those keys. Daddy laughed and said she'd not lost her touch, so I suppose she could get a job if she wanted one.'

'But I expect she doesn't want one,' Mabel said. She looked thoughtfully at the younger girl. 'I wonder how long it will be before you move on? She was really upset over the bathroom, wasn't she?'

Eve sighed and looked round wistfully at the room

in which she and Mabel stood. The ceiling sloped on one side almost to the floor, and the view through the thatch-framed windows still showed the green and gold of summer. 'Don't say that. It's lovely here. Surely she won't want to move?'

It was Mabel's turn to shrug. 'Well, it did seem to me that she wasn't the sort of lady to help stack the wheat or take the tea out to the harvesters. But maybe I'm wrong. After all, she wanted a safe place for you to stay and you can't get much safer than this.' She cocked her head on one side in a listening attitude. 'I hear the grandfather clock in the hall striking the hour. Are you hungry? It'll be a grand tea because Auntie Bess is never mingy and always feeds us well. She keeps warning everyone about this rationing thing they say is coming but I can't see that it's made much difference so far.' She turned to head for the stairs, smiling at Eve over her shoulder as she did so. 'I didn't tell you, because it won't affect you, but Miriam, one of the land girls, snores, so I always try to be asleep before she gets into her stride. But Auntie Bess has put you and your mum and Chrissie in the best front bedroom, and even Miriam's snores won't penetrate that far.'

The tea was as wonderful as Mabel had predicted. And the land girls, bronzed from the sun and full of chatter about their work, took pains to include both Eve and her mother in their conversation.

Uncle Reg was a small man, dwarfed by his wife. He had thin greying hair, very pale blue eyes and a quiet voice. He only spoke twice, once to acknowledge his

40

wife's introduction to the Armstrongs, and the other when he bade Chrissie goodnight. But he had a charming smile which transformed his otherwise rather dour features, and when one of the land girls made a joke his face lit up with amusement and Eve found herself liking him despite his quietness.

Chrissie had been put to bed some time previously and must, Eve thought, be very tired indeed since he did not attempt to lure his mother up to their room with requests for a drink of water, his favourite teddy or the worn old blanket, known as his num-num, which he liked to have wrapped around his shoulders at bedtime no matter how warm the weather.

As soon as the meal was over and it was growing dusk outside, everyone settled down to their various tasks. The land girls cleared the table and washed up then went into the dining room to write their letters home, or so Mabel informed Eve, and Mr Faversham, heaving a deep sigh, crossed to his desk, got out a large ledger and began to enter figures in it. Mrs Faversham produced a tapestry bag from which she pulled a quantity of knitting and Mrs Armstrong, having found a pile of very old magazines, began to leaf through them with a discontented expression on her face. Presently she turned to their hostess.

'Mrs Faversham, I promised my husband to let him know when we had settled in at Drake's Farm. I don't know whether he's at sea at present, but if so I can leave a message with the number he has given me. May I use your telephone?'

Mrs Faversham stared. 'Bless my soul, we've no call

for a telephone here,' she exclaimed. 'But there's a box in the village, right outside the post office. There's a bicycle the land girls use in the big barn, if you'd like to speak to your husband from there. Do you have change?'

Eve waited for a grumble which did not come. To be sure her mother heaved a sigh, but then her face brightened. 'Is there a cinema in the village, or a library?'

'Oh aye, there's both,' their hostess said. 'Cinema once a month in the village hall, library open whenever Miss Maple decides she can spare the time, 'cos it's in her back room.' She grinned widely. 'There bain't much choice of reading matter, but you'll have books of your own, no doubt. I takes *Woman's Own* and Reg there has the *Farmer's Weekly*. Have you read *Lorna Doone*? That's a book I like so well I bought meself a copy. I'll lend you that wi' pleasure, for 'tis a grand tale and set in this very county. Then tomorrow mebbe you can ride into the village and telephone Plymouth. We bain't usually so quiet,' she added apologetically, glancing around the room. 'We makes our own butter and cheese, to say nothing of cream, but I kept this evening clear, thinking you might be tired and not want to be working.'

Eve, sitting cross-legged on the rag hearthrug, looked up into her mother's face, expecting an indignant response, but instead of disclaiming any intention of working on any evening, her mother got slowly to her feet and smiled sweetly at the older woman.

'It's not dark yet, though dusk is falling,' she remarked. 'I think I'll take up your suggestion. If Eve will show me the way to the village . . .'

'Oh, Mummy! I don't know the way to the village,' Eve said hastily. 'Mabel does though, I'm sure.'

Mabel, who had been covering pages of an exercise book with neat handwriting, looked up quickly and laughed. 'You can't miss it, and it's perfectly safe if you go the back way, the way Eve came,' she said cheerfully. 'When you reach the end of the lane turn right, and keep on for about a mile. Honestly, Mrs Armstrong, you can't get lost. And of course the telephone kiosk is bright red so you can't miss that either. You'll be fine, honest you will. I'm writing my war diary, otherwise I'd come with you. It's a nice walk, honestly, Mrs Armstrong.'

The older woman looked undecided for a moment. 'Well, if I get lost I shall know who to blame,' she said at last, giving Mabel a roguish look. She crossed the kitchen, went into the small hall and took her coat from its hook, gesturing to Eve to follow suit. Eve did so, but ventured to suggest that her mother would be fine on her own.

'What if Chrissie wakes?' she asked hopefully. 'He might cry for one of us.'

'Oh, nonsense. Once he goes off he never wakes until morning,' Mrs Armstrong said untruthfully. 'Don't you want to accompany your mama? It will do you good to get some exercise.' As she spoke she slipped Eve's school mac round her daughter's shoulders, and Eve gave way to the inevitable. Reluctantly, she followed her mother into the farmyard, afraid the older woman would find fault with everything on their walk and thus spoil her own pleasure in this magical place. But on this occasion at least she was spared.

'We'll go the long way round, not down that nasty muddy lane,' Mrs Armstrong said as soon as they were out of earshot of the farm. 'I don't mean to wreck my only decent pair of shoes. There isn't a pavement this way either, but at least the road is tarmac and quite respectable. Come along, Eve. I really must tell Daddy we can't possibly spend more than a couple of days here; he must find us somewhere else. I'm sure he never realised there was neither a bathroom nor a WC at Drake's Farm. Once I tell him he'll start looking for alternative accommodation, and the sooner the better. Step out, Eve; don't dawdle.'

Eve obeyed, and they were soon in the village. Eve looked around her: there was a village green, and a sizeable pond through which a tiny stream chuckled and gurgled its way, Eve assumed, to the sea.

It was an attractive place. The green was surrounded by thatched cottages with whitewashed cob walls. All the front doors were identical, but outside one a plum tree flourished and another boasted an apple tree still heavily laden with fruit. Eve would have liked a closer look, for she had noticed a fat tabby cat curled up on one doorstep and sweet-smelling pinks on either side of another short path, but Mrs Armstrong hurried on. All the front gardens surrounding the green were well tended, making Eve think of gossiping women exchanging the latest news whilst they worked on their plots. One of the cottages had a bow window display-ing various commodities, and she saw the red Post Office sign on the door frame. So this was their destin-ation! She had a sudden urge to produce her Saturday sixpence, go into the shop and spend lavishly, but then realised that at this time of day the sign on the door must mean what it said, which was 'Closed'.

Eve was about to point out the Post Office sign to her mother when Eleanor Armstrong grabbed her arm to steer her towards a shiny red kiosk. Here, they both knew, was housed the public telephone. Eve would have followed her mother into the booth but Eleanor shushed her away, so she sat on the post office wall and waited with what patience she could muster. For a miracle her mother managed to get hold of her husband at the very first attempt, and from that moment on Eleanor simply complained about everything. The farm was too small, the lack of a bathroom and lavatory unbelievable in this day and age. The tea had been far too lavish for Chris's delicate stomach; the animals were certain to bring fleas and filth into every room in the house. Eleanor had closed the door behind her so that Eve should not hear her end of the conversation, but the spring on the door no longer worked and every word she uttered could be clearly heard by her daughter. Eve felt her face grow hot with humiliation. It simply wasn't true. The farm was lovely, the galvanised tin bath which hung on the scullery wall plenty big enough for a weekly bath, and the food nicer than anything the Armstrong children had ever tasted before. And then, when it sounded as though Mr Armstrong had actually been getting cross with his wife, Eleanor had played her trump card. She had told Daddy about the arrangement Mabel's mother had made for her daughter, and pointed out that whilst Eve and Chrissie stayed safely at the farm she herself could be doing useful war work, for her secretarial skills must be needed by someone.

'Wouldn't you be proud of me if I joined one of the services as my contribution to the war effort?' she said hopefully. 'And I can drive, which many women can't. Oh, Bill, if I have to spend more than two or three days at Drake's Farm I'll go mad, honest to God I will. Please say I can leave Mrs Faversham to take care of the children and come back to civilisation. I promise you I'll visit them whenever I'm not working to make sure they're all right, but I *can't* stagnate in that dreadful place! I wouldn't dream of bringing them to Plymouth if you honestly think it will be targeted by the Luftwaffe, but out at Drake's Farm they'll be safe as houses. If the Favershams are willing I'll start looking for lodgings tomorrow. Do you agree?'

Mumble, mumble, mumble went the telephone. But though Eve could not hear her father's side of the conversation she knew very well how it would end. Her mother would dump them at Drake's Farm, trusting the Favershams to look after them, and would rush down to Plymouth where all the things that mattered to her could doubtless be found in abundance. Eleanor Armstrong adored the cinema and the theatre and loved the admiration which was usually her lot, for she was a very pretty woman. And presently, when Eleanor finally said goodbye to her husband and replaced the receiver, Eve's delight was almost as great as her mother's. With or without Mrs Armstrong, it looked as though she and Chrissie would remain at Drake's Farm, which was all that mattered.

There was a small mirror in the telephone kiosk, and after she put the receiver down Eleanor checked her appearance in the spotted glass, even going to the length of producing a comb from the pocket of her coat and tidying her hair. Then she emerged from the box and took Eve's hand. They walked for a moment in silence before Eleanor turned to her daughter.

'I hadn't realised the door to the box didn't close. You must have heard just about every word,' she said. To Eve's relief she did not sound angry. 'How would you feel if I joined Daddy in Plymouth and left you and Chrissie at the farm? You see, I've never lived anywhere so primitive, and when I realised that that girl Mabel's mother – is her name Mabel? – has got herself a job instead of staying here I thought I might follow suit. How would you feel about that? You'd have to be responsible for Chrissie, but I dare say he'd behave himself better if I wasn't around to give him his own way all the time. I'd come and visit you often, of course, so we could see how it was working out.' Her voice sharpened. 'Well, miss? Why so silent? You're usually all too happy to give your opinion, especially when Daddy's around to take your part. If you don't like the idea we could look for somewhere different, I suppose, but it would be a great help if you were prepared to stay at Drake's Farm without me.'

To Eve's amazement there was actually a note of pleading in her mother's voice, and she couldn't help giving a little smile. For once, she and her mother were in complete accord; Eleanor wanted to exchange the primitive farmhouse for something quite different, and all Eve wanted was to remain at Drake's Farm for as long as she possibly could. The only snag, in fact, would be Chrissie. Eve did not relish the prospect of being in charge of such a self-willed little boy, but perhaps Eleanor was right and he would not be so naughty once he was away from his mummy. She thought back to his behaviour that afternoon. He had responded well to Mabel's threats and promises, and in any case, once school started he would be the responsibility of someone else. She looked up into her mother's face and read hope there.

'Well?' Eleanor said impatiently. 'Do you want me to look for another place, one on a bus route perhaps, with a proper bathroom and an indoor WC?' Once again her voice sharpened. 'Would that suit Madam better?'

'No,' Eve said quickly. 'I won't leave the farm and nor will Chrissie. The Favershams don't mind no bathroom, so why should we? You can tell Daddy me and Chrissie want to stay right where we are.'

Eleanor Armstrong gave a little purr of satisfaction, and squeezed Eve's hand. 'Good,' she said decidedly. 'Then tomorrow I shall get a taxi into the city and start looking for lodgings nearer civilisation than Drake's Farm – for myself, I mean.'

By the time they re-entered the farmhouse Mabel and the land girls had disappeared to their beds, since they started work at the crack of dawn. By a great piece of good fortune Chrissie had not woken and Eve was not surprised to be told to go straight up to their room, since her mother had some business to discuss with Mrs Faversham. She crossed the kitchen and headed for the stairs, guessing they would be talking about Eleanor's new scheme. If Mrs Faversham were to refuse . . . but she could not bear the thought and put it out of her head. Her father had a saying which came, she rather thought, from a song: 'Never trouble troubles till troubles trouble you.' Downstairs she could hear the hum of voices, but she did not even attempt to listen. Suddenly, she was sure that all would be well.

Next morning, Eve was awoken by something heavy landing on her chest, and a voice shouting in her ear.

'Wake up, wake up, Evie Armstrong! I want my breakfast egg what Mabel promised me, and Mummy says I can have soldier boys to dip in the yolk and milk from the cow to drink.'

Eve opened reluctant eyes, wondering for a moment where she was, then remembered and sat up with a jerk, tipping Chrissie on to the floor and making him give a wail of protest.

'You can't have breakfast until you're dressed,' she told him, scrambling out of bed and noticing with some surprise that their mother was nowhere to be seen. 'I'll do your buttons, but you can put your own clothes on.'

'I can't. You know Nanny Burton puts me clothes on,' Chrissie said quickly.

Eve laughed at the mental picture of Nanny Burton in Chrissie's blue shorts and chequered shirt, but she picked her brother up and sat him on top of the chest of drawers.

'All right, but you'll have to wear yesterday's shirt and shorts, because Mummy hasn't unpacked yet,' she said. 'We'll have our breakfasts and then come back and start.'

Eleanor Armstrong was not usually an early riser, but when Eve and Chrissie entered the kitchen she had already left the house. Mabel, sitting at the table crunching toast, informed Eve that Mrs Armstrong had gone out some time previously.

'I imagine she went to order a taxi to drive her to Plymouth,' she said. 'I don't know what she wanted to do there, but she was awfully eager to get away before Chrissie woke.' She eyed Eve narrowly. 'Do *you* know why she lit out at such an early hour? It's got to have something to do with that telephone call last night.'

Eve was about to explain when Auntie Bess bawled: 'Brekker up! Chrissie has the blue egg cup with the picture of a cockerel on one side; Eve, yours is the white one. Mabel's been let off her own work today so she can explain the chores you'll be doing the rest of the week.'

Anxious to please, Eve bolted her breakfast, which was delicious, and watched Chrissie slowly dipping soldier boys into his egg's golden yolk whilst Mabel and Mrs Faversham cleared the table round them. Finally she got to her feet and shook her head at Chrissie, who promptly tried to hurry and then wailed when he got eggshell in his mouth.

'Quiet, you!' Mabel said sharply. 'You can't come with your sister and me because you'll slow us up. Be a good boy and do as Auntie Bess tells you, and we'll see you at dinner time.'

Chrissie gave a shriek of protest and pointed to the piece of brown shell which he had just spat into his palm. 'You're a naughty girl, Eve Armstrong,' he wailed. 'Mummy said you were to look after me; I won't be left with this nasty old woman, I won't, I won't!'

Eve was horrified by her little brother's outburst but Auntie Bess did not seem perturbed. 'You'll do as I tell you,' she said equably. She jerked a thumb at the back door and winked at Mabel and Eve. 'He'll bide wi' me, no question,' she said. 'No need to take him with you; I've found up my box of old toys and it'll keep him happy sortin' them out. And there's the Noah's Ark. When my lads were young and it were too rainy to go out they'd spend hours pairing the animals up and having mock wars. Afore you goes off, Mabel, you might bring the play box through – it's on a chair in the dining room – and Eve, since his lordship has stopped bellowin' you might as well clear his place at the table. Then he can spread everythin' out on that until 'tis time for me to cook dinner.'

'He could play on the floor and save you trouble,' Eve said rather timidly. She could imagine all too well how her brother would react if he was told to move everything off the table in the middle of a game with some Noah's Ark animals, but Auntie Bess, though she smiled, shook her head.

'I don't want him underfoot while I'm gettin' the ingredients for my baking,' she explained. 'I dare say he'd like to give me a hand when I'm ready. I always used to give my boys a piece of pastry each which they could make into any shape they liked.' She frowned thoughtfully. 'Mebbe they was a little older than his lordship here, but I expect we'll manage to amuse each other.' She gestured towards the back door. 'Off with you, girls, and be thankful he's too small to reach the handle. You won't need your coats, for 'tis a warm day.' She smiled kindly at Eve. 'No need to worry about your brother. I've reared a family of my own and know all the tricks, though 'tis a long time since my own boys rifled the toy box.'

Opening the door and slipping out into the farmyard, Eve waited for a shriek of protest, but it did not come, and presently she and Mabel strode out into the lane, since Mabel had announced her intention of taking her new friend to see the village school, and the rectory where children too young for school would be cared for while their older siblings were in class.

As they entered the lane and saw the orchard on their right Eve suddenly remembered the boy in the apple tree and opened her mouth to ask Mabel who he was, but then remembered his hushing gesture. Hastily, she closed her mouth again, but though she looked hopefully up at the trees with their prolific crops of colourful fruit there was no sign of the boy. She supposed he must have been stealing apples, though why he should feel the need to do so when he might fill his pockets with windfalls until he could carry no more she could not imagine.

Mabel was chattering away, explaining that the chores of which Auntie Bess had spoken were pleasant ones: feeding the hens, preparing the food for the pigs and then tipping it into their troughs, brushing down the farmyard and transferring the steaming pats of cow dung from the cowshed to the muck heap. Then there were tasks with which Eve could help, although she would not be able to manage them alone: harnessing the pony which pulled the trap, forking hay down from the loft into the mangers for the two big carthorses, and transferring milk from the shining galvanised pails to the big churns which, Mabel informed her, would be collected by the dairy lorry as soon as milking was finished.

By the time all this information had been absorbed by Eve the two girls had reached the ford, where they stopped to gaze into the limpid waters.

'I always leave Drake's Farm earlier than I need, because everyone likes to play with water even when they're nearly thirteen,' Mabel said instructively. 'Bob – he's Auntie Bess's younger son – has told me some great stories. In another month he says the hazelnuts will be ripe for picking, and a week or two after us kids have stripped the hazels the sweet chestnuts start. They're more difficult to gather because of their prickly shells, but Bob says he and his pals always found a way to get them so we shall too. I tell you, living at Drake's Farm is just about the best thing that could happen to you . . .' she glanced rather guiltily at her companion, 'except living in your own home, of course.'

Eve thought of her home, with its electric lift which could whisk you up to the third floor in a magic moment. In her mind she thanked George, the lift boy, crossed the gleaming parquet flooring of the corridor and entered her flat. She stood for a moment, listening to the familiar sounds – a clatter of crockery and cutlery and the soft murmur of cockney voices – and smiled to herself. That would be the maids, tackling the breakfast washing up, which was usually their first task. Bertha would wash up one day whilst Catherine dried and put away, and the next day Bertha would dry and Catherine wash up. At the weekend, and during school holidays, as soon as breakfast was cleared away Eve and Nanny Burton, with Chrissie sitting comfortably on Nanny's hip, would follow Mummy into the morning room, where Nanny Burton would be given Mummy's orders for the day. Often, these did not concern the children. They would go to the playroom and Eve would read a book or paint a picture or learn poetry by heart whilst Mummy, already beautifully dressed and made up, would telephone her friends and arrange to meet them for coffee in Swan & Edgar, or for lunch at Fortnum & Mason. Nursery luncheon, as Eve had been told to call it, was a dull meal. Chrissie would have sardines on toast followed by rice pudding, and Eve, who hated sardines, might be regaled with luncheon meat. Nanny Burton, a large woman with a large appetite, had much more interesting food and sometimes she would share it with the children, having first made them promise not to tell, but generally their meals could be described as plain but wholesome. Afternoons were only spent in the flat when it was raining or too cold to go out. Otherwise they went for invigorating walks through the London streets, visiting museums, art galleries and even, once, a picture house, where Nanny Burton informed her charges that the lady and gentleman they were watching were not actually in the theatre itself but miles and miles away. Eve pretended to understand the events unfolding on the screen but Chrissie, who had slumbered peacefully throughout, showed an alarming tendency to ask questions about what little he had seen. Thinking quickly, Nanny Burton told Mummy that he had fallen asleep as they walked across Hyde Park and must have dreamed the whole thing, so Mummy had never guessed that on one occasion at least the children had not been enjoying the park's fresh air, but had been sitting in a stuffy cinema watching a matinee performance of *Trouble in Paradise*.

'Did you see that?' Mabel's voice brought Eve abruptly back to the present. 'It was a brown trout! The stream's very shallow here, but there are two big deep pools where water drains off from a steep hillside, and that's where the trout lie up. Bob used to fish for them when he lived at home, but he doesn't get the opportunity all that often now he's in the Navy. Did you see it? The trout, I mean?'

'No, I was looking for mermaids,' Eve said unguardedly, then gave a little laugh. 'I know there's no such thing, of course, but this is such a magical place . . .' Her voice trailed away and she looked anxiously into her companion's face, fearing to see amusement or even contempt in the older girl's expression.

But Mabel was nodding and smiling. 'You're right there,' she said. 'I've been staying with Auntie Bess all summer, and though of course I miss Mother and Father I'm very happy here. We came from Norfolk, which is beautiful too, but very different from Devon. I know what you mean when you call this place "magical", and it's always changing. Auntie Bess says in winter the stream doubles or trebles in size, so we shan't be crossing here when we go to school, but will go by bridge, so to speak. I expect you've got wellies?' She chuckled. 'We'll need them in the winter. *Devon, Devon, glorious Devon, always rains six days out of seven.* I wouldn't go so far as to say it rains as much as that, more like four days out of seven, but still a lot more than it did in Norfolk.' She cocked her head on one side in thought. 'But it's gentle rain, soft and warm, and no one takes any notice save to say . . .' and here Mabel's voice changed and deepened to that of an elderly Devonshire man: "tis good for the crops, my handsome.'

She laughed, and Eve laughed with her as they skipped quickly across the stones and entered the beech wood. The trees still wore their summer foliage, and the girls strolled companionably along under the canopy of green and gold until they reached the village, where their first visit was to the church, a little grey building standing amidst very old gravestones and wild grasses which were already whitening after the long hot summer.

'If we see them I'll introduce you to the rector and his wife,' Mabel said. 'Mrs Ryder will be in charge of the crèche, or whatever it calls itself, so we can tell her about Chrissie. Things are still in an awful muddle at the village school, apparently – it seems they sent two schools here instead of one, and then there are the local children as well, so no one knows when term will start.' She pointed to a small grey stone building adjoining a playground which was like all the school playgrounds Eve had ever seen. 'That's the school. There's talk of taking over the village hall for some classes, but it's still all up in the air.' She grinned mischievously. 'So us kids are having a sort of extended holiday whilst the teachers sort themselves out. Ah, there's Mrs Ryder. Come on – I'll introduce you.'

But the rector's wife eyed them with some surprise. 'What are you two doing here?' she asked briskly. 'It's registration day; you were supposed to be at the school no later than nine o'clock. I'm afraid you're bound to get into trouble for turning up thirty minutes after everyone else has left.'

'We're not evacuees, Mrs Ryder,' Mabel said quickly. 'It's me, Mabel Davies, and this is my friend Eve. We're living with Mrs Faversham at Drake's Farm and nobody told us anything about having to register today.'

Mrs Ryder was a small, middle-aged woman with a flat bosom and shrewd dark brown eyes. She looked rather fierce and Eve shrank closer to Mabel as the older woman produced a pair of steel-rimmed spectacles from her jacket pocket and placed them on her nose. Suddenly she smiled.

'Mabel, dear. I'm so sorry I didn't know you, but I've seen so many children over the past couple of days that I don't believe I'd recognise my own if they turned up unexpectedly.' She peered at Eve. 'And you'll be the young lady whose father is at sea. Mrs Faversham told me you have a little brother who will be coming to my crèche.' She whipped the spectacles off and placed them carefully back in her pocket, then held out a hand and shook Eve's warmly. 'I'm sorry I can't stay to chat and make you welcome,' she said apologetically, 'but I'm just off to a meeting in the next village. No doubt we shall meet again.' Without giving either girl a chance to reply she climbed into the driver's seat of a small and very old motor car, started the engine and departed with a great crashing of gears. Mabel giggled.

'She's a funny old dear, but although you might not think it, young children adore her,' she said. 'I believe her youngest is not much older than Chrissie, so she's probably had plenty of practice. Auntie Bess says she has a way with children, even though she doesn't look the cuddly kind.'

They walked round the school, looking for a way in, but all the doors were locked. It was a typical Victorian building with high windows which let in light but could not be seen out of unless you were a good deal taller than most pupils. The village hall next door was simply a long room with windows on the side overlooking the street, below which were a great many cheap folding chairs. At one end was a rudimentary kitchen and at the other an equally rudimentary cloakroom with pegs for coats. The floor, however, was wood block and well polished, which surprised Eve until Mabel told her that dances were held there monthly. The chairs beneath the windows were for seating the audience when films or indeed any other forms of entertainment were showing.

When Mabel had conducted Eve on a tour of the premises the two of them visited the village shop. Mabel produced a little red purse and, having given some serious thought to her choice, bought two ounces of humbugs. When one of these was comfortably tucked in each girl's cheek, they emerged into the street once more.

'Well, you've seen just about all there is to see of the village,' Mabel said. She pointed to a large shed, before which was a solitary petrol pump. 'That's the black-smith's forge; he shoes horses *and* mends cars, only there aren't many cars in the village yet. He's Mr Pryde; he's nice. I'd introduce you, but he drives the local bus and he won't be back yet – he'll have taken the older kids to register at the big school in town.' She glanced at the sun now high above their heads. 'Oh, dear, it's taken longer than I thought it would to show you round. We'll be late for lunch; I just hope Auntie Bess has saved us some grub.'

Eve set off at a brisk pace the way they had come, but Mabel laughed and tugged at her arm. 'No need to hurry. I was only teasing you about being late for lunch. It's usually what they call a "ploughman's": Auntie Bess's fresh-baked bread, the onions she pickled last year, a big bowl of lettuce and tomatoes, and cheese. The farmhands – Mr Trevalyn and old Mr Smith – eat with us if they're working near enough, and if not Auntie Bess packs a lunch for each of them and some-one takes them down a jug of tea. That will probably be our job most days until school starts.'

Eve gulped. 'Will you be going to school in town? I do hope not, otherwise it's going to be horrid. All the evacuees will know each other and no one will know me. Well, there is one boy I sort of know, but he'll be in a separate building, won't he?'

Mabel frowned, then laughed. 'You really don't know anything, do you?' she said. 'I take it you didn't go to a village school – well, obviously you didn't. Girls and boys are taught together here.' She laughed again. 'Just imagine trying to separate pupils by sex as well as by age and ability. But no, I'll be coming here with you – a lot of the local kids stay on until they're fourteen.'

'Thank goodness for that,' Eve said, giving a sigh of relief. 'It's not that I'm frightened exactly, but it's so hard not knowing anyone. Suppose they pick on me? There was a girl at my old school who'd had an operation on something called a cyst and the nursing home had shaved her head. The other girls were horrible to her. They called her Baldy and said she'd had nits, whatever they may be, and wouldn't sit next to her in class. Even the teachers made remarks; I should think she was the only girl in the school to be glad when the war started, although of course I haven't seen her since July; perhaps her hair has grown again by now.'

The two girls had reached the wood as they talked and now Mabel stared at her companion, wide-eyed. 'What a horrible school yours must have been,' she said frankly. 'You won't get anything like that in the village, I promise you. Oh, you may get teased, but you won't get bullied. And you say the teachers never told anyone off for the way they behaved?' She snorted. 'Of course there *may* be one or two of the evacuees who aren't nice at all, but they'd have to be really horrid to make fun of someone who'd had an operation.' She looked at Eve accusingly. 'I trust, Eve Armstrong, that you did not join in what I can only describe as persecution?'

60

'No, of course I didn't,' Eve said indignantly. 'And you're right, it was a horrid school. Daddy was furious when I told him about the girl being called Baldy, and complained to the headmistress, but it was nearly the end of term and I don't think she did anything about it.' She looked thoughtfully at Mabel. 'If someone threatened to give you a bloody nose, would that be persecution?'

Mabel laughed. 'Course not, unless they actually did it. Why? Has someone said that to you?'

Eve looked fixedly ahead of her and a rhyme popped into her mind. *Tell tale tit, your tongue will be split, and all the little pussycats will have a little bit.* She had heard the cockney kids playing street games using the rhyme to tease each other, though with no malice in their cheerful voices, so rather than risk being a tell tale she shook her head.

'One thing I do hate is tale-bearing,' Mabel said rather primly. 'Want another humbug? Once we get to the stream we can have a drink of water, because don't humbugs make you thirsty?'

Chapter Three

When Eve and Mabel entered the kitchen Mrs Faversham had cleared the table and was washing up. She turned and gave the two girls a broad smile, jerking her thumb at Eleanor Armstrong, who was drying the dishes and piling them up on the scrubbed wooden table.

'Well, your mother has found herself lodgings nearer Plymouth, Eve, and she'll be leaving us in a few days' time,' she said bluntly. 'You and Chrissie will be staying here with your uncle Reg and me, and very glad we are to have you, pet. Now, are you hungry? I saved some grub for you and Mabel; it's in the meat safe, so get outside of that and then you can amuse yourselves until tea time. I shall need the table in here, so you can take your plates through into the dining room and clean up when you've ate.'

Eve smiled to herself. All her worries had been for nothing, because it was pretty plain that her mother was as keen to leave her children as they were to be left. When it came to the actual parting Chrissie would undoubtedly cry, for his mother was always showering him with little treats, but he was at the age when getting his own way was more important even than little treats, and he doubtless thought he could bend Mrs Faversham and Eve herself to his will just as he did his mother.

'Well?' The impatience was back in Eleanor's voice. 'You said last night you thought it was a good idea. Don't say you've changed your mind!'

'Of course I haven't,' Eve said indignantly as Mabel emerged from the pantry with two plates of delicious-looking food. 'Don't worry – we'll be fine without you.'

At the end of the week Eve and Chrissie waved their mother off with a show of affection so convincing that Mabel asked anxiously if Eve was sure she had made the right decision in remaining on the farm. Eve smiled.

'Yes. Mummy finds me a wretched nuisance most of the time and isn't afraid to say so, and this last week Chrissie has behaved so badly that she's been avoiding him as much as possible. She's got her own life to lead, and I know she'll come and see us as often as she can.'

They had walked to the end of the lane to wave the taxi off, and now Mabel took one of Chrissie's hands and Eve the other and they swung him between them all the way back to the farmhouse, much to his enjoyment. He shot into the kitchen, informed Mrs Faversham that his mother had gone, and demanded one of the scones she had just brought out of the oven. Mrs Faversham smiled at him, but Eve thought there was steel behind the smile.

'Not till tea time, and that's not for a couple of hours

yet,' she said firmly. 'Off with the lot of you. I've been up to your bedroom, Eve, and it's a rare disgrace. What's more, you and Chrissie here will be swapping rooms with Lily and Miriam. You three will have more room in the attic and the land girls won't have to worry about waking Mabel when they're on early milking.'

Eve stared. She had been aware that various changes would follow Mrs Armstrong's departure but she did not think there had been any mention of giving up their room to Miriam and Lily. In fact she was pretty sure that her mother had assumed they would keep the existing arrangement for whenever she or Daddy visited the farm. She opened her mouth to say so but Mrs Faversham cut her short.

'Don't worry, my duck, there's the little spare room at the foot of the attic stair. We've arranged that if your mother or father wants to sleep over they can go in there. After all, the last thing they want will be Mr Gabble here' – she jerked a thumb at Chrissie – 'interrupting their sleep.'

Eve smiled. It was the perfect solution, and though their mother might grumble at losing the use of the larger room Eve knew she would much prefer an uninterrupted night's sleep to sharing a room with Chrissie.

So the three children mounted the stairs and began the gargantuan task of clearing the Armstrongs' room before climbing the second flight of narrow steps to the attic, where they found Lily lying on her bed reading a letter. Eve knew the older girl had a boyfriend who flew fighter planes; his name was Colin, and Lily wrote to him most days, receiving replies on thin airmail paper, for Colin had been posted abroad – to South Africa, Lily believed. He clearly missed his 'golden Lily', as he called her; a nickname which Eve considered entirely appropriate, for she thought that Lily, with her golden hair and slender figure, was the most beautiful girl she had ever encountered. But now Lily laid aside Colin's latest missive and smiled at them.

'Hello, kids,' she said cheerfully. 'Come to claim your new room?' She stood up. 'Give me two ticks and I'll be out of your way – as you can see, Miriam's packed her stuff already, so we're nearly all set.' She thrust the last of her things into a knapsack as she spoke, pulled the cord tight and hefted the bag on to her shoulder. 'Right, that's it. So if one of you could hand me Miriam's pack, please, I'll leave you to it.'

As soon as the changeover had been completed the children clattered down the stairs and into the kitchen, just in time to see Mrs Faversham take a large casserole dish out of the oven and place it in the middle of the table.

'First hot meal of the day is always the best – not counting breakfast, o' course,' she said cheerfully. 'Spuds is bubblin' on the range so they'll be ready in five minutes, and Lily and Miriam will be here in no time, hungry as hunters as usual.' She turned to Mabel and Eve. 'Now, you two, Mrs Ryder popped in while you were upstairs to say that school starts next week. You've to go to the village hall at nine o'clock tomorrow morning to get your instructions.'

'What about me?' Chrissie said plaintively. 'Eve mustn't go anywhere without me; Mummy promised.'

Mrs Faversham shook a chiding finger. 'You'll go to the rectory, young man, and take your orders from Mrs Ryder. And don't you think you're going to spoil my tea by whining and trying to upset your sister, or it'll be straight to bed for you and not a taste of my good stew will you get. Which is it to be?'

Chrissie sniffed the succulent smells which emanated from the casserole and turned worshipful eyes on Mrs Faversham. 'I loves you, and I loves your cooking,' he assured her. 'Is there plum pie for afters? I did love your plum pie.'

Next day Eve and Mabel ate their breakfast porridge and hurried off to the village hall, dropping Chrissie off at the rectory on their way. When he realised he was being left he began to grizzle and clutch at his sister's hand, but Mrs Ryder picked him up and took him to the conservatory where a number of children were already playing with the various toys the rector's wife had collected. There was a large sand tray, a big box of wooden building bricks and a pile of rather tattered books, and to Eve's relief Chrissie rushed straight to the sand tray, although she was slightly dismayed to hear him announcing boastfully that he would make a much better sandcastle than the one a small boy of about his own age was trying to construct there.

Mrs Ryder smiled reassuringly at Eve. 'He'll be fine once he's learned to mix with other children,' she said in a low voice. 'I take it he's never attended a nursery school or play centre before?'

Eve shook her head somewhat guiltily. 'We had a

nanny; Nanny Burton. She stopped him playing with other children in the park in case they were a bad influence. What time shall I call for him, Mrs Ryder?'

Mrs Ryder smiled. 'When Miss Matheson has finished with you,' she said matter-of-factly. 'Off you go now. You'll be told to which group you will belong and whether you are doing mornings or afternoons in school next week. Don't worry about Chrissie; he's an attractive little boy and will soon settle down.'

The girls made their way to the village hall. They were by no means the first to arrive, since it was a good three miles from the farm to their destination, but others were even later and it was well past nine o'clock when the teacher addressed them. She explained that they would be divided into two groups, one of which would do their lessons in the morning for the first week whilst the second would be taught in the afternoon; the second week they would swap. They were to be divided roughly by age, and when Eve was asked how old she was she gave that useful reply 'Going on twelve', which meant she would be placed in the same group as Mabel. She wanted to stick as closely as she could to the only girl she knew in the entire crowd and expected that Mabel would feel the same, but her hopes were dashed when Mabel gave a squeak of delight and rushed to a tall dark-haired girl who looked about thirteen. The two hugged.

'Joyce!' Mabel squealed joyfully. 'Whatever are you doing here? Auntie Flo told Mum you were being evacuated with your school to some place in the wilds of Wales. Are you going to stay at Drake's Farm? That's where Eve and I are living. Oh, I haven't introduced you to Eve. Her parents are in Plymouth too . . . but oh, Joyce, it's grand to see you again. I'm sure you've grown six inches since Easter.'

Joyce was rosy-cheeked, her dark hair cut short in a Dutch bob. The glance she gave Eve was perfunctory. 'Hello, Eve. I'm Joyce Epplethwaite, Mabel's cousin,' she said, and then turned her attention back to Mabel. 'No, I'm not staying at Drake's Farm, wherever that may be. I got a billet with the Huddlestons at the manor. Wouldn't it be grand if you could move in there too?'

'Oh, but the farm's lovely,' Mabel said rather uncertainly, 'and Mrs Faversham's a wonderful cook. Now if you could move in with us . . .'

The two began an animated conversation and Eve turned away from them, sick at heart. Although she had barely acknowledged it until now she had secretly hoped that she and Mabel might become best friends, but this now seemed an empty dream.

She looked wildly round at the mass of children and thought miserably that she had been foolish to pretend to be older than she really was. Should she confess to the teacher that there had been a misunderstanding? As she stood wondering what to do, she found herself suddenly addressed.

'I say, Eve, we're supposed to be separating into our groups now, you know,' Joyce said. She smiled quite kindly at the younger girl. 'Shouldn't you be with the others of your own age?'

Eve hesitated. It was the ideal opportunity to confess, to admit that she had fibbed in order to stay with

Mabel, for she still had a lingering hope that when Joyce took herself off to Huddleston Manor Mabel would become, if not her best friend, at least a close one. Accordingly, she mumbled something to Joyce and then spoke directly to Mabel.

'I fibbed about my age so that I could stay with you,' she said defensively. 'But I'm quite clever; I was head of my year at my old school so I dare say I'll manage to keep up.'

Mabel laughed, but Joyce's smile had disappeared. 'Self-praise is no virtue,' she said. 'Mabs and I were top too but you won't hear either of us boasting.'

'I wasn't . . . I didn't . . .' poor Eve stammered, hoping Mabel would take her part, but it seemed that the conversation, so far as the older girls were concerned, was over.

'Come on, Mabs, let's find ourselves a quiet spot somewhere, away from all these kids,' Joyce cut in. 'We're supposed to be writing down the work we'll be expected to do on our own . . .'

Eve turned away blindly, ashamed of the tears which rose to her eyes and blinking furiously to get rid of them. If Mabel moved to Huddleston Manor she supposed another girl would be evacuated to Drake's Farm. She might be nice, of course, friendly and forthcoming, or she might be some stuck-up self-satisfied beast like Joyce, but whichever she was Eve would have to put up with her. But for the time being she must be sensible, and join her own group, so she straightened her shoulders and marched through the milling throng of children towards a kind-looking elderly man who was perched on one of the desks and was clearly there to answer questions. Eve smiled at him and held out her notebook.

'I'm in the wrong group,' she informed him. 'I'm nearly ten, not nearly twelve. I wasn't evacuated with my school or anything like that; my mother and father have left me and my baby brother in the care of the lady who owns Drake's Farm . . .'

When the alarm went off Eve was already awake. Listening to the noises coming from the farmyard below, she glanced across the long low room at the sleepers in the other two beds, and sighed. Much to her dismay, Mabel had managed to get a billet at Huddleston Manor so that she and Joyce could be together, and that, of course, left an empty place at Drake's Farm.

Mrs Faversham had been disappointed to lose her paying guest and had intended to advertise for a replacement, but the authorities had, for once, been on the ball and before many days had passed Mabel's place had been filled by a genuine evacuee, a girl of around Eve's own age who had missed the first wave of evacuation due to a nasty attack of mumps.

The newcomer, Connie Hale, was nothing like Mabel. Although she was pretty, with curly dark hair and a pair of wide blue eyes, she was no substitute for the girl Eve had hoped to make her friend. For one thing, it soon became apparent that she was not happy. She hated the country and made it pretty plain that for two pins she would have returned to the city whence she had come. She boasted of her home life in Liverpool, of a large and imposing grocery shop owned by her father, of the staff he employed and the school she had attended. She had assured Eve that she had come top of her class so often that she was taught amongst children at least two years older than herself, and though she ate everything which was put before her she never admitted that the food was anything special and assured Eve, and anyone else who would listen, that her mother provided meals far superior to those enjoyed by the inhabitants of Drake's Farm.

Eve had been prepared to try to like Connie, but it was hard going and very soon impossible. Connie boasted of her educational superiority, but since her spelling was atrocious, her arithmetic worse and her reading, so far as Eve could see, about the level of a seven-year-old's, Eve soon learned to take everything Connie said with a pinch of salt; a very large pinch. Eve's own full name was Eve Deborah Armstrong. Connie claimed her middle name was Ariadne, after a Greek goddess of amazing beauty, but by the time she told Eve this, Eve was already wise to her stories and simply stared without comment.

'It *is* Ariadne,' Connie had said angrily. 'Just because you tell fibs, Eve Armstrong, that doesn't mean I do. Why, I bet you don't even have a middle name, so no wonder you're jealous of mine. I'll tell Auntie Bess you called me a liar, and she'll be mad as fire.'

'Tell her what you like,' Eve had said placidly. 'And I *do* have a middle name, but I don't go telling everyone about it. In fact I don't like it much; it's too fancy, so I never use it.'

'Oh,' Connie had said rather blankly. But after a moment or two the blank look had disappeared. 'Well, if you're ashamed of your middle name, that's up to you. I'm *proud* of mine. I was called after my great-grandmother, who was a famous singer in the music halls.' She had grinned spitefully at Eve. 'I just thought you'd like to know.'

From that point on things had gone from bad to worse between the two girls. But now, peeping out of the window, Eve saw that it was one of those autumn days which come so rarely but are so delightful, with soft sunshine, a warm breeze and the ground thick with the gold and brown of fallen leaves. Lily and Miriam had obviously finished milking and were herding the cows back to their pasture, so Eve pushed her head a little further out of the window and waved violently, giving vent to a quiet 'Whoopee' as she did so.

'Who's champion cow this morning?' she called. 'When *I* learn to milk it will be Rosaline, because she's my favourite and Auntie Bess says cows give down more milk if they're being milked by someone who's fond of them.'

Lily looked up and grinned. 'Today's champion is Snowdrop. She filled her pail so full I had to fetch another. If you come down you can have a glass of milk whilst it's still warm.'

'Yuck!' said a scornful voice behind Eve. 'I *hate* warm milk; it's bad for you. My father says . . .'

'Oh, shut up,' Eve said, though not maliciously. 'Milk's not bad for you; why do you think the school gives us those little bottles to drink with our elevenses? Why should your father think it's harmful? Doesn't he sell it in his shop?'

'He does sell it in his shop,' Connie said sulkily. 'Well, he would if there was a call for it, but folk in Liverpool buy their milk direct from Mr Hastings. They come out with jugs and he fills them from a great big can on the back of the cart . . . it's the best milk in the world, the stuff Mr Hastings sells.'

Eve sighed and turned away from the window. Why did Connie have to be so argumentative? Why couldn't she, just occasionally, agree with what one said? Eve looked back on the halcyon days when she and Mabel had shared their thoughts and wished with all her might that those days could return. They might, of course; she knew that. It would soon be December and Connie had been loud in her determination to return to Liverpool for the Christmas holidays.

'I'm not afraid of bombs,' she had said scornfully. 'I'd risk more than bombs to be in dear old Liverpool for the festivities. My mum will get a big chicken and Dad will give her extra housekeeping money and Auntie Bess was talking about handing out sticks of sprouts and a bag of potatoes to anyone who went home around Christmas.'

A dozen snappy retorts rose to Eve's lips and were banished. What was the point? As she turned from the window Chrissie clambered out of his cot, scooped his clothing off the little chair by his bed and gave his sister a seraphic smile.

'I washed whilst you were looking at the cows,' he said untruthfully. 'But there's strawberry jam on my shirt; shall I get a clean one out?'

Eve tutted. 'You have *not* washed, so you can do that now, if you please. Give me the jammy shirt and I'll rinse it off in the kitchen when we go down for breakfast. Hurry up; it's a glorious day so we might as well make the most of it.'

Ten minutes later, scrubbed and brushed, Chrissie chuckled as they entered the kitchen. 'Mrs Ryder says she's going to light a fire in the drawing room and roast chestnuts today,' he said gleefully. 'Are you in school this morning, Evie? I don't *think* you are, so you might come and help Mrs Ryder and get some roast chestnuts for yourself.'

Eve smiled at her small brother; there were occasions now when she really loved him and did not have to put on an act. 'You're right, it's the other group who are having lessons this morning,' she assured the little boy. 'It's kind of Mrs Ryder to roast the chestnuts and I must say I'd appreciate a share. But come and sit down, darling, and eat your porridge, otherwise there'll be no roast chestnuts for either of us.'

Over the last few weeks, Eve, Connie and Chrissie had formed the habit of walking down to school with the evacuees from the neighbouring farms, for all of whom the lane that led past Drake's Farm was the quickest way – and the prettiest, Eve thought. After breakfast, when they gathered outside the gate, she looked around at the assembled children as she always did, wondering whether she would see the boy who had been so rude to her at New Cross station. She knew his name now – Johnny – and that he lived with three other boys at Spindlebush Farm, about a quarter of a mile up the road, but apart from that he was still a mystery. He seldom joined the other children in their games and seemed content to keep to himself, not having any particular friend, it seemed, amongst the other children at the school. There were a good few more boys than girls, since most of the farmers had stated bluntly that they would prefer boy evacuees to girls, since boys could help on the farm.

When she heard this Eve had been rather annoyed, for she thought girls could be every bit as useful as their male counterparts, but rather to her own surprise she had soon found she got on very well indeed with the boys. They were a nice crowd, always willing to help with homework or heave a girl over a stile, and today Eve had no qualms about cross-questioning Robbo, as the other boys called another of the lads from Spindlebush Farm, about the evacuee called Johnny.

'Though I've never exchanged so much as a word with him,' she hastened to explain. 'I saw him on the station platform in London and he was quite rude, so I just want to ask him why he didn't like me.'

'Oh, that's Johnny all over,' Robbo said cheerfully. 'There weren't nothin' personal in it, you may be sure; he were just so full of beans that he had to let them out on someone and you must've been the nearest. Don't give it a thought. He ain't avoiding you, it's just that he's having a bit of a laugh seeing you looking out for him all the time.'

'Well, he's a mystery to me,' Eve said stubbornly. 'Have you ever read *Alice's Adventures in Wonderland* – or is it *Through the Looking Glass*? I'm never quite sure which is which. Any road, he's like the Cheshire cat. I catch sight of him, up to some mischief no doubt, and then he fades away before I can grab him, leaving nothing behind but a grin.'

Robbo gave a snort of amusement. 'Wait till school starts properly after Christmas,' he suggested. 'Up till now, things have been in a rare muddle. What with all the coming and going teachers are finding themselves trying to take classes of kids from six or seven to thirteen or fourteen. The little 'uns don't understand a word they say and the big 'uns get bored and start to play up. But they're sortin' themselves out, and after Christmas we'll be in proper classes with registers an' such, so Johnny won't be able to slope off on his own affairs the way he does at present.'

As he spoke, Robbo looked curiously at Eve. They were strolling along the stretch of tarmac road on the last lap of their walk to the village and now his dark eyebrows rose quizzically. 'Why do you care? There's plenty of boys who are rude to girls just to get a rise out of 'em. Why pick on Johnny? I gave you a shove when we were both after the same lovely big chestnut, *and* I called you a name, but all you did was laugh. What's so special about Johnny?'

Eve shrugged, then scowled down at her feet. It was a fair enough question. Why *did* she care what Johnny thought? Sure, he had been rude to her, but so had a dozen other people. Come to think of it she had been rude to Johnny, or as rude as she dared be with her mother's eagle eye upon her. But Robbo was staring at her, clearly curious, and she made haste to answer. She stopped contemplating her stout lace-up shoes and met Robbo's glance with an assumption at least of frankness.

'Out of all the kids who've been dumped on the village there's only one face I've recognised, and that's Johnny's,' she said truthfully. 'But it doesn't matter; I guess you're right, and after Christmas I'll maybe find out what he's got against me.'

Robbo sighed. He was an attractive boy with a dimple in one cheek and floppy dark hair which he was forever pushing back out of his eyes. 'I keep tellin' you, Johnny will have forgotten whatever it was he said to you weeks ago. Still, if you end up in the same class you'll be able to ask him yourself. How old are you, anyway?'

'I'm nearly ten,' Eve said. 'Younger than Johnny, I think. Younger than you, for that matter. How old are you?'

'I'm nearly twelve, same as Johnny,' Robbo said promptly. They had been dawdling along the verge but speeded up as the cottages of the village came into view. 'I know you're not in school with us this morning, so I guess you're helping out in the nursery, in which case both of us had better get a move on.' He chuckled. 'Your little brother's joined up with Alex Ryder and the Caldecott twins, and between the four of them poor Mrs Ryder will have her hands full without you wandering in late.'

Eve sighed. Privately, she considered her time spent helping at the nursery to be purgatory, but it would not do to say so. 'Yes, I'm helping Mrs Ryder today,' she said resignedly. She smiled at her companion. 'Usually I don't enjoy it very much, but it's not so bad now that Christmas is getting close. We're making paper chains and other decorations for the village hall, because as you probably know they're having a big party there for all the evacuees; and later on, nearer the time, we're going to make food for it: little buns and sausage rolls and so on, which should be fun. Better than trying to interest the little blighters in Bible stories, anyway, which Mrs Ryder *will* insist are told to the children at least three times a day.'

Robbo whistled under his breath and cast his eyes heavenwards. 'I thank the good Lord my ma was never blessed with children younger'n me,' he said piously as they reached the rectory gate. 'Want me to tell Johnny you've been askin' for him? I don't mind acting as go-between if it'll help.'

Eve felt a blush burn up her neck and into her cheeks and shook her head decidedly. 'Don't you *dare*,' she said forcefully. 'Johnny's nothing to me.' She put a hand on the gate and swung it wide. 'Please, Robbo, don't say anything. As you say, when things get sorted out . . .'

'Robbo!' The shout came from an older boy who had been designated a prefect and whose job it was to try to sort out who should be where and when, an unenviable task.

Robbo sighed and gave Eve a shove towards the

78

rectory. 'All right, Mac,' he called. He winked at Eve. 'Just seein' me girlfriend gets to work on time, then I'll be at your service.'

Eve, hurrying down the brick path towards the solid bulk of the rectory, turned to pull a face at him, but she was too late. Robbo and Mac, deep in conversation, were already crossing the playground towards the old Victorian school.

Chapter Four

The Christmas party was every bit as much fun as they could make it, and the children almost forgot there was a war on. Some of the evacuees had even returned to their families for the holidays, a few of the more home-sick ones vowing never to return, but Eve and Chrissie, with Connie, Lily and Miriam, remained at Drake's Farm, much to the Favershams' delight. 'For it'll be our first year without Bob and Richard, and Christmas wouldn't be Christmas without some young folks in the house,' Auntie Bess had confided to Eve as she was cutting the tops for mince pies and Eve was spooning the delicious-looking mincemeat into the waiting pastry cups. 'I always think children round off Christmas the way candles round off a Christmas tree – they add the sparkle, and everyone feels happier because they're there. That's what you and Chrissie – and Connie, of course,' she added, looking rather conscious, 'will be this year – our Christmas candles.'

And then, before the memory of paper chains and sausage rolls and Auntie Bess's miraculous Christmas cake had even begun to fade, Eve woke up one morning to find that the long-promised snow had come at last.

Sitting on her bed with her blue woollen dressing gown tightly buttoned against the cold, she watched, enchanted, as the falling flakes, white against the grey of the sky, began to settle. The locals had been muttering about significant snow for several days and now Eve could see that they had been right. A bitter but brisk wind whirled the flakes this way and that, and watching from her eyrie Eve could see Miriam slogging across the farmyard, her woolly scarf tied tightly under her chin and her land girl's waterproof already bearing small pyramids of snow on either shoulder.

Eve went to the washstand, where to her secret delight she had to break the ice on the ewer, but she soon discovered that the business of cleaning off the previous day's grime with water whose temperature barely exceeded freezing point was not a pleasant one. After performing the sketchiest wash she could manage she eyed her slumbering companions as she dressed. After several sleepless nights in the Armstrongs' old room Lily had returned to the attic to escape poor Miriam's snores; her bed was empty, of course, but Chrissie was still dead to the world in the deep sleep of childhood, while Connie lay curled up into a tight little ball, her clothing spread out over the top blanket along with a rather threadbare winter coat and a bright red pixie hood which had been a Christmas present from her mother and father and was, she assured Eve, all the rage in her home city. Alone amongst the evacuees Connie came from Liverpool and so was able, Eve thought resentfully, to tell any number of tall stories about the place without fear of being branded a liar. Eve sighed and thrust her arms into the thick scarlet jumper which had been part of her own Christmas present from her parents. If only Connie had been more like Mabel! Mabel never sneered at anyone, but there was scarcely one evacuee who had not suffered from Connie's malignant tongue, which had become even sharp since her parents had refused point-blank to allow her to make the journey back to Liverpool for Christmas. In fact the only person Connie had time for was the golden Lily. She fawned round the older girl, offering to do any small jobs for her, but Lily, though always kind, refused such offers as politely as she could.

'That Connie! She's lonely and miserable but has too much pride to admit it,' Lily had once confided to Miriam when they were milking the cows, unaware that Eve had entered the shed. 'If only she wasn't so critical! I've tried telling her that she'll never be popular if she finds fault all the time, but she just says she doesn't want people to like her.'

Miriam, her head tucked into her cow's smooth flank, was busy stripping the last teat of its contents. 'They shouldn't have billeted her round here, where most of the other evacuees are from London,' she remarked. 'Naturally it gives her the perfect excuse to say anything she likes without fear of contradiction. But I dare say all they thought about was finding her a bed and a school place anywhere there was room.'

Lily picked up the two full buckets and set off to

pour the milk into the cooler. Over her shoulder, she put her own optimistic seal on the conversation.

'She'll settle in; they all do, in the end, and you couldn't ask for a better billet than Drake's Farm.'

But that had been weeks ago, and so far as Eve could see Connie was still as objectionable as ever. She knew for a fact that the good marks which the other girl had got in the rather rushed arithmetic test had been the result of peering over her neighbour's shoulder and copying both her workings and her results. Eve, who had never cheated in her life, had longed to tell; why should Connie benefit from the hard work of others, after all? But when she had found Lily alone in the scullery one day the older girl had put her straight.

'In the end, cheats get their come-uppance,' she had assured Eve. 'Why don't you try to be a little kinder to her – Connie, I mean? She must be miserably unhappy to spend all her time being so nasty. I've done my best to make her feel at home and see she gets her share of any little extras going, but so far she hasn't appeared to notice.'

'Oh, but you are the one person she really likes, Lily,' Eve had said quickly. 'Do you remember, when we had rabbit pie and apple crumble for supper, how she went on about being patriotic and said that Auntie Bess should think of our poor soldiers and sailors instead of feeding a lot of useless evacuees?'

Lily had chuckled. 'I do indeed! I bet she'd shout louder than anyone if Auntie Bess gave us bread and dripping instead of that rabbit pie. Look, Eve, I'm doing everything I can to try to help, but you must do your best as well. Believe me, Connie is absolutely miserable. I doubt if she's ever visited the country in her whole life; certainly she's never lived in it. That's why she keeps telling us that Liverpool is so wonderful. Well, it might be, for all I know, but so is Devon, and it's up to us to see she's happy here. Are you game to try?'

'I have tried,' Eve had said indignantly. 'Honest to God, Lily, I've done my best. I heard her crying one night when she was still quite new and hadn't lived here very long. It was a freezing cold night but I got up and went and sat on the end of her bed, asking her what was the matter and could I do anything to help. She lay there quite quiet for a minute and I started to tell her how we were all homesick at first but we soon settled in, and do you know what she did? She bunched up like – like a sort of steel spring, and kicked out so hard that I shot across the room and bruised my shoulder on the washstand. And she called me a nosy cow and said she wasn't going to take cheek from me. Then she hunched the covers over her shoulders, said three bad words in a row, and said she hoped my shoulder was broken. Honestly, Lily, she isn't a nice person at all.'

Lily had put a comforting arm around Eve's shoulders. 'Deep unhappiness sometimes comes out in the oddest way,' she said. 'You go on being nice to Connie and she'll come round and show a side of herself that you've not yet seen. Next time you catch her out in a lie, pretend you think she was just kidding. No one's all bad, Eve; it's just insecurity which makes her tell such whoppers. Last time I heard her boasting about

her life in Liverpool and her rich relatives I pretended
I knew the city quite well, and she shut up like a clam
and changed the subject. She'll come round, you'll see.'

This conversation had taken place some days earlier
and now Eve stared across at Connie's rumpled head,
just visible in the light which flickered palely through
the attic window. Perhaps Lily was right and Connie
was just lonely and unhappy and would gradually begin
to show her nicer side. If she's got one, Eve thought
rather doubtfully. She remembered her promise to be
nicer to the objectionable newcomer and sat up a little
straighter on her bed. She would try, she really would.

She was about to go downstairs and start on her
chores, but then a thought struck her and instead she
went over to Connie's bed and perched on it, whisper-
ing, 'Connie, the snow's ever so thick and the land girls
will be carting the milk down to the end of the lane
presently. If you hurry you could come with me and
give them a helping hand.' She was watching Connie's
face as she spoke and saw the bright blue eyes open
and fix muzzily on her face.

'Is it time to get up?' Connie asked in a slurred, sleep-
blurred voice. 'Don't say it's seven o'clock already?'

'I dunno what time it is,' Eve said. 'But all our normal chores get turned upside down when the snow's
on the ground, Uncle Reg said so at supper last night.
So I thought I'd get up early and see what I could do to
help. There's still the hens and the pigs to be fed, and—'

Connie's eyelids had been gradually lowering, but
suddenly they shot open again. 'Bugger off!' she said
loudly. 'No wonder I never heard the alarm, 'cos it

didn't ring, did it? You're just trying to smarm up to Lily, because you know I'm her favourite.' She smiled suddenly, but it was not a nice smile. 'Want me to kick you into the bloody washstand again? I could, you know; I'm quite strong enough.'

With these words she humped the blanket over her shoulders once more and Eve turned away, shocked to the core. Two bad words before breakfast, she thought, scandalised. Before she came to Drake's Farm she had not heard even the mildest of expletives, but here the farmhands frequently cursed when a cow trod hastily or a horse accidentally bit the hand that fed it. Amongst the children, however, swearing was much frowned upon by Auntie Bess, for on her only visit so far Mrs Armstrong had mentioned that she had heard one of the farmhands using what she described as 'bad language'. It might not have mattered, but Chrissie had seized upon the offending word and even Auntie Bess, a broad-minded woman, had not liked to hear a three-year-old cussing like a man grown.

As usual Eleanor had blamed Eve for letting her little brother learn such words, but Auntie Bess had shaken a reproving head.

''Tisn't as though the child knew what he was sayin',' she told Eleanor. 'If you make somethin' of it we'll be hearin' that word twenty times a day for the next three weeks. If you ignore it, the lad will forget it in an hour. And as for its being anything to do with young Eve here, what's she supposed to do? Stuff the kid's ears with cotton wool?'

Eleanor had laughed. 'There I go, over-reacting as

usual,' she had said lightly, and the matter had been allowed to drop.

Now Eve resisted the temptation to say something sharp to Connie and headed for the stairs, clattering down both flights noisily and hoping that, if she woke Chrissie, he would begin to bellow, so that Connie would either have to get out of bed and help him to dress or be in trouble with Auntie Bess. One of the few rules the latter imposed upon her charges was that no one would allow Chrissie to come to harm, and trotting around the farmhouse in his nightwear in such freezing weather could easily lead to a bad cold in the head, if nothing worse.

Eve burst into the kitchen and saw that she was certainly not too early. Auntie Bess believed everyone worked better in snowy conditions if they had a good hot meal inside them. She would serve the usual porridge, Eve knew that, but there would also be bacon sandwiches: thick slices of home-made bread between which would nestle equally thick slices of bacon. The land girls and Uncle Reg would have waded into breakfast this morning with a will, happy to know that an equally substantial meal would be provided at the end of their working day. Eve herself, Chrissie and Connie did not need the sandwiches, but would be given something extra, perhaps a second boiled egg, sitting in a little china egg cup and awaiting their pleasure.

Mrs Faversham, standing at the stove, looked up and smiled as Eve entered the room. 'Is that dratted brother of yours with you?' she enquired. 'He likes a three minute egg so's he can dip his soldiers into the yolk, but as I tell him, I can't foretell the future, so I doesn't put his egg on to boil until he's finished his porridge. And you'll have to get on with your chores without him today, 'cos the snow's too deep for a little 'un. If I were to let Chrissie go out in this weather it would come over the tops of those little wellies what your mum bought him, and that would never do.'

As Eve went out of the kitchen to fetch Chrissie she could not help smiling. They had been at the farm now for over three months and though school was still what you might describe as a bit of a muddle Mr and Mrs Faversham saw to it that the farm was run efficiently, everyone knowing their jobs and feeling proud when they were congratulated by the farmer and his wife on the way they'd handled their chores. In fact, Eve thought, running quietly up the second flight of stairs, apart from Connie things could scarcely have been better. Once animals were fed, horses groomed and stables and sties swept out and laid with fresh straw, the young inhabitants of Drake's Farm could do more or less as they liked provided they arrived promptly in the kitchen at meal times. Mrs Faversham told them frankly that to waste food in wartime was wicked.

'Keep your ears open for the sound of the church clock and you won't go far wrong,' she had told them. 'During the holidays, once you've done your chores the rest of the day is your own. Just remember to come in for dinner and tea and don't get benighted; we've not got the time to go quartering the countryside looking for kids who might've fallen in the snow and bust both their ankles.'

Eve had just reached the top of the stairs when Chrissie's shrill treble sounded in her ears, along with a more muffled sound which she guessed must be emanating from Connie. She shot across the landing and threw open the bedroom door, to see Chrissie tugging at Connie's bedclothes whilst Connie shouted at him to get out and go down for breakfast.

'I'm skippin' the meal for the sake of my figure,' she informed Eve. 'It's about time you did the same. You're getting as fat as a pig, Eve Armstrong.'

Eve scooped Chrissie up and carried him over to the washstand to wash his grubby little face and fingers in the icy water. At the mere touch of the flannel he shrieked and hit out, but Eve went grimly on with her task until her little brother was clean and then dressed him as swiftly as possible, completely ignoring Connie when she shot up in bed, tousle-headed and sleepy, to demand that Eve should get her brother out of the attic before she landed them both a good hard thump.

Only when she had finished with Chrissie did she turn to the other girl. 'Are you sure you're not coming down for breakfast? I don't honestly think you're ever going to get fat, you lucky thing.'

She spoke as pleasantly as she could, still mindful of Lily's suggestion that she should try to find Connie's nice side. After all, if you looked at it practically, Connie did have a nice side, but she kept it for grown-ups – and Lily, of course. To the other evacuees – and Eve now counted herself and Chrissie as evacuees – she was sharp and bitter if she did not simply ignore them, though Eve had noticed that she was nicer to the boys than to the girls; nicer even to the old farmhands than she was to their wives. However, Eve continued grimly to be nice to Connie, or as nice as she could bear to be in the face of the other girl's antagonism, so now she continued, 'Are you getting up or not? Do you want me to tell Auntie Bess you've decided to have a lie-in? I don't mind doing your chores if you really don't want any breakfast.'

Connie sighed deeply and threw off the covers. 'And you'd eat my egg, no doubt, as payment,' she said bitterly. 'All right, all right, I'll be down in ten minutes. I'll tell Auntie Bess you forgot to wake me.'

Eve clamped her lips together tightly, but Chrissie, now warmly clad in thick knitted jersey and trousers, dashed towards the door.

'Eggs, eggs, eggs!' he shouted. 'And you are a fibber, Connie Hale. Eve did wake you, you know she did, so if you tell Auntie Bess she didn't you'll go to the Other Place, which Mrs Ryder told us was a polite way of saying hell.'

'Oh, shut your bleedin' face,' Connie said rudely.

Eve lifted Chrissie up, rested him on her hip and left the room, giving him a secret little smile as she did so. It was obvious that though Chrissie was a boy he did not yet count as such so far as Connie was concerned. Eve wondered at what age her little brother would start to receive polite treatment from the other girl, but then realised that Connie was unlikely to be around as Chrissie grew older. Connie was a city girl to the marrow of her bones, and her oft-repeated promise to leave

Drake's Farm just as soon as she could always sounded as though she meant it.

Eve and Chrissie arrived in the kitchen just as Auntie Bess finished spooning porridge into two dishes and raised her brows at Eve.

'No Connie?' she asked, giving Eve a confidential little grin. 'That girl do hate it when 'tis her turn to clean the beast housin', but whilst she's under my roof she'll live by my rules. Ah, I hear footsteps.' She began to ladle porridge into a third bowl just as Connie entered the kitchen and slid into her accustomed place, turning to give Mrs Faversham a broad but sleepy smile. 'Sorry I'm late, but Eve didn't wake me,' she said, giving Eve a malicious glance.

Mrs Faversham chuckled, but Chrissie, beginning work on his porridge, shook his curly golden head. 'Only bad children tell fibs,' he announced chattily. 'Eve did wake her, only she used a naughty word and wouldn't get up. Don't know why, because the boys from Spindlebush Farm is going sledging. I've never been sledging but I want to go.' He turned wide, appealing eyes on his sister's face. 'You'll take me when your chores is done, won't you, Eve?' he enquired. 'There may be snowball fights later, and Robbo said that when the snow came they'd have a compe-whatsit to see who could make the biggest snowman. I *like* the snow; I wish it would snow all winter.'

Connie grunted. 'I've got a pain in my back,' she said pathetically. 'Someone else will have to clean out the cowshed. I can't bend and straighten to get the muck into the wheelbarrow.' She turned eagerly to the older woman. 'I'll help you in the house, Auntie Bess. I can lay fires and make pastry . . .'

Eve smiled to herself. She had watched the farmyard cats, who seldom if ever came indoors, picking their way distastefully across the snowy yard to reach the comparative safety of the big barn, and thought now that Connie was just like one of them. She hated the cold and the snow and simply wanted to be tucked away in the warm kitchen. But it was her turn to help the farmhands to muck out the cowshed and no amount of pleading that she had a headache, could feel a bilious attack coming on, or suspected that she had broken her ankle would make the slightest difference. Auntie Bess would laugh, rumple Connie's dark brown curls and give her a push towards the back door.

'You're a one, you are,' Auntie Bess said now. 'Do your share, young woman, and before you know it the job will be done. Mr Smith's got a real bad go of arthritis and he's going to feed the poultry so it'll just be you, Mr Trevalyn and Miriam. It's not her turn to muck out but she's a good girl. Lily had tackled nearly all the milking before she'd sat down for breakfast. So you get on, like the rest of us, and I don't expect to see you inside this kitchen until you pop in for elevenses.'

Chrissie sniggered. 'When I'm a man I'll have arthuritis and I'll muck out the cowshed even if me bones hurt,' he said boastfully. 'But I aren't a man yet so I'll help with the little jobs and then Eve will take me to Spindlebush Farm and show me how to sledge.'

Upon these words he scraped round his now empty

porridge dish and began on his egg. Auntie Bess had already taken the top off for him, and now he dipped bread and butter fingers into the golden yolk with great enthusiasm. 'You'll take me sledging, won't you, Eve?' he repeated, and it occurred to Eve that his sojourn at the farm had already greatly improved not only his manners but also his speech. Once away from the influence of a too-fond mother he was becoming quite a nice little boy; indeed, when Eleanor had visited at Christmas she had been surprised and perhaps even not quite pleased at the change in her favourite child. But right now Eve feared that her little brother was in for a disappointment. Auntie Bess had said he was not to go out into the snow, and Eve knew that she would not change her mind. It was not that she was unyielding and cruel; quite the opposite, in fact. She planned her days carefully, and though she had not said so Eve knew that by keeping Chrissie indoors, unpopular though it may be, she was trying to ensure that the little boy did not catch cold, slip on the ice or otherwise come to grief. It was true that she did not have time to nurse him, but Eve was sure that her primary concern was for Chrissie's well-being and not her own.

But Chrissie was dipping his last soldier boy in the egg and then beginning to scoop out the delicious white. 'I can go sledging, can't I, Eve?' he persisted.

Eve finished her own egg and looked rather helplessly at Chrissie's rosy expectant face. She had opened her mouth to begin a placatory reply when Auntie Bess took things into her own hands. She came away from the stove and lifted Chrissie from his high chair.

'You're getting so big and strong I think you can sit on an ordinary chair in future,' she said. 'As for them boys from Spindlebush Farm, they'll have a mort of jobs to do before they can play in the snow. It wouldn't surprise me if they took the sledge into the village to fetch pig meal and such and didn't get to throw a single snowball.'

Chrissie's face had fallen as he gazed up at Auntie Bess. 'Well then, I'm going to make a slide right across the farmyard. I'll hide in the tack room and watch people fall over and break their bleedin' ankles, so I shall.'

Eve giggled and so, rather to her surprise, did Connie, but Auntie Bess did not.

'Don't you go repeatin' what the farmhands say; that's bad talk and you know it,' she said reprovingly. 'And as for makin' slides and watchin' people have nasty falls, you can forget that. No, I've a much better idea. You and me will have a bake day and you can be my chief taster. We can't have icing sugar but there's nowt to stop us makin' a batch of gingerbread, and when we've done that I'll show you how I make dumplings to go in the stew we're having for our tea tonight.'

Eve saw Chrissie open his mouth to object to this tame pastime, but at the mention of stew and dumplings he looked thoughtful. It was his favourite meal, and much though he had wanted to play in the snow the temptation to be the chief taster, when his favourite meal was on the menu, was strong. I'm not the only one who knows Auntie Bess won't be persuaded to do what she thinks is wrong, Eve told herself. And if I get away quickly, as soon as I've helped with the chores,

I'll be able to explore a bit more of the countryside, snow or no snow. It will be the first time I've not had Chrissie hanging on to my hand and making me carry him as soon as his legs get tired. He's not a bad kid, in fact he's getting better every day, but it will still be a relief not to have him chattering away beside me.

She looked across the kitchen to where Auntie Bess was carrying the dirty dishes over to the sink, and Auntie Bess smiled at her and winked. Eve smiled back, delighted to see understanding in the other's face. Auntie Bess was a wonder! She understood Chrissie and was not fooled for an instant by Connie's pretended sweetness. Auntie Bess knew Connie was lazy and bad-tempered, but she never let it influence the way she treated her, which was just how she treated Eve herself.

Right now Chrissie was chattering away to Auntie Bess, very much as though it had been his own idea not to go out in the snow. Eve was most impressed; how had Auntie Bess done it? She had managed to make a day in the house sound the sort of thing Chrissie would most enjoy. Sledging, if it involved going into the village to fetch pig meal, became an unwanted chore, and making a slide in order to watch people fall over – though it might have been fun – was not the sort of thing a nice child would even contemplate.

Whether he would let his sister escape without him, however, was another thing altogether. He had grown increasingly fond of Eve and she knew he thought of her as a sort of mother substitute, but mothers cannot spend their whole lives pandering to their children's whims, and even Chrissie must be aware of this, so

95

Eve was not too surprised that he took no notice when Auntie Bess told her to get her coat on.

'You can do my marketing, little Eve,' she continued. 'I've got a list as long as your arm for Mrs Shelborne, and perhaps you'll persuade her to explain about this 'ere rationing, what the wireless announced t'other day. It seems if you keep hens instead of buyin' eggs they'll give you poultry feed, but I'm not sure how it works.' She sighed. 'All these ministries of this and that, poppin' up all over the place, tellin' you one thing one moment and somethin' different the other. 'Tis a good thing we're remote, like, and on the small side, but no doubt they'll get round to us sooner or later and I don't want to be in trouble, so I hopes Mrs Shelborne can explain.'

'All right, Auntie Bess,' Eve said joyfully. She could go into the village by her beloved old lane, sauntering along at her own pace, enjoying the crisp air and scuttling through the three or four inches of snow until her boots met the crackling golden-brown leaves of the previous autumn. She wished Mabel was still at Drake's Farm – she wished this a dozen times every day – but she had always had a lively imagination and could pretend that her friend was with her, anxious to hear her news and to pass on her own.

Auntie Bess had a small notebook in her hand and was frowning down at it, clearly checking the shopping list before handing it over to Eve. 'Mrs Shelborne will sort out what I can have and what I can't,' she remarked as she did so. She glanced significantly at the pantry where Chrissie, muttering to himself, was selecting items which he thought Auntie Bess would need for her baking. 'Go you off, child, before young master decides to try to go with you,' she said in a low tone. She jerked a thumb at Eve's coat and hat hanging on their hook by the back door. 'Unless you want to hear wails of protest you'd best slip off while his lordship is fully occupied.' She smiled conspiratorially at Eve as that young person began to don coat, hat and boots. 'There's no hurry for the shopping, but you'll be wanting your lunch so listen out for the church clock and be back in time for whatever I'm serving.'

'I will, Auntie Bess,' Eve said, and slid out of the back door as stealthily as any mouse. She crossed the snowy farmyard at a trot, glancing apprehensively over her shoulder as she did so, but all was quiet. Chrissie had not missed her yet, or perhaps he had simply decided that assisting Auntie Bess with her baking was probably more fun than a chilly trek into the village and back.

Eve turned out of the gate and set off in the direction of the village, giving herself an ecstatic hug. This was the first time she had been alone in the lane since that wonderful day when she had seen Drake's Farm for the first time. There were many games which the children had used to shorten the long walk into the village in the weeks since then, but Eve had never revealed to anyone but Mabel those first magical moments when she had imagined fairy folk sculling tiny acorn boats across the still waters amongst the beech tree roots. Today, however, she could please herself. When she reached the stream she could wander along to the deep pool where the brown trout lurked and spend as much time as she liked simply watching them. It would be impossible to play games such as the three billy goats gruff, but what did that matter? And it would be rather fun to walk in her stout wellingtons amongst the frosted reeds, breaking the ice, and wading across by the ford, instead of using the bridge which looked so frail but was, in fact, extremely tough, since the farm horses came this way on occasion and the bridge scarcely creaked under their considerable weight.

Eve had been walking slowly anyway, but now she slowed even more. On her right was the old orchard, looking wonderfully festive with snow on every branch. She had never seen the orchard when the blossom was out, but now, with the snow taking the place of the apple flowers, she could imagine it in all its beauty, and determined to ask Auntie Bess when she could expect to see the first frail pink and white of the petals.

She passed the spot where she had seen that solitary wild strawberry growing on the mossy bank, and remembered that Uncle Reg had told her that in summer the bank would be scarlet with berries and she would be able to fill a basket for Auntie Bess, who, like Nanny Burton, vowed and declared that the flavour of a wild strawberry would never be matched by the cultivated kind.

But now it was winter and even the moss on the tall banks was covered with snow, so when she heard a soft thud, though it made her jump, she immediately concluded that it was the snow sliding off one of the big fruit trees which lined the lane and would have continued dreamily sauntering onwards had a hand not gripped her shoulder and an accusing voice spoken practically in her ear, making her jump quite six inches and squeak with fright.

'You've been talking to Robbo about me; asking questions and that. Well, now you can ask me to my face. Go on, what's your interest in Johnny Durrell?'

It was none other than the boy from New Cross station. Recovering a little from the initial shock, Eve spoke slowly. 'It's because when I first came here yours was the only face I recognised, but whenever I tried to speak to you you always seemed to disappear,' she said. 'I told Robbo you were like a Cheshire cat; I'd catch sight of you amongst the other kids in the school playground or making for home at the end of the day, but before I could reach you all there was left was a Cheshire cat grin because the rest of you had buzzed off. I only wanted to ask you why you didn't like me, but you never gave me the opportunity. As I said, you just pulled off your disappearing trick so naturally that I thought you were avoiding me, and I wanted to know why.'

All the time she was talking she was staring at Johnny. He was tall and sturdily built, with straight blond hair which fell over his forehead and was constantly flicked back, eyes of so dark a blue that one had to stare in order to make certain that they were not black, and a determined chin. He had eyebrows so fair that they were almost white, and as Eve came to the end of her explanation they drew together in a puzzled frown.

'Let me get this right,' he said. 'You claim to have recognised me, but I don't see how you can have, because I don't know you. Were you at St Cuthbert's primary? You could have been, I suppose, though I can't remember seeing you there. So where are we supposed to have met one another? Or were you just telling whoppers to make yourself more interesting?'

Eve stiffened indignantly. 'I've got no need to tell horrid lies to do that,' she said crossly. 'My old English teacher in London used to say one of the girls put on airs to be interesting; I suppose that's what you meant, isn't it? Come to that, someone who keeps deliberately disappearing . . . oh, never mind. No I did not go to St Cuthbert's, wherever that might be, and if you can't remember seeing me before I came to Drake's Farm you can't. Who cares?'

For a moment the boy looked surprised, then he shrugged. 'If you don't want to tell me, that's fine by me,' he said. 'You're only a little kid, after all. If you're going into the village we might as well walk together.' He grinned suddenly. 'And to make the walk more interesting you can give me a clue – a clue about where we met, I mean.'

Eve hesitated, but only for a second. She had been looking forward to revisiting the magical spots, and pretending that Mabel was with her, but heaven knew she had waited long enough to find out why Johnny had first been rude to her and had since kept out of her way. She might not get such an opportunity again, so she glanced sideways at him and then nodded.

'Right,' she said, 'only you have to answer my question

first. Why did you disappear whenever I tried to have a chat? Is that fair?'

'Yeah, I suppose so,' Johnny said thoughtfully. 'In fact I might have spoken to you sooner, when Robbo said you'd been asking about me, but I never saw you alone. Either you were with a group, or you had that kid hanging on to your sleeve, the little one with yellow hair. I don't like kids; they're a perishin' nuisance, and I didn't want him taggin' on to me the way he tags on to you. Robbo told me he were your brother, but as I said I'm not fond of kids.'

'I'm not too keen on them myself,' Eve said ruefully, 'but I don't have much choice; Mummy made me promise to look after Chrissie – that's his name, Chrissie – and he kicks up such a fuss if I leave the farm without him that it's easier to take him than not. But Auntie Bess – that's Mrs Faversham – takes him off my hands when she can, and this morning she promised to let him be chief taster whilst she did the baking, so he let me come out without any bother. Daddy's in the Navy and Mummy's in Plymouth with him, so Auntie Bess is in charge.'

She chanced a glance up into Johnny's face and saw that he was looking slightly contemptuous. She did not have to ask him why. 'You think it's babyish to call my parents Mummy and Daddy,' she said shrewdly. 'I did try using "Mother" when she got something she called a forty-eight at Christmas and came rushing up to Drake's Farm. She brought our Christmas presents, nice thick jumpers and stuff like that for us both and a pink teddy with blue eyes for Chrissie to cuddle when he goes to bed. Chrissie and I agreed that we would call her Mum or Mother, which is what most of the evacuees call their parents, but she just got cross, so we've reverted to Mummy and Daddy – for a bit, anyway.' She giggled. 'It was made worse by Chrissie throwing the teddy bear across the living room and saying he was a big man now with Arthur Askey – he meant arthritis – and didn't want a baby's teddy bear, especially not a pink one.'

She did not add, as she might have done, that Mummy had scolded her for encouraging Chrissie to forget his darling baby ways, and whilst she was considering whether to ask if Johnny had little brothers and sisters he suddenly stopped dead and pulled her round to face him.

'Mummy!' he crowed triumphantly. 'That's the clue. Mummy! New Cross station! Gosh, you've changed. You were such a prim little thing, with your hair in plaits and a panama hat plonked dead straight on top of your head.' He chuckled. 'Of course, I never expected to see you again or I might have been a bit more polite. What did I say to you that you've remembered all these months?'

Eve smiled. 'Your words are burned on my brain,' she said teasingly. 'Can you truly not remember? Honest Injun?'

Johnny shook his head and gave her a wicked grin and Eve could not help thinking how nice he looked when he smiled. 'I suppose I'm not surprised you've forgotten – or at least are pretending to have forgotten,' she said chidingly. 'It was very rude. *We're gettin' on a better train than this one. This one's for kids. Us older ones is goin' to the country, so yah boo and sucks to you!'*

Johnny laughed. 'Well, that's put me in my place,' he said. 'If I think it's childish to call your ma Mummy, then I admit it's just as childish to shout insults through a train window, so shall we call it quits?' He held out a square and rather dirty hand. 'Shake on it, buddy,' he said in his best American cowboy accent. 'Tell you what, how about you and me being mates? You're not much younger than me, and if you can get rid of that little brother of yours you me and Robbo can have a good time, one way and another. I've seen you with another girl – dunno her name, but she looks a good sport. What say we make up a foursome? We can do all sorts when summer arrives. What do you think?'

Eve had been about to accept the suggestion with real pleasure, but now she hesitated. Was Johnny thinking of Mabel? Surely he could not have taken a liking to the detestable Connie Hale? How could she find out which of the two girls he meant? After a moment, she cleared her throat.

'Do you mean Mabel? She's got very pale blond hair and blue eyes and she's a bit older than me; well, quite a bit older actually. But she's left Drake's Farm so that she can be with her cousin Joyce. We see each other at school sometimes but it's not the same.'

Johnny scowled at his booted feet, then raised his eyes to Eve's and heaved a sigh. 'Why would I suggest a foursome with a girl who doesn't live here any more?' he asked impatiently. 'I've seen you with a girl who's got sort of dark hair, but I couldn't tell you the colour

103

of her eyes or anything like that. You and she usually come out of the farm together.'

'You must mean Connie Hale,' Eve said, after giving the matter some thought. The last thing she wanted was a foursome which included the horrible Connie, and with her luck she would find herself bracketed with Robbo whilst Johnny and Connie became close friends. She opened her mouth to tell Johnny that she and Connie were anything but mates, then changed her mind. See how it goes, a small inner voice advised her. You like Johnny already, despite how badly he behaved at New Cross station. See how it goes, Eve Armstrong. 'I don't know her very well yet, but that sounds fun,' she said rather doubtfully. 'But what about Chrissie? I can't guarantee that I shan't be landed with him, you know.'

Johnny laughed, put his arm around her shoulders and propelled her forward. 'I'm sure we'll manage something somehow,' he said cheerfully. 'Are you in a hurry? If not, there's something in the wood I'd like to show you, so long as you promise not to go telling every Tom, Dick and Harry.'

'Ooh, secrets!' Eve said happily. 'I shan't say a word to anyone, but I can't guarantee Connie won't talk; she's a bit of a blabbermouth, or that's what Lily – one of the land girls on the farm – called her.'

'But she isn't here,' Johnny pointed out. He looked shrewdly down into Eve's face. 'You don't like her, do you? But from what you've said she hasn't been with you very long, so perhaps your judgement is a bit hasty. Incidentally, do you know how far this wood extends?'

By now they were under the branches of the great beech trees and beneath their feet the snow had given way to a mere sprinkling of frost.

'I've no idea,' Eve said truthfully. 'Although Chrissie and I have been at Drake's Farm for ages I haven't had much opportunity to explore, but I do remember old Mr Smith telling a story once about a time when the snow was so deep that it came above his boots. It was about some child getting lost in the wood and when he was discovered old Mr Smith said he was stiff as a board and dead as a dodo. He said if it hadn't been for the farm dogs starting to dig in one of the snowdrifts they mightn't have found the body until spring.' She gave a shudder. 'So I suppose the wood must be a lot bigger than the little bit we see on our way to and from school.'

Johnny nodded. 'It's immense,' he told her, 'but fortunately the snow isn't too deep, and even if it was . . .' he pulled her to a halt and pointed to the trees by which they were surrounded, 'it would have to come awfully high to cover the markers. Can you see them?'

Eve looked around her. Mostly, the trees were fully grown and mature, but every now and again a brave sapling raised its head; Eve felt she could almost see the little trees straining towards the blue sky above. But Johnny was looking at her expectantly and she broke into hasty speech.

'Do you mean the little saplings on either side of us? I remember one of the farmhands saying that every five years or so someone comes along and thins out the big trees to give the little ones a chance, only I don't see how you can tell . . .'

Johnny laughed. 'No, it's much simpler than that.' He went over to a mighty beech and pointed to where an axe had chipped a V-shaped scar in the grey bark just above shoulder height. 'See that? The trees with those marks trace the main path through the wood.'

'That's brilliant,' Eve said admiringly. 'But if it was me by myself I might simply go deeper and deeper into the wood just by following the axe marks.'

Johnny grinned. 'You aren't as daft as you look,' he said. 'If you go closer you'll see there's a sort of red blob near the axe mark. The red blob shows the way to the lane and a green blob to the other side of the wood; get it?'

'Yes I do, and it's brilliant,' Eve said again. 'Only you haven't said what there is at the other side of the wood. Does it go to the village? Don't say it goes all the way to the town!'

Johnny shook his head. 'Someone told me it leads to the forestry part,' he said. 'That's where the authorities plant trees which will be harvested at a certain time of year, just as though they were apples or sprouts or something. They're very hardy and can grow higher than the broadleaf trees; broadleaf means beeches, elms and oaks and such like – anything which sheds its leaves in the autumn and grows new ones in the spring. The forestry trees don't have leaves, they have needles.'

'I know; like Christmas trees. I think they're called conifers,' Eve said, remembering something Daddy had once told her.

Johnny nodded. 'When I'm old enough to get a job I want to work with the forestry people so I'm learning all I can about trees. Or I might go for farming – something outdoors, at any rate.'

Eve was about to suggest that cutting down trees might not be much fun if you loved them, but at that moment Johnny pulled her off the path and into the wilderness of young trees and frosted grass. Naturally enough, having heard Mr Smith's awful story and seeing no marked trees on either side, Eve resisted.

'The trunks of these trees don't have blobs on,' she said. 'Oh, Johnny, I don't want us to be like the babes in the wood!' She glanced fearfully around her, then gave a nervous laugh. 'What if I found myself knocking at a gingerbread door and being pulled into a marshmallow cottage by some old witch? If there are marks on these trees I can't see them, and I don't believe you can either.'

Johnny grinned. 'You're right, but don't get in a state,' he said cheerfully. 'I know where I'm going, and fortunately I've got a good sense of direction. I don't want to leave a trail because some of the country people, the farmers in particular, would— Aha! We've arrived. *This* is what I wanted to show you.'

He pointed, but all Eve could see was a largish area of beaten snow and what looked like a very large rabbit hole. She looked questioningly up at her companion.

'What a whopping rabbit burrow. But I've been noticing them – smaller ones – all over the place, so what's different about this one? Apart from the size, I mean?'

Johnny gave a small snort of triumph. 'It's clear you don't know much about the country yet,' he said mockingly. 'This, my dear Eve, is most certainly not a rabbit burrow. In fact it isn't a burrow at all, but a sett. And do you know who lives there?' He sank his voice to a whisper. 'It's a badger's house, just like the one in that book by Kenneth Grahame. I can't remember what it's called, but . . .'

'Do you mean *The Wind In The Willows*?' Eve said. Secretly, she was more than a little disappointed. After the long walk she had expected to be shown something really exciting: a tree house or a log cabin which Johnny and Robbo had built for themselves. But she knew better than to show Johnny a disappointed face. Instead, she smiled brightly at him and lowered her own voice. 'I say, Johnny, how clever of you to find Mr Badger's very own front door! If we were small enough and could walk into the hole I'm sure we'd find a little green-painted door and a gilt knocker. Did you find it yourself, or did one of the forestry men show you? I wish—'

But at this point Johnny's hand clamped over her mouth and muffled the words which were about to emerge from between her lips, and he pointed to something Eve had not noticed before: a little path down which was coming a figure she recognised only from books and stories. The badger was returning from his night's wanderings.

The two youngsters watched in awe as he padded along his narrow path, paused to look around him carefully and then disappeared into his sett. For a moment neither spoke. Eve realised she had been holding her breath and released it in a long low sigh.

'I never thought I'd see a badgers' sett, let alone a real live badger,' she said. 'How many people know about this, Johnny? Does the badger have a wife down in that hole? And little ones?'

Johnny shrugged and drew her back the way they had come. 'Hush,' he whispered. 'Wait till we're out of earshot. If the badger knew we'd watched him he might abandon the sett and go and live somewhere else.'

Eve nodded and neither said another word until they were well clear. Only then did Johnny answer her question. 'So far as I know I'm the only person who's ever spotted so much as a whisker of the badger, let alone his sett,' he said. 'And now there's you, of course.' He grinned down at her, his eyes still alight with the wonder of what they had seen. 'I was telling you; some of the local farmers have queer ideas and blame the badgers for passing on tuberculosis to their cattle. It's all rubbish, of course, but I've actually heard people say they've watched badgers drinking milk from a cow's udder. So you see I don't mean to tell anyone else about what we've seen today. I only found it yesterday and I was longing to tell someone, but I wouldn't dream of putting the badgers' lives at risk.' He turned to look down at her, his face still flushed from excitement. 'We mustn't make a path straight from the lane to the sett because someone else might follow it. One of the farmhands at Spindlebush once told me quite proudly that he'd killed a badger with a spade and dug out the sett in order to kill its mate. With folk like that around . . . well, I daren't even tell Robbo, but you're a girl, and girls don't even like squashing spiders or batting wasps away from cake, so I decided I could let you into the secret. Only you must promise to keep it to yourself.'

Eve licked her finger and drew it across her throat in the time-honoured fashion. 'See this wet, see this dry . . .' she began, but Johnny interrupted.

'Don't worry. I could tell you weren't the blabbing sort or I'd never have shown you,' he assured her. 'But don't forget this is just you and me. What is it that wall poster says?'

Eve giggled. *'Be like Dad and keep Mum,'* she quoted. 'Are we nearly back at the lane? Only I promised Auntie Bess I'd be home in time for lunch and I haven't done the shopping yet.'

Chapter Five

The old woman sitting on the mossy log smiled to herself as the memories flooded in. The badgers' sett! She had not thought about it for years, and yet at the time it had seemed so important. It had been the first secret between herself and Johnny, who was determined not to let even a hint of its whereabouts become known. Anything which led to its discovery, he had said impressively, would be bad news not just for the old badger but for his young as well.

The old woman played the memory back and frowned a little. Surely they had discovered the sett in winter, so why did her mind show her the green of young beech leaves against a sky of brilliant blue? She shrugged to herself; perhaps, after all, memories were not always more accurate than dreams, because she knew perfectly well that Johnny had talked of not visiting the sett again whilst their tracks in the snow might give the animals away. Of course there must have come a time when the weather had improved, but she was almost certain they had not visited the badgers' sett for months after that first occasion. She had a vague feeling that there had been something else on their minds as the fragile beauty of April gave way to the warmth, sunshine and birdsong of May. Luxuriously, she remembered the brilliant weather, the wonderful early summer which had followed the harsh winter. It was then that she had really tried hard to get to know Connie, but whenever she asked if the other girl would like to join her and Johnny on one of their many expeditions, Connie would either make a dismissive comment or sneer at the suggestion that she should spend any time with Eve at all. Deep down this had suited Eve very well, and she and Johnny had had many wonderful times together, just the two of them.

Even as the thought entered her mind the pictures began to form. She and Johnny lugging a large sack between them, a sack full of acorns for the two pigs who lived in the sty. Eve smiled to herself. She could not have said how old she and Johnny were at the time; she could only remember the happiness. They had picked blackberries as well, delving into many a copse, scratching and bruising themselves but presenting Auntie Bess with what she described admiringly as the biggest and best blackberries she had ever seen.

There were other memories, too. Sledging trips and forgetting to brush the snow off a wonderful slide she and Johnny had made between them, so that Willy the postman had stepped unwarily upon it and whizzed the length of the farmyard whilst Johnny and Eve had clutched each other, helpless with laughter. Willy had cursed them roundly and made them gather up all the letters which had flown out of his bag during his unexpected and headlong journey, and then, steady on his feet once more, had begun to laugh every bit as helplessly as they.

With determination Eve tried to remember why she and Johnny had not visited the badger again once the better weather had arrived and it was safe to do so, and suddenly, almost blindingly, the reason came to her. Of course! Uncle Reg had bought a wireless set and it was by this means that they heard that the BEF – the British Expeditionary Force – was being brought home from the Continent. No explanation that she could recall had been given, just a frantic appeal to anyone owning any sort of boat that they should set out for the beaches of northern France to bring back the British troops. She heard again Mr Churchill's deep rumbling voice.

We shall fight on the beaches, we shall fight on the landing grounds, we shall fight in the fields and in the streets, we shall fight in the hills; we shall never surrender . . .

He had said that immediately after the evacuation, and she thought now that his words had moved a nation, and resonated down through the years. There was a speech by Henry V, something about St Crispin's Day; she could not remember all the words, but the sentiment was the same.

He that outlives this day and comes safe home will stand a tiptoe when this day is named and rouse him at the name of Crispin . . . Then will he strip his sleeve and show his scars and say, 'These wounds I had on Crispin's Day.'

As she sat there, under the canopy of green leaves, the pictures began to come. All the evacuees from the surrounding farms had gathered in the Favershams' kitchen and heard it was not only little boats which were needed. Every man, woman and child on the south coast of England must do their bit to help.

'But what can kids like us do?' someone had said, and it was Uncle Reg who had answered.

'The fellers will want feedin',' he had said. 'They'll be hungry and thirsty and some may be hurt . . .' He had pointed at his wife. 'Make up packs of grub and bottles of cold tea and put together as much first aid stuff as you can find. We'll take the truck into Plymouth and distribute 'em to anyone in need.'

*

Eve had never dreamed that there were so many soldiers in the world. Every man she could see on the docks around her was grey-faced with fatigue, wet and filthy, thirsty and starving, and desperate for news; news which was not forthcoming, because nobody knew anything save that the BEF had drawn back. Not a retreat – Eve had heard the words a thousand times – but a strategic withdrawal, and Johnny, who was standing by her side, handing out packs of sandwiches and bottles of cold tea to the men as they passed by in their hundreds to make way for the next wave of returning troops, reminded her of what he had said earlier, as they had gone together to fetch more supplies from the temporary depot where more volunteers were feverishly making sandwiches: that Wellington preferred to fight a battle on ground of his own

114

choosing, which is why his troops had fallen back to the village of Waterloo.

Eve had no time to do more than smile quickly at each man as he passed her, taking the tea and the sandwiches eagerly and begging for news she was unable to give. So far as she could see it was just one terrible muddle, but a large white-haired woman standing within a few feet of her was giving what comfort she could. 'Our aircraft are up there doing their best,' Eve heard her repeating over and over. 'Mr Churchill will tell us what's going on as soon as possible, and in the meantime the orders are you're to go to your homes, stay there and prepare for whatever lies ahead.'

The lines of disembarking men seemed never-ending, and soon Eve found herself moving like an automaton, reaching for sandwiches and tea, pressing them into outstretched hands, and scarcely even glancing at each face as it passed. Indeed, when the man opposite her spoke to her directly she thought he must be addressing someone else and looked behind her to see who it was.

'Sweetheart!' the man was saying incredulously. 'For God's sake, sweetheart! What the devil are you doing here?'

Eve's head jerked back round. The voice was husky with fatigue, the face above her own drawn and weary, and the clothing bore little resemblance to what had once been a naval uniform, but as she automatically thrust a packet of sandwiches and a medicine bottle of cold tea into his grimy hands she knew him at last.

'Daddy!' she said in amazement. 'Oh, Daddy, I never

115

thought . . . I thought you were far away, somewhere safe, in your ship! What happened? Oh, Daddy . . .'

Bill Armstrong made a brave attempt at a smile, but somehow it slipped and Eve saw a tear trickle down through the dirt on his face.

'A direct hit when we were making our umpteenth trip across the Channel. But how did you get here? What on earth—' He broke off. 'I must get word to Eleanor; have you seen her?' Before he could say any more someone further along the line came over and seized his shoulder in a not unfriendly grip.

'That head wound needs attention, sailor, and you're holding everyone up,' the newcomer said. 'There's a dressing station a few hundred yards further on. You'd better stop making up to this young lady and get seen to before you go on home.'

Bill stepped obediently out of line, but when Eve would have followed him he shook his head. 'I'll find your mother myself, just as soon as I've had my wounds dressed,' he said. 'She won't be far from her little girl, I'm sure of that.'

Eve said nothing but watched him go, feeling puzzled. In all the vast crowd of helpers, she told herself, it was only natural that she should not have thought to look for her mother. Why should she, indeed? Eleanor Armstrong had visited the farm only twice, and on both occasions she had been in a hurry to get away. No doubt Daddy would run her to earth without any help from Eve herself. Not without relief, she reached for another food pack and bottle of tea and handed them to the next man in line, dismissing everything else from her mind.

By the time the bright June day began to fade into evening, Eve was exhausted. When Auntie Bess came along to collect her, she asked rather timidly if the older woman had seen Mrs Armstrong, only to receive a decided shake of the head.

''Tis impossible to pick any one woman out amongst so many,' Auntie Bess said comfortably. 'Who were that you were talkin' to, young woman? The tall feller?'

'It was Daddy,' Eve said, and could not keep the incredulity out of her voice. 'Did you see him, Auntie Bess? His uniform was in shreds. He said his ship had received a direct hit, and then he asked if I knew where Mummy was, and of course I didn't.' She looked up at the older woman's rosy face. 'Mummy'll be all right, won't she?'

'Your mum will be safe and doing something useful, you can be sure of that,' Auntie Bess said firmly. 'Now come along, out of harm's way until Uncle Reg and I can take you home.'

Eve pulled back. 'Where's Johnny?' she asked wildly. 'Oh, Auntie Bess, Johnny went off to get fresh supplies, and if I'm not here when he gets back he'll be frantic with worry. I must try and find him before . . .' She expelled her breath in a relieved sigh. 'There he is! He must've met up with Robbo, 'cos they're both heading this way. Oh, thank God!'

*

How could I have forgotten the evacuation of Dunkirk, the old woman marvelled to herself, staring into the sparkling waters of the stream. Why, it was one of the most important points of the war, that we managed to get so many members of the BEF safely back to Britain. Not that it was so very safe, for the Germans continued to attack our troops even when they were wading out to the boats, and in the ships – like my father's – bringing them back home. And no sooner had they re-formed than the Battle of Britain started. Do I really remember watching the dog fights between the RAF and the Luftwaffe, or am I just remembering what was reported in the newspapers? What I know I remember is the brilliant weather, the sun glinting on the cockpits of the Spitfires . . . oh, dear God, sitting here is bringing everything back, both the things I want to remember and those I would rather forget. The day we watched a Spitfire and a Messerschmitt attacking one another, the flame from their guns . . . it was a school day, I remember that. We were in the playground and the teachers shouted at us to come back to the classroom and crouch under our desks, but of course no one took the slightest notice. We couldn't stop watching the fight going on over our heads. I can even smell the lilac flowers on the tree which leaned over the playground fence, and feel Connie's hand gripping mine as the boys screamed their support for the Spitfire as though they were watching a football match.

She was back in the school yard, the years rolling away, the children's shouts becoming louder. She saw Chrissie standing by the Ryders' gate, his face red with excitement; heard his shrill little voice as he encouraged the Spitfire above him to 'kill the wicked bugger'.

But his encouragement was not needed. Suddenly the German aircraft was no longer involved. It was plunging earthwards in a column of black smoke and roaring flames and Eve had felt vomit rise in her throat.

'There's a man in there,' she had said huskily. 'Oh, Connie, I hope to God he's dead and can't feel anything . . .'

Then there was a dull explosion as the burning plane crashed somewhere on the moors. Several of the bigger boys tore through the school gate and began to dash along the road, crowing with delight that 'their' plane had won and shouting that they must see what was left of the enemy.

Eve had uttered a long sigh and released Connie's hand. For a moment they had been sisters in sorrow, hating the war as much for the pain of the German pilot as for the Englishman who had downed him. Then Johnny had come into the playground with Robbo in close attendance and Eve had seen, with a rush of relief, that both boys were pale, clearly sharing her own feelings. Neither spoke but words were not necessary. The incident – if you could call it that – had brought home to them all the full horrors of war.

Johnny had been the first to break the silence. 'One of them had to win,' he had said, and his voice had shaken a little. 'Naturally it was horrid watching someone get killed, but that shouldn't blind us to the fact that the Germans are the enemy. We didn't ask them to come over here and shoot up our railway lines, kill our soldiers and sailors and try to enslave us. For all we know the pilot in that Messerschmitt could have been a hero, but he was still our enemy. We have to remember that, but it shouldn't mean we're pleased to see him suffer. I don't want to sound like a prig . . .'

Robbo had cut across him. 'You're right, of course,' he had said slowly. 'This isn't a game, it's deadly serious, and we oughtn't to gloat when we see someone on the other side die a horrible death.'

Johnny had agreed. 'No, we oughtn't,' he said. 'But being grateful isn't gloating, so we can be grateful that at least there's one plane that won't be attacking us again.'

The old woman adjusted her position on the mossy log to try to sort herself out. She had come here to remember not the war but the lives she and the other evacuees had lived during their sojourn in Devon. Despite the fact that Johnny and Robbo lived at Spindlebush and she and Connie at Drake's Farm they spent most of their free time together, and now she realised, as perhaps she had not done before, that the war had just been a background to their life and not really a part of it.

They listened regularly to the wireless which now took pride of place on the kitchen dresser, but somehow nothing that they heard seemed real. Reality was deciding how to cross the stream when it swelled from a summer's storm; should they wear boots and tackle the ford or should they use the bridge? Even the constant murmurings voiced by the grown-ups that after Dunkirk an invasion must be imminent did not really affect them. They had been warned to watch out for parachutes gliding gently on the summer breeze, had been told that the seeming nuns floating earthward might be stormtroopers in disguise, come to rape and pillage, but somehow they found this quite impossible to believe, even though they promised their seniors to be on the alert for any stranger who might come amongst them with questions, lightly put, which they should on no account answer.

When a middle-aged couple living on the outskirts of Plymouth were found to have a foreign newspaper in their salvage collection the children were thrilled rather than terrified; even when the couple mysteriously disappeared one dark night, Robbo, Johnny, Eve and Connie simply thought it was just another tall story, put out to make everyone wary.

What was real was the effort everyone made to provide food for the nation, food which had once been brought by ship from various parts of the world but could be so no longer. Bananas, pineapples and oranges disappeared from the shelves, though rumour had it that the rich still managed to obtain the forbidden delights. But the youngsters living at Spindlebush and Drake's Farm did not miss what they had never had, for even the Armstrongs had drawn the line at such unnecessary expense.

What mattered now was gathering in the crops, and as the war entered its second year Mr Faversham told Eve and Connie to tell their teacher that they would shortly be helping to harvest the potato crop from the ten-acre, so would be unavailable for lessons for some time to come.

It was hard work, delving amongst the soil loosened by the blade of the big tractor to find every single potato; back-breaking, you could say, for old Mr Smith was smitten by a bad attack of arthritis and had to retire from the fray whilst his wife rubbed goose grease into his aching back and shoulders and scolded him for being a silly old fool. But the youngsters enjoyed what for them was a holiday from school; hard work it might have been, the old lady reflected, but it had also been fun.

September 1940

Eve opened an eye to peer round at the other beds as the sunshine crept through the window and lit up the attic room. Lily was on early milking so her bed was empty, and Chrissie and Connie were still asleep. Eve smiled to herself. It was a potato day, and she loved such days with a passion. Not only would she miss school, a treat in itself, but she would spend the day following the tractor, grubbing in the earth for what she thought of as precious pearls, the crop that would not only feed the inhabitants of Drake's Farm but also help to feed the nation.

She squiggled round in her bed so that she could see the clock and once more smiled to herself. She could have another lovely half-hour in bed, though judging from the sunshine just peeking above the distant hills everyone but Chrissie and Connie would soon be up and working as hard as they could. There was corn to be harvested, potatoes to be dug up, cleaned and sacked, apples and plums to be picked and preserved, and blackberries and nuts to be gathered in, to say nothing of the acorns that the pigs so adored.

Eve sat up on one elbow and contemplated her room-mates. Chrissie was fast asleep on his back, giving little purring snores, but Connie had turned her face away from the light and now muttered a protest.

'The alarm's not gone off,' she mumbled. 'Oh, I'm so tired! Pull the blackout curtain across, will you?'

'Not worth it; the alarm'll be going off in a minute, so there's no point in you trying to get back to sleep. Anyway, you know we're digging out the rest of the potatoes in the ten-acre today, and Uncle Reg said he wants all the help he can get,' Eve said virtuously. 'And you know what Chrissie's like; once he's awake he'll want his breakfast, and it's no use telling him Auntie Bess will still be cooking the porridge because he'll simply ignore anything we say. In fact he's quite capable of going downstairs in his pyjamas even though he knows that Auntie Bess won't feed him until he's properly dressed and ready for school.'

At that moment the alarm went off and Chrissie's reaction was immediate. He sat up, rubbed his eyes and climbed out of his little bed, heading for the washstand.

'I'm going to play with the bricks,' he announced. 'Me and Alex are going to take our share and build a huge castle . . .'

He began to try to lift the ewer and Eve, seeing disaster ahead, jumped out of bed and went to his assistance. She began to ply the flannel on his face with more enthusiasm than Chrissie liked, saying as she did so: 'What's this about bricks? Now you're starting real school I shouldn't have thought you'd want to play with bricks.'

123

Chrissie stared at her. 'I forgetted,' he breathed. 'Mrs Ryder says I'm her best pupil and today I can give out the work books.' He eyed his sister anxiously. 'Am I clean? Why are you holding those rompers? Mummy bought me a proper boy's shirt and proper boy's trousers too, remember. Schoolboys don't wear rompers; they're for babies.'

'Oh, I quite forgot,' Eve said mendaciously, pulling open Chrissie's drawer and producing the desired clothes. He pushed his arms into the grey shirt but Eve hesitated before adding the smart green and red jumper. 'Are you sure you want this, darling?' she asked, eyeing the smart new garment. 'It's going to be a warm day and you don't want to take the jumper off and leave it where some other child might mistake it for his.'

'Oh, you mean someone might steal it?' Chrissie asked. His eyes flashed with indignation, and a brisk discussion began, only to be interrupted by a moan from the now only occupied bed.

'Shut up, you two; I've got a real bad headache and you're making it worse. You can tell Auntie Bess that pulling those bloody potatoes yesterday has given me a migraine so I shan't be coming down to breakfast. Well, not until later, anyway.'

'Auntie Bess won't save breakfast for you on a potato day,' Eve warned the other girl. 'But if you're not hungry ... well, it's up to you. You can choose between breakfast and a headache. I don't care either way.'

Connie gave a loud moan but slid out of bed and ambled over to where her clothes lay. She made no attempt to wash but heaved her pyjama jacket over her head and pulled on the clothes she had worn the previous day, then put on her slippers. Chrissie turned wondering blue eyes on his sister.

'Connie's a dirty cat,' he said in a conversational tone, and then, discretion being the better part of valour, he set off at a brisk pace, ignoring the cry of '*What did you say?*' which floated after him as he charged down the attic stairs, closely followed by the enraged Connie, still threatening to box his ears.

Eve, who had washed and dressed with all possible speed after their departure, reached the kitchen to find Auntie Bess ladling out their porridge. She frowned at Eve's tardy arrival, reminding her sharply that if she wanted a lift up to the potato field on the trailer she had better hurry herself. Eve sighed. How was it that Connie could get away with being late every day, for every meal, and never find herself in hot water; whilst she, Eve, was scolded for being just a few minutes behind? Spooning porridge as quickly as she could, she told herself ruefully that it was because Connie was so pretty, and had such charming manners towards grown-ups that even Auntie Bess was sometimes taken in. Worse, Connie's good manners worked their magic not only on adults, but on boys as well. Over the last few months she had had Johnny dancing attendance on her as though she were someone of importance. If she was asked to run an errand which involved using the rusty old bicycle kept in the Favershams' barn, she only had to look at Johnny for him to offer to go himself. And when Eve had told him about the time when Connie had calmly taken a beautifully darned sock from Eve's work basket and replaced it with her own cobbled and uncomfortable mend, he had simply laughed at her.

'What does it matter which of you did it?' he had enquired with a grin. 'Don't tell me you can tell one darn from another, because I'm damn sure you can't.'

Eve had stared at him, open-mouthed, but had soon rallied. 'She doesn't darn, she cobbles; that means she doesn't make a neat sort of pattern which you can't feel when you put it on, but bunches all the material up together so that walking on it is really painful. Honestly, Johnny, I bet every woman in the village knows her own darning from everyone else's.'

'Well, it sounds pretty silly to me; the sort of thing no feller would even dream of worrying about,' Johnny told her. 'Besides, if she can't darn, she can't, and you should be happy to do her mending for her. I expect she does things for you, doesn't she?'

'No she doesn't,' Eve said baldly, and turned away when she saw the disbelieving look in Johnny's dark blue eyes. 'Oh, I'm sorry I mentioned it.' She gulped. 'Only it's horrid having to watch everyone admiring work that I've done and hearing them say how clever she's been.'

She did not add, as she easily could have done, that she believed Connie had taken the shilling which Uncle Reg had given her for helping out when Mr Smith's back had kept him off work. Connie herself had not lifted a finger; she had complained of a headache – her headaches were becoming legendary – but the next day Eve had discovered that the shilling had gone from her pocket. When she told Auntie Bess about her suspicion Auntie Bess had shaken her head warningly, but later, without comment, she had handed Eve another shilling.

'In future, give me your pocket money and I'll keep it for you,' she had said. 'In fact, why don't I take that back?' She had paused, frowning slightly as though wondering whether to say something else, and then had added, 'Don't worry, my chick. Not everyone likes the countryside nor hard work, but I'm a great believer in letting things sort themselves out.'

Eve had longed to ask whether she thought Connie had taken the money, but even as she opened her mouth the older woman shook her head again.

'Give she time,' she said softly. 'There's good and bad in everyone, and sometimes it's a fight to see which wins. And don't forget I've got your shilling.'

Chapter Six

The war dragged on, but sometimes it seemed to Eve that it never affected either Spindlebush or Drake's Farm, although everyone except Chrissie listened avidly to the nine o'clock news. Throughout the spring the bombing raids were getting heavier; London seemed to be their main target, but soon enough the Luftwaffe began to attack the ports. Like Eve and Chrissie, all four boys at Spindlebush Farm came from London, and everyone was edgy, waiting for news of their family and friends, but dreading the wrong sort.

In April, when Plymouth was bombed – Blitzkrieg, the Germans called it – they saw the fires blazing even across the miles which separated them from the city, and in the days which followed Eve could not rest until she heard that her mother was safe. Her father, too, was unhurt, having been out at sea protecting an Atlantic convoy carrying desperately needed goods from America to Britain. America was still a neutral country, but such convoys showed that she was already fighting in one way or another for the beleaguered Britons.

But still the war did not seem real to any of the evacuees. They continued with their lives, rejoicing in the wonderful summer weather which had followed a harsh winter. They knew that certain foods were getting scarce and that rationing was strict, but living deep in the countryside with all the bounty of nature at their disposal they hardly noticed the significance of the queues outside virtually every food shop when they visited the town.

The Spindlebushes and the Favershams had come to an arrangement by which they pooled their rationed commodities, and in return for the Spindlebushes' larger contribution Auntie Bess agreed to provide all the evacuees with a sandwich at noon and a big meal in the evening. Eve in particular was delighted by this arrangement, for it led to a closeness between her and Johnny which would not have been possible had they not had their meals together.

Lily and Miriam now shared their milking duties with the two younger girls. Eve loved the feel of the teats as they slid through her fingers, loved the hissing of the milk into the galvanised buckets, and seeing the younger girl's aptitude Lily took her under her wing and taught her as much as she could. Eve soon learned the little peculiarities of each cow: Rosaline had to have her tail loosely tied to her hind leg or she would constantly flick it into your face as you milked; Snowdrop kicked, that odd slanting sideways movement which could send the bucket flying if you weren't prepared for it. Maud would turn in mid-milk to stare into your face, which always made Eve giggle, and Ellie seemed to think human hair was edible and constantly licked your head if you didn't watch out.

Connie, on the other hand, absolutely hated milking. She found the feel of the teats between her fingers disgusting, and she was constantly getting her feet trodden on because she did not listen when Lily explained each cow's behaviour. As a result, she whined all the time, even promising to muck out instead if it would get her out of milking.

At last Auntie Bess grew tired of Connie's behaviour and took her into the kitchen, teaching her to make bread – not an easy task – and handing out other work as the need arose, always making sure that such jobs were performed to her satisfaction. Sometimes she put her in charge of Chrissie, insisting that she keep the little boy with her and entertain him with some suitable employment. With both Chrissie and Connie occupied elsewhere, Eve spent many hours with Lily, and soon came to admire the land girl more than almost anyone else on the farm. In fact Lily was a favourite with everyone; Uncle Reg loved her because she threw herself into any job she was asked to perform with such enthusiasm, and Auntie Bess for the fact that she was always clean and tidy at mealtimes and never needed to be reminded to scrub up before eating. From herding the cows, feeding the pigs or digging potatoes Lily went straight to the scullery to pump a bucket full of water, grabbing the rough towel off its hook as she passed.

'You do as Lily does and you won't go far wrong,' Auntie Bess was fond of saying. 'Miriam's a good girl and does her best, but she's not a country girl. Lily isn't either – brought up in a cathedral city, she was – but she picks things up easily. When I tell her something, once'll be enough, whereas when I tell Miriam I have to repeat it two or three times.'

By the time the war was entering its third year Uncle Reg was beginning to count Eve and Lily together, so when he asked Lily to bring the cattle down from the pasture furthest away from the farm he did not deem it necessary to add that she would be assisted in her work by Eve as well as by Shep, the black and white collie who knew almost as much about herding cattle as Uncle Reg himself.

Eve was no longer frightened of the beasts the way she had been when she had first come to Drake's Farm, but she still armed herself with a large stick, not to hit but to guide them, and to discourage the young bullocks from trying to go in the opposite direction from the way she wanted. You could rely on the fact that every gateway you passed would seem to have some strange attraction for even the most docile animals, so Eve had grown accustomed to going ahead to shut gates and bar gaps as they went.

The walk up to the pasture known as Pete's Patch was a pleasant one. A ditch ran along the left-hand side and in spring it was the ideal place to watch for toads, frogs and newts, and Eve had on several occasions got good marks at school for her knowledge of the amphibians. Connie shrieked and ran at the sight of a froggy face, however, and though the idea of teasing her by producing a tiny frog in the palm of one's hand was tempting, Eve never did so. She herself had no great liking for either worms or house spiders, to say nothing of snakes, even the harmless sort, and though she believed Connie was also afraid of such things she was uneasily aware that if Connie found someone's weak spot she would probably take advantage of it. Certainly, Johnny and Robbo would! They often boasted they were frightened of nothing, even announcing that they could pick up an adder without getting bitten if they had a forked stick. Eve, who had never even seen an adder, had pulled a disbelieving face, but always looked carefully at thick clumps of grass and heather when they were out on the moors. It was one thing being brave and quite another courting trouble.

On the other side of the track the hedges were red with unripe blackberries, the hazel trees already sporting the green nuts which would later provide a feast for the evacuees, and in the fields beyond the poppies and cornflowers swayed with the golden wheat in the gentlest of breezes.

Eve looked round her with great content. She no longer felt guilt over the fact that she was happier here than she had ever been in London. It even seemed as though her mother, too, was content here, for on the last occasion when she had visited the farm she had scarcely found fault with anything Eve had done, and had actually congratulated her on Chrissie's improved manners.

'He was getting more than I could cope with,' she had said, her tone almost apologetic. 'I blame Nanny Burton; she gave him his way rather than correcting him when he did wrong, and that made him difficult, to say the least.'

Eve had opened her mouth to point out that since her mother had only visited the farm three times in almost two years she hadn't had to cope with her son very often, then shut it again. She had no desire to say that it was not just herself who had contributed to Chrissie's improved behaviour. Auntie Bess had known just how to handle him from the start, and even Mrs Ryder had played a part by simply treating Chrissie as though he were a good little boy and not a spoiled and demanding wretch, which he had most definitely been when they first arrived.

Eleanor was still exclaiming at how proud she was of her children, and Eve had no intention of souring the atmosphere by disclosing that Chrissie still occasionally behaved badly. The trouble, Eve knew, was that her little brother was a good deal brighter than anyone else in Mrs Ryder's nursery school. His reading was excellent and his writing almost as good. He was a great favourite with Mrs Ryder, who had given him the title of 'monitor', and though his friend Alex followed close on his heels so far as education was concerned Chrissie made sure that he always stayed just ahead. When Eve and Connie – and quite often Johnny and Robbo – sat down at the kitchen table in the evenings to do their homework, Chrissie often followed suit, eager to prove that he was every bit as clever as his big sister.

'Hey, dreamy!' Lily's voice cut across Eve's thoughts. 'What are you thinking about? Auntie Bess was telling me that there's to be a jumble sale in the village on Saturday, so how about coming with me? I'm in desperate need of some khaki wool to finish off the mittens and balaclava I've been knitting for Colin, and I wouldn't mind some new boot socks; next winter is bound to be a bad one and I've a hole as big as a pigeon's egg in my old ones.'

'I wonder why everyone uses pigeon's eggs as a measure?' Eve asked idly. 'What's wrong with a hen's egg? But if you're really good, Lily, and we find your khaki wool, I'll darn your socks for you.'

Lily laughed. 'For a start, they're green socks, not khaki,' she pointed out. 'You and your darning! I shall not forget the fuss when you darned one of Uncle Reg's best socks and Connie claimed it for her own work. As I recall it Auntie Bess had to intervene when Johnny started to put his oar in.'

Eve chuckled. 'Yes, I was a twerp,' she admitted freely. 'But I hadn't then realised that Connie was in the habit of doing things like that.' She looked curiously at Lily as they strode side by side up the track. 'Lily, do you mind if I ask you something?'

Lily laughed. 'Ask away,' she said gaily. 'I don't promise to answer, but there's no harm in asking.'

'It's nothing terribly important, but I'd just like to know what you think,' Eve said. 'You know Robbo? Well, of course you do; you know everyone I know, I suppose.' She hesitated for a moment and then blurted the words out, feeling foolish but hoping to get a helpful answer. 'Lily, wouldn't you say Robbo was a really handsome bloke? I mean *really* handsome,' she added with emphasis. 'He's at least four inches taller than Johnny – I know that, because they were measured in school the other day – and he's easy-going and he laughs a lot . . .'

Lily grinned. 'You sound as though you're in love,' she said jokingly. 'But you're right, of course; in a couple of years he'll have all the girls chasing after him, so if you want to stake a claim you'd better do it now.'

'Well, I don't want to stake a claim,' Eve said quickly. 'No, what I wanted to ask you was why Connie likes Johnny so much and scarcely takes any notice of Robbo. And you know what Johnny looks like – his hair is the colour of hay and his face is covered in freckles. Next to Robbo he's not even a little bit handsome. But Connie follows him round like a tame lamb. She helps him out with schoolwork even though we're not in the same group, and she's actually letting him teach her to ride Flurry, Auntie Bess's old pony, when everyone knows she's scared of horses.'

She looked up at Lily and saw that her friend's face wore a look of slight puzzlement. 'Do you know, it's never occurred to me before, but you're quite right,' Lily said slowly. 'Johnny's very nice, but in the looks department he simply isn't in the running against Robbo. And does he return her feelings?'

Eve shrugged, then pulled a wry face. 'I'd like to say no,' she admitted. 'Not because I don't like Connie – though I don't – but because it riles me to see her walking off with Johnny and leaving me behind. But I must admit he seems to like her a lot and often takes her side against mine. So what is it that Johnny's got and Robbo hasn't? Any ideas?'

Lily ruminated for a moment then shook her head. 'If Johnny was older I'd suspect him of having sex appeal, but he simply isn't old enough. And it's not as though like was calling to like, because Johnny's really straightforward, wouldn't you say? He doesn't hide his teeth, but comes straight out with whatever he's thinking, whilst Connie never lets anyone know what goes on in her pretty little head.' She looked speculatively at Eve. 'Do you mind if I'm equally frank, Eve?'

Eve giggled. 'I know what you're going to say. You're going to say I'm not pretty and Connie is, but that isn't the point, is it? I just want to know why Connie likes Johnny best.'

Lily laughed, but by this time they had reached the field and were beginning to round up the bullocks, so the subject was shelved until they were walking back down the hill with the beasts scrambling ahead of them, when Lily gave Eve the only answer she could think of.

'Haven't you noticed, when you've been in town or on the bus, how often a pretty woman is sitting next to an ugly man, and it's clear that they're married to one another? There's no accounting for tastes, chick.'

Eve's forehead wrinkled. 'I know what you mean,' she said slowly. 'But surely that's different? Look at Mr and Mrs Smith, for instance; she's really pretty still with lots of wavy white hair and beautiful skin, whereas old Mr Smith always reminds me of a toad because his eyes bulge and he's usually grinning. But I suppose life has been harder on Mr Smith, because farm work truly *is* hard, isn't it, Lily? And of course Mrs Smith spends most of her time indoors.' She considered for a moment before speaking again. 'Johnny will never be handsome, like Robbo.' She sighed. 'It was a daft question, anyway. Only . . . Johnny and I used to spend almost all of our free time together, and now he mostly goes off with Connie. But I suppose it doesn't matter at all, really. Forget I even mentioned it.'

Lily was about to agree when a thought seemed to strike her. 'There might be another reason,' she said slowly as Shep guided the bullocks out of the lane and into the farmyard. 'I've met girls in my time who simply want whatever somebody else has. Could that be the answer?'

It was Eve's turn to shrug. 'Dunno,' she said. She grinned at her companion. 'But if you're right I'd better start making up to Robbo; then perhaps Connie will direct her attentions at him.'

*

The old woman sat on her mossy log trying to sort the memories into their proper place in her mind, but she soon realised this was impossible. She had never kept a diary, never dreaming that she could forget the wonderful years she had spent at Drake's Farm. And she had not forgotten, or not *what* had happened, at any rate. What she had forgotten was the order in which these momentous events had occurred. She could run through her mind every aspect of each harvest tea but had no idea which one was which, although she remembered holding Chrissie firmly by the hand and promising him treats if only he would not try to join the workers as they sweated and strained to gather the sheaves into stooks before it grew too dark to see what they were doing.

She herself had always been allowed to help with the hay harvest, she knew. She remembered bright June sunshine, riding home to the farm on the hay wain, and watching Mr Trevalyn as he arranged the harvested crop into intricate ricks. But were the memories from 1940, 1941 or 1942? She did not know, could not remember, and in any case what did it matter? What mattered was recapturing a young girl's happiness, though she also remembered that there had been aspects of bringing in the wheat which in those early years Auntie Bess had thought the evacuees would not enjoy, so that the younger children had been removed from the field as darkness began to creep across the land.

Sitting on her comfortable perch in the dappled sunlight, the old woman made one last attempt to recall her very first wheat harvest, but it was no use. Telling herself she had not returned to Drake's Farm to compile a chronological – and probably very boring – list of her experiences, she leaned back in her seat and allowed her eyelids to droop. Tiny pictures bright as jewels began to appear in her mind's eye, and she surrendered to their charm. They were what mattered, after all.

September 1942
The week during which they were due to harvest had been wet and overcast and Mr Faversham had not been the only farmer pulling a long face as he looked at his

rolling fields of rain-soaked wheat, but one morning Eve was woken at an early hour by sunshine falling on her face and sat up with a jerk. She glanced at the alarm clock and then over the hump in Connie's bed to Chrissie, who was stirring sleepily and trying to avoid the sun's rays. The previous day the gentle rain of Devon had ceased around lunchtime, and now Eve remembered that Mr Smith, a good weather forecaster, had prophesied that they would have sunshine in which to harvest the desperately needed wheat. Mr Trevalyn had pulled a doubtful face, but sure enough, by the time the children were ready for bed, Mr Faversham had been making his plans for an early start.

'But won't the wheat still be wet?' Eve had asked, when he had announced that he had discussed the matter with the neighbouring farmers and they had agreed to start cutting the next day. Mr Faversham had shaken his head.

''Tis the breeze what'll dry out the crops,' he explained kindly. 'Don't 'ee worry, maid; by the time 'tis light enough to work we'll have a binder down the lane and everyone assembling.' He grinned at Eve, standing at his elbow and thinking doubtfully about the sodden wheat. 'Now, we'll be glad of your help tomorrow, but don't forget, building stooks has to be learned; you can't just pile 'em up any old how. But if Mr Smith says the weather will stay good – and he does – then it looks as though we're all set for a grand harvest.'

So now Eve hopped out of bed and poked her head out into the early morning sunshine and felt it warm on her face. She gave a muted crow of satisfaction and heard Chrissie's bedsprings creak. It was a case of all hands to the pump at harvest time, and Auntie Bess had explained that everything, but *everything*, stopped until everyone's wheat was gathered in, so Chrissie would have to go to the rectory with the other children too small and young to assist and be kept an eye on by Mrs Ryder and anyone else who was not taking part in the harvest. Chrissie had not been pleased, especially when he heard that Connie, whose claims of a bad back had reached their climax the previous day, was one of the volunteers who would look after the little ones.

Initially, Chrissie had admired Connie greatly, saying over and over that she was the prettiest girl he had ever seen and much nicer than Eve, but that had been during what Lily had called the honeymoon period, before the reality of Connie's selfishness became apparent even to him. Other volunteers might play games with the children, give them piggy backs round the rectory garden or take them to the post office to buy a few off-ration goodies, but Connie was not one of these. She did not make the children work, because that would have meant doing something herself, but she insisted that her lightest commands were obeyed, rigorously enforced an hour's sleep after their sandwich lunch, detached them from their favourite toys, and would not let them play in the sand tray or with modelling clay because she said she had better things to do with her time than to clear up after snotty brats.

Chrissie had been downright delighted when he was taken out of the nursery class and put in what he called 'real school', but because of the harvest he would have to join the other youngsters again and he had told Eve the previous evening that Connie would be nasty to him as soon as she got him away from the adults.

'She don't like me,' he wailed when he realised who was going to be in charge. 'Why can't I come with you? I'm a big boy now, Eve; I've been in real school for nearly two years!'

Eve hesitated. She knew Chrissie was right: Connie did not like him – or indeed any other young children – but it would be Mrs Ryder who was truly in charge and she would not let Chrissie be bullied, especially if Eve had a word with her first. So now Eve padded across to the washstand, poured out water and soaked the flannel. Soap – and toothpaste – were two of the commodities which had disappeared from the shops, and ingenious though Auntie Bess might be she had not yet found a substitute for either of these. When she and Mrs Spindlebush took their fruit and vegetables into the town to sell them to those less fortunately placed she offered to barter anything in season in return for soap or toothpaste, but this ploy did not work every time, presumably since everyone was in the same boat. Eve summoned Chrissie over to the stand and washed him vigorously, pointed to his clothing and told him that if she had a good report from kind Mrs Ryder about his behaviour she would try to persuade Uncle Reg to let him come to the harvest field with the others the following day.

Chrissie had been inclined to whine and threaten bad behaviour but this remark made him cheer up wonderfully.

'I'll be good as gold; I'll help Mrs Ryder with the kids in the baby class and I won't grumble,' he promised. 'How old do you have to be to help with the harvest, Eve? Will I be old enough next year?'

Eve, dressing herself and watching with some amusement Chrissie's attempt to get both arms down the same sleeve of his shirt, pretended to consider, although in reality she had no idea of the age of the youngest harvesters, though she thought it was probably nine or ten. After all, she had been helping with the harvest ever since they had arrived at the farm and no one had objected.

She was turning towards the door when she remembered that Connie was supposed to be at the rectory in time to welcome Mrs Ryder's charges, and turned back to give the other girl's shoulder a brisk shaking.

'Get up, get up, get up, you lazy devil,' she chanted. 'I feel so sorry for you . . .'

Connie groaned and put her head under her pillow to muffle the sound of Chrissie imitating a bugle call to arms, and though Eve was tempted to give her a salutary slap she refrained, since she suspected that Connie would take it out on Chrissie if she did something so unwise. However, when Connie made no further move Eve sighed, picked up the end of the bed and tipped its occupant out on to the bare boards of the floor.

'I said get up,' she repeated. 'And don't think I'm not wise to your nasty little ways – I know you only said you had a bad back to get out of helping with the harvest, though goodness knows why you'd want to. Anyway, it means you're stuck with looking after the youngsters today, so *do* come on.' She sniffed loudly. 'I smell porridge! Well, shall I go down and tell Auntie Bess that you don't want any breakfast?'

Connie sat up and Eve noted bitterly that the other girl looked even prettier flushed and tangled in her blanket on the floor whilst glaring up at her tormentor.

'All right, all right, I suppose for once you have a point,' Connie said peevishly. 'And now you can jolly well get out and let me dress in peace. Did you leave me some clean water in the ewer? Or do you expect me to go traipsing off downstairs for more?'

Having seen Connie struggling out of her bedding Eve moved towards the door. 'You can do as you please,' she said airily. 'I take it you're helping with the harvest tea? I heard Auntie Bess saying yesterday that Mrs Ryder was going to make the tea on a Primus so people can have more than one cup if they want – the men will have cider, of course, and the kids will have milk, I expect, so you're going to be pretty busy.'

Connie moaned and tipped the dirty washing water into the slop bucket, then damped the flannel and washed her face, not bothering with her neck, arms or indeed any other portion of her anatomy. Auntie Bess said that children who didn't wash properly got spots, warts and various other unsightly ills and for many weeks Eve had watched hopefully for Connie's smooth skin to become appropriately blemished. But for some reason Auntie Bess's rule did not seem to apply to Connie, who remained spot-free and, presumably, dirty. Eventually Connie responded to Eve's question.

'Make the harvest tea when I've got those bloody

kids to keep an eye on? Don't make me laugh,' she said scornfully. 'Mrs Ryder is in charge so she can damned well produce her own share of the grub.' She began to tick items off on her fingers. 'Mrs Spindlebush has made the biggest apple pie you've ever seen and the lady from the post office – can't remember her name – has made the harvest cake, using chopped-up carrots in place of dried fruit. It sounds horrible, but Auntie Bess says it's just grand. There's a pork pie made from the meat the government let Uncle Reg keep and I guess there'll be no end of sandwiches; Spam, corned beef, cucumber, tomatoes . . .'

'Well, don't go feeding your face on what's meant for the harvesters,' Eve said. She knew the other girl was quite capable of secreting upon her person any little extra that took her fancy, but Connie just sniggered and followed Eve and Chrissie as they clattered down the attic stairs.

'I don't eat nearly as much as you, Fatty Arbuckle,' she said spitefully. 'And though I shall have my share of the harvest tea I'm going straight to bed afterwards, so it won't be me doing the washing up.'

'Bed?' Eve echoed. 'What on earth are you talking about? It'll be too early for bed.'

They had reached the kitchen by this time and Connie gave Eve a withering look. 'You don't suffer from migraines the way I do, and after a full day with screaming brats I dare say my head'll be fit to pop!'

Eve had opened her mouth to make a retort when Auntie Bess cut in. 'Eat up and shut up,' she said cheerfully. 'Speaking for myself I'd rather work at ten

144

harvests than look after those children for a whole day, especially if one of them is Chrissie.' She wagged a reproving finger at Connie. 'And don't you think you can abandon poor Mrs Ryder to those little monkeys because in my opinion she's got enough on her plate with the harvest tea. I'm just worried that someone might run into the road or fall into the pond or get in the way of the binder, because you'll be expected to shepherd all the kids up to the field as soon as she gives the word.'

Connie looked both startled and annoyed. 'No one told me I'd have to take the little beasts up to the field,' she said huffily. 'I just wish someone had trained Shep to herd kids instead of sheep and cows.' For once she looked at Eve with an almost pleasant expression on her pretty face. 'Can't you come down to the rectory and give me a hand?' she pleaded. 'It wouldn't hurt you to help me out, just this once.'

Eve was about to retort indignantly that she would have quite enough to do without adding Connie's work to her own when it occurred to her that this was a chance to show both Auntie Bess and Lily, who were watching her as they ate their porridge, that she really was trying to be nice to the other girl. She was beginning to say that she would do her best to get away when the back door opened and Mr Smith entered the kitchen. The fine weather had obviously affected him, for his face wore a large smile, though his words were spoken in a mournful tone.

'That porridge looks good, missus. Can I scrape out the pan?' he asked. 'My good woman ran out of milk this mornin' and had to make our oats wi' water. Imagine that, young Chrissie.' He winked at the assembled company, giving Auntie Bess such a droll look that she laughed, dished out a plate of porridge and pushed it over to the empty place before him.

'One of these days you'll burst, Sam Smith,' she said as he began to eat. 'I dare say you're eager to start, so I take it Mr Faversham has told everyone what jobs they are to do?'

'He has that,' Mr Smith said through a mouthful of porridge. 'I'm in charge of the binder, which will be pulled by Dapple and Flicker, and the land girls will be collectin' the sheaves and makin' them into stooks. The kids – the Spindlebush lot and young Eve here – will be digging up the potatoes in the far field and putting them into buckets, whilst Mr Trevalyn oversees the normal farm work – the essential stuff, that is.'

Auntie Bess smiled at Eve. 'And I want you to be sure to keep Chrissie with you when tea's over, because Uncle Reg will have his gun out and we don't want no one peppered by mistake.'

'What will he be shooting at?' Eve asked. She knew the farmer went out, usually first thing in the morning or last thing at night, to shoot rabbits for the pot, saying with satisfaction as he brought the dead bunnies into the kitchen that they'd been eating his crops so the more he shot the better.

'Vermin,' Mrs Faversham said. 'He reckons that for every rat he puts out of action he saves a good bucket of poultry feed, because them rats get into everything, you know, even the metal bins which some people' – and here she looked very hard at Connie – 'leave the bin lids up instead of closing them.'

Eve carried her empty porridge dish over to the sink and turned a puzzled face to Auntie Bess. 'I don't understand,' she said. 'Uncle Reg often takes a gun out after rabbits; why should today be any different?' She was watching Auntie Bess as she spoke and saw a look that could almost have been regret cross her foster-mother's face, but her reply, when it came, was practical.

'While the binder's cuttin' round the edge of the wheat the rabbits and rats and so on retreat towards the middle, thinkin' they can hide there. But as the horses come closer the critters realise their safe refuge isn't safe at all so they bolt for the hedges and ditches and the men are waitin' to pick them off.' She smiled a little uncomfortably at Eve. 'You don't want to find yourself peppered with shot, do you?'

'No, I don't,' Eve said fervently, 'only what about the harvest tea? Will the little ones be safe?'

Auntie Bess nodded. 'Course they will, my lovely. Take my word for it: everything stops for tea, even potting rabbits!'

Eve dropped the last potato into the bucket and stood up to ease her aching back, then nudged Johnny who was just finishing his own row.

'Have you done?' she asked hopefully. 'If so you might walk with me down to the village to collect the kids from Mrs Ryder's. I promised Connie to give her a hand because Auntie Bess says they can come to the harvest tea and poor dear Connie feels she can't bring them up on her own.' She tried to make her voice sound teasing and friendly but realised she had failed as Johnny cast her a reproachful look.

'Nasty, nasty!' he exclaimed. 'Why don't you like Connie? Surely you're not still angry with her for pinching your darning?'

Eve turned to face him, trying to look bewildered. 'Why do you say that? I'm doing my best to get along with Connie, but it isn't easy. Anyway, are you coming?'

Johnny shrugged and lifted his laden bucket of potatoes. 'No, I think I'll take these spuds up to Drake Farm and knock the worst of the dirt off them in the scullery,' he said. 'You go and fetch your brother and I'll see you at the harvest tea.'

Eve sighed, but set off for the rectory willingly enough, and later, when the harvest tea had been eaten and Uncle Reg and the farmhands were taking up their stations round the edge of the field, she was glad she had done so, for Connie, clearly trying to repay her for her help with the little ones, offered to take Chrissie back to the farmhouse before the shooting began. Eve accepted both the olive branch and the suggestion gladly.

'Thanks ever so much, Connie,' she said with real gratitude. 'I hardly ever get a chance these days to have a bit of time to myself, so that would be lovely.'

Connie looked gratified, and for the first time it occurred to Eve that the other girl might be as glad to end their feud, if you could call it that, as she would be herself. She cast her mind back to the day when Connie had first put in an appearance and realised, with a stab of guilt, that despite telling herself she would try to be friends she had actually resented the other girl just for not being Mabel, so now she smiled at her and promised to be back no later than ten o'clock.

'Not that I'll be that late, I don't suppose,' she added. 'But if you really don't mind keeping an eye on Chrissie, Connie, I'd love a chance to wander around the woods.' She turned to Johnny. 'Want a moonlight walk later? We could visit—' She shut up abruptly as Johnny's elbow caught her a severe blow in the ribs. Hastily she changed what she had been about to say to something innocuous and was pleased when Johnny took her hand and gave it a squeeze.

When Chrissie was told that Connie was to be his companion on the walk back to the farm he began to grizzle, but Connie put a stop to his complaints by offering him a toffee from the tin which the Favershams had given her. Each child had been presented with a similar tin, of course, but Chrissie, who had eaten his own toffees long since, gave a delighted crow and trotted off happily, chattering away to Connie as though they had always been the best of friends.

Johnny and Eve grinned at each other. 'There's diplomacy for you,' Johnny said. 'Who'd have thought it? But at least we'll get a chance to take a walk without Chrissie demanding an explanation for every word you speak.'

'Oh, he's not that bad,' Eve said tolerantly. 'As brothers go, he could be a lot worse. Indeed, my mother wants to take him into Plymouth the next time Daddy's home so that he can see all the ships. She wouldn't have done that a few months ago.'

'He'll like that . . .' Johnny began, but Eve, filled with a fresh determination to do Connie justice, interrupted him.

'Johnny, I've never asked – have you not told Connie about the badgers' sett, or the foxes' earth . . . stuff like that? I'm sure – oh, listen! They're starting to shoot. Oh, the poor bunnies – they're terrified. And look – there are rats, and mice – or are they voles? Oh, Johnny, it's horrible, isn't it?'

Johnny sighed. 'Yes, it's horrid to watch,' he said, 'but just think how grateful Mrs Faversham will be when she sees all that fresh rabbit meat. It must be awfully hard feeding us all every day, what with rationing and so on. And rats eat anything they can get their teeth into, which makes things difficult for Mr Faversham too, so really the men are only doing what has to be done, however sweet the bunnies might look when you see them in the meadows.'

Eve saw the logic of this, of course, but she still hated seeing the rabbits leap into the air as the shot killed them, and later, following this train of thought, she suddenly said, 'Do you remember what I was saying before, about telling Connie about the badgers' sett? Don't you think we should?'

They were walking down the lane in the direction of the stream, and already they could hear the water gurgling under the little bridge. For a moment, Johnny didn't answer.

'I haven't made up my mind,' he said at last. 'I like Connie, of course I do, and I'm sure she wouldn't give away secrets on purpose, but I've been afraid she might do so by accident. And you know how the farmers are always going on about the threat badgers pose to their milking herds. Connie might not realise that if she told anyone about the sett, accidentally or on purpose, they might consider it their duty to destroy it.' He sighed. 'Sometimes I just don't understand what makes farmers tick, but whatever it is it's not worth running that risk. But you know best, Eve. You must have got to know her pretty well, sharing your bedroom and taking it in turns to look after Chris. Is she to be trusted, do you think?'

The last rays of the sun were sinking over the distant moors, and Eve stood for a moment watching the deepening green of the leaves and wondering how to reply. She had tried once or twice to alert Johnny to Connie's habit of slithering out of any unpleasant task, but that did not mean the other girl was untrustworthy. Eve looked around her. Wild roses grew in the hedges, tall foxgloves added their white and purple beauty to the scene, and on the far side of the hedge they could hear the murmurs of the harvesters as they cleared up after the day's work. She turned her head to glance at Johnny and realised she still had not answered his question.

'I don't think she'd give away a secret,' she said slowly. 'Not on purpose, at any rate. Why, even Chrissie has learned to keep his mouth shut. He told the children at the village school about some birds' nests he'd found and heard later that the boys took the eggs to make decorations for their mothers' cottages. He cried at the thought of the sad blackbirds, thrushes and chaffinches when they found their nests empty, and vowed he'd never tell anyone about a nest again.'

'Don't they know nothin', those boys?' Chrissie had said tearfully. 'I remember you tellin' me, Eve, that if you take birds' eggs you must always leave one or two in the nest. Then the mummy bird will sometimes lay more and still be able to bring up a brood.'

When Johnny gave her hand a reassuring squeeze Eve was glad she had given Connie a clean bill of health, so to speak. He was beginning to say that he would show Connie the sett at the very next opportunity when an unexpected noise made them both jump.

'What was that?' Eve asked uneasily. 'It sounded like an animal in pain, but I expect it was just one of the harvesters mucking about.' She would have walked on, but Johnny stopped her by grabbing her arm.

'Hang on,' he said tersely. 'You're right: something's hurt. That cry came from quite near . . . ah, I see it. It's a young rabbit. Oh God, oh God, oh God!'

As he spoke he plunged into the ditch, and in a moment he came out bearing a young rabbit streaming blood, with something metallic attached to its leg.

'Johnny?' Eve said timidly. 'Is it badly hurt? Oh, the poor creature. Can you get that thing off?'

Johnny had knelt on the edge of the ditch and when he looked up at her she saw that his eyes blazed with fury. 'Hold the rabbit!' he ordered. 'I'm going to get the trap off. Can you wedge a bit of really thick branch between the teeth if I pull them apart? Wait till I show

Uncle Reg. I asked him once and he swore that he never let anyone use traps on his land, so we'll see what he says about this.'

Between them they managed to get the rabbit's leg out of the metal jaws. Johnny tucked the trap under his right arm and cradled the rabbit with infinite gentleness in his left as they started back to the harvest field to find Uncle Reg. It was not long before they caught sight of him, with Mr Smith and Mr Trevalyn, heading homewards.

The rabbit lay still and quivering in Johnny's arm and the men did not at first realise that it was still alive.

'Hey, young Johnny, that'll make half a dozen rabbits for the pot,' Mr Smith said jovially, indicating the limp bodies slung over his own shoulder. He chuckled. 'Though I must say, that 'un you got could have done with another month's fattening before bein' eaten. I were just tellin' the master here . . .'

He was interrupted. 'Uncle Reg, you swore to me you never had traps on your land, so who set this?' Johnny thrust the cruel metal object under the farmer's nose. 'I know you wouldn't do anythin' so wicked, but somebody did, and I want your given word that you'll find out who and see that he's punished.'

The farmer took the trap from Johnny, wincing as the bright metal caught the dying rays of the sun.

'I dunno who'd dare to set a trap on my land, knowin' how I feel,' he said. He gestured to Johnny to put the rabbit down, and cocked his shotgun. 'That leg won't ever bear weight again, so I'll put it out of its misery. I'm sorry that you should've been distressed, lad. I'll destroy this trap and speak firm, but I doubt I'll ever find out who set it.' He turned angrily on Mr Smith and Mr Trevalyn. 'Do you realise what might have happened if Johnny had found it with his foot? Or young Chrissie had walked into it? Someone would have been up in court, war or no war.' He turned back to Johnny, 'Lay him on the path, lad.'

Eve prepared to close her eyes, shuddering at the sight of the rabbit's mangled limb, but Johnny was shaking his head. 'No, Uncle Reg, this is one rabbit you're not going to get for the pot,' he said firmly. 'I'll look after him whilst the wound heals and set him free when he's fit to be released. And I shan't let him go where there's any danger of his being shot . . .'

'It will never survive,' Uncle Reg said gently. 'When I said I'd put it out of its misery I meant every word, so if you lay it down . . .'

Accepting the inevitable, Eve leaned forward to stroke a caressing hand between the big drooping ears. Then she faced Uncle Reg.

'I think it's dead already,' she said, her voice trembling.

Tears sparkling on his cheeks, Johnny laid the rabbit down on the verge, nodding sadly as the creature's head lolled in death.

'Traps like that are illegal, aren't they, Uncle Reg? I think we should tell everyone where we found it and what it did . . .'

' . . . or what it could have done,' Uncle Reg said grimly. 'Don't you worry, I'll put the word around that we've a wrong 'un somewhere in the neighbourhood.

That's a punishable offence, setting a trap like that one. If we ever find out who did it we'll set the law on him all right.' He put a heavy hand on Johnny's shoulder, then bent to pick up the small corpse before moving off again, walking slowly, his eyes scanning every inch of hedge, ditch and verge as he went.

Behind him the farmhands were having what to them was a quiet conversation, but Eve caught the gist of it and felt the hairs rise on the nape of her neck.

'I reckon 'twere meant for that plaguey badger,' Mr Smith said, but out of the corner of her eye Eve saw Mr Trevalyn shaking his head.

'Too small for a badger,' he opined. 'No, no, I reckon someone was trappin' for the pot and when they hear what happened they'll be up out of here and off to try elsewhere.'

Mr Smith was opening his mouth to argue the point when the farmer turned and wagged his finger. 'That's enough about killing,' he said. ''Tis bad luck to go after badgers save to drive them off your own bit of land. I've heard there's one of the beasts with a sett and young 'uns somewhere in the woodland but so far as I can see they've done our herd no harm. It might not be true anyway; I've not actually seen a badger myself for at least two years.'

This could have been the moment to test Connie's trustworthiness, Eve thought, but of course Connie and Chrissie were safely tucked up in the farmhouse by now, and Connie did not yet know about the sett in any case. She sighed. She had been looking forward to a moonlight walk with Johnny – how romantic that sounded – but now it looked as though they would have to go their respective ways before the moon was up.

When they reached Drake's Farm she jerked Johnny's elbow and whispered as much, but he raised his brows.

'Why should we go in?' he demanded. 'You promised Connie that you'd be back by ten; it's a long way from that yet. I wouldn't suggest the woodland, just in case whoever set that trap is skulking in the beeches. Since traps like that are illegal he might be willing to commit any sort of crime in order not to be caught. How about going back to the stream? Have you ever walked up towards the source? The further up you go the wilder it gets, and we've had enough rain this week to mean it will be running quite fast. Or what do you say to nipping into the house and seeing if Chrissie's fallen asleep yet? If he has, and I'd put money on it, we could collect Connie and we can all go. If we're lucky we might see all sorts of wildlife. It's beautiful even by moonlight; you and Connie will love it, honest to God you will. There are water voles and . . . oh, all sorts, and of course once you get out of the trees you can see someone coming a mile off, so we'd be in no danger.'

'I don't think we'd better fetch Connie, though,' Eve pointed out. 'Chrissie may be asleep, he probably is, but Lily won't have gone to bed yet and if he wakes up and finds himself alone there'll be all hell to pay. Auntie Bess lets him have a night light floating in a saucer of water, but there are nights when the shadows thrown

156

by the candle frighten him almost more than the dark, which is why I usually have to be in the house in case he cries.' By now the little party was crossing the farm-yard and Eve stole a glance at Johnny's face. 'That's why I was looking forward to a moonlight walk. It's something that hasn't previously come my way. But look, if you'd rather take Connie than me . . .'

Eve was astonished at herself for making the sugges-tion. But as it happened Johnny shook his head firmly and seized her elbow, steering her away from the farm-house and towards the open countryside. Eve glanced back over her shoulder at the farm. It reminded her of a crouching animal with its thatch pulled down over the bedroom windows and the glass in those windows reflecting the last rays of the dying sun. She waited for Johnny to remark on the beauty of the building with its whitewashed cob walls, the flowers in the beds on either side of the back door and the general air that it had grown where it was rather than been built. But this apparently had not occurred to Johnny. When they emerged on to the lane he raised his brows.

'Left or right?' he asked prosaically. 'We can't go as far as the source of the stream and get home before dawn tomorrow, so shall we simply stroll along until we get to the deep pool? One of the Spindlebush farm-hands who came home on leave told me he'd seen an otter there once, but I don't know whether to believe him. Come to think of it, we might find out, because otters lie up during the day and go about their busi-ness at night.'

Eve agreed that this was a good plan. It had occurred

to her that this was the perfect moment to try to find out a little more about Johnny's past, for while she told herself that now they knew each other so well he would not resent being questioned, she had always hesitated to put that theory to the test. She glanced sideways at Johnny. He had never mentioned parents, or any other relatives for that matter, but then she had never asked. It was simply, she thought, that they had both left their pre-war lives behind and had no reason to discuss their past. Well, that was about to change.

'Johnny, I hope you don't mind my asking, but what do your mum and dad do?' she said. 'You know my father's in the Navy and Mummy's joined up too: she was an awfully good secretary when Daddy met her and she's doing the same sort of thing now. What about yours?'

Johnny laughed and skirted a puddle, grabbing Eve's hand and steering her around it as well. 'I wondered when you'd ask,' he said, and Eve could see his teeth gleaming in the light of the rising moon as he spoke. 'My dad's in the army – his unit was posted to Burma, or one of those outlandish places – and my mum firewatches or mans the WI wagons. She can drive, got her licence and everything, and she taught my two older brothers, who are both drivers in the army now.' He stopped walking and turned his head to look down at her, and she read curiosity in his glance. 'I gathered from what you said that your parents are stationed in Plymouth, which isn't that far away. I should have thought they would have visited on a more regular basis. Still, it takes all sorts; I suppose you keep in touch by letter.'

Eve stiffened. This sounded remarkably like criticism of both her parents, and indeed when she looked at Johnny he was grinning as though aware that she would not take his observation lightly.

'My parents can't just please themselves,' she said, a touch coolly. 'Daddy's at sea most of the time and really busy when his ship's in port, and I expect Mummy's in the same boat . . .'

Johnny sniggered. 'In the same boat; a very Navy way of putting it,' he remarked. 'By the way, have you asked Connie about her family? Or are you only nosy about me? She's had it pretty tough, you know. She lives very near the docks and she's an only child. Her father owns a greengrocer's and her mother's like mine, helping out with the war effort in any way she can . . .'

'Or at least that's what she told you,' Eve said tartly, and could have kicked herself when she saw the disapproval on her companion's face.

But when he spoke, it was mildly. 'Why should she lie about a thing like that? You really do dislike her, don't you? And as far as I can make out, for no particular reason.' Once more he caught hold of Eve's hand, pulling her round. 'We're not going to get as far as the otter pool – it's after half past nine, so we'd better turn back here or you'll be in trouble,' he said cheerfully. 'Look, I wasn't quite fair just now. Connie does tell the occasional whopper, everyone knows that, but I'm sure it's only to try to make herself sound more interesting. I suspect most of us tell the odd tall story for that reason, so why don't you forget all that stuff and try a bit harder to discover the real Connie? Honest to God, Eve, there's a really nice person hidden away inside that girl. If I can see that why shouldn't you?'

They were back at the enormous puddle and Eve skipped round it, giggling. 'I *am* trying, really hard,' she promised. 'Just you wait and see; me and Connie will get along much better now I know a bit more about her. And you're right about telling whoppers. We may not all tell downright lies but most of us exaggerate a little. Next time when I'm tempted to challenge her I jolly well won't.' She peered anxiously up into Johnny's freckled face. 'The truth is that I've been jealous of Connie from the start. She's so pretty!'

Johnny laughed. 'She *is* pretty, isn't she? But what do looks matter? My dad says it's character that counts, and he's right, you know.'

They reached the farm, and as Johnny led the way across the yard Eve said what was on her mind.

'Do looks really not matter, Johnny? Wouldn't you like me better if I had golden curls like Chrissie's? And big blue eyes?'

Johnny laughed and pushed open the back door for her. 'I'd like you just as much if you were plain as a pikestaff,' he said. 'And now go and get your beauty sleep and perhaps tomorrow when you get up you'll have been transformed into Shirley Temple! Goodnight, young Eve.'

Eve opened her mouth to ask another question, then closed it again. What was the point? She had said she would try to get to know and like Connie and she meant to do just that. She remembered a saying which Mr Trevalyn was fond of quoting. *Fine words butter no parsnips*, he would say, so she would start this very minute by going upstairs and thanking Connie for keeping an eye on Chrissie. She might even take her up a cup of cocoa as a sort of thank-you present. She was filled with a grim determination both to take Johnny's advice and to find herself a proper friend in Connie.

As she stepped into the kitchen several pairs of eyes swung round to stare at her. Mrs Trevalyn and Mrs Smith had come over to join their husbands, and now the four of them were sitting round the green baize card table with mugs of cocoa and Auntie Bess's ginger biscuits before them. Auntie Bess herself was putting the rest of her baking away in the pantry and her husband, scowling, was filling in one of the interminable ministry forms which seemed to arrive with every post. On the kitchen table was a pile of dead rabbits from which Eve, with a shudder, dragged her eyes. She had no wish to relive the horror of finding the trap, and went straight over to the dresser.

'Has Chrissie been good?' she asked hopefully. 'I thought I'd take Connie a mug of cocoa as a thank you. It was lovely to have time to myself just for once. He's not a bad little boy but he never stops talking.'

Auntie Bess closed the pantry door behind her and smiled. 'He's been very good, but I checked on them five minutes ago and they were both fast asleep, so it wouldn't do to disturb them.' She smiled reassuringly at Eve. ''Tis time you were in bed yourself, else you'll be no manner of use in the morning.'

161

Chapter Seven

Despite her busy day, Eve woke early on the following morning. Connie still slumbered, Chrissie was giving little purring snores and the sunshine streaming through the window proved Mr Smith's weather forecast right. Eve yawned and stretched luxuriously. Lily's bed was, as usual, empty; Eve, who was often awake before the alarm went off, thought it was Lily's departure to milk the cows, quiet though she tried to be, that woke her.

If she was awake before Lily left she usually got up as well, because she loved the early milking. She was becoming increasingly adept with the cows and Lily often told her what a help she was. Lily was always kind but she was truthful, too, so Eve valued her praise, and when writing to her parents usually included a reference to her favourite land girl. Today, however, Lily was not on early milking, so Eve slid out of bed and washed as quietly as she could, intending to join her friend for breakfast. She was about to slip through the door when a querulous voice stopped her in her tracks.

'Evie! You left me with Connie for ages yesterday. It

isn't school today, is it? Can I come with you? I'll be ever so quick . . .'

Eve sighed, but nodded. 'Yes, if you like,' she said resignedly. 'But I'm not sure what I'll be doing later, so if I'm busy and you can't help you'll have to find some way to amuse yourself, all right?'

But Chrissie was already at the washstand dipping his flannel into the cold water and rubbing enthusiastically at his small, rosy face. True to his word he was soon ready and brother and sister went down to the kitchen, where Auntie Bess, no doubt having heard them coming, had already got the porridge dished out. Lily smiled a greeting over her own portion, and presently they were joined by Miriam and Uncle Reg, and a few minutes later by Mr Smith, who often popped in to talk over farming matters and to have a share of the porridge which he vowed and declared was a good deal better than that which his wife made.

Chrissie was the first to finish. He scraped up the last spoonful of porridge, slid off his chair, and tugged urgently at Eve's sleeve.

'You did say I could come with you today, didn't you, Evie?' he said, and Eve, smiling down at him, thought she read desperation in his expression.

'Of course I did,' she said. She lowered her voice. 'What's the matter, Chrissie? Don't say Connie was unkind to you?'

'Not exactly,' Chrissie said. 'Only I got a secret. Can we walk down the lane? Then I'll tell you what I done. Did, I mean.'

'Right,' Eve said, making up her mind. 'When we've

done our chores we'll walk to the village and see if we can buy some sweets. You'd like that, wouldn't you?'

Before they set off to start their chores Eve ran upstairs to the attic to ask Connie whether she wanted to come to the village with them. She was not surprised, however, when Connie moaned 'No ta' and burrowed deeper beneath her blankets. The other girl frequently spent a couple of hours in bed when she was neither working on the farm nor due at school, so her refusal was typical; Eve only wondered how she could bear to waste her time in such a way. She was about to go downstairs again when another thought struck her. She had wanted to thank Connie for looking after Chrissie; if she did Connie's chores as well as her own Connie might lie in bed until lunchtime. She made the suggestion somewhat tentatively, half expecting a rebuff, but Connie opened her eyes and actually smiled.

'That would be grand,' she said gratefully. 'Thanks, Eve.'

So when Eve descended the stairs she felt she had made a good start in her efforts to get along with Connie, and with Chrissie's help the chores were done in no time. They took the eggs they had collected back to the kitchen and reported to Auntie Bess, who reminded them to be back in time for lunch and waved them off quite cheerfully.

It was a fine day, the sunshine dappling the lane with leaf shadows, but Chrissie, who normally ran ahead shouting back comments to anyone who would listen, was, Eve thought, more subdued than usual. She remembered that he had begged her not to leave him behind and wondered what had happened to make him reluctant to stay in the house with Auntie Bess. He had said something about a secret; no doubt she would find out what was on his mind in the fullness of time.

When they reached the bridge he went and stood in the middle of it and Eve assumed he wanted to play the three billy goats gruff. Sometimes he took the part of the troll and sometimes he was the biggest billy goat, but on this occasion it seemed he only wanted to talk. When Eve would have pretended to dodge past him he grabbed her sleeve, shaking his head when she tried to get free.

'Hang on, Evie,' he said urgently. 'I want to tell you my secret. You know Connie took me back to bed before you came home last night?'

'Yes, of course I know. Auntie Bess thought you wouldn't like it because the men had to kill the rabbits and rats that were hiding in the last of the corn. Not for fun: meat is scarce because of the war, and you know how you love Auntie Bess's rabbit pie; and as for the rats, they eat the corn that's meant for the farm animals, so in a way it's a sort of competition. Can you understand that? No one wanted you to be upset, so you went back to the farm whilst Johnny and I had a bit of a walk around. And since Connie had said she'd keep an eye on you I knew you'd be all right. She wasn't unkind to you, was she?'

Chrissie shook his curly head. 'No, but she fell asleep all hunched up under the covers whilst I was still awake and it was still daylight outside so I thought I'd come and find you. I put on my blue dungarees, my wellingtons and my jacket and sneaked out of the back door without anyone seeing me. I went back to the field where they were cutting the corn, but I didn't see you and the men were making such a hullabaloo that no one even noticed me, and just as I was thinking I'd best get back to the farm before it got really dark a rabbit bolted out of the hedge practically into my arms. It didn't even try to escape when I pushed it into my jacket. It knew I was a friend, Evie, and when a couple of farmhands from Spindlebush came crashing after it and asked if I'd seen which way it had run I just shook my head. It was hurt, Evie. There was blood on his foot so I carried him back to the farmyard because I knew there was a big old cardboard box there, and shut him inside it. I fetched hay from the barn so he'd have somewhere nice to lie down and then I carried the box as far as I could, which was' – he waved a hand vaguely in the direction of the woodland – 'in there, in one of those clearings where the grass and the weeds are as high as my waist.' He looked guiltily at Eve. 'And I stole two big handfuls of grain, because rabbits must like it, wouldn't you say?'

'Oh yes, definitely,' Eve said. 'But Chrissie darling, you really shouldn't go wandering around the woods on your own. Last night, Johnny and I found a rabbit in a trap down by the stream. We told Uncle Reg and he's taken the trap to the police, because he wants to find out who set it so he can order them off his land.'

Chrissie looked stricken. 'Was it a big rabbit with a white bobble tail?'

Eve shook her head. 'No, it was only a baby; I'm sure

your rabbit would have been quite happy with the hay. Only you can't keep him in that box. You must let him go to be with his brothers and sisters. He'll feel like a prisoner in even the biggest box; it's freedom he'll want before everything. So let's go and find him and take him back to his own place, where he can live a happy and free life like all the other wild rabbits.'

She looked hopefully at her small brother but was not really surprised when he looked earnestly up into her face. 'I want him for my own pet. People do keep rabbits as pets; one of the boys in my class at school has a white one with pink eyes, so why shouldn't I have a nice brown one which is just my friend and no one else's?'

Eve sighed. She thought of all the complications which keeping a rabbit would bring in its wake. Feeding it would be easy and cleaning the cage would be Chrissie's responsibility, but she could just imagine the wailing and gnashing of teeth which would follow if a fox or Shep the sheepdog fancied a plump caged rabbit for his dinner. Yet how could she deny her little brother the chance to have his own pet? Choosing her words carefully, she said, 'We can talk about that when we've found him. But honestly, Chrissie, I don't think you can expect the Favershams to welcome another responsibility. Auntie Bess is ever so kind – Uncle Reg too – but they've got a lot on their plates at the moment. So don't get your hopes too high.' She indicated the three tiny narrow paths which led into the woodland and eventually through it to the forestry. 'Which way?'

Chrissie took her hand and began to tow her along the little track which led off to the left, plunging on to another little path and then another. Finally they came to a clearing where grass and weeds forced their way up in competition with a great many saplings, and Chrissie came to a stop.

'It's here, by that big patch of brambles,' he said, and Eve recognised the hope in his voice. 'I remember those brambles because Auntie Bess said she'd make us bramble jelly if we'd pick the berries for her. I pushed the box well into cover.' He bent and peered at the luxurious growth, then straightened and turned towards his sister. 'He's gone!' he said, his voice trembling. 'The box is here but the rabbit's gone. He must've tipped the box over and escaped.' He gulped, but then he added bravely, 'And I'm glad, because it must mean that he was strong enough to get back to the field and find his friends, and he'll be happier with them than with me. It's best for wild animals to live in the wild, isn't it, Evie?'

Eve looked at her brother with admiration. How could I have been so blind as to not realise how he's changed, she asked herself. He isn't a baby any more. 'Yes, it is, darling. And now we must get back because you know Auntie Bess is really strict about mealtimes,' she reminded him. She held out a hand to take his, then saw the look on his face and hastily withdrew it.

He smiled. 'Thank you for coming to find the box with me,' he said. 'I feel a lot better now I know he's safe in the field.'

*   *   *

'Evie, you'll never guess!' Chrissie said excitedly. 'Auntie Bess told me that Mummy and Daddy are coming for a visit in a couple of weeks – the same weekend as Lily's birthday – so I asked Auntie Bess if we could have a party that weekend and she said yes. Colin can't come, of course, because he's teaching flying abroad, but Mummy and Daddy will be there, and the Spindlebush lot, and I'm going to help Auntie Bess make a birthday cake for Lily and lots of other things for a really special tea . . .'

Auntie Bess was at the sink washing up the breakfast things so Eve picked up a tea towel and began to dry the china and cutlery. 'That's a fantastic idea, Chrissie,' she said. 'Tell you what, if you go on being so clever I think we might ask Auntie Bess if we can go into town and choose a present for Lily: something pretty, or some scented soap, if we can find any; Lily always smells lovely.'

Auntie Bess turned from the sink to inform them that the Armstrongs would enjoy the party, but Eve had her doubts. She knew her mother's idea of a birthday treat would be a film show in a real cinema, and thought she might greet the idea of a party tea with something less than enthusiasm. But when she put her fear to her father in one of her letters his reply was immediate and cheerful.

So long as it doesn't rain I'm sure Mummy will make a big effort and come to the farm for Lily's birthday tea, he replied. *Remember, darling, Mummy is a Londoner through and through, but she's really looking forward to seeing you both and I'm sure she'll tuck in with the rest of us.*

'I'll tell Mummy how disappointed we would be if she didn't come,' she told Chrissie, having read the letter aloud. 'After all, this is Lily's birthday party, and I know Mummy's very fond of Lily. Everyone is.'

The weather had been good for so long that when Eve woke on the morning of the surprise party to find a fine drizzle falling on the window she could scarcely believe it. How could fate be so cruel? She had said her prayers every night for a week because she knew it meant a lot to Chrissie to have his mother with them. She herself had been extra specially good, helping Auntie Bess in every way she possibly could and doing her maths homework without pestering Johnny to check her answers; a considerable sacrifice, for he was much better at arithmetic than she and she knew how pleased both Mummy and Daddy would be if her homework merited a star.

However, even though it was raining now it might not be raining by the time their parents set off for the farm. Daddy had arranged to borrow a car from a friend and had assured them gaily, in his latest letter, that their mother would feel like a princess being conveyed on a magic carpet to Drake's Farm.

'There will be plum pie and ice cream because Auntie Bess promised,' Chrissie remarked now, scrubbing at his hands and face in the nice cool water which Eve had fetched up in its jug and poured into the basin. 'When will you put your party dress on, Evie? I'm going to wear my new shirt, my school trousers and the shoes with the laces, because Mummy likes her boy to look smart.'

Eve giggled; sometimes Chrissie was so grown up that when he reverted to baby speak it always made her laugh.

'Evie, I said when are you going to put on your party dress?'

She sobered. 'Never, unfortunately,' she said ruefully. 'It was too tight under the arms the last time I put it on in London, and now I can't even get it over my head, so I'll be wearing the only other respectable dress I own, which is my blue gingham school one.' She looked across the room to where her small brother was examining himself critically in Lily's mirror. 'But I don't think you ought to wear your school trousers, because birthday parties aren't really posh occasions,' she went on. 'Didn't Auntie Bess say we should wear our oldest things, because Johnny and Robbo will want to play what Mummy would call nasty rough games and we're bound to get dirty, especially if it goes on raining?'

'If it goes on raining we shan't be playing out of doors,' Chrissie said unhappily. 'If it goes on raining there won't be a party, not a proper one. I was going to show Mummy the pond we're digging out to give the ducks somewhere nice and big when they come for a swim.' He sighed deeply, then went to the open window and looked anxiously up at the grey clouds scudding across the sky. 'Oh, Evie, I did so want nice weather, because Mummy hardly ever comes to the farm and I want her to learn to love it, like we do. Only she won't if it rains, because whatever we wear Mummy will wear something smart and she'll be afraid the rain will spoil it.' He sighed again. 'In her last letter she said she was bringing a present for Lily, which she wouldn't have said if she didn't mean to come, but if she decides not to because it's raining . . . oh, Evie, I'll be *soooooo* disappointed . . .'

'I'm sure she'll come,' Eve said, crossing her fingers behind her back. 'After all, if the weather's bad we can play games in the house, and that'll be fun, won't it?'

'A birthday party? Just for me?' Lily's astonishment seemed real, but Eve was aware that almost everyone in the village had been let into the secret and guessed Lily knew as much about the 'surprise' party as everyone else. For one thing, presents had had to be bought and wartime shortages made this a mammoth task. But they had managed, each one of them, to get Lily something they knew she would like. Chrissie, Eve and Connie had put their money together and managed to find a small bar of scented soap, to be presented with a soft and fluffy face flannel made out of an old towel and carefully hemmed by Eve's willing hand. Miriam had decided on a small bar of chocolate which she had been saving for some such occasion. The farmhands presented their colleague with flowers from their own gardens and the blacksmith, though he was unable to attend the party, had nailed a horseshoe to the attic bedroom door, assuring all and sundry that it would bring Lily good luck.

The Armstrongs were not expected to arrive at the

farm until late afternoon, but to Chrissie's joy they arrived before lunch, having accepted a lift from a friend in an official car. The children happened to be out in the farmyard when the shiny black vehicle drew to a halt no more than a hundred yards from the farm gate, and naturally enough they raced up the lane to see who was calling. It might be a ministry inspector, but they soon discovered it was no such thing. A handsome man in naval uniform sporting a great deal of gold braid got out of the car and went round to open the front passenger door just as Bill Armstrong got out of the back seat and grinned at the assembled company, for even Auntie Bess and Uncle Reg had come out of the house to see who their visitor was.

Eleanor Armstrong, looking incredibly smart in a navy suit and crisp white blouse, addressed herself to Auntie Bess. 'We're awfully early, but Captain Carruthers offered us a lift and says he'll call for us at around six o'clock, if that's all right? The car Bill was going to borrow fell through and I didn't fancy the bus – it's always dirty and crowded – so when the captain offered to pick us up as well we just couldn't resist, could we, Bill?' she concluded, smiling blindingly at Captain Carruthers.

'No indeed; we're very grateful,' Bill said, but Eve, hovering at the back of the small crowd, thought he sounded less than delighted. Before she could begin to wonder just who this Captain Carruthers was Uncle Reg surged forward, a hand held out.

'How do you do, captain? It's awfully good of you to

173

bring our guests, and if you would like to join in the birthday fun you're very welcome. My wife has prepared enough food for an army – or should I say the Navy? – so one extra is no problem and you would be very welcome.'

Captain Carruthers smiled, showing gleaming white teeth. He was a handsome man with a neatly trimmed black beard and bright blue eyes, reminding Eve of the picture of the sailor on a packet of Player's cigarettes. 'It's very kind of you, but I have an appointment, rather an important one, in the dockyards at Devonport, so I'm afraid I can't accept your invitation.'

'Surely you've time for a quick cup of tea?' Aunt Bess suggested. ''Tis fresh made.'

The captain smiled and nodded. 'Well, five minutes won't hurt.' Once inside the Favershams' large and homely kitchen he glanced around the table then turned to Eleanor Armstrong. 'I'm warning you, young woman, that if you ruin your uniform playing party games I'll have you on a charge. I did tell you to wear old clothes, but would you listen?'

Lily struck in. She was laughing. 'Captain Carruthers is right, Mrs Armstrong, but I've a spare pair of dungarees and wellingtons which you can borrow. They'll keep you clean as a new whistle.' She stood up. 'You might as well come up to my room right now and try them on, but we're about the same size, I would say. Want to give it a go?'

Eleanor pouted but agreed that it might be sensible and Auntie Bess glanced at the clock on the mantelpiece. 'Lunch in ten minutes,' she reminded them, handing Captain Carruthers a large tin mug of tea. 'Off with you, young ladies.'

By the time the table had been set for two extra diners Lily and Eleanor were on their way downstairs, both dressed in Land Army working clothes, and when they came into the kitchen and stood side by side Bill Armstrong laughed and said they could be twins. Both had golden hair, though Lily's was more wheat-coloured than her companion's, and they were roughly the same height and build.

Bill pulled out a chair for his wife just as Captain Carruthers stood up. 'Best be on my way or I'll be in trouble,' he said breezily. He turned to Eleanor. 'My meeting will be over by eight o'clock at the latest so I'll pick you up soon after that.' He grinned at Bill. 'I rely on you, old fellow, to see your lovely lady doesn't keep me waiting.' He raised his hand in a mocking salute. 'Have a grand party; I only wish I could join you, but, as everyone keeps reminding us, there is a war on. Goodbye everyone; nice to have met you. No, don't get up, or I shall be in trouble for delaying this good lady's lunch.'

He grinned round at the assembled company and left the kitchen, shutting the door firmly behind him.

Auntie Bess was about to give Chrissie the plates to hand out when she noticed his grubby little paws. 'Look at your hands, young man,' she said. 'And that jersey is filthy. I know I said old clothes but I didn't mean *that* old.' She turned to Eleanor. 'I hope you don't think I'd let him sit down to a meal in that state. Normally I'd send him to the scullery, but there's a bit of soap in his room and a clean shirt.' She turned back to

Chrissie. 'Off with you and don't come back down until you're clean as a new pin.'

Chrissie grinned and slipped off his chair, and was already climbing the second flight of stairs when Eleanor suddenly clapped a hand to her forehead. 'Oh, what an idiot I am!' she said. 'I left Lily's birthday present in Skip's car. I hope he hasn't left!' She jumped to her feet and ran out of the kitchen before Lily, who had stood up as well, could call her back.

'What a good thing it's a cold meal,' she said teasingly, sitting down once more. 'I'm sure my present could have waited, though why Mrs Armstrong bought me anything in the first place I can't imagine . . . although of course I'm extremely grateful,' she added, smiling at Bill.

Bill grinned. 'An impetuous lady, my wife,' he said proudly. 'She clearly wanted you to have it at once. She's like that; she can never bear any delay . . .'

He was interrupted by the return of his wife, who came breathlessly back into the kitchen, pink-cheeked from running but waving a small parcel triumphantly. 'Caught him up before he'd gone more than a couple of yards,' she said, and sank into her chair just as Chrissie came clattering down the last flight.

'I'm clean, I'm clean!' he announced, taking his own place at the table. He glanced across to where Lily sat, a brown paper parcel in her hand. 'Is that from my mummy and daddy? Are you going to open it now?'

After lunch everyone played various party games until they were called in for the birthday tea. Auntie

Bess had done wonders, Eve knew. It was simply not possible to buy dried fruit or exciting fillings for sandwiches, but looking at the laden table, Eve thought, you would never know it was wartime. The sandwiches contained delicious mashed-up egg, cucumber from the post office's ancient greenhouse or tomatoes from the same source. There was one of Auntie Bess's famous rabbit pies and any number of crumbles and tarts made from the fruit which was ripening in the orchard. Eve noticed that Johnny and Robbo scarcely waited for Uncle Reg to give the word before they began to reach for the food. Eve had often suspected from the way the boys ate at Drake's Farm that even the breakfast Mrs Spindle-bush provided did not compare with what Auntie Bess had to offer.

When everyone had eaten their fill the plates were cleared and a beautiful birthday cake was carried in and placed reverently before Lily.

'We couldn't find twenty-one birthday candles,' Uncle Reg said apologetically. 'But Mother found one in a dresser drawer, which is better than nothing, so I'm afraid you'll have to make do with that.' The candle was lit, Lily blew it out with her first attempt, the big knife was plunged into the heart of the cake and the slices were handed round. Even Connie, who seldom congratulated Auntie Bess on her cooking, admitted that the cake was downright pre-war, despite the substitution of candied carrot for the unobtainable dried fruit. It was typical of Lily that she took a couple of slices to be given to Mr Pryde and his wife, saying that they should enjoy their share of the cake in return for her lucky horseshoe.

Chrissie was alight with happiness, his beaming face almost outdoing Lily's. As they crossed the farmyard he caught at Eve's arm.

'Wasn't it a good idea to have a party for Lily?' he enquired. 'Everyone is having a wizard time ...' he puffed out his small chest, 'and it's all because of me. And Mummy's enjoying herself, isn't she? Can we tell her the party was my idea? She'll be so proud of her boy.'

Eve neglected to point out that Eleanor had already been told by both Auntie Bess and herself that the party had been Chrissie's idea, and though she had smiled absently and said what a clever boy he was she had not shown any particular interest.

'Have Daddy and Uncle Reg finished the washin' up yet?' he went on, fortunately not waiting for Eve's reply to his previous question. 'When everything's cleared away we're going to have a game of rescue – what some of the others call Relievio. Mummy and Daddy are going to join in; Daddy, Connie and you will be the searchers and the rest of us must hide. Connie says we can hide anywhere on the farm or in the woods but not in the house because that's where you go when one of the hunters finds you. Doesn't it sound great, Evie? Fancy Mummy saying she'll play as well! I always knew Daddy would. I'm glad I thought of this party because it's already been lots of fun and it goes on getting better and better. And it was my idea, wasn't it, Evie? Not just the party but the sort of game that grown-ups can enjoy as well. And even Connie is having a lovely time, she told me so. The hunters will count up to a hundred, quite slowly, so the hiders will have plenty of time to choose a good place where they won't be seen. Lily says we shouldn't hide in a bunch but one by one.' He puffed out his chest again and beamed up at Eve. 'Bet I'm the last one to be found because I'm the smallest and can get into the tiniest spaces. And Mummy will be found first because she doesn't know the countryside like we do, does she, Evie?'

'True,' Eve said. 'They've just finished washing up and they want me to get everyone into the kitchen so they can start the game, because Mummy and Daddy will have to leave as soon as Captain Carruthers arrives.'

By the time they re-entered the farmhouse everyone had assembled and Bill was running through the rules of the game.

'When a hunter finds you and puts a hand on you you're out and have to return to the kitchen. The last one to be found will be the winner.'

Very soon the hiders had disappeared as if by magic. Bill, Eve and Connie completed the count and strode into the farmyard, shouting, 'We're coming to ge-et you!'

'You two girls check the outbuildings whilst I search the garden,' Bill went on. 'Then we'll start on the woodland. We'll divide it into sections and I bet you that in twenty minutes or so we'll all be back in the kitchen. Mrs Faversham – Auntie Bess to you – has made a big batch of scones and there will be mugs of cocoa for losers as well as winners. Only we must get a move on because Mummy and I will have to leave very soon.'

'All right,' Eve said briefly, hiding her disappointment that her father would not be searching with her. 'I'll do the lofts and the stables while Connie does the cowsheds and the shippon.' She set off at brisk pace and soon found her first victim. Johnny had made himself a nest in the hay and was lying there comfortably reading a book and eating an apple. He grinned at Eve as she slapped him on the shoulder and shouted 'Gotcha!' and scrambled out of the hayloft, making straight for the kitchen and the beautiful scones which he knew awaited him there.

Having toured the farmyard the three of them took to the woodland and Eve's next find there was Chrissie. He had tucked himself away in a hollow tree and Eve was about to grab a protruding foot when her conscience smote her. Chrissie was only a child, after all, and to be found amongst the very first would take some of the pleasure out of the day for him. So she walked past the tree and continued to look to left and right, trying to make as little noise as possible. She spotted Robbo under the bridge across the stream and then, in a mossy dell, saw Miriam's red skirt as the other girl shrank deeper into the cover of ferns and brambles. In the end Chrissie was the last to be discovered, though Eve guessed that their father too may well have seen that protruding foot and decided, as she had herself, to pretend otherwise.

When they were all assembled in the kitchen eating scones and drinking cocoa Bill gave a deep sigh, glanced at his watch and announced that the captain would be reaching the main road at any minute.

'It's been the best day I could possibly imagine,' he said. He turned to Lily. 'The best day ever,' he repeated with a grin. 'You've made me feel young again; I wish you were twenty-one three hundred and sixty-five days of the year. But one thing is certain: I'll never forget today if I live to be a hundred.' He turned to his wife. 'You'd better take off your borrowed plumage, my love, otherwise Captain Carruthers may find himself with the wrong young woman at her desk tomorrow.'

Eve saw her mother stiffen and knew the comparison was not a welcome one. She gave a secret smile: although Eleanor would never admit it, she was nowhere near as beautiful as Lily. Eleanor's bright gold hair came out of a bottle and there was a hardness about her features, but Eve knew it would never do to say so.

Once the Armstrongs were gone the party broke up quite quickly, the farmhands disappearing to their cottages and the Spindlebush boys heading back up the lane to their beds. Eve looked at Chrissie's half-closed eyes, picked him up and told Auntie Bess that he was far too sleepy to sit chatting and drinking cocoa.

'I'll take him upstairs and let him lie in tomorrow,' she said. 'And for once he won't complain, because I'm telling you, Auntie Bess, if I'm to get my chores done tomorrow I ought to be in bed myself the moment I've tucked Chrissie in, which will be just as soon as I can manage.' She was as good as her word, tumbling the little boy into his bed the moment he had had a quick wash and donned his pyjamas.

'Night night, Evie,' he said drowsily. 'Weren't it a wonderful day, though? I'm so glad that Mummy and Daddy came to the party. Wasn't it nice of Captain Carruthers to bring them? Lily must have been glad too because she rushed out to say thank you just before he left. I was watching from the window and I saw her leaning into his car and giving him a big kiss.'

Eve had been about to turn away but her little brother's words stopped her in her tracks. 'She kissed him?' she asked incredulously. 'But she doesn't know him! When was this, Chrissie? I'm sure you must have got confused. Grown-ups don't kiss other grown-ups unless they know them awfully well. It can't have been Lily.'

'Well, it was, because she was in her uniform. And she did know him,' Chrissie said drowsily. 'She put her arms round his neck and they had an oogly-googly kiss; honest, Evie, they did.'

Eve shrugged. The ways of adults were strange to her but she supposed that sometimes people who hardly know each other might exchange kisses of thanks, or of greeting or farewell. But why would Lily be kissing anyone except, of course, Colin? The more she thought about Chrissie's words the more unlikely they seemed. She thought she knew Lily pretty well by now and it was just not in character for the other girl to go cuddling a virtual stranger.

On the very verge of sleep, she remembered how muddled Chrissie could get if he stayed up past his usual bedtime. That must be the answer. Chrissie had imagined the whole thing and her best course now would be to forget all about it. Satisfied, Eve slept at last.

Chapter Eight

Auntie Bess cleared away the last of the uneaten food – not that there was very much – and then settled down at the table with a nice hot cup of cocoa before her, smiling as she did so. Peace had descended at last, leaving just her, Uncle Reg and the land girls in the kitchen.

'The pair of you worked like the Trojans you are,' she told them. 'Oh, I know it was all supposed to be great fun, but fun has its price and you'll pay it in tiredness.' She chuckled. 'In half an hour there won't be one person still awake at Drake's Farm and that's as it should be.' She turned to Lily, eyebrows rising. 'Well, how does it feel to be twenty-one years old? I only wish we could have found ourselves a magic carpet and brought your young man home on it, if only for half an hour. But this war can't go on for ever, or so I tell myself, and you and your Colin will be together sooner than you may think.'

Lily stood up and went round the table to give Auntie Bess a kiss on her round, pink cheek.

'Thanks for a wonderful day,' she said. 'As you say,

it would have been marvellous if Colin could have come, but so long as he's safe and happy I don't grumble.'

'And now it's time you two girls went to bed, otherwise you won't be much use to anyone tomorrow,' Auntie Bess said. She held out both hands to help Uncle Reg to his feet. 'We've all had a wonderful day, thanks to you, Lily my dear, but the party's finished now and tomorrow the work starts all over again.'

Lily lay on her back in the darkness staring at the ceiling, which was low and covered in fine cracks. Ever since she had arrived at the farm and been installed in the attic bedroom she had planned to get hold of some whitewash from somewhere so that she could erase the lines. But gradually she'd grown to rather enjoy the many pictures which her imagination created above her head. There was an old man with a pipe in his mouth and a bulgy woman aboard what looked like a ship, and now Lily found she had no desire to get rid of them. Instead, she made up stories about them, though usually not for long since sleep came rapidly when one lived an active outdoor life.

However, on this occasion no new adventures befell her hero and heroine. Her thoughts were racing, and to control them she decided that she would relive as much of the day as she could, whilst waiting for her companions to fall asleep. She had no intention of opening the envelope from Colin, let alone reading its contents, before she could do so in complete privacy.

For a moment she lay in the dark, listening to the

stirring of her companions. She had had a busy morning pretending to ignore the preparations for the
'surprise' party, and had entered the kitchen not long
before lunch knowing that already there was a small
pile of presents by her plate, which she would open
when everyone was assembled. She had seen her
mother's familiar handwriting on top of the pile of half
a dozen envelopes, and recognised her pal Mary Jane's
careful script peeping out at the bottom.

Auntie Bess had turned and beamed a welcome.
"Twon't surprise you to know there's a letter from
your young man,' she had said cheerfully. 'In fact it
arrived yesterday, but us held it back 'cos we guessed
'twould be birthday wishes.' She had glanced at the
clock ticking away on the kitchen mantelpiece. 'Give it
another five minutes and everyone will come rushing
in and the fun will start. Do you want to take your feller's letter up to your room so's you can read it in
private?' She had chuckled. "Tis quite a thin letter for
a change, so it maybe only says happy birthday, but it's
up to you, of course.'

Lily had picked up the letters and was surprised to
find that Colin's envelope was the lightest of the bunch.
He must have been in a hurry because usually his letters were long and chatty, the sort that everyone likes
to receive. For a moment she was tempted to see what
the blue airmail envelope contained, but then she had
changed her mind. She would save it until all the
excitement was over and then enjoy it when everyone
had gone and the youngsters were asleep. Accordingly
she had put the other letters back on the table and

headed for the stairs, calling over her shoulder as she mounted the first flight: 'Thanks, Auntie Bess, but I won't read it yet. It'll be the perfect end to what I'm sure is going to be a perfect day.' She had gone straight to the attic and pushed the letter under her pillow, though with a twinge of regret that she could not enjoy it twice over, once now and once when everyone else was safely asleep. Sometimes she wanted Colin so badly that she shed tears into her pillow, but today she had a party to distract her.

In the doorway, Lily had hesitated. Suppose there was some exciting news in the letter? For all she knew he might have been posted back to England; he might be on his way now! Perhaps that was why the envelope only held, at most, a couple of sheets of thin airmail paper. He wouldn't want to waste time giving her much news in a letter when he would shortly be home to tell her himself. As a trainer he would fly home, not have to suffer the tedious ocean trip. Just suppose . . . but a voice from below was calling her name and Lily gave one last rueful look at the corner of the blue envelope with its well-loved writing and then left the room, shutting the door firmly behind her. The letter would lie beneath her pillow like the gold at the foot of the rainbow, waiting for her to enjoy at the end of what looked like being a wonderful day.

But now Lily lay for a little longer, forcing herself to have patience. She waited until Chrissie's bubbling snores and Eve's and Connie's steady breathing told her they were all asleep, and only then did she fish under her pillow and bring out the letter. With trembling fingers she lit her candle, stood it on the box which did duty as a bedside table and slit open the envelope. She pulled out the thin airmail pages, so delighted at the sight of Colin's well-remembered script that she could have laughed aloud if she hadn't been determined not to wake her roommates. She hitched herself up on one elbow, spread out the letter and began to read.

My dearest Lily, how I miss you. You are the best thing that ever happened to me and I hope to God, my darling girl, that what I am about to say will neither hurt you too much nor come as a great surprise. I've met someone else. Her name's Valencia and she's a blue-eyed blonde and so like you to look at that you might be twins. I told her about you as soon as I realised she was beginning to mean a lot to me, and she insisted that I must tell you at once how we felt about each other.

Dear Lily, you will always hold a place in my heart, and I hope with all my soul that you will meet a better man than me and fall truly in love, as I have.

Please forgive me for what must seem like disloyalty, but I couldn't help myself. Valencia means the world to me. I should've written this letter six months ago, but Lily, darling, I simply could not make up my mind whether it was Valencia I was in love with or you. It was a dreadful decision to have to make, and even though I've been back in Britain for three weeks I still find this letter very difficult to write. But in the end I knew I wanted to spend the rest of my life with Valencia and must break the news to my old love. Please try to understand, darling. I will never forget you, and I envy the man who wins you. Colin

Lily read the letter through tear-blurred eyes, and then with trembling breath blew out the candle and crumpled the letter into a tight little ball. She and Colin had been boy and girlfriend for seven years; their romance had been the envy of her friends, so how to explain Colin's change of heart? It was not only sad – it was humiliating. He had met her parents and liked them, knew many of her old school friends, had slipped easily into the role of Lily Kendal's boyfriend, and now all that was over. And explanations would be called for. Oh, not from the folk at home, but from those here at Drake's Farm, some of whom had envied her starry-eyed love affair and others who had simply taken it for granted that Lily and Colin were made for each other. Lily had spoken often about Colin, mentioning marriage and the family they hoped to have one day. And on the first occasion that Colin had visited Drake's Farm he had immediately struck a chord with Auntie Bess and Uncle Reg, who said that he reminded them of their own son.

'Such a handsome fellow, and it's plain to see he's deeply in love with his "golden Lily",' Auntie Bess had remarked. 'You only have to walk into the room, my dear, and his whole face lights up. You're a very lucky girl. It's not often true loves comes along, but when it does you must grasp it with both hands. He's clearly devoted to you and will make you a wonderful husband.'

How can I go downstairs tomorrow morning and tell them, Lily asked herself. Oh, how can I face them? Sleep was impossible. She simply lay on her bed phrasing and rephrasing what she would say at breakfast next morning. And then, as though the idea had been in her head all the while, a tide of longing, deep and passionate, washed over her. She sat up, aware that this solution to her problem was the right one. She would go home! She had never taken so much as a day's leave from her work as a land girl, and as far as she could make out there was nothing to stop her from taking that delayed leave now. It would not take her long to pack her few possessions into the knapsack which hung on the end of her bed. Miriam would do her work, or more likely little Eve. Moving silently around the darkened room, Lily began to pack.

Auntie Bess was always first down in the morning and as soon as she entered the kitchen she saw the note propped against the marmalade pot. She stared at it for a moment and then saw that it was addressed to herself and picked it up. It was written on lined paper and consisted only of half a dozen lines.

Dear Auntie Bess, the note read. *I am taking some leave to go home and see my parents. I hope I have not made things difficult but I have to go. The letter from Colin told me he's met someone else. If I stay here every bit of the farm will remind me of him and I'm not strong enough to face it yet. Yours with love, Lily.*

Auntie Bess sat down on a chair with a whump. For a moment she simply could not take in what she had read. Like everyone else at Drake's Farm she had thought Lily and Colin were simply waiting for Colin's return before they got married. It seemed unbelievable that what she had secretly thought of as the love affair of the century could be finished, and that by a letter which he must have realised would arrive around Lily's twenty-first birthday. The note clenched in her hand had been written on a page torn out of an exercise book, and she turned it over in the hope that there would be a postscript on the back saying that the note had been a joke, but of course there was nothing.

She got ponderously to her feet and climbed the stairs which led to the attic. Lily's bed had been neatly made up. Her clothes were missing, as was the knapsack in which the girl had kept her personal possessions. Auntie Bess heaved a sigh. Lily had gone, all right, and suddenly she realised that she must get downstairs and start thinking about how they would manage. She scanned the note again; it gave no clue as to how long Lily would be away. In the meantime, until they could replace their best worker, Auntie Bess must wake everyone, tell them that Lily had gone home on unexpected leave and start reallocating the day's work. I'll get Eve to do Lily's milking and old Mr Smith can get off his behind and clean the milking parlour, Auntie Bess told herself. Young Chrissie can go up to Spindlebush, explain what's happened and get them to lend me one of the lads for a day or two, just until we sort ourselves out, and in the meantime I'd best stir myself or everyone will be coming down and the porridge won't even be started. Thank God for the Aga; *that* won't let me down!

Lily walked up the familiar road towards where the great bulk of the cathedral announced that her home was only minutes away. Home! She had been born here and had lived here all her life until she had answered the cry for girls to work on the land, to take the place of fighting men who had been called up. She had gone to school here, had proudly worn the uniform first of the Brownies and then of the Girl Guides. She had met Colin here; her heart thumped painfully at the recollection. She had gone with a crowd of friends to a dance at the Gala Ballroom and the handsomest man there – Colin Tunstal – had not only asked her to dance but had walked her home afterwards. After that he had met her parents on several occasions, impressing them with his easy charm and delightful manners. He had soon become a regular visitor, and though he never overstepped the mark it soon became clear – or so people said – that they were made for each other. They had similar tastes, both loving the countryside and country pursuits. And very soon Colin was accepted as the man she would marry one day. Neither had ever been out with anyone else, nor had they wished to. Colin was Lily's idea of the perfect mate and when he was posted abroad she had been heartbroken, but, as everyone kept repeating, there was a war on, and simply by taking their separation as a part of her war effort Lily had felt she was doing her bit.

She had joined the Land Army only a few weeks after Colin had been posted. They had exchanged letters almost daily and telephone calls whenever they could get to a phone, and in all her wildest nightmares Lily had never dreamed that Colin would meet someone else and cast her aside, not even in person, but by a letter so cruel that she could scarcely believe it had come from the man she had loved so passionately.

Lily reached the white wicket gate which led to her house and stood for a moment staring at what had once been a beautiful front garden. She supposed she had expected change, but not quite like this. The flowerbeds, the shrubs and the lawn had all disappeared, to be replaced by neat rows of vegetables. Only the old lilac tree which leaned over the wicket gate and the climbing rose which clambered up the stone walls were unaltered. Lily smiled to herself. There had been keen competition amongst the tenants of the Close as to who had the loveliest garden, and for a good few years now her father and mother had won hands down. Lily assumed that her love of the countryside had come directly from her parents, for the house had a long back garden which they kept in apple-pie order. There were asparagus beds, great clumps of rhubarb, half a dozen blackcurrant bushes and several raspberry canes which had supplied the household with pounds of delicious fruit which the Reverend Michael Kendal vowed were the best in the city.

Well, they won't have rooted up the back garden, Lily told herself hopefully. And the house shouldn't be so very different. It was too small to be taken over by the military and too near the many airfields in Norfolk to be a home for evacuees. Her mother had said vaguely that they had an injured officer billeted on them but Lily had no idea whether he was still with them or had re-joined his unit. There had been some accident or other at his base, and her mother, having been a nurse, had offered to take the wounded man in.

Now, leaning on the wicket gate, Lily wished she had paid more attention to her mother's letters, but she had been so wrapped up in Colin and his various items of news that she had rather skimmed over her mother's lengthy epistles. She pushed open the wicket gate and entered the front garden, nodding approvingly to herself as she passed between the rows of vegetables. There wasn't a weed in sight, and when she peered at the big round green cabbages no caterpillar reared its hopeful head.

Lily smiled to herself; knowing her father's ways he would have advised any humble caterpillar to go elsewhere. Father would set his choirboys to collect the pests and would pay a penny a dozen – or that had been the old rate – to any boy who had the patience to catch enough offenders and take them proudly into the Reverend's back scullery, where they would be painlessly destroyed.

Lily gave one last valedictory glance at what had once been the most beautiful garden in the Close, and looked up at the house, thinking hopefully that she might find little change once she got indoors. And after the most perfunctory of knocks – for who could be in the kitchen except her mother or father? – she pushed open the door, knowing that her parents had never locked it before and never would.

'There's nothing to steal, and anyone who wants a few blackcurrants or some sticks of asparagus is welcome to them,' the Reverend was fond of saying. 'Not that anyone has ever helped themselves yet.'

Lily entered the kitchen and found, as she had expected, that it was exactly the same: the big wooden table on which Mrs Kendal had once cooked enormous meals for fundraising events, the tall dresser which reached up to the ceiling and contained a motley array of mismatched china and glass, the six or eight wooden chairs which provided the Kendals and any visitors with somewhere to sit, and the cracked linoleum on the floor which her mother scrubbed optimistically every morning and sighed over pessimistically every evening, for though they often talked of replacing it that had never happened. One end of the room was taken up with the ancient range in whose depths there smouldered the remains of yesterday's fire. Lily knew fuel was scarce and guessed that her mother only lit the range now when she was baking.

She looked around her and saw a big old-fashioned glass vase full of late roses, from the climber that adorned the outside walls. She crossed the room, dumped her bag next to the dresser and bent to sniff one of the blooms. It was an old-fashioned variety, no longer much grown, but the scent was sweet and all pervasive once you got near enough, and suddenly it all seemed too much. Lily plonked herself down on a chair, spread out her arms on the table and laid her head upon them. And then, without any sort of warning, everything caught up with her. The journey from the farm had been a long and complicated one. Catching the right connection at the right time had not always been easy, and she had had to spend the night in the waiting room of a tiny station somewhere in the wilds of the countryside. She was deathly tired, so tired that even Colin's treachery – for she was beginning to regard it as such – no longer consumed her thoughts as it had two days ago. Feeling the first slow tear form in her eye, she winked it away and told herself that she would never love again, not if she lived to be a hundred. Colin could marry his Valencia with her good will; she would dance at their wedding, she would congratulate Colin on his beautiful bride, and then she would never see him again.

When a hand touched her shoulder she was so sure that it must be Colin's that she did not even look up, but remained with her head on her arms and a sob beginning to try to escape from her dry throat. He hadn't meant what he said. He had sent the cruel letter as a rather bad joke and now here he was, claiming her for his bride.

'Lily? What's happened? We had a telegram from Mrs Faversham saying you were coming home. Oh, my darling girl. Is it Colin? Has he – is he . . .'

Lily moved her head from her arms and swivelled round in her chair to look up into her mother's strained and anxious face. 'Colin's all right,' she mumbled. 'He's very well, in fact. Oh, Mother, he's met someone else and I don't think I can live without him.'

Her mother took hold of both her hands, pulled her to her feet, and gave her a hard, comprehensive hug. Lily looked at her through a blur of tears, then wiped them away with the palms of both hands. 'I don't know why I'm crying when I'm so lucky,' she muttered. 'I've got you and Dad to support me through whatever lies ahead, which is more than a lot of girls can say. I can't show you Colin's letter because it hurt me so much that I threw it away, but you can imagine it upset me dreadfully. He actually had the cheek to say he would always love me . . . oh, Mother, I wish I'd kept it now because you would understand how betrayed I felt. He's been my boyfriend for so long, and the awful thing is that I can't hate him. In fact if he walked in here right now I'd probably throw myself into his arms and forgive him everything.'

Mrs Kendal sat down in the chair next to her daughter's and shook her head. 'No you wouldn't. You've got more spunk than that,' she said firmly. 'Colin has dealt you a terrible blow and you've come home – very sensibly I might add – to get over the shock of it. And I'll tell you something I've never told anyone before. I never did like your Colin. Oh, I agree he was handsome and charming, but his eyes were too close together, and though he was proud to be a Brylcreem boy I always thought he was too slick to be the right mate for my lovely girl.'

Despite herself, and with tears still dappling her cheeks, Lily could not forbear to chuckle. 'This is very sudden,' she said. 'I thought you adored Colin as much as I did. I thought you were planning to borrow Maisie O'Hara's wedding dress so that we could be married despite the war. I know you told me you'd met Colin's mother and thought she was somewhat overbearing, but . . .'

Mrs Kendal snorted. 'She boasted about her flight lieutenant son who was teaching other men to fly

Spitfires, but when I told her my girl was in the Land Army she brushed it aside. In fact, she sneered.'

Once more, Lily chuckled. 'You didn't say any of this in your letters,' she reminded her mother. 'I did get the impression that you were not too keen on Mrs Tunstal, but not that you actually disliked her.'

'How could I say such a thing when you meant to marry her son and seemed to be deeply in love with him?' her mother asked reasonably. 'But now that it's all over between you I shall be frank. Neither Michael nor I thought he was worthy of you, and we both hoped the friendship would not last.' She beamed at her daughter. 'The world is full of modest and delightful young men, many of them old friends of yours. You were carried away by Colin's looks and charm, but looks don't last and charm isn't always sincere. Oh, my darling, I know that right now you feel that you could never love anyone but Colin, but you're wrong, you know. Your heart is sick after the blow he's dealt you, but you'll recover, I promise you. Why, you're twenty-one years of age – I hope you had a lovely birthday, by the way – and you've only ever been out with one young man. If you'd joined one of the armed services you would have met a great many delightful fellows, but stuck away on that farm miles from anywhere you've had virtually no opportunity to meet anyone else. I've never forgotten you telling me that you didn't even join the other land girls when they went off to a dance in the town because you felt it would be disloyal to Colin. When you go back to Drake's Farm you must hold your head high and attend every social event as though Colin had never existed. And whilst you're with us you must do the same.'

Lily sighed. 'I'm going to ask for a posting somewhere far away from Drake's Farm,' she admitted in a small voice. 'I just can't face them, Mother. I've gone on and on about Colin; how can I eat my words and go back there? And besides, I did go to one dance and there wasn't one man present that I would have looked at twice. I'm better away from Drake's Farm, honestly I am.'

Mrs Kendal considered, head tilted slightly to one side. She was a pretty woman, very like her daughter, though her thick fair hair was streaked with white and her figure hinted at the plumpness of middle age. She thought for a moment, then smoothed the hair off her daughter's forehead and smiled triumphantly.

'Do you remember Mr Parker? Oh, you must do – he and his wife farm no more than two or three miles outside the city. You used to love going there to give a helping hand when you were only ten or eleven. Remember?'

'Yes, but does he employ land girls?' Lily said doubtfully. 'Didn't he have a daughter who helped him and his wife to run the farm? You can't be suggesting that they might get rid of her and employ me, because I'm sure it's most unlikely.'

Mrs Kendal tutted. 'Silly girl, of course I'm not. The thing is, Peggy Parker left the farm a year or two ago to become a driver in the air force and though they've applied for a land girl Mrs Parker was telling me only the other day that they had had no luck. Another thing

198

in your favour – if you apply for the job, that is – would be that you wouldn't need living accommodation. So I'm sure if you went and saw Mr Parker he'd be delighted to give you a try. And now, darling, go upstairs, take off those clothes, have a wash – I'm afraid it will have to be cold because I don't think there's any hot water – and put on a clean summer dress. It will make you feel much better, I promise.'

Lily stood up and bent to kiss the older woman's smooth cheek. 'Int you a wonderful woman, Mrs Kendal?' she said in the broad Norfolk accent which the children at school had used when no teachers were around. 'I won't say I'm completely cured of Colin, because that wouldn't be true, but I feel so much better already, you wouldn't believe. Oh, how I wish I hadn't thrown the letter away! You might even be able to make me see the funny side of it!'

Abruptly, she clapped her hand to her mouth. 'Mother, I threw it into the wastepaper basket in the attic where we all slept! I scrumpled it up, but it would be just my luck for one of the girls to read it. Well, that settles it. I'm *not* going back, not to Drake's Farm at any rate, and if I could get a job on the Parkers' place that would be perfect.'

Giving her mother a final kiss, Lily mounted the stairs and stood on the landing for a moment looking out through the window at their long back garden. The asparagus season was over but its delicate fern still flourished, and even from here Lily could tell that the blackcurrant bushes had been harvested. By standing on tiptoe she could see, in the distance, the rolling fields of what she was almost sure must be the Parkers' place. She told herself joyfully that she could walk there if necessary, but thought it quite likely that her mother had kept her old school bicycle, which would halve the journey time. Smiling to herself, she opened her bedroom door, meaning to dump her knapsack and then go along to the bathroom – what luxury – for a thoroughly enjoyable, and much needed, strip-down wash.

Slinging her bag ahead of her, she was almost inside the room before she realised it was already occupied. Lying on her bed and smoking a cigarette whilst reading a book which had certainly not come from her father's shelves was a young man. He was in shirt, trousers and boots, and when he saw her staring at him he sat upright and cast down his book, though he continued to hold the cigarette.

'What the hell . . . ?' he said.

Lily allowed her gaze to travel from his not very clean boots to the top of his head. He had bright ginger hair, white lashes and brows and he looked as though he could do with a darned good shave. He grinned at Lily's astonishment, which annoyed her and made her straighten her back and give him one of her coldest looks.

'What are you doing in my bedroom?' she asked frostily. 'I've just been talking to my mother and she didn't say there was anyone in the house beside ourselves. What the devil are you doing here?'

'I could say the same,' the man said. He had an American accent, Lily realised. 'I don't suppose Mrs

Kendal knows I'm home yet. But what about you? You barge into *my* bedroom without a word of explanation, chuck your knapsack down on the foot of *my* bed and all in all act as though you own the place. Who are you, anyway? Mrs Kendal never mentioned . . . oh, I get it. You're the long lost daughter who's on a farm some-where in Devon.' He grinned at her. 'Am I right? Only nobody mentioned you were coming home on leave, and when I came in and there was no one home I just came up to my room to snatch an hour or so's rest before going downstairs to see what's available for lunch.'

Lily gasped. What a nerve the fellow had! *His* room indeed. Why, she had been sleeping in this room ever since she could remember. This impudent young man must be the officer who had been billeted on her parents when he had been injured in an accident – now that she looked at him more closely she could see stitch marks, pale but clear, standing out against the tan on his cheek. However, she certainly did not intend to share her room with this rather crude colonial. Once more, she swept him with a disdainful look. She had never liked red-haired men, and this one added to his lack of charm by having a snub nose, about a million freckles and slightly rabbity teeth. Lily drew herself up to her full height and jerked a thumb at him.

'Out!' she said briskly. 'This is *my* bedroom, and I am about to clean up and get rid of the travel stains. Col-lect your traps, whatever they may be, and take them up to the attic. There's a folding bed up there and I'm sure my mother will find you sufficient bedding for it, but I certainly don't intend to move out of my own bedroom just for your convenience.'

The young man did not move. 'If there's only a camp bed remember I'm a good deal taller than you,' he pointed out. 'If anyone sleeps up there it ought to be you. And anyway, first come first served.'

Lily came right into the room and flung open the wardrobe doors. 'Please clear your things out at once,' she said. 'There's no point in arguing. You will simply have to make do with the attic, because I'm hoping to get a job near here so I can live at home. But you were right: I am the Kendals' daughter. So who are you?'

He sketched a salute. 'I'm Captain Hank Ruskin; I fly Liberators.' He gave her a lopsided grin. 'Anything more you want to know?' He rubbed his eyes and swung his legs off the bed, and for the first time Lily realised that though he had been reading his book and smoking a cigarette he had been doing so despite being almost asleep. For a moment she felt a pang of remorse and was tempted to tell him to stay where he was whilst she used the bathroom, but then she decided that that might well make him think she was backing down, which she had no intention of doing. Now that he was on his feet she could see he was well over six foot tall, and she noticed for the first time that one of his legs seemed to be bandaged from thigh to ankle. Lily felt guilty. How would he manage with his wounded leg? She could scarcely expect him to climb the narrow attic stairs, which weren't stairs at all, really, but a ladder which one pulled down whenever ascending to or descending from the attic above.

Lily took a deep breath and prepared to apologise. It was scarcely his fault that she had come home unexpectedly, or that it had not occurred to her that her mother's wounded officer might be occupying her old bedroom. And he certainly could not have been expected to scramble up the ladder whilst her own room was unoccupied and, he must have thought, would continue to be so.

'Look, Captain Ruskin,' she said awkwardly, 'I've been travelling for two days and I'm afraid I lost my sense of humour and a good many other things as I crossed the country. I hadn't even noticed your bandaged leg when I started in on you. I'm truly sorry. Please leave all your things in this room and consider it your own until you are able to return to your station.'

She half expected a snub, because she had been pretty unpleasant before, but the grin he gave her was friendly.

'It's all right,' he said. 'And it's a base, not a station. I dare say your mom told me you were expected, but the message never got across.' He jerked a thumb at the bandaged leg. 'I'm only here until this heals, which shouldn't be long, I hope. My co-pilot's a great guy, but he's a little on the skinny side and you need good leg muscles to fly a Lib, so the sooner my leg's operational again the happier everyone will be.' He grinned at his own choice of words. 'Including you, I guess. Now you're home I'll ask Mrs Kendal to find me another billet.'

'Oh, please don't,' Lily said, dismayed. 'I'm sorry I was so horrible to you, and I promise I'll be perfectly happy to sleep in the attic whilst you recover.' She gave the young man her most winning smile. 'Please don't make me feel worse by refusing. If my mother knew how rude I've been to a guest she'd be very angry.'

Hank had been collecting his various pieces of property from around the room, and now he dumped them on the bed and returned Lily's smile. 'It's real good of you, ma'am – Miss Kendal, I mean,' he said. 'I would offer to take your stuff up to the attic but you could do it yourself twice as fast. And now you'd best get off to the bathroom before you have your mom climbing the stairs to find out what's going on. She must be the least curious woman in the whole world, because she lets me come and go just as I like. The doors are never locked, and there's always food of some description available for a hungry guy who's missed out on a meal.' He glanced at the large watch on his wrist. 'Or maybe you'd best leave your wash for now. Your mom serves what she calls a luncheon at noon and it's ten to twelve already.'

'Right, then we ought to go down in a minute,' Lily said briskly. She grinned at him. 'Did I tell you my name was Lily and I prefer to be called that rather than Miss Kendal? But tell me, is Hank a real name or did you make it up?'

The young man laughed. 'I was christened Henry but no one ever calls me that,' he said. 'Lily; what a pretty name. It suits you. Back home on stateside I've an uncle with a big yard who grows lilies – I think they're called regal lilies, or something like that. You look a bit like one, with all that pale gold hair.'

Lily blushed. 'Do your crew call you Ginger?' she asked, to change the subject. 'If you were an Englishman they'd call you either Ginger or Carrots.' She gathered up an armful of discarded clothing and began to hang it in the wardrobe. She thought that however great a pilot he might be he was the untidiest man with whom she had ever come into contact. Then she chided herself. He'd had no time to tidy the room before she had burst in upon him.

'I do get called Ginger sometimes,' he admitted, 'but not twice! And now let's go down to the kitchen. If your mom was surprised to see you she'll be even more surprised to find I was upstairs all the time.'

During the meal Lily had the opportunity to study her new acquaintances as he and her mother chatted, and she realised that Hank reminded her strongly of someone she knew. But who? She searched through her acquaintance in her mind and at last came up with the answer. Who did she know with clumpy hair, a snub nose and a million freckles? Which of her admittedly narrow circle had light brows and lashes and a tendency to turn every remark into a joke? Before she could stop herself the name had slipped from her mind to her lips: 'Johnny Durrell!'

Mrs Kendal stared. 'What on earth made you say that?' she asked. 'Isn't he one of the workers at Drake's Farm? I know I've heard the name before and I'm pretty sure it was in relation to the farm.'

Lily laughed. 'He's a worker all right, but not a farm worker; an evacuee. He doesn't actually live at Drake's Farm, but he's a nice lad and will always help out when he's needed, and to tell you the truth he's rather like Captain Ruskin here to look at.'

They were sitting round the kitchen table and Hank puffed out his chest. 'A handsome guy, I guess,' he said, and smiled as the two women scoffed.

'You're neither of you what I would call good-looking,' Lily said honestly. 'In fact if you saw him you probably wouldn't think you looked a bit alike. It's just something in your expressions, I suppose. I must write to Eve and tell her.' She smiled a little sadly at Hank. 'She's an evacuee too and I suppose you could call her Johnny's closest friend, but I know she'll be expecting me back and what I really need to tell her is why I shan't be returning to Drake's Farm.'

There was a short pause before Hank spoke. 'Are we allowed to know the reasons' he asked mildly, 'or is it something personal?'

Lily opened her mouth to make some innocuous remark, and realised she couldn't. 'I'll tell you one day, perhaps, when we know each other a bit better,' she said. 'Would you like a little more soup? If so, pass your bowl.' He did so, and Lily, replenishing it from the big saucepan, went on brightly, 'Mother makes all her soups from our own garden vegetables. It was the same at the farm – almost nothing was bought in.' She smiled at Hank across the table, telling herself that he might be the plainest man in the whole of the American air force but that was no reason to make him feel uncomfortable. After all, she had fallen in love with Colin, the handsomest man she had ever met, and look what had happened there. She handed him the bowl of soup and cut a large slice off her mother's homemade loaf. 'There you are, eat up!' she said. 'If you're anything like Johnny you won't be fussy and you'll polish off anything on offer.' She sighed reminiscently as a picture of Johnny and Eve popped into her head and for a moment she actually contemplated returning to Devon. After all, she had good friends there. Why let one unfortunate experience change her whole life? But it had, for the time being at any rate, and she would write to Eve that very evening to apologise and explain.

She helped herself to another slice of bread – it was nearly as good as that made by Auntie Bess – and found herself wondering what Eve and Johnny would be doing now. Playing some game, she supposed, for the evenings were drawing in and they would have finished their chores for the day. Her thoughts were so far from the present that she jumped when her mother said chidingly: 'Eat up, Lily darling. Concentrate on your food and stop thinking about Drake's Farm. We'll go to see the Parkers first thing tomorrow and discuss what to do for the best. All right?'

Chapter Nine

Autumn 1943

When Eve awoke it was raining; not viciously or even particularly hard, Eve thought drowsily. It was the same rain which had started three days ago and continued without pause ever since, the soft and gentle rain of Devon which could soak you to the skin without your really noticing.

Eve groaned and opened one eye to look at the alarm clock, then remembered that early milking this weekend fell to the lot of Miranda, the new land girl. She wasn't new at all, really, for Lily had been gone the best part of a year and Miranda had come in her place only a month or so after she left. Eve sighed. It seemed as though she was fated to lose her best friends, though Johnny was a good substitute.

After Lily went there had been a short period when everything seemed upside down and topsy turvy, and in desperation the Favershams had asked for the loan of one of the boys from Spindlebush Farm.

'But there's no use lendin' us a complete beginner,' Mrs Faversham had explained worriedly. 'Suppose we take on young Johnny Durrell? He's a handy young chap, and though he can't share the attic with the girls he can sleep in the little spare room. After all, the Armstrongs have never used it. But can you manage without him? I wouldn't want to put you in a difficult position, losin' young Durrell.'

Mrs Spindlebush had laughed. 'He do spend most of his time with you anyway,' she pointed out. 'We'll get the paperwork sorted out and carry on regardless, as the old song says.'

So now Johnny was a permanent member of the Drake's Farm team. The only disadvantage to this scheme was that Johnny, like Connie, could sleep the clock round, so Eve had the more or less permanent job of descending the attic stairs and making sure Johnny was awake in the morning before she began to wash and dress herself.

Miranda was nice but, in Eve's eyes at least, no substitute for Lily. The most you could say was that she tried hard and was always jolly, even when everyone was cross with her because she had made some foolish mistake. Fortunately, she was a light sleeper, and even before the alarm clock got into its stride Miranda awoke, sat up with a reluctant sigh and then stretched and yawned.

'Morning, young Eve,' she said amiably. 'Why're you awake? I'm on earlies this week, aren't I?'

She did not attempt to keep her voice down and Eve looked anxiously over to where Connie and Chrissie were cocooned in their blankets. Neither stirred, and she breathed a sigh of relief as Miranda swung her legs out of bed, padded over to the washstand and dipped a flannel into the pitcher. When the older girl had gone she meant to enjoy the luxury of a strip-down wash before the others woke up, and then go downstairs and give a hand with anything Auntie Bess required. After that she was sure she could employ herself usefully, though the rain made outdoor work difficult.

Descending to the kitchen, she wondered whether the longed-for letters from her parents had arrived at last. Lily, now working at Parker's Place and living at home, had invited Eve to stay with her for a week or two when Auntie Bess and Uncle Reg could spare her. Eve had been thrilled and delighted at the invitation and had written at once to both her parents asking permission to visit the Kendal family, but so far neither Bill nor Eleanor had replied. To be sure, Eleanor had said she would visit Drake's Farm at the very next opportunity since she wanted to have a chat with her eldest child. But she had not even mentioned the Kendals' invitation so Eve, with a resigned sigh, had written again, and now every morning when she entered the kitchen her first action was to see if there was a letter for her.

For once, Johnny was down before her, and when she had checked whether there was any post for her – there wasn't – she asked him how he intended to spend the afternoon once his chores were done.

'Taking a bus into town and meeting Robbo for tea,' he informed her. 'Want to come along?' He sighed. 'Life's not fair, is it? Robbo's the same age as me but he looks a lot older, so when he told the recruiting officer that he was seventeen he said the chap didn't even look surprised.' He peered into Eve's face. 'How old do you reckon I look?'

Eve pretended to consider. 'I should think nine or ten?' She grinned as he tried to punch her but deftly avoided the blow. 'Well, you did ask,' she said reproachfully. 'Are you really going to meet Robbo? Can I come? I can whizz through my chores and be ready as soon as you are.'

'Oh, all right,' Johnny said with pretended reluctance. 'But have you any money? I'm meeting Robbo at Jackson's. You can't go into a café without any and I can't afford to treat you.'

'Auntie Bess keeps my pocket money, but I think at the last count I had two or three bob,' Eve said. 'Is it a date, then? We'll go to meet Robbo together?'

But a disappointment awaited them. Just as they started down the lane to catch the bus they saw the telegram boy cycling towards them, and both felt a stab of apprehension. Telegrams could bring good news or bad, but this time the telegram boy was grinning quite cheerfully, which would not be the case if he was the bringer of bad news.

'Afternoon, Freddie,' Johnny said, indicating the envelope the boy was holding. 'Who's it for? Shall we save you a journey and take it to the farm?'

Freddie grinned. 'It's for you and it's from your mate Robbo,' he said shamelessly. 'He's been sent off on some course or other – he can't say more 'cos walls have ears – so that's your meeting knocked on the head.'

Johnny gave an exclamation of dismay and snatched

the telegram from Freddie's hand. *'Don't come, stop, off on course stop see you next week, stop, Robbo,'* he read aloud, his brow clearing. 'It's not a put off, just a delay. Thanks very much, Freddie. There's no need to reply.'

The boy turned his bicycle round and Eve and Johnny headed back towards the farmhouse. 'I wonder what sort of course it is?' Eve said idly as they crossed the farmyard. She looked hopefully up into the grey sky. 'Oh, Johnny, if only it would stop raining! I don't feel like staying indoors. I feel like . . . oh, playing cricket or football, or netball maybe. I'm just full of energy and I want to use some of it up. Let's go back to the kitchen and ask Auntie Bess if there's anything we can do for her. Or Petal's due to calve any day now. As it's her first, Mr Trevalyn says he wants to be around when she begins, so we could go and sit in the hayloft and warn him if she looks as though she's starting.'

Johnny looked at his watch, a new acquisition from his father to mark his sixteenth birthday. 'Much energy that will use up,' he said mockingly. 'Tell you what, hang the weather. Let's go down to the end of the orchard where the ruined greenhouses are and play French cricket. Why don't you go and ask Auntie Bess if we can use the flat piece of grass where they're going to plant new apple trees? We can't do any harm down there; the greenhouses are ruined already, and it will do us good to play out for a change.'

Eve looked doubtful. 'But suppose she says we can't? They prepared the ground for planting apple trees, not for playing French cricket.'

Johnny frowned. 'If we don't get permish we might

get into trouble,' he pointed out. 'Look, tell you what, I'll round up anyone who wants a game and you go and make sure it's all right to play by the greenhouses. I should think Auntie Bess would rather we played at the end of the orchard than in the farmyard, after what happened last week.'

Eve giggled. Last week, despite the rain, they had been playing tag in the farmyard when someone had collided with the milk churn and sent it rolling round the yard and making the most awful din. Unfortunately, it had been that time in the afternoon when the Favershams were having their nap and the sudden clatter of the falling churn had apparently jerked Uncle Reg out of his sound sleep, convinced that they were being bombed, or at the very least shot at. It had taken Auntie Bess several minutes to convince him that it was only a milk churn that had been injured, if you could count a slight dent in its smooth side as an injury. Unfortunately, it was Johnny who had been the main perpetrator of the milk churn's downfall, and now he scowled at Eve's giggle and turned away to speak to Connie, who had just appeared in the farmyard.

'It's still bloody raining; Auntie Bess thought it had stopped,' she was saying disgustedly. 'I asked if there was anything she would like me to help her with and she bit my head off. She said Uncle Reg was still recovering from our last bout of helpfulness, thank you very much, and she'd be obliged if I'd get out of her hair.'

'That's not like Auntie Bess,' Eve observed. She looked hopefully at Johnny. 'Why don't you do your own asking? I'm sure she'll say yes.'

Johnny shook his head. 'She still hasn't forgiven me for nearly giving Uncle Reg a heart attack,' he pointed out. 'You go, Eve. You're her favourite, we all know that. Where's Chrissie? You could take him with you, to melt Auntie Bess's hard heart with his winning ways.'

Eve opened her mouth to reply, but Connie cut across her. 'Your wretched little brother is probably the reason Auntie Bess's grumpy,' she said nastily. 'You Armstrongs are enough to annoy a saint. But if you really want him you'll find him in the cowshed, watching Mr Trevalyn bringing Petal's calf into the world. My mother would say it wasn't fitting for a child to watch a cow giving birth, but at least it will keep him out of the way for a bit.'

Eve gave Connie a baleful look but then changed it – she hoped – to a friendly smile. Everyone was edgy because of the constant rain, so it was no good getting at each other.

'All right, I'll go,' she said. 'And I'll ask if I can fetch the old tennis racket and ball from the sports chest whilst I'm at it, though usually Auntie Bess positively encourages us to play with them. They were her sons' in years gone by and she likes to see them being used.' She turned to Johnny. 'You'd better round up everyone who isn't busy, because I'm sure Auntie Bess will be downright glad to see us out of the farmyard and well away from the milk churns. I'll meet you down at the ruined greenhouses in five minutes . . . no, better make it ten, though I don't think Auntie Bess will take much persuasion.'

She did not wait for Johnny's and Connie's reactions

but set off at once for the kitchen, where Auntie Bess, normally the most easy-going of women, greeted her with something very like a scowl. She looked up as Eve came in but continued to wield her rolling pin on the ball of pastry on the table before her.

'What do *you* want?' she said disagreeably. 'I hope you don't think you can disturb me when I'm cooking because I won't have you children perpetually under my feet, and if you imagine you can help me you're wrong. This here rationing is making even the simplest job difficult, so if you don't want to be outside you can clear off up to the attic. Where's that young devil of a brother of yours? He was in here earlier driving me mad with questions as to why I wanted Petal to have a heifer and not what he termed a "boy calf". And when I told him, he burst into tears. So now what do you want?'

Eve glanced at the clock above the mantel. At this hour in the afternoon both Auntie Bess and Uncle Reg should have been comfortably ensconced in the small dining room, Uncle Reg with a handkerchief over his face and Auntie Bess with her head cuddled into the red velvet cushion. She opened her mouth to ask Auntie Bess what had happened to change her routine, then thought better of it.

'Please, Auntie Bess, will it be all right if we all go down to the ruined greenhouses and play French cricket with the tennis racket and ball from the oak chest?' she said instead. 'We'd be out from under your feet until at least six o'clock, or even later.'

Auntie Bess gestured with her rolling pin at the door which led into the hall. 'Do as you like,' she said impatiently. 'But keep that plaguey brother of yours under control. Mr Trevalyn don't want him in the cowshed so you tell him from me he's to play with the rest of you and not to come bothering.'

'Thanks, Auntie Bess,' Eve said humbly and shot into the hall, heaved at the heavy lid of the chest where Auntie Bess kept what she called her sports equipment and shot out again, shouting over her shoulder 'Thanks again, Auntie Bess' as she left the kitchen and closed the door carefully behind her.

Outside in the yard, faces were turned hopefully towards her. No one had made it down to the orchard, because Petal's calf had been safely delivered and Chrissie was telling everyone that it was a girl cow – a heifer – and the prettiest little creature Mr Trevalyn had ever seen. Eve saw that Johnny had managed to winkle out Bunny, a Spindlebush boy who rarely left his studies even for French cricket; then there was Connie, of course, and Miriam and Miranda – the terrible twins, Uncle Reg had dubbed them – had very sportingly agreed to play too, which would make it much more fun.

'Did she say yes?' Connie said eagerly, just as Johnny demanded: 'Did she bite your head off?' which made Chrissie frown.

'People don't bite heads off unless they're nasty Nazis,' he said. He looked accusingly at Johnny. 'If anyone's cross and biting heads off it ought to be Uncle Reg. He was the one who thought the milk churn was a bomb.' He looked slyly at his sister. 'Silly old fool,' he said in a low voice. 'Bombs don't sound like milk churns.'

Eve was shocked. She gave his arm a smart smack. 'Don't you *dare* say such a thing when Uncle Reg and Auntie Bess have been so good to us,' she snapped. 'Now come along. It's time to start this game if we're going to get it over by teatime.'

The small group headed doggedly down to the orchard, with Chrissie in his over-large raincoat and hat leading the procession, until they reached the flat plain where very soon now the new apple trees would be planted.

'We won't pick sides because there still aren't enough of us,' Johnny said authoritatively. 'It's every man for himself.' He produced a coin from his pocket. 'We'll toss for who goes first, but I think it should be Chrissie. If we all remember our own scores then we should end up with a winner.' He grinned round at them. 'In you go, Chrissie, and may the best man win.'

Eve had felt sure that if the rain carried on the game would soon be abandoned, but this did not prove to be the case. Everyone carefully kept their scores except for Chrissie, who said he was so far ahead of everyone else on points that Eve said grumpily an inability with figures must be a family failing. Actually she was not doing too badly, having caught Miranda out with a flying leap which caused everyone to give a round of applause. Emboldened by this, when she took the racket she smote the ball with such fury that it soared into the air like a rocket and came to earth somewhere in one of the ruined greenhouses, though no one could say with any certainty which one.

After ten minutes of diligent searching Chrissie had had enough. 'There's only one place it could have gone and that's down the big chimney which Mr Trevalyn told me was what they used to keep the greenhouses warm in the olden days,' he said, 'when old Mr Drake what built the farm tried to grow peaches and nectarines for his market stall.'

Everyone stared up at the chimney which, Eve thought, had suddenly begun to look incredibly tall. Miranda put into words what they were all thinking.

'Well, it was a pretty ragged ball anyway.' She turned to Eve. 'Were there any others in the chest?' She grinned at the younger girl. 'Since you were the one who whacked it up there I think it should be you who tells Auntie Bess what happened and fetches a replacement. It's a shame to abandon the game when everyone's doing so well. In fact, if we say the first one to reach a hundred wins, the game should be over just in time for tea.'

'Oh, but it'll take ages to go all the way back to the farm and start rooting around in the chest,' Eve said, dismayed. 'I know it was my fault for hitting the ball so hard, but I don't fancy facing up to Auntie Bess again. I don't know what's happened to make her so cross but something must have, because she was really fed up. She more or less made me promise not to keep popping in and out of the kitchen whilst she was trying to cook. Can't someone else beard the dragon in her den? One of you grown-up land girls?'

Miriam had been sitting on the tumbledown wall of what had once been a greenhouse, but now she gave a resigned sigh and stood up. 'I suppose if someone has to go it might as well be me,' she said. 'I could take a look at the new calf whilst I'm up there, but don't any of you try climbing that chimney because it doesn't look very safe to me.' She shook an admonitory finger at Chrissie. 'I know the moment I'm out of sight you'll start boasting that you can fetch the ball, no bother, but it really isn't safe, Chrissie. Will you promise me you won't try to find it whilst I'm gone?'

Chrissie shook his head. 'Course I won't, because I'm coming with you,' he said firmly. 'Evie should go really, because it was her wallop what sent the ball up so high, but Auntie Bess likes me more'n she likes Evie, so she's sure to let me hunt in the chest for another one.'

'That's right, old chap, there's bound to be at least one more lurking under all the old rubbish in the sports chest,' said Johnny cheerfully. 'Off you go, you two, and try to be tactful if Auntie Bess grumbles at being disturbed.'

'Right,' Chrissie said, gambolling ahead as the two of them set out. 'But I don't *think* I'll go into the house at all. You can find a tennis ball without any help from me, can't you?' He turned to smile winningly at Miriam. 'Auntie Bess is never cross but she did seem to get annoyed when I asked about boy calves.'

Eve watched her brother and Miriam out of sight, then turned to Johnny. 'I don't want to depress you, but I had to rummage really hard to find even one ball in the sports chest, and I doubt if Miriam and Chrissie will have better luck. I think we'll have to give up on French cricket for today.'

The five remaining players mooched around, gazing

219

hopefully back towards the farmhouse, but Miriam and Chrissie didn't reappear and Johnny, with a resigned sigh, announced that as far as he could see Eve was right and they might as well admit that the game was over for the day.

'Can everyone remember their scores?' he asked. 'We can continue playing tomorrow, if everyone's agreeable.'

Eve had begun to say that she had completely forgotten hers when she stopped abruptly with a little squeak and pointed upwards. 'Look!' she said. 'It's been there all along but we were so sure it'd gone higher that we didn't really look at the stack itself. The reason we didn't see it was because it's wedged in the gap where a brick once was and a fern's growing over the top.' She stood on tiptoe but could not quite reach the ball. 'Oh damn, I'm nearly tall enough, but not quite. If I stood on a couple of bricks I would be able to get it, I'm sure.'

Johnny began to collect the fallen bricks that were lying around and pile them into a rough sort of ladder. 'What idiots we were not to look lower. Stand back, you lot – I'll soon get it out of there, and then when Miriam and Chrissie come back we can finish the game.'

Eve looked at the rather shaky pile of bricks resting against the wall and tugged Miranda's arm. 'That chimney stack looks as though it might keel over at any minute,' she said. 'Tell him it's too dangerous, Miranda. He won't take any notice of me, but you're a grown-up; he might listen to you.'

Miranda agreed. 'Don't do it, Johnny,' she said

urgently. 'It isn't worth getting hurt just to finish a game . . .'

Johnny was almost level with the tennis ball now and half turned as Eve added her own plea to Miranda's. 'I'm there now,' he said as he reached for the ball and began to pull it from its hiding place. 'You see? Easy, once we . . .' And then there was a sort of rumbling and both Johnny and the chimney stack disappeared in a cloud of dust.

Auntie Bess had got over her ill humour almost as soon as Eve had rushed from the kitchen clasping a tennis ball in one hand and an ancient tennis racket in the other. The trouble was, today should have been the day of the WI tea, a social gathering which she much enjoyed. It had been Mrs Brown's turn to host it, at Heathcliff Farm, but she had sent a message round to all the members with one of her sons – she had three, all under ten – to say that she had her old father in bed with a shocking case of influenza and had to cry off because her kitchen was probably positively buzzing with germs.

By the time the message reached Auntie Bess it was too late for her to inform everyone that she would be happy to have the meeting at Drake's Farm instead, so as a result the one social event which she looked forward to had been cancelled and the large tray of fruitless scones, her contribution to the tea, would go unappreciated except by the inhabitants of Drake's Farm.

Consequently, her normal good humour had deserted her, and when Chrissie had come barging into the kitchen demanding to be told why a boy calf could not stay on the farm, she had forgotten tact and told him the simple truth: bull calves would spend the rest of their short lives with the other bullocks until the time came for them to be slaughtered and turned into food for the hungry nation.

Chrissie had never thought to wonder where the bullocks went when they were taken off to market, and now that he had been told he was heartbroken.

'Not my dear little calves,' he had said pitifully, and when Auntie Bess had explained rather brusquely about food shortages he had first burst into tears and then rushed out of the room. Guilt had been added to Auntie Bess's irritation, causing her to snap at both Connie and Eve, but by the time a commotion broke out in the farmyard she had recovered her equanimity and simply assumed that the game of French cricket had been spoiled by the rain. She was just thinking it was fortunate that the range had been lit for her baking activities and had actually started to lower the drying rack when the back door burst open and Connie and Bunny shot into the room, pushing Miriam and Chrissie ahead of them.

'What on earth . . .' Auntie Bess began, for all four were talking at once, making it difficult for her to understand just what the panic was about, save that someone had been hurt and might need hospital treatment. She hauled the clothes dryer up to the ceiling again and raised her voice above the tumult. 'Who's hurt, and how badly?' she said briskly. 'Should I wake Uncle Reg, or is it something I can deal with?' She

222

smiled comfortably. 'I've a first aid box with all sorts inside. I'm sure I could find something . . .'

Bunny cut across her. 'It's Johnny, Mrs Faversham; we were playing down by the old greenhouses and part of the chimney collapsed on him. I don't think your first aid box will be enough. I've done anatomy at school and I think he's broken his left leg, because it's at a funny angle, and he's probably damaged his ribs as well. Oh, Auntie Bess, if we took a door off its hinges, like they do in books, we could carry him up from the old greenhouses whilst we wait for the ambulance.'

Auntie Bess gave a little shriek. 'Wake Uncle Reg,' she ordered Connie tersely. 'Bunny, go and get Mr Spindle-bush and explain what's happened, and ring for an ambulance while you're about it.' She turned to Chrissie. 'You stay with me, my lad; I'm too old and fat to be much use and you're too young and skinny. But you can take me down to the old greenhouses and show me just what happened and where. Then we must go up to the main road so we can guide the ambulance to where it's needed. If Johnny can talk, he can tell us where he's hurt . . .'

Johnny lay in darkness without moving, aware something had happened though he could not imagine what, but somewhere quite near someone was banging on a drum which sent reverberations of pain through his aching head. He thought he opened his mouth to ask whoever it was to stop but no sound came out, or no sound that he could hear, at any rate. He tried to move but could not, so he lay still. He was thirsty, but though he was sure there were people around him he realised he had no way of contacting them. His voice did not appear to be working, and when he tried to move his hand it felt like a lead weight and stayed exactly where it was. Then he became aware that the darkness was lit now and then by flashes of light and with an enormous effort he managed to open his eyes. He was lying on something very hard and uncomfortable whilst rain pattered down on his face, and someone, he did not know who, was crying. He wanted to tell whoever it was to bring him a drink, only the words would not come, and trying to force his reluctant body to wake – if it was sleep which gripped him – was too much like hard work. Then, for the first time, he realised that someone was speaking, and though the words did not make much sense he thought that perhaps when the darkness shifted away completely he would be able to understand. But presently the bed on which he lay – only it could not possibly be a bed because it was much too hard – gave a sort of jiggle and the movement hurt Johnny so much that he felt himself collapsing once more into the dark.

Later, he did not know how much, he found that he could hear a voice and make sense of what it was saying.

'Johnny dear, the ambulance has arrived and the fellows are going to lift you off the door and on to the ambulance bed. The driver says it may hurt you a little but I'm going to do my best to hold you steady. Can you hear me, dear? It's your Auntie Bess talking and I'm going to come with you in the ambulance to hold you steady, because movement hurts, doesn't it?'

Johnny opened his eyes and thought he probably nodded whilst saying in a shred of a voice, totally unlike his usual tones: 'Movement hurts.'

'It would,' Auntie Bess's voice said, clearly trying to be reassuring. 'The ambulance man says you've broken your leg, a real nasty break, but just you lie quiet and remember everyone's doing their best. There's a doctor coming to give you a shot of something to help with the pain. The ambulance driver won't so much as start his engine until the doctor arrives, so just you lie still and before you know it you'll be nicely plastered up and starting to walk again.'

The voice had been coming from a short distance away but now it moved closer and Johnny opened the only eye which seemed to want to open and saw Auntie Bess's round pink face only inches away from his own. She was trying to smile but it was a poor effort and in fact it frightened Johnny more than anything else, for Auntie Bess was not one to show emotion and in the short glimpse he had had of her face before his eye closed again he had seen tears glistening on her cheeks. I must be really bad to make Auntie Bess cry. I should try to reassure her, he thought, and was still trying to think of comforting words when there was a sharp pain in his arm, sharper than he could bear. Without at all meaning to do so, he gave a yelp, and even whilst the doctor was assuring him that once the drug started working the pain would ease off Johnny slid, gratefully this time, into pain-free darkness.

He did not return to consciousness until he was ensconced in a hospital bed with Dr Randolph standing beside him and both Auntie Bess and Uncle Reg at the foot of his bed. Auntie Bess was saying in a worried voice that he was an evacuee and his father was serving abroad, but she had already sent a telegram which should bring his mother to her son's side.

Johnny opened sleepy eyes, the lids so heavy that they might have been made of lead. 'I'm all right,' he whispered, 'but my leg does hurt. I'm sure it's broken.'

'It is,' Uncle Reg said. 'It's what I heard one of the nurses call a greenstick fracture.' He grinned down at Johnny, his usual cheerful grin, and Johnny found it more reassuring than any words.

'Good,' he said vaguely. 'Can I go home soon? My mother was a nurse in the last war and she understands about broken legs and things.'

The doctor smiled down at him. 'We've been more worried by the crack on the head you took,' he said. 'At one point . . . but we won't go into that. According to your young lady it was a falling brick, and of course you lost quite a lot of blood. But as soon as you recover from that – maybe after the stitches come out – you'll be able to go back to Drake's Farm, but not home, because I understand that your mother lives in the heart of London and that's no place for a lad with a broken head, let alone a broken leg. Do you understand?'

Johnny nodded wearily. Suddenly complete exhaustion had set in. He was hungry but no longer thirsty, so he assumed someone had given him a glass of water at some point. Then he saw the tube leading to his wrist and the bottle of transparent liquid on a hanger beside his bed and realised it must have been feeding water into him whilst he was unconscious.

Now Auntie Bess was leaning over and doing what she had never done before, which was to give him a kiss. 'You're a brave lad, Johnny Durrell,' she said huskily. 'I've not got the whole story out of young Connie yet but she's stuck to you like glue. She's in the waiting room now and I know she would like a word, even if it's only to bid you goodnight. Can I send her in?'

Johnny would have liked to say no, but that would have been rude and ungrateful so he nodded drowsily and presently Auntie Bess's place was taken by Connie, who fell to her knees beside the bed, the jolting sending arrows of pain through Johnny's head and leg.

'Oh, Johnny,' she wailed. 'Are you terribly hurt? If only Eve hadn't made you turn round just as the tower began to topple, none of this might have happened. I wanted to come in the ambulance with you but Auntie Bess came instead. Eve just went back to the farmhouse and started getting everyone's tea. She must have known she wouldn't be much use, not with the doctor saying you must be kept quiet.'

Johnny felt her fingers clasp his own and in the back of his mind an unworthy thought arose. Connie was enjoying the drama of the situation. Suddenly it was all too much. He was too weak even to escape the clutch of Connie's hand. He realised he had no idea what Connie was talking about; even less what the doctor had meant about a brick. Surely no one had been throwing bricks? His eyes closed in sheer exhaustion, and he felt rather than saw Auntie Bess seize Connie's shoulder, give it a shake, and pull the girl to her feet.

'Don't you start filling his mind with your twaddle,' he heard her say reprovingly. 'When he's better he'll remember what happened of his own accord. As it is, the doctor says he doesn't want Johnny excited or disturbed, so come along. Uncle Reg has brought the truck round to the front of the hospital and I want to get back to the farm just as soon as I can, else those gannets will have ate all the baking I did today and probably tomorrow's as well.'

He was aware of Connie leaning over him and giving him a kiss. 'I'll come and see you tomorrow. You be good now and get yourself fit and well because we want you back at Drake's Farm . . .'

'Oh, be *quiet*, Connie,' he heard Auntie Bess say. 'Can't you see that all the lad wants is a nice long sleep? You can come and see him tomorrow evening, if you've done your chores and I can spare you. He'll be feeling better by then.'

Johnny tried to nod, but his head was too heavy. It reminded him of the big pink cabbage rose which grew by the cowshed and had a flower so big that Uncle Reg tied it to a stake every year in order to stop the magnificent bloom from simply breaking off. That was how Johnny felt now, like a head-heavy rose. Slowly he turned his head into the pillow, enjoying the feel of the cool linen on his cheek. Somewhere, a voice was calling him, and then the voice faded away and was replaced by pan pipes. Johnny had no idea what they were doing on a hospital ward but very soon it did not matter. Nothing mattered. Johnny slid into sleep.

Chapter Ten

Johnny's mother visited him within a couple of days of the accident. Eve did not know quite what to expect, for Johnny had never described Mrs Durrell to her, but she had pictured her as plump and easy-going, regarded by her sons with tolerant affection and playing down her role in the war effort. The reality, however, was very different. Eve was sitting by Johnny's bed in hospital when his mother arrived and she jumped to her feet at once to fetch an extra chair, surprised to see that Mrs Durrell looked far too young to have two sons in the army, and was dressed in a smart grey suit, shining black shoes, and what looked like black silk stockings. Her fair hair was twisted into a bun on the nape of her neck and she bore very little resemblance to Johnny, though when she smiled and greeted him with a kiss Eve thought she caught a fleeting likeness.

Johnny had been sleeping, but he awoke as his mother's hand smoothed his rough hay-coloured hair off his forehead and a smile lit up his face.

'Oh, Ma, I knew you'd come,' he whispered feebly.

'This here's the pal I told you about . . .' He tried to hoist himself further up the bed but his mother pushed him gently back against his pillows.

'It's all right. Connie and I will chat and get to know one another until you feel like talking.'

'I'm Eve, Mrs Durrell,' Eve said shyly. 'Connie and I take it in turns to visit Johnny – Auntie Bess says he should only have one visitor at a time, because if we were both trying to talk to him we'd tire him out in no time. I'm sure that doesn't apply to you, though. Has someone told you what happened?'

Mrs Durrell smiled. 'I had a word with Matron before I came on to the ward and she put me in the picture. I'm sorry I got your name wrong – you're the one with the little brother, aren't you? Johnny's very fond of you both, I know, and of this Connie, of course.' There was a rattling in the background and a woman in a stained white pinafore entered the ward by bashing the doors with a large trolley. 'Ah, here comes your tea, young man. Eve, do you think that lovely lady would be very kind and let me have a cup? The train did stop a good many times but I was so afraid it might carry on without me if I joined a queue that I'm dry as dust and could drink a gallon of anything on offer.'

'I'll ask her,' Eve said doubtfully, for her experience with the trolley-pusher was that she regarded the tea and the rather stale-looking sandwiches she dispensed as her own personal property, but Mrs Durrell's winning smile did the trick and the tea lady handed over a brimming cup without a word of complaint.

When visiting hour was over, Eve led Mrs Durrell to

the parking area where she knew Uncle Reg would be waiting with the truck to give them a ride home. He greeted Johnny's mother warmly, and made haste to offer her the hospitality of Drake's Farm for as long as she was able to stay.

'You can sleep in young Johnny's room,' he assured her as he started the engine, got the truck into gear and drove cautiously out of the parking lot, 'so no need to feel you're taking anyone's place. You wouldn't want to share with Miriam – snores louder than this 'ere engine, that one do – still less bunk down in the attic with young Eve and all the rest.' He turned his head to wink at Eve, causing him to swerve dangerously towards oncoming traffic. Eve gave a moan of protest, reminded yet again that Uncle Reg was more at home driving the pony in the trap than negotiating what little motor traffic there was through the town centre, and swivelled quickly to address Mrs Durrell, sitting by the window on her other side.

'Auntie Bess used to keep the room where Johnny sleeps for my parents, if they ever wanted to stay over,' she explained. 'But Daddy's in the Navy and often away at sea and Mummy works in the naval offices as a secretary, so they don't get many chances to come and visit. And Connie's parents are in Liverpool so really it's been Johnny's room since he left Spindlebush Farm. How long will you be able to stay, Mrs Durrell?'

Mrs Durrell had jumped when the truck lurched towards the other side of the road, but she answered Eve's question with aplomb. 'Well, as it happens, I was planning to stay for a whole week. I've brought my ration card, of course, which I will give to Mrs Faversham so she won't lose out by having to feed one more.' She smiled. 'It's very good of you, Mr Faversham, and I should be glad to accept your kind offer. I know Johnny is very happy at Drake's Farm, though I think he still has every intention of joining the air force as soon as he's able. He was very envious when his pal Robbo was accepted. But that's still in the future; for now he's learning about farming, and loving every minute of it, judging from his letters.'

'Well, if he changes his mind and decides to stay with the land, we shall be very happy to employ him,' Uncle Reg said. 'He's a grand lad, but like all the young 'uns he won't listen to advice. I'm telling you, Mrs Durrell, we've warned him and warned him that the life of a Spitfire pilot isn't all glamour and girls.' He chuckled. 'Ah well, time will tell. He may change his mind yet. After all, every boy in blue isn't necessarily even aircrew, let alone a swaggering young fighter pilot.' He shrugged. 'If it weren't for this dratted war he'd start at the bottom in the cookhouse and work his way up. Mebbe he'll get to be a pilot and mebbe he won't; we must all wait and see.'

After Johnny's mother's departure, Connie made sure she was always first in line to see Johnny. This made Eve cross, and it was particularly galling when Johnny's memory began to return in great leaps, because the other girl had somehow managed to convince him that the accident had been largely Eve's fault.

'I don't see why he should believe you and not me,'

Eve said one evening as the girls were getting ready for bed. 'He was quite cold to me this evening and scarcely thanked me when I gave him a copy of that book about the air force he'd said he wanted. I'd like to know just how you can make out that I was responsible for the accident. I was only warning him not to do anything foolish. Miranda was too, weren't you, Mandy? Do *you* think it was my fault that he turned round at that particular moment?'

'Of course not. Johnny's falling had nothing to do with you.' Miranda glared at Connie. 'You're a trouble-maker, you are,' she said angrily. 'How could Eve have possibly made the chimney fall on Johnny? I shouted a warning too, remember? Why haven't you tried to blame me?'

Chrissie, with his pyjamas buttoned wrongly and his num-num clutched to his chest, pointed an accusing finger at Connie.

'You don't want Johnny liking anyone but you,' he said. And Eve watched with some pleasure as the colour rose up Connie's neck and dyed her cheeks pink.

'How *dare* you, you nasty little boy,' Connie said furiously. She had just jumped into bed, but got out again with the clear intention of boxing Chrissie's ears, though Miranda soon put a stop to that. Eve smiled to herself. As they grew to know Miranda better they had all realised that there was steel beneath the land girl's easy-going air.

'Get back into bed, Connie Hale,' she ordered now. 'Chrissie's right and you know it, so don't you go thinking that I'll allow you to give him a slap for telling the truth! Now settle down, because we've a full day ahead of us tomorrow and making sure that everyone has a turn at visiting Johnny doesn't make it any easier.' She turned to Eve. 'Don't worry, love. Johnny's had a hard time of it what with the crack on his noddle and a broken leg. When he gets back on his feet he'll begin to see things the way they really are and the two of you'll be pals again.'

Christmas passed and Johnny's health improved, although he still walked with a very noticeable limp. And it was his limp which was on his mind one day in June as he lay in his bed, gazing up at the ceiling through a blur of shameful tears. He had practised disguising it for the entire week and then, to prove how fit he was, he had walked all the way into town to the recruiting office. Once there, he had lied valiantly about his age and had admitted that he had suffered an accident from which he had now completely recovered.

The sergeant behind the big desk had eyed him keenly. He was a large man, square-faced and long-nosed, and the eyes which fixed themselves on Johnny's face were unfriendly. When he smiled, tauntingly, his mouth turned down at the corners showing yellow teeth and a good deal of unpleasant-looking fat tongue. Johnny had disliked him on sight, though he did his best to hide it, and soon realised that the feeling was mutual. 'You've gorra limp, wack,' the sergeant had said unkindly, in an accent not unlike Connie's, Johnny thought. 'And you don't look as old as you claim. Come back in a year or two and mebbe I'll change me mind, but as things stand at the moment the air force can manage without the services of a lad what'll never be able to march one mile, lerralone twenty.'

Deeply humiliated, Johnny had returned to Drake's Farm and met Eve and the others in the yard, Eve all eager interest and Johnny still smarting from the sergeant's words.

'How did you get on?' Eve had begun, and then looked up into his face and wished she had not spoken. She sighed. 'Was it your limp? Oh, Johnny, I'm so sorry.'

She had tried to take his hand but Johnny had jerked away from her. 'So you should be,' he had said furiously. 'It's all your fault, so you'll probably be quite pleased to learn that they turned me down. Said it was useless to apply again for at least six months. I never even had a chance.' He had gulped down the sob that was fighting to get out of his throat and brushed a hand across his freckled face. 'I hate you, Eve Armstrong! I don't believe I'll ever get accepted for any of the forces, thanks to you.'

Eve felt as though she had been kicked in the stomach; she actually bent forward as though she had received a blow. Even allowing for his disappointment his reaction had been cruel, and looking round the faces of the others – Connie, Chrissie and the farmhands – she saw shock written plainly on their features. And oddly enough it was Connie who spoke up in her defence.

'I've been having a think, and I don't believe it was Eve's fault you fell. No one asked you to climb the chimney stack . . . indeed, as I recall it Eve told you not to do any such thing.' She shook a reproving finger under Johnny's snub nose. 'And it's certainly not her fault that you look young for your age. You wanna eat them words, Johnny Durrell, and say you're sorry for putting the blame where it don't belong.'

She seized one of Johnny's fists and tried to uncurl his fingers, then took Eve's hand, now wet with tears, and tried to press it into Johnny's.

'Go on, you know I'm right,' she said.

Johnny took a deep, unsteady breath and uncurled his fingers, but the subsequent 'I'm sorry' was said with his eyes on the ground and Eve realised that though the other girl had meant it kindly Johnny resented being forced to make an apology which, had Connie left things alone, he would eventually have made of his own accord – and, she hoped, meant what he said.

The farmhands had unobtrusively melted away and Auntie Bess, who had been a silent witness of the entire scene as she stood in the kitchen doorway, must have been holding her breath, for she gave a long, whistling sigh.

'Eve, come in and lay the table. 'Twon't take you a minute, for Miriam did most of the work before she went up to Pete's Patch. Johnny, you'll want to get out of them Sunday clothes and into something more comfortable. And let's forget all about joining the forces for the time being. Come along in now and get on with some work.'

At supper that evening conversation might have been difficult, but Uncle Reg, a wise man, had no intention of letting an atmosphere develop in his house and said so. He looked keenly round the table whilst his wife was serving the vegetable pie then tapped his mug briefly with his spoon, bowed his head and spoke out clearly.

'For what we are about to receive, may the Lord make us truly thankful,' he said, and looked round the table again. 'Now let's have a little less sulking over what can't be helped, young Johnny. I refuse to have my supper spoiled by your temper. I gather you're angry because the RAF turned you down. Have you never heard the story of Robert the Bruce and the spider? You've had one try and given up, and if that's all you intend to do you're not the lad I know. But you're still living under my roof, so I want to know exactly what happened at the recruiting office.' He smiled kindly at Johnny. ''Tis your pride which is hurt. *We* know your worth, so try, try and try again and before you know it you'll be in uniform. And don't you pull a long face at me, because I believe in telling the truth.' Once more he looked round the table. 'Why's no one eating? There's apple crumble for afters.'

For some reason this made Connie start to giggle, and very soon Johnny was describing the sergeant in highly unflattering terms and saying what he would like to do to him if he ever met him in a dark alley, which made Chrissie choke over his mouthful of Woolton pie. He turned to Johnny.

'Would you really pull his long nose until it reached his knees? Oh, I'd love to see a man with a trunk like an elephant.' He turned to his sister. 'You'd help Johnny by holding on to the sergeant's arm so he couldn't get away, wouldn't you, Evie?' he said. 'Every time I go past the recruiting office now I shall peep in to see if he's still got a trunk instead of a nose. You are funny, Johnny, and I must say I like it best when you're here. Whilst you were in hospital we missed you ever so, didn't we, Evie? I think I shall call that sergeant Jumbo and offer him a bun. Do you think he'll take it in his trunk and shove it into his big old mouth?'

There was no doubt about it, Chrissie's contribution had broken the ice. Everyone was laughing, advising Chrissie to steer well clear of the sergeant if he really intended to make such an offer, and very soon talk became general.

Eve, watching Johnny covertly, saw that he was smiling, and when he noticed that she was looking at him he winked, his expression so normal and friendly that she took heart. Everyone was chattering, and though Connie was sitting next to Johnny she was talking to Auntie Bess, so Eve risked a friendly overture.

'Are you still keen to see the training film about the RAF, Johnny? It's being shown on some of the newsreels and the lads who've seen it say it's pretty good. I could find out where it's showing and we could catch a bus into town . . .'

She was watching Johnny's face as she made the suggestion and saw his expression change to one which she could almost describe as weary resignation.

'Do you want to come with us?' he asked. 'Is that what you're trying to say? Because Connie's already got it in hand and we're going into town on Wednesday. You can come if you like, but I thought you were more interested in the land than the air.'

238

Eve pushed her plate of food away and stood up. 'Oh, I don't want to interfere with your arrangements,' she said bitterly, and turned to Auntie Bess. 'I didn't tell you while we were all so worried about Johnny, but I've finally heard from Daddy that he and Mummy are quite happy for me to accept Lily's invitation to stay with her in Norfolk. So if it's okay with you, Auntie Bess, I'll leave as soon as possible.' She gave a watery sniff; tears filled her eyes and she wiped her hand across them, muttering that she thought she had a cold coming and ought to go upstairs to fetch a clean hanky. She made a rush for the attic but when she got there she turned angrily towards Connie, who had followed her. 'What do *you* want?' she said rudely.

Connie raised her brows. 'You needn't bother to run away, Eve Armstrong. You're welcome to go to the flicks with Johnny. He's not my type, especially now when all he can talk about is the boring old RAF. So just you come downstairs and tell Auntie Bess you won't desert her.'

Eve's back stiffened and she felt heat rise in her cheeks. 'Don't you try to tell me what to do or where to go,' she said furiously. 'And if Johnny's foolish enough to prefer you to me then that's his lookout.'

'Oh, go to hell, Eve Armstrong,' Connie said spitefully. 'If that's how you feel, the sooner you leave the better!'

'Goodbye, be good, and come into the village to phone me at least once a week to tell me you're well,' Eve shrieked at the diminishing figures on the platform. She waited until she could see only the countryside whizzing past then leaned back in her seat and smiled at the only other passenger, a fat lady holding a large wicker basket containing vegetables. She had been accompanied on to the train by two small and quarrelsome children, but they had left the compartment as soon as the guard started closing the doors, so Eve hoped to have a peaceful journey at least until her first change.

Auntie Bess, when appealed to, had heartily endorsed the plan. 'You tell that Lily she'll be welcome as the flowers in spring if she'll visit us at Drake's Farm,' she had said. 'But in the meantime, young lady, just you forget about work and enjoy yourself. I dare say Lily's already planned a great many things for you to do, so don't you go wasting your holiday. Visit the cathedral, do some sightseeing . . . oh, you know the kind of thing.'

'I will, Auntie Bess,' Eve had said humbly. 'It's awfully good of you to take charge of Chrissie while I'm away. Mummy said she'd come over to the farm whenever she could and take Chrissie off your hands, but of course she's very busy . . .'

Auntie Bess had laughed. 'Amn't we all?' she said cheerfully. 'But your little lad is growing up to be a real help around the place. I don't mind telling you that a few months back I'd have palmed him off on someone else, but not now. Now, when he's given a task he does it as well or better than some who shall be nameless.' She smiled widely. 'But don't you go telling him, or he'll get that swollen-headed there'll be no bearing him.'

Thus reassured, Eve leaned back to enjoy at least a

part of her long journey, then checked her possessions to make sure she had everything. She had slung her haversack up on to the string rack above her head but, like her travelling companion, she clutched a wicker basket containing two packets of sandwiches – one ham and the other strawberry jam – a small flask of tea, and a great many somewhat withered apples, the sort Eve particularly liked. Peeping into the basket, mouth watering, she saw that Auntie Bess had included one of the large custard apples as well, and was tempted to take a bite but resisted. After all, before she had left Drake's Farm everyone had assembled in the kitchen for a hearty breakfast and Auntie Bess, as she placed a loaded plate before Eve, had said briskly: 'Get outside of that, young woman, and you won't need feeding until you reach this here Close where our Lily lives. Rail journeys is dusty uncomfortable things at best; I dread to think what they're like in wartime. If I'm to believe what I've heard there'll be trolleys with tea urns at a good few stations, though of course you'll need the conveniences if you drink too much and that might be difficult, and don't forget to ring the village number just as soon as you arrive . . .'

But at this point the door of the compartment burst open to admit a young man in naval uniform who slumped into the seat opposite Eve, grinned sleepily around and within half a minute was snoring even more loudly than Eve's favourite sow.

Eve, who had jumped and squeaked when the sailor entered, hoped devoutly that he would sleep all the way to the next station, and then reminded herself that Lily wanted her to 'broaden her experience' and gave a smothered giggle. It was certainly true that she had often sung 'What shall we do with the drunken sailor?' but she had never dreamed she would be accompanied by one on her long journey to Norwich!

The train drew in to a large and busy station and Eve jumped to her feet. She had to change trains and was grateful when the sailor took her haversack from the rack and helped her shrug it on to her shoulders. It had turned out that he was not drunk at all but merely exhausted and was on his way home for precious leave, the first for over a year, he had told her. They got quite friendly before reaching the point where he went off to one train and she to another. She did not manage to find a seat on this particular train, but a polite little boy gave up his place to her in return for two apples, which made Eve smile. She remembered her last encounter with a boy on a train, when the boy had been Johnny. Amongst all that motley throng on the platform he had stood out because he had been loud and obnoxious. Eve smiled to herself at the comparison. Johnny might have been nicely brought up but his manners on that occasion had been anything but. This boy, on the other hand, having thanked her for the apples, perched on his suitcase and informed her that he was being met in Norwich by his uncle, an impatient man, and therefore hoped very much that the train would not be late.

'I'm being met there, too,' Eve informed him, thinking to herself that there are certain advantages in wartime travel. 'In the peace', as they were now calling it, folk did not speak to each other on trains.

Presently, Eve fell into an uneasy sleep and woke with a start, remembering all too vividly the words which Johnny had flung at her, the words which had led to this journey, if she was honest. *I hate you, Eve Armstrong! I don't believe I'll ever get accepted for any of the forces, thanks to you!* Even his mumbled apology could not lessen the pain as his words had struck home. Was he right? Had it really been her fault that the recruiting sergeant had rejected him? She could not tell, but hoped his resentment, whilst real enough now, would begin to take some more logical form than a wholly undeserved allocation of blame once she was beyond reach.

Eve settled back in her seat and soon she was in the land of dreams herself. The overcrowded railway compartment gave way to sunny skies, and the voices of the passengers surrounding her became birdsong and the splash of the stream as it made its way under the wooden bridge and down to the sea.

She was happy, even in her dream, and somehow Johnny's words were no longer a thorn in her flesh. In her heart she should have known he would never say such a cruel thing in order to hurt her. He had simply been hitting out at the fat old sergeant and was almost certainly regretting the spurt of temper which had caused him to accuse Eve of being to blame. Then, in her dream, the train was chugging into Norwich Thorpe and there on the platform was Daddy, smiling a welcome, helping her down to the platform. In the dream now, there was an anxiety which she could not quite explain, which was reflected in her father's eyes. Why was Daddy here and not at sea? Why was he so anxious to tell her something? She must give him an opening or she would never know.

'Daddy? What is it? Are you unhappy? Have I done something wrong?'

'You've done nothing,' her father said reassuringly. 'Don't worry about Mummy and me. These things happen in wartime . . .'

In the dream she was still standing on the platform and the train was making steam, clearly about to move off. Eve tried to remember something that she had meant to ask Daddy, but the scene was fading and even as she tried to catch her father's hand a voice far too near her ear bellowed 'Norwich Thorpe, all change here for . . .' and then listed place names of which she had never heard. Someone shook her shoulder and Eve opened her eyes. For a moment confusion reigned. She had been talking to Daddy, wanting to reassure him that she was fine and everything was all right. But someone had lifted her haversack down from the rack and picked up her jacket, which she had cast off when the compartment became stuffy, and a man in service uniform was shepherding her into the queue of people slowly descending from the train. Eve looked up at her rescuer, if you could call him that, and rubbed her eyes.

'I fell asleep,' she said wonderingly. 'I've travelled all the way from Devon, and then when we've nearly arrived I go and fall asleep.' She peered ahead of her

244

into the Stygian gloom, looking hopefully for a tall slender figure topped by flaxen hair.

The man chuckled, and then as they reached the doorway he lifted her down on to the platform. Eve was beginning to thank him and to wonder what she should do if there was no sign of Lily when she heard her calling her name. 'Eve! You're here at last! You poor little thing, what a journey you must have had! Do you know your train is nearly four hours late? I was beginning to think they'd cancelled the connection and you wouldn't arrive until tomorrow, but I hung on when a kind porter told me the train was on its way.'

'Oh, Lily,' Eve said gratefully, falling into her friend's welcoming embrace. 'It was good of you to wait. I'm so glad you did.'

Lily turned to the man who had lifted Eve down. 'Thank you *very* much. Now we'd best fight our way through this crowd and make our way home as soon as possible.' She turned to Eve. 'How you've grown, my love. I was looking for a little skinny waif and almost missed the young lady in the old school mac.' She gave Eve another reassuring hug. 'Come along; if we step out we can be home in fifteen or twenty minutes.'

Eve had got off the train still more or less in a daze. Lily insisted on carrying her haversack, but even without the weight of it on her shoulders she had difficulty in walking the short distance from the station to the Close. In fact, had it not been for the enlivening effect of the night wind she was sure she would have fallen asleep on her feet long before they got there. As they walked Lily kept up a constant stream of chat, probably guessing that Eve was feeling shy about meeting her parents, but in fact the first thing that struck Eve when she was ushered into the Kendal kitchen was an elusive likeness to the kitchen at Drake's Farm. It was not as big and a good deal more modern, but there was something about it which Eve recognised as being from the same mould as Auntie Bess's domain.

As soon as Eve entered the room the woman standing at the kitchen table slicing a loaf looked up, put down her bread knife and came over to give her a spontaneous hug. She was tall and blonde, her hair lightly streaked with grey, and the blue eyes which rested on Eve's tired face were kind and very like Lily's.

'Welcome to our home, little Eve,' she said, smiling. 'I'm sure you've already guessed that I'm Lily's mother because people are always telling us we're very alike. Take off your jacket and make yourself at home. You must be worn to the bone and wanting nothing more than your bed, but I've made a thick vegetable soup which you shall sit down and enjoy before I'll let you so much as climb the stairs.'

Eve beamed at her hostess. She looked around the pleasant kitchen; the dresser twinkled with china, strings of onions hung close to the fire in the stove, the big kitchen table bore a blue bowl of apples and a glass bowl of pears, and there was enough homely clutter to convince Eve that she was going to be comfortable here. She dug her spoon into the soup and took a mouthful; it was thick, as promised, and very good.

'Thank you,' she said shyly. 'I *am* very tired, but this soup is so delicious that I'd like to finish every drop. Only I'm rather afraid I shall fall asleep and my head will flop straight into my plate.'

Mrs Kendal laughed. 'As soon as you've finished your soup Lily will take you up to her room, which you are to share whilst you're with us. Don't worry about oversleeping tomorrow; it will do you good. I have to go out in the morning so if I've left by the time you come downstairs you must simply help yourself to anything you fancy. Lily tells me that kind Mrs Faversham has taught you all to make porridge so you can start off with a big bowl of that and fill up the chinks with my homemade bread. Later on either Lily or I will show you round and introduce you to my husband when he comes in.' She smiled as she watched Eve use a piece of bread to mop up the last of her soup. 'I do hope you enjoyed that; it certainly looks as if you did. And now off with you, girls, and get your beauty sleep. If I don't see you in the morning, Eve, I'll be around later, and if you come across a young man in the uniform of an American flyer that will be Hank. He's a nice guy – dear me, I'm already speaking his language – and he came to us – oh, it must be getting on for two years ago now – when he'd hurt his leg pretty badly in some sort of accident at his airfield and couldn't fly for a while. He's quite fit again now, of course, but his plane – only he calls it a ship – was shot down a few weeks ago, and apparently he's grounded until they can find him another one. He's around the place quite a lot, so I thought I should tell you in case he came in tomorrow when you were here on your own.' She crossed the room with a swift light step and smoothed a hand down Eve's cheek. 'Poor little Eve,' she said kindly. 'Here am I, gabbling away and keeping you from the rest you're obviously in need of. Night night, girls; sweet dreams!'

On that first morning Eve slept deeply, not even waking when Lily crept out of the room. She left a note for Eve explaining that she was on early milking at Parker's Place but that was all, so it was quite a surprise to Eve when she went downstairs to find a tall young man whistling a popular tune below his breath and stirring porridge in a large pot.

'Oh!' Eve said, taken aback. She had a vague recollection that Mrs Kendal had mentioned a member of the American air force, but she had not realised that she would meet him quite so soon and so unexpectedly. He was obviously amused by her surprise, and gave her an infectious grin.

'You'll be Eve Armstrong, late of Drake's Farm, and I'm Hank Ruskin, an American flyer, as you can see.' He tipped porridge into two blue bowls and pulled out a chair, indicating that she should sit down, then took the place opposite her. 'What'll we do today?' he said cheerfully. 'Lily thinks you might like a quick tour of the house and garden. Then we could walk into the city and have a snack lunch somewhere before going up to the castle to take a look around. You'll get a magnificent view from there, I promise; I was very impressed when Lily insisted on dragging me up so she could point out various landmarks. What do you say? Does that appeal to you?' He grinned again. 'Or have I made it sound like a lecture?'

'No, no, it sounds grand,' Eve said hastily. 'And this porridge is grand, too.' She cleared her throat. 'I know you're in the air force, but are you in the cookhouse? Is that where you learned how to make porridge? Oh, and do I call you sir, or aircraftman, or what?'

'Call me Hank,' the young man said equably. 'We don't stand on ceremony, us Yanks. But actually I'm a Liberator skipper waiting to be assigned to a new ship, so until that happens I'm at your service, ma'am. And as for the porridge, my mother taught me to make it when I was just a kid.'

Eve had thought she was tired after the journey but she found Hank's company invigorating, for it seemed as if he must know as much about Norwich as Mrs Kendal herself. First of all they went round the large garden admiring the neat rows of vegetables, then they toured the house, which was large and warm; Eve took to it at once. After that they went into the city and found an extraordinary little old street – Elm Hill – where a pavement café provided them with baked potatoes and thinly sliced corned beef. Eve would have sworn that after the porridge she needed nothing more, but somehow she managed to devour the food, and as they left the little café Hank turned to her, giving her his rabbity grin.

'Not worn out yet?' he enquired jovially. 'Have you still got the energy to climb the castle mound? It's real steep, so if you're tired we could do the cathedral next and leave the castle for another day. How do you feel, Eve? Can you make it to the top?'

Eve tilted her head back and looked up and up until her eyes rested on the castle which must, she thought, overlook the entire city. 'I'm game to have a go,' she said boldly. 'Remember, I've been working on a farm for years now and farmers don't exactly encourage their people to give up just because the ground's a bit steep. And the view from the top must be incredible.'

Hank smiled and gave her shoulder a reassuring pat. 'You're a gal after my own heart,' he said. 'And the path doesn't go straight up; that really would be a bit much. Instead, it meanders so that when you reach the top you shouldn't be gasping for breath. And as you say, even if you were the view would be worth it.'

Eve was very impressed by the castle and enjoyed her visit, though from the top of the keep she was sad to see how much of the city had been destroyed by the Luftwaffe. Hank had not yet arrived in England when the worst of the raids took place, but he had heard about those terrible days from the Kendals.

'The market used to be four times the size it is now,' he told Eve, 'partly because the blackout means that in winter the stalls have to open late and close early, and also because the shops simply don't have all that much to sell.' He pointed to a large hole below them. 'That was Curls, a huge department store. It received a direct hit, and Mrs Kendal told me it was the first place to be cleared away because the remains were so dangerous.' He chuckled. 'But the people of Norwich are a tough lot, and they made good use of that big old hole. They installed enormous water tanks in it so that the firemen putting out the incendiary bombs didn't have to interfere with the domestic water supply. Other people were fighting the war in their own way all over the place. Mrs Kendal told me that she was passing Greens, the school uniform outfitters, and happened to glance into the ruins. She said the only thing left standing was the wooden horse, still rocking gently, and smiling at passers-by as though to say "We ain't beat yet".'

'And all this was going on whilst we were tucked away in Drake's Farm, not realising what the Blitz meant,' Eve said in a small constricted voice. 'If we'd known . . . but in a way we *did* know, because Plymouth was bombed pretty heavily too. We just didn't see the results, not with our own eyes. My family lived in a flat overlooking Blackheath in London. My mother told me once that there had been a bomb or an incendiary or something further along our street and she had gone up there as soon as she could to make sure nobody we knew needed help. I'm ashamed to say it meant nothing to me. I don't know what sort of damage I thought a bomb might wreak . . .' She turned impulsively to her companion. 'We listened to the radio and read the newspapers but I promise you, Hank, we didn't really understand the terrible things that were happening.'

Hank shook his head. 'And that was how it was meant to be. You kids were evacuated before the war even got properly under way, because your parents needed to know you were safe. How old were you, when the war started?' And then, before she could answer, 'Too young to be of any use, believe you me.

My dear child – not that you're a child any more – the whole point of the evacuation was to keep your generation safe and as far from the war as possible. Admittedly, if Lily had known that Norwich was about to be attacked she wouldn't have stayed on that farm for five minutes, but in her way she and the rest of the Land Army were fighting back, hitting the Luftwaffe by feeding not just civilians but the troops too. And that applies to you kids as well, so don't you go blaming yourself because you'd found a safe haven. Be thankful that you could do your bit without having to face the terrible destruction the Nazis inflicted.'

He looked down at her and patted her on the shoulder, his ugly face suddenly lit by his endearing grin. 'Well, that's it; lecture over. At the time the Kendals thought it was a bloody miracle that the cathedral and the castle were undamaged. I'm not a religious man, but without wishing to sound silly I think the hand of God must have been over those particular places. After all, so far as I heard the only cathedral which was really badly damaged was Coventry, and I believe they're already making plans to rebuild it as soon as the war is over. Although we mustn't forget the doodlebugs. They're the new weapon the Nazis have developed – have you heard of them? They're flightless, pilotless bombs which are being launched at Britain from certain parts of France. When their engines cut out they fall out of the sky and do considerable damage, so we mustn't think England's reached its safe haven yet.'

'I've heard of those things,' Eve said thoughtfully as they descended from the castle mound, 'but I thought they were aimed at the Channel ports? And poor old London, of course.'

Hank gave a short bark of laughter. 'They are what I would call an imprecise weapon of war,' he said. 'We aren't the only ones who don't know where they're going to land – the Germans don't know either. They simply launch the things from some airfield as near the coast as possible and wait for news. Quite often they land in open country, or in the sea, and at least one has flown straight into the path of a Messerschmitt, causing both aircraft and doodlebug to explode on the spot. I don't imagine there would be much left after a collision of that nature.'

By now they were at the foot of the mound again and crossing the wide street which Hank informed her was called Castle Meadow. Eve imagined that they were heading home until her companion swerved to one side and led her down a flight of steps into a narrow street where a green iron table and two small chairs stood on the pavement outside a tiny café.

'I'm parched,' Hank said frankly. 'How about a nice cuppa, as you Brits call it, and a couple of sticky buns? Lunch seems a long time ago and I dare say you could do with a bite.'

Eve's expression probably said it all, for he settled her on one of the chairs, waved a hand to a passing waitress who looked as though her feet were killing her, and ordered tea for two and a couple of sticky buns. The waitress creaked into the café and then popped her head back out of the open door.

'Would your young lady prefer a nice fresh-baked scone?' she asked. And though Eve said no, she would like the sticky bun, she felt a glow of pride because the waitress had taken her not for Hank's little sister, but for his girlfriend. However, when she looked again at Hank's homely face, with its snub nose and the stitch scars which lifted one corner of his upper lip, she was not too sure that the mistake had been a compliment. Nice though he was, Hank was no beauty. In fact she had never, so far as she could recall, met an uglier man. She knew Lily liked dark-haired men and Hank's red hair couldn't even be described as ginger; it was the colour of a new carrot and clashed horribly with his reddish skin and white brows and lashes. Then, as she took the first bite out of her sticky bun, Eve chided herself. He was friendly, generous and amusing, and what more could anyone ask? A nicer person than me would say that appearances don't matter, she told herself. A nicer person than me would not even notice his rabbity teeth – which only look like that because of the stitches in his cheek, I expect – and his overly large feet. And even the size of his feet might be put down to the fact that he's wearing his flying boots.

She drained her teacup with a satisfied sigh and smiled gratefully at her companion. 'That was just what I wanted,' she said. 'You are clever, Hank, to find this odd little place. How long have you been in the city now? And how old are you anyway? Or is that a rude question?'

'I'm twenty-four,' Hank said at once, 'and I've been in the UK now for nearly two years. As I expect you know I came to stay with the Kendals after my accident, when the USAAF had been appealing for billets. Mrs Kendal took me in because she used to be a nurse, and she's taken better care of me than my own mother could have done. But I'm back on base now, of course, and I'll be in the air as soon as they find us a new ship.'

'Oh, but you don't *have* to fly again, do you, Hank?' Eve asked anxiously. She had already realised that she liked Hank immensely and would worry dreadfully if he had to go back in the air. She said as much and he gave her a friendly punch on the shoulder.

'The Huns are still dropping bombs, you know, though God knows why they haven't simply realised that they've all but lost the war.' He grinned down at her, pushing his cap to the back of his head. 'You've come in at the end of the battle, baby, but just be grateful for that and don't try to do me out of my last chance of glory!'

This made Eve laugh, but she realised there was a strain of seriousness behind his words. So when she was hauled from her bed that very night, a blanket wrapped round her shoulders and a basket of provisions, carefully selected, placed in her charge, she was not entirely unprepared. She looked up at the night sky, crisscrossed by searchlights and alive with the humming of aero engines, and felt the first icy prickle of fear. She grabbed Lily's hand as they hurried down the concrete steps into the shelter, where Lily settled Eve on a bench amongst other residents of the Close and gave her hand a comforting squeeze.

'Mother and Father are ARP wardens so they've gone to their posts; I have to be at the Guild Hall on fire watch,' she said. 'Don't worry – I don't have to do much except report fires, obey orders and see that everyone is safe until the all clear sounds. Meanwhile, Eve dear, I want you to stay exactly where you are. I know it's very tempting to push aside the curtain and climb up the steps to see what's going on, but you really mustn't do that. Promise me you won't try?' She consulted her wristwatch. 'It's ages since we had a raid. Of course it had to happen on your second night here, but it shouldn't last long. The ack-ack batteries and the boys on the searchlights will make sure of that. I'll come and find you when it's over.' She would have turned away but Eve caught her arm. 'Where's Hank?' she enquired urgently. 'Will he come down to the shelter presently? Only I don't know anyone else and if a bomb does hit . . .'

She saw Lily's white teeth gleam in a reassuring smile. 'He'll be back at the base by now, I'm sure. You see, the RAF bombers fly at night but the US Liberators fly during the day, and there's all sorts of stuff to be seen to once they're safely home. Since Hank's not flying at the moment he helps out whenever he can.'

After Lily left her Eve expected to feel very lost and alone, but to her surprise she found several kindred spirits in the shelter, girls like herself who had similar interests and were beginning to think of themselves as young women. In fact, she realised she was enjoying her enforced incarceration, and when one of the girls suggested that they should get together that evening and go to the dance at the Samson and Hercules ballroom she accepted unhesitatingly. Had Lily not said that this holiday would help her to meet other young people of her own age?

When the all clear sounded, shortly after daybreak, Lily met her at the top of the shelter steps and the two of them walked back to the Close together. They entered the kitchen to find a jubilant Hank awaiting them.

'I've seen the CO and they've found us a new ship,' he said joyfully the moment they opened the door. 'Now my crew can get back to teaching the Jerries a much needed lesson at last.'

Halfway through her first week in Norwich, during which time she had attended three dances at the Samson and Hercules, Eve realised that at least half the USAAF were in love with Lily. Between dances they clustered round her, each man intent upon catching her notice. Tall ones, short ones, dark ones, fair ones, they all thought Lily an English rose beyond compare, and would have fought over her had Lily not made it plain that she wasn't hanging out for a boyfriend. When Eve teased her, she just smiled and said they would get over their infatuation as soon as they returned to their homeland. In the meantime it was a rare day when she did not receive boxes of what the American airmen called candy, bouquets of flowers, or anything else which would cause her to look upon one or another with approval.

Eve guessed it was a sort of game; the men loved her delicate looks, her gentle voice and above all, perhaps, her English accent. They vied with each other to amuse her, acquiring cars from unknown sources to take her to the cinema, the theatre, or even up to London, where Eve gathered they were welcomed with respect even at the grandest places.

However, there was one person who made no attempt to lure the golden Lily to his side. He liked her, but then he liked Eve as well, and when he could have claimed her for a dance he usually gave way, with a rueful grin, to any member of his crew who hankered after the girl he teasingly called 'the blonde bombshell'. This made Eve laugh, because Lily was certainly no bombshell, but when she showed no sign of favouring one over another, and gave no hint of feeling more than a friendly interest in any of them, Eve was forced to conclude that her love for Colin must have gone deeper than she, Eve, had realised. In fact, she often thought that Lily's love for Colin had never truly died, and one day at the beginning of the second week, whilst the two girls were in their bedroom getting ready for the latest dance at the Samson, she asked Lily outright just how much Colin's defection had hurt her.

Lily was applying a delicate smear of colour to her long and curling eyelashes and jumped when she heard the question.

'Oh, Eve, I nearly poked my eye out,' she said reproachfully. 'Colin who? I mean, I know at least three Colins; one's English and the other two are Americans.'

Eve giggled. 'When you were at Drake's Farm you were in love – or thought you were – with Colin Tunstal,' she said. 'We all thought you'd come back to Drake's Farm once you got over him, but you didn't. I suppose I thought he'd put you off men for life; is that true? If you

258

think I'm being really cheeky I'm sorry, but I've grown up, Lily, and there are things I want to understand. There's one man in the USAAF who's absolutely crazy about you – you must know the one I mean. His name is Alvin something or other, and he's so good-looking the girls nearly swoon if he asks them to dance. But he only asks them when you're on the floor already, and then he keeps trying to get near you and doesn't care that his partner hates it and everybody else is laughing at him.'

Lily had been making up her face – a dab of powder on her nose, a dab of lipstick on her mouth and just a smear of mascara on her long gleaming lashes – but now her eyes met Eve's in the little mirror and she gave a subdued chuckle.

'That chap? I suppose he is rather handsome, but there's nothing in his noddle apart from his own looks, you know. Haven't you noticed how dreamy he seems half the time? That's because he sees himself as a sort of Prince Charming and believes that at one kiss from him I'll buckle at the knees, dismiss all the other nice boys and dance off with him into the sunset.' She chuckled again. 'My love, you've got to start recognising sincerity when you see it. That little fair chap, Tommy Roberts, the one who flies a Mosquito and thinks he's in love with me? He's not, you know. When he goes home to his little village in Wales and sees his Sian again – a girl who has written to him every week since the war started and loves his personality and not just his fair hair and blue eyes – he'll not give me a second thought. Can you understand, sweetie? You don't fall in love with someone just for their looks – it's much more meaningful than that.' She turned away from the mirror and smiled at her companion. 'You've come away from Drake's Farm now because Johnny was in a temper and said things he didn't mean. Picture his face beside Alvin's and see which one is really your friend.'

'But you haven't answered my question,' Eve pointed out. 'I've heard someone say that because of what Colin did to you you'll never marry anyone else. That's not true, is it? Did he really hurt you badly enough to put you off men for ever?'

Lily began to brush her hair rhythmically, then tied it back from her face with a blue ribbon which exactly matched her eyes.

'I'll tell you something I've told nobody else, sweetie,' she said after some thought. 'Colin wrote to me . . . oh, weeks ago . . . saying that he had come to his senses and wanted to resume our relationship. He wanted to see me, and I agreed; why not? He and I go back a long way. He was my first boyfriend. So we agreed to meet at the Dorchester of all places and talk over what had happened. Eve, I got there first and watched him walking across that enormous dining room, looking for me – or at any rate looking for the girl he had left behind – and I knew I had narrowly escaped making the worst mistake of my life. I suddenly realised he's frightfully handsome but not particularly nice, and by the time he reached the table I just wanted to get on the first available train back to Norwich. I didn't want to shame him in front of all the other diners, but I didn't want him to leave with the impression that I still had any feeling whatsoever either for him or for our relationship, which was finished so totally that even my smile must have looked rather fraught. You see, my feelings for Colin weren't real feelings at all. He was just another fellow who liked pretty blondes and I was no longer just a pretty blonde.' She smiled suddenly, then pulled a face. 'I knew it was useless to try to explain, so I just said I had an appointment and walked out on him; dumped him with even more force than he had dumped me. And as I hurried to catch the train a tremendous feeling of lightness came over me. I was sorry for Colin, and I suppose there will always be a place in my heart for the first boy who meant anything to me, but it's over. I wrote him a letter telling him I didn't wish to see him again and I suppose he went back to the girl he left me for, but whatever he did is no concern of mine and I'm happy to have it so. And now, shall we go down to the kitchen and wait for our escorts to take us to the dance?'

Eve had not said a word throughout this explanation, but as they descended the stairs she took her friend's hand and gave it a comforting squeeze.

'I'm glad you told me,' she said. 'Suppose you had never received that letter and went ahead with your plans for a wartime wedding? Oh, Lily, I think I understand now why you're what they call "fancy free", and I'm glad. There are lots of very nice boys chasing round after you and you're all having a good time, but in a way you're playing a game and so are they, and when the war's over and the glamour's gone you might settle down with one of them or you might not. Is that right?'

At the bottom of the flight Lily stopped and wagged an admonitory finger at the younger girl.

'You asked me and I told you because I trust you, little Eve,' she said seriously. 'I don't mean to encourage anyone to believe that I'm on the hunt for a husband, because I'm not. In fact of all the crowd of young men that I've met since I took the job at Parker's Place there isn't one I'd look at twice. For a start, I'm British through and through and wouldn't dream of moving abroad. I know I'm a city girl and before the war I'd probably have worked in an office and been happy enough, never knowing what I was missing. But now when the war is over I mean to look for a job on the land. I'm good with stock and Mr Parker needs another cowman or woman, but even if he doesn't take me there'll be jobs for land girls who have already proved themselves, so I'm not worried. I may not make much money but I'll be doing the work I love, and since I learned to love it at Drake's Farm I'm going to come back for a visit very soon. I shan't be able to stay long, of course, but I must see the Favershams to thank them for everything, and apologise for running away.'

'They'll understand,' Eve said at once. 'We all miss you dreadfully, Lily, but to have you back at the farm for a while would be wonderful. And don't you think you ought to tell them that you have discovered Colin is a rat?'

Lily chuckled, but shook her head. 'He's not a rat, just a very ordinary young man; war fooled him into thinking he was in love with me when all we were, in truth, were friends. So let's forget the whole thing and enjoy the dance.'

Chapter Eleven

The talk with Lily had opened Eve's eyes to a great many things, and that evening, when she danced, as she did, with several young men who asked her to partner them, she found herself looking at them with different eyes. They were nice, friendly and eager for the war to end, and because of the talk with Lily Eve realised that she was able to think of them simply as friends.

She had not expected her mother to visit her whilst she was in Norwich and was surprised one bright afternoon to find, when she returned from a last visit to the cathedral, her mother sitting at the kitchen table, talking in the friendliest way to Mr and Mrs Kendal. Eve stared. She hadn't seen Eleanor since Lily's twenty-first birthday party, and could not help wondering why she had taken the trouble to come all the way up from Plymouth when her daughter had been within far easier reach in Devon. The matter was soon explained, however. When Eve started to ask her why she had come so far her mother gave a rather artificial laugh.

'I'm a driver as well as a secretary, you know, and I had to bring the admiral up to Norwich to attend a very important meeting,' she said. 'I left him at the city hall whilst I arranged overnight accommodation, and then of course I remembered that my one and only daughter was somewhere in the city, enjoying the first little break she's had since the war started.' She glanced around the table. Mr Kendal smiled politely back but said nothing. He was a tall, thin, dreamy clergyman, always a man of few words, and now he left his wife to maintain the conversation. Mrs Kendal turned to Eve.

'Aren't you a lucky girl? Your mother has come a long way to see you, Eve. I put the kettle on as soon as I heard who she was, but I'm afraid the only food I had to offer was some rather boring oatmeal biscuits.'

'Oh, don't worry about food; the admiral has already booked a meal for all of us at somewhere called the Library Tavern,' Mrs Armstrong said gaily. She glanced at her wristwatch, then addressed herself to Eve. 'Darling girl, I have exactly half an hour before the forces catch up with me again. Tell me all your news; have you thought at all about what you want to do when the war's over?'

Eve stared. 'Well, I suppose I'll go back to London with you and Daddy and try for the grammar school – the teachers here said I'd certainly done well enough at least to apply for a place. But what about Chrissie? Are you going to take him on again?' She smiled. 'He's a bit of a handful, but you've always been able to manage him, though I can't imagine that he'll find life back in London attractive.'

Eleanor was looking a little startled. 'Well, I'm afraid you'll both have to stay where you are for the time being,' she said. 'I've no idea when Daddy and I will be able to take up civilian life again. Chrissie will be happy to stay on the farm until then, won't he? And you can start to study for grammar school on your own, you know.'

Eve laughed. 'I'm not too sure about that, but Chrissie will be delighted, and so will Auntie Bess. Indeed, she's said several times that she doesn't want to lose us Armstrongs when the men come back from the war.' She looked up at her mother. 'Some of them have come back already, because captured German soldiers are working on the land and have to be supervised. We evacuees couldn't possibly do that, and we're kept as far as possible away from them. Mrs Shelborne at the post office says some of the Jerries are real nice guys, and I think she's right. Chrissie, of course, speaks to everyone, and one prisoner who knew a bit about woodwork carved a beautiful horse for him. He keeps it on the windowsill in the attic and is ever so proud of it.'

'Yes, well,' her mother said awkwardly. 'You can scarcely blame Chrissie for fraternising with the enemy when they give him gifts.' She turned suddenly on Eve, a sharp expression on her beautifully made-up face. 'It's happened now, and can't be undone, but you should keep a closer eye on your brother and tell him that the man who carved that horse might easily be the one who led the bombardment against Plymouth earlier in the war.'

Eve did not say anything. She was remembering how her mother had constantly snubbed her, and recalling also that it did not do to complain. Better to say nothing, for in twenty minutes or less – Eve glanced at the clock on the mantel – Mrs Armstrong would have left and Eve would probably not see her again for months. After all, a mere thirty miles or so had separated them in the past and her mother had rarely made the effort to come to the farm and see her children even then.

A knock on the back door interrupted her train of thought and as soon as a rosy face appeared around the panel Mr Kendal stood up.

'I can see I'm needed,' he said with mock resignation. He gave a little bow and held out a firm white hand. 'Goodbye, Mrs Armstrong; so nice to have met you. I hope we shall meet again, but just now my colleague here has need of my services.'

He left the kitchen and Eleanor got to her feet. 'It's time I was off as well,' she said, and there was definitely relief in her voice. She turned to Mrs Kendal. 'Thank you for what you've done for my daughter; she works very hard at the farm and I'm sure this break will have done her good.' She held out her hand, and then Mrs Kendal accompanied both her and Eve down the short path to the front gate. Mrs Kendal gave her guest her usual sweet smile. 'Any time you come up to Norfolk we shall be delighted to entertain you,' she said rather formally. 'It's a pity your daughter has been billeted so far away, but we must all expect to be moved around in wartime and from what I've gathered your

Eve is very happy in Devon. And now I must start preparing our evening meal, since we're expecting guests. I've invited a young American airman and a chap who drives a Wellington bomber, so I had best start making a very large and very delicious rabbit and vegetable pie.' She smiled at her visitor as an official car turned into the Close and drew up alongside them.

It was the sight of the official car, Eve thought afterwards, which brought vividly into her mind a long-ago conversation with Chrissie. She had told herself over and over that it was Chrissie's imagination which had led him to believe that Lily had kissed the driver of the car which had brought their parents to the farm on Lily's twenty-first birthday. She had tried and tried to make sense of it, to convince herself that Lily, who had such high principles, had allowed herself to be half pulled into a big black car in order to be passionately kissed, but she had never really succeeded. It just did not ring true. She simply could not imagine her friend behaving in such a fashion.

Eve frowned. Chrissie had said Lily was in her working kit: fawn-coloured overalls, a yellow shirt and long green wellies. Miriam had been on early duty that day and had found time to change into a skirt after finishing her morning chores, so the only other person in land girl kit had been Mrs Armstrong. But I must stop worrying over trifles, Eve told herself determinedly. I suppose it doesn't really matter, but I hate to think of dear Lily behaving so badly.

It was not until she got into bed that she admitted to herself that, if it had *not* been Lily, the only other explanation was that her own mother, a married woman, had shared an 'oogly-googly kiss' with a naval officer who was not her husband.

For what seemed like most of the night Eve tossed and turned. And in the morning, pale-faced and red-eyed, she cornered Lily when they had finished washing up the breakfast pots and without preamble told her the whole story. 'So if it wasn't you, Lily, and I don't think it was, it must have been my mother,' she said in a low voice. 'If my father knew . . .'

Lily turned to Eve and gave her a reassuring hug. 'No, it wasn't me,' she said. 'But don't worry – these things happen when someone is off their guard in wartime. That kiss wouldn't have meant anything; it would just have been a sort of joke between two friends, nothing serious. But your father might not like it, so if I were you I shouldn't mention it to him. Will you promise me something, darling? Will you pretend the incident never happened? Because it can't have been important, and I'm sure Chrissie has already forgotten it completely. Eve?'

'I promise,' Eve said at once. She smiled lovingly at Lily. 'I never meant to burden you with my worries, but I couldn't bear . . . oh, never mind. I shan't ever think of it again, and I feel sort of light, as though you've taken a burden off my shoulders.'

'Good,' Lily said approvingly. 'Now, what would you like to do today? There must be things you'd rather do than come to work with me at Parker's Place. Mr Parker has bought a large number of pigs – I don't know how many yet – and wants them rehoused in the sties nearest the house; I think they're in-pig gilts, so he wants to keep an eye on them. But it doesn't seem fair to ask you to herd pigs on your last day.'

Eve laughed. 'A busman's holiday, don't they call it? When you do the same thing on holiday or at work? But I'm one of the lucky ones; I love my work and wouldn't want to do anything else. Besides, I don't suppose the pigs will take up the whole of the day; we can come home and de-piggify ourselves, then go to one of these tea dances you've told me about.' She looked sideways at Lily as they crossed the kitchen and headed for the back door. 'Do you remember me mentioning a chap called Robin Maddon? He's ever so nice, and he's like us, Lily, he loves the land, though at present he's a mechanic looking after aero engines. He wants to see me again before I go back to Drake's Farm. Would you mind if I invite him to the tea dance as well? The minute you appear half the USAAF will arrive on the doorstep, so you won't lack for partners.' She smiled at her friend. 'You are lucky. You've never been a wallflower, standing at the side of the dance floor and waiting for some kind soul to take pity on you and ask you for a dance.'

Lily laughed. 'I can remember being a gawky young girl positively praying for someone to ask me for a dance,' she assured Eve. 'And I haven't noticed you being short of partners either. So is it a date? We'll move the pigs, clean up, and go to the tea dance. Can you get a message to your Robin?'

Eve pressed her hands on her hot cheeks. 'I'll manage somehow,' she mumbled, suddenly aware that the relief of unburdening herself to Lily was very much with her still. She had a great deal of respect for the older girl and could not imagine her behaving in the fashion Chrissie had described. True to her promise, she determined to put the whole thing out of her mind, and after they had finished at Parker's Place and were on their way back to the luxury of a bath it occurred to her that there was something else she wanted to ask her friend. As they entered the Close and ascended the stairs to their room she shot a sideways glance, pregnant with mischief, at her friend.

'I've got another question for you,' she said gaily. 'You aren't influenced by looks and I know you like him, so why don't you go dancing with Hank?'

'Because he's never asked me,' Lily said promptly. 'I agree he's a nice guy, but he's just not interested in being anything but friends.'

Eve's eyebrows shot up until they nearly touched her hairline. 'He's never asked you?' she said incredulously. 'If so, he's the only American airman who hasn't. And why wait for an invitation? If I were your age I reckon I'd ask him myself.'

'Nice girls wait to be asked,' Lily said. 'Fast girls may cut a man out from the herd, but I am *not* a fast girl. If Hank wants to dance with me there's only one thing stopping him.'

Once more Eve's eyebrows climbed. 'And what's that?' she asked suspiciously. 'Don't say he doesn't like you, because I know he does. Does he prefer to dance with girls who aren't as tall as you? But he likes you as a person and surely that's more important. So come on, Lily, what's stopping Hank asking you to dance?'

Lily giggled. 'He's got two left feet,' she said. 'Have you ever seen him dancing? He simply has no sense of rhythm or anything. He's certainly no Fred Astaire!'

It was Eve's turn to giggle. 'Now you come to mention it he really doesn't dance, does he? Once when we were doing the St Bernard's Waltz and needed him to make up a set I remember he gave up after two or three attempts and sat it out, as they say.'

'So now, Miss Nosy, you know why Hank doesn't dance. I never knew him before his accident, when for all I know he might've danced as well as the next man.' She looked hard at Eve. 'He never talks about what happened, but it must have been much worse than he ever lets on. So don't ask awkward questions, young woman, because you might not like the answers.'

'Oh, poor Hank!' Eve said, honestly dismayed. 'Lily dear, I'm so sorry. I should never have asked. Please don't let him know that I did, and in future I'll keep my big mouth shut. Only you and he are my best friends – apart from Johnny, of course – and I couldn't help thinking it would be rather nice if you got together.'

'Well, now you know. And now, young woman, who's going to have the first bath?'

Eve had hoped to see Hank on her final morning in the Close because next to Lily she regarded Hank as her best friend in Norwich. It had been he who introduced her not only to the beauties of the city but also to a great many friendly and likeable people, including Robin Maddon. However, on the day of her departure a big raid was planned and Hank was determined to be flying his Liberator.

'This may well be the last raid of the war,' he had told her seriously. 'And I intend to be a part of it.'

The conversation had taken place whilst the three of them were sitting on the small chairs provided at the Samson and Hercules for those who were not dancing. Lily, seated between the other two, looked very hard at Hank.

'I wish you didn't have to go,' she said slowly. 'Surely you've done enough tours of duty? I know very well that you could have gone back stateside after your accident two years ago, but you're still here. Why tempt fate?'

Hank had shrugged. 'It's my decision,' he said mildly. 'When I start something I like to finish it. I can't tell you where the raid will be heading, or what sort of resistance we'll meet. All I can say is what we've been told ourselves; every available air crew has to be on the alert.'

It was Lily's turn to shrug. 'Do as you please,' she said rather pettishly. 'My feelings don't count, of course.'

Hank had laughed and reached across the space between them to squeeze her hand. 'Don't you worry yourself about me, Lily; I'm like a cork, the sort that always bobs up to the surface just when you think I've gone for good. Let's change the subject, shall we?' He turned to Eve. 'Well, honey? Have you enjoyed your break from routine? Lily tells me that she's planning to visit you all at Drake's Farm before too long.' He gave a short bark of laughter. 'I gather that things are a lot quieter in the depths of Devon than in Norfolk, and that Mr Faversham is a good deal easier to work for than Mr Parker.'

Eve had begun to reply when Lily jumped to her feet and addressed herself to Hank. 'Oh, you make me sick, Hank Ruskin. You talk of the war as if it were some sort of a game, which it most certainly is not. You're like a foolish child, ignoring reality and thinking yourself invincible. Well you're not! You're just an ordinary guy caught up in extraordinary circumstances. And until you come to your senses and act like a man instead of a silly boy who doesn't know any better you can find someone else to sit out dances with.'

Eve's mouth had dropped open and her eyes had rounded with horror. To be sure, she had only known Hank a couple of weeks, but she had known Lily much longer and had never heard her friend utter so much as one unkind word. Lily just wasn't like that. She never got cross or lost her temper. She was gentle and thoughtful and until that moment Eve could not have imagined the older girl ever losing control. But when she looked up into Lily's face she saw her eyes sparkling with anger and her cheeks pink with it. Instinctively, she also got to her feet.

'Lily?' she said uncertainly. 'What's the matter? What's Hank said which has made you so cross?'

She had expected a soft answer, but Lily whirled on her, her face still suffused with anger. 'Don't you see he doesn't care what happens to him?' She was almost shouting. 'Well, if he's got a death wish he ought to be in a mental institution and not in charge of an aeroplane. I'm going home; you can come with me if you like or you can stay here, I don't care.'

This was so unlike the Lily she knew that Eve's jaw dropped again, but seeing other people staring she pulled herself together. 'Was it something I said?' she asked humbly. 'Dear Lily, I didn't mean to make you cross, and wherever you're going I'll come with you.' She turned to Hank, who was still sitting on his chair, seemed unmoved by the scene which had just been enacted. 'Did I say something wrong?' she asked anxiously. 'I can be awfully tactless . . .'

'No one said anything wrong, except me, and all I can do is apologise,' Hank said, though neither his face nor his voice looked at all repentant. In fact, Eve thought, he looked rather pleased with himself. Lily too, as she fished out the cloakroom ticket and gave it to one of the workers in exchange for their coats, appeared to have calmed down. She put her arm round Eve's shoulders and gave her a hug. 'I'm sorry, darling. It was nothing to do with you,' she said reassuringly. 'I just got into a state for no real reason. Do you want to sit out the rest of the dance, or shall we look for a taxi?'

The three of them made for the exit and Hank took one of Eve's small hands in his own large one and tucked one of Lily's in his other arm. 'You mustn't worry about me, either of you,' he said. 'I'll be fine. And as for death wishes . . .' he turned to Lily and pinched her cheek, 'you're crazy as a coot if you think that. I wouldn't risk life and limb of any one of my crew, I can promise you. I intend to take nine men out and bring nine men home again.' He smiled at her. 'Should I apologise? Only I don't quite know what I would be apologising for.'

There was a short pause before Lily spoke. 'I don't know what came over me,' she said in a small voice. 'We all have a job to do in wartime, but everyone keeps telling us the conflict is nearly over and I suppose I thought you'd done your bit.' She looked shyly up into Hank's homely face. 'Will you forgive me? I said things I didn't mean and I'm heartily ashamed of myself. Please, Hank, can we forget every word I said? Because they weren't my words, not really.' She gave a tiny chuckle. 'I bet you never thought you'd see me lose my temper. Well, now you know I'm just a shrew with a spiteful tongue which I have to be careful to keep under wraps. Oh, Hank, you're the best friend I've ever had and it would break my heart to lose you. Say you forgive me! Say you'll forget every word I uttered. Say . . . ah. Here's a taxi with his flag down.'

Hank smiled at Lily and raised a white eyebrow. 'Forgive you? For what? Just get aboard that taxi, my woman. Isn't that what they say round here?'

As she lay in her small bed in the attic, Eve remembered how on her last evening in the Close she had realised that she could not wait to return to the life she loved.

She had had a wonderful holiday, a real break from routine. She had met a great many people, some of whom she liked very much, Robin Maddon for one. At the tea dance he had promised to write to her and to come to the station the next day to see her off. He had even promised to spend his next leave at Drake's Farm if they could put him up for a couple of nights, but as she had packed her suitcase Eve had thought that this promise was unlikely to be kept. Robin was kind and good-looking and obviously attracted to her, but she was several years younger than he, and once she got back to Devon she doubted that she would think of him as anything more than a pen pal. Her old life would take over and she would seldom think of the friends she had made in Norwich, though Lily of course was different. The bond between her and Eve was warm and strong and would never be forgotten. Furthermore, Eve had learned important lessons from the older girl. The realisation that it was character which counted, and not looks or charm, had made her see everything in a clearer light, and on the day she returned to Devonshire and stepped off the train in the familiar little station to see Johnny, Connie, Chrissie and Uncle Reg lining the platform, tears of joy had literally spurted from her eyes, making the waiting committee laugh.

Eve gave a watery smile. 'I'm crying for joy, not sorrow,' she explained. 'I had a lovely holiday, Lily made sure of that, but I was terribly homesick for Drake's Farm and missed every single one of you.' She glanced around her. 'It's been so long since I lived anywhere but Devon that it's more my home – my real home – than that horrid London flat could ever be. Even if Chrissie and I could go back there, we wouldn't want to. It's odd, but somehow the farm has become our home and the flat seems to belong to Mummy and Daddy and have no connection with us. Did you bring the trap, Uncle Reg? It'll be a bit of a squeeze, won't it?'

Uncle Reg led the way out of the station and pointed with a flourish at the vehicle which awaited them. 'We brought the old hay wain, because since everyone wanted to meet the train we needed plenty of room,' he explained. 'Hop aboard, the lot of you; there's a grand supper all laid out on the kitchen table to welcome our best girl home. All aboard? Off we go then.'

Eve, squeezed between Connie and Johnny, had never felt happier. One glance at Johnny's freckled face with the broad grin that revealed a chipped tooth was enough to tell her he regretted the way they had parted.

'Are you all right?' he asked. 'Golly, we missed you! No one ever realised how much work you did, but Chrissie's been a real help, never grumbling no matter what he was asked to do. Now tell us, did you have a good time? I reckon you met plenty of fellers all eager to take you dancing and show you the sights. Reckon you never gave us a thought once you settled in.'

There was not much space even in the hay wain, but Eve swivelled round and gave Johnny a good old-fashioned glare.

'You may be fickle, Johnny Durrell, but I'm not,' she said severely. 'I met lots of people, some nice, some nasty. There was one in particular, an American Liberator pilot called Hank. He was nice. I suppose we were friends, but other than that there was nobody to compare with my pals here.'

'Well, if you say so, but a couple of letters came for

you this morning. Auntie Bess wouldn't let us open them so they're waiting by your plate.' Johnny scowled. 'One of them has S.W.A.L.K. written on the back.' He ground his teeth. 'Bloody silly thing to write on an envelope, I thought. I was in two minds whether to chuck it on the fire, but Auntie Bess said you weren't likely to take it seriously, not once you were back at Drake's Farm.'

Eve laughed. 'Now I'm back nothing else matters,' she said joyfully, recognising that the time had come to ask the question which had been uppermost in her mind since she left the Close. 'Oh, Johnny, I missed your ugly mug so much. Have you missed me?' She was watching his face as she spoke and saw the colour rise from the collar of his open shirt, but knowing Johnny – and she *did* know Johnny – she doubted very much whether he would put his feelings into words. However, he punched her shoulder rather hard, making her squeal in protest.

'I missed you at milking time and when we were rounding up the cows at the end of the day,' he admitted. 'But now you're back, and that's all that matters.'

When the hay wain drew up in the farmyard Eve was the first to climb down, though Chrissie came a close second, bubbling over with excitement at seeing his sister back on Drake's Farm once more. Together they ran into the kitchen, where Eve flung her arms round Auntie Bess and kissed that lady's florid pink cheek.

'It's so good to see you, Auntie Bess. I've missed you so dreadfully,' she said. 'Gosh, you've spirited up some jam and cream! I never had anything near so good in Norwich and can't wait to sink my teeth into one of your gorgeous scones.' She picked up the letter that had so outraged Johnny and ripped it open, scanning the contents swiftly. As she had guessed, it had come from Robin, and contained only the promise that he missed her and would write weekly to give her all the news he thought would interest her. 'Well, nothing much has happened since I left,' she said. 'But I suppose it's kindly meant, so I won't throw it away until I've answered it.'

As she picked up the second letter Chrissie gave a squeak of excitement. 'That one isn't just for you, it's for me as well. I recognise the writing,' he said triumphantly. 'Is she coming to see us? It's been ages since she visited the farm.'

Reading, Eve shook her head, then looked sadly at Chrissie. 'Oh, darling, I'm so sorry to be giving you bad news. Mummy's boss has been posted to the north of Scotland and has asked her to go with him – apparently she's the best secretary he's ever had. She doesn't say so, but I'm sure she'll do her best to come and see us before she leaves.' She smiled reassuringly at her small brother. 'Look, Chrissie, the war will soon be over, and then we'll be able to see Mummy whenever we want. We may even be able to go back to the flat; would you like that?'

Chrissie's lower lip trembled and his blue eyes filled with tears. 'I don't want to go back to the flat,' he said sullenly. 'Suppose one of those doodlebugs gets us? But I'm only staying with Auntie Bess until Mummy finds us somewhere nicer to live. I hate it here, Eve Armstrong, and I hate you!'

Eve gasped. When Chrissie was in a temper she knew he said spiteful things which he did not really mean, but this seemed unusually bitter. After all, he had been nothing but a baby when they had left the flat, and Mummy had come to the farm so rarely that Eve had imagined his memories of her would be very hazy. It seemed she was wrong. She began to say, soothingly, that there was nowhere nicer than Drake's Farm in the whole country, but Chrissie, his eyes still narrow with rage, turned on her and punched her in the side as hard as he could.

'You!' he exclaimed. 'You don't care what happens to Mummy, and she doesn't care what happens to you. You don't like her and she doesn't like you, not even the tiniest bit. If she goes off to Scotland and you never see her again you'll be quite happy.' He glared defiantly up at her. 'You'd like to live at Drake's Farm for the rest of your life so long as you could see Daddy now and then. Well, I don't care what happens to you and Daddy. It's Mummy who matters to me.'

Uncle Reg leaned across the table and caught hold of Chrissie's clenched fist. 'I think you'd best unsay those remarks,' he said quietly. 'I know you're disappointed because your mother is going to be a long way away for a while, but that's no reason to insult folk who've done their best to make you feel at home. I thought you loved the farm and were happy staying here. Well, perhaps I'm wrong. Perhaps you would really prefer to go to the wilds of northern Scotland to be with your mum.

If so, I can arrange for that to happen tomorrow. How would that suit you? Eve wouldn't go with you, of course, because we need her here on the farm, but after the things you've just said – if you meant 'em – I don't s'pose that would bother you.'

For a moment Chrissie just stared around the table, as though looking for support. Then he burst into tears, jumped off his chair and cast himself on to Auntie Bess's lap, burying his face on her ample bosom and flinging his arms round her neck.

'I didn't mean it, I truly didn't mean any of it,' he cried. 'Drake's Farm is the loveliest place in the whole world, and I wouldn't change it even if I could. I don't want to go to Scotland, but oh, it's such a long time since I've seen Mummy, and now she's going so far away from me and maybe I'll never see her again.'

Auntie Bess kissed the top of his curly head and stood him down beside her. 'For a little 'un you've a rare nasty tongue,' she said with a chuckle, although Eve thought her eyes looked suspiciously bright. 'You've insulted every single person sitting round this table without any cause. You say your mummy doesn't love Eve, but how do you know that? After all, when she comes to visit it's as much to see Eve as it is to see you, Chrissie. And saying you hate it here isn't very kind to Uncle Reg and me, is it?'

Chrissie grabbed her hand and planted a kiss on her palm. 'I didn't mean it, I didn't mean it,' he wept. 'I don't want to go back to the flat when the war's over nor I don't want to go to Scotland. Oh, Auntie Bess, let me stay with you, please. I'm truly sorry I said what I did, and I didn't mean a word of it.' He turned round to face Eve. 'I do love you, Evie, honest I do, and I s'pose Mummy does too, even if I'm her favourite.' He turned to Uncle Reg. 'Must I say sorry to every single person round the table,' he asked hopefully, 'or can I just say a big sorry to everyone?'

'A big sorry will do,' Uncle Reg told him. 'As for being Mummy's favourite, just you remember, young man, that there's enough love to go round for everyone. Of course it's meant to be spread evenly, but I bet most mums and dads, in their secret heart, have a favourite child. After all, you said yourself that you have a favourite parent! Now come and sit down and let's finish our tea.'

Now that he was back in the air, Hank hoped that the dreams – or rather the nightmares – would stop. They all started the same way: climbing into the ship with his crew and carrying out the pre-flight checks. Only then did the true nightmare begin, for he found himself in a strange aircraft with no idea what his checks should be. He was on his knees in the dark, gazing around him, a bit like Jonah in the whale, and he needed to get to the tail end. The tail gunner, a friend of long standing, would be waiting for him. Crouching, for there was not a great deal of head room, he made his way towards him just as the aircraft gave a warning shudder, someone shouted something, the ship speeded up and then smoothed out and he knew they were airborne. Someone near him muttered that it would be a fair while before they were over the target and he realised, with a sinking sensation in the pit of his stomach, that several hours of boredom awaited him, as well as the fear which clutched at every heart aboard though not one man would admit to it.

He was halfway back to the tail when he recalled that he was the skipper and should be up front. What use was he stumbling along in the dark of the fuselage? Time concertinaed; he was in his seat, they were over the target, he could see buildings below, and he turned his head to apologise to the co-pilot for his temporary absence. The person sitting next to him was Lily. She put out a hand and gripped his knee.

'The bomb aimer's bought it,' she said quietly. She smiled at him, a very sweet smile. 'We're on the way home, dear Hank, and won't need to keep radio silence once we've crossed the Channel. Will you be all right if I leave you? I won't be gone long.'

He heard the Messerschmitt before he saw it, seized the joystick and turned to the navigator.

'How much further have we got to go?' he said, and even as he spoke the Messerschmitt dived and Hank heard the rip of the bullets as they hit their target. Someone screamed – he thought it was himself – and then they were spiralling down towards the North Sea. He pulled himself to his knees – suddenly he was back in the fuselage of the mighty plane – and then the pain was such that he knew he'd been hit.

Hank sat up and pushed a hand through his damp hair. Phew. The bed was narrow and he must have turned too suddenly on his still sensitive leg and woken himself up. He glanced at his wristwatch and heaved a

sigh. It would be three hours before he could reasonably get up and start a new day, and he was sure he
wouldn't be able to sleep again. The curtains were drawn
back, and when he propped himself on one elbow he
could see there had been a frost during the night. The
branches of the trees outside were white with it, and
the grass too. Hank told himself he should think of
home and see if that helped to calm him, but before he
could even visualise the small farmhouse in Connecti-
cut his head had fallen back on the pillow and he was
fast asleep.

Chapter Twelve

Eve opened sleep-blurred eyes and took stock of her surroundings. She was in her little bed in the attic, which was now only occupied by herself and Miranda. Chrissie had moved into the small room at the foot of the attic stairs, the one which Johnny had once occupied, and Connie had gone home to Liverpool. Propping herself up on one elbow, Eve knuckled her eyes as she peered at the alarm clock which stood on the stool between her bed and Miranda's. Two a.m. No wonder she felt so tired. She wondered what had caused her to wake up, but could think of no reason. Slowly, she lay back down and rolled on to her side. It had been eight months since she had returned from Norwich and an awful lot had changed in that time, not necessarily for the better.

Eve had picked up her share of the workload with ease and thoroughly enjoyed throwing herself back into the daily routine. Once again she and Miriam would do one milking shift whilst Johnny and Miranda did the other. Chrissie too was getting to be a dab hand around the livestock and connected well with the cows, the pigs and the poultry. Eve smiled to herself, thinking that this was probably because at some stage or other most of the livestock had mistaken Chrissie's golden curls for hay or corn. She had seen Daisy trying to grasp his locks with her long tongue and ending up licking the side of Chrissie's face, causing him to giggle and squirm.

Robin Maddon had stayed true to his word and wrote to Eve regularly, to Johnny's obvious annoyance, telling her all about life in the army and how everyone believed that the war would soon be over. He never went into too much detail about how the war was affecting him or his friends, but she knew that he loved receiving her letters about life on Drake's Farm. He would ask after the cows by name, and who had been champion milker that week. Eve was always eager to fill him in on all the details concerning the various animals, but quite early on she realised that she never mentioned Johnny in her letters to Robin, although she was not entirely sure why. She supposed it was because she thought Robin would not be interested in the human inhabitants of Drake's Farm, as he had never met any of them.

Then had come the day when everything changed for ever. It was a clear winter morning and everyone was eating breakfast when Auntie Bess had walked slowly into the kitchen, a handful of letters in her floury hand, and handed them over to their various recipients.

'Two, no three, for our Eve,' she had said as she passed the envelopes over Chrissie's head to his sister. 'One for you, Reg – looks like it's from the Ministry – one for Connie, from your ma if I'm not mistaken, and one for you, Johnny.' She turned to stare at him. 'It looks official.'

The room had fallen silent as Johnny fingered his letter before picking up a knife and slitting along the top of the envelope. He pulled out the sheet of thin paper within and read what was typed thereon, then placed it back in the envelope. When he looked up his eyes met a sea of expectant faces.

His own face had been flushed, and he was beaming. 'I'm in,' he said, unable to keep the excitement out of his voice. 'I've got a week before I have to go, but I've finally been accepted.'

Uncle Reg had whooped and clapped him on the shoulder, and Auntie Bess had beamed at him. Chrissie had looked at him in awe.

'Crikey, Johnny, just think. You'll be flyin' in one of them Spitfires soon, or a bomber! Wow!' he said, his eyes sparkling with admiration.

Johnny had looked proudly at Eve and Connie. 'Not going to congratulate your old pal? All this time I've been hoping and praying, and now . . .'

Eve had stood up and walked round the table to place both hands on Johnny's shoulders. 'If it's what you want, then of course I'm pleased,' she said, 'but I won't try to pretend that I'm not frightened for you, or that I won't worry about you.' She leaned forward and gave him a peck on the cheek, and as she did so she saw that he was looking past her towards Connie, his brows rising.

'Well?' he said.

Connie shrugged. 'Good for you! At least you'll get away from this place, so it can't be all bad.' She stood up and headed towards the stairs, calling over her shoulder as she went, 'I shan't be here too much longer myself. My mother has written to say that I can come home now that it looks as though my auntie Cassie has found somewhere else to live. Her place was hit by an incendiary bomb and she's been staying with them ever since, but they think she'll be gone soon. They're hoping so – my father has reopened the shop and could do with my help.'

Eve and Chrissie had exchanged glances, then Chrissie spoke up. 'That'll mean it'll be just you and me, Evie.' He looked perplexed. 'We'll be the only children at Drake's Farm.'

Eve nodded and sank back into her chair. All this change in one morning's breakfast. She couldn't quite believe it. It did seem that the war would soon be over, and she had always thought that the day peace was declared would be the best day of her life, but now she realised that it wouldn't just be the war that would end, but her life as she knew it at Drake's Farm as well. With Johnny leaving, the farm would not be the same. Yet the cows would still need milking, the hens and pigs want feeding, the horses need grooming . . . in fact there would be an awful lot more work to do when Johnny was no longer there. She had said as much to Auntie Bess.

The older woman had shrugged. 'We'll cope, dear, we always do. If you remember, Eve, before you came to the farm there was only Lily, Miriam and Mabel here to help, and even with Johnny gone there'll still be you, Connie, Chrissie and the terrible twins, so there's no need to fret.' She smiled at Eve's concerned face. 'Although I think it's more the company you'll miss than the help. Lord knows we all will. The farm is a livelier place for having a bunch of youngsters around, so you're not the only one who'll feel the impact when Johnny leaves.'

Auntie Bess had stood up to start on the dishes, handing a tea towel to Chrissie as she did so. 'I'll wash and you can dry,' she said. 'Everyone moves on; that's what happens in life. Our Bob has a sweetheart in France and from what I can gather from his letters it appears that she's not keen on coming over here to live. What's more, her father has a large farm and could do with Bob's help . . .' She shook her head sadly. 'When this war does end it will be a wondrous day, but not without cost.'

Now, lying in her small bed, Eve wiped a tear from her cheek. Auntie Bess had been right. Within a couple of weeks of getting his papers Johnny had left Drake's Farm. They had had a farewell supper for him the night before he was due to catch his train, and when everyone had finished eating Auntie Bess had sent the children off for a walk around the farm whilst she, Miriam and Miranda cleared everything away.

Johnny, Eve, Connie and Chrissie had visited each of the animals in turn, Johnny ruffling manes, patting the prickly hairs on the pigs' backs and stroking the cows' foreheads as he said his goodbyes. Once he had finished his farewell tour, he turned to the others.

'Now what? How about a moonlight stroll down the lane?'

'I'm not walking down that lane in the pitch dark! If you two want to go wandering around the woods at night, tripping over tree roots, that's your lookout, but I won't be coming.' Connie had turned to Chrissie. 'You'd better come back with me, 'cos Auntie Bess'll be ever so angry if she thinks I've let you go wandering around at night with these two.'

Chrissie had opened his mouth to object, but Eve had said quickly, 'She's quite right, Chrissie. Auntie Bess doesn't like you being out after dark.'

Chrissie had been about to argue, but thought better of it and followed Connie back to the house, dragging his feet a little but making no further protest. Johnny watched them go, then turned to Eve.

'How about going to say goodbye to the badgers?'

Eve had gaped at him. 'Gosh, Johnny, I'd forgotten all about them! Do you suppose they're still there?'

'I don't know – I haven't been to look for months.' He had smiled at her. 'But let's see, shall we?'

They had turned into the lane and started to stroll down towards the stream when Johnny suddenly caught hold of Eve's hand and gave it a friendly shake. 'Do you realise, Miss Armstrong, that this is the first place we met, officially I mean? I don't count the time at New Cross station.'

Eve had smiled and squeezed his fingers. 'Yes, I remember. Gosh, Johnny, how long ago was that now?' She cocked her head on one side. 'More than five years! But it doesn't seem that long at all.' She slid her hand from his and tucked it into the crook of his elbow. 'I never thought the war would last this long, or that I would end up thinking of Devon as my home and not London.' She looked up into his sparkling blue eyes and thought how he'd grown. 'Do you see Devon as your home more than London too? Or is it just me and Chrissie?' Before Johnny could reply, she continued, 'I suppose it's different for you, because your mother is very loving and homey . . .'

Johnny had stopped walking and was looking at Eve with his head tilted on one side. 'I'm sure your mother loves you, Eve; she's just not what you'd call a typical mother. She's more of a career woman.' He ruffled her hair. 'Who couldn't love our little Evie?' he said, a broad grin spreading across his freckled face.

Eve had felt a hot blush spread up her neck and invade her cheeks, and she gave him a playful shove. 'You haven't answered my question. Do you see London as your home, or Drake's Farm.?'

Johnny had gazed through the bare branches of the trees at the silver moonlight as he considered the question. 'Well, I guess if you can say that home is where the heart is . . .' he looked down into Eve's face, his eyes twinkling, 'then I guess my home would be here. With Auntie Bess and Uncle Reg and you . . . oh, and everybody.' He took Eve's hand again and gave it a small squeeze.

By now they were quite close to the badgers' sett, and suddenly Eve stopped and pulled Johnny to a halt beside her, placing a finger to her lips and pointing between the trees. Shuffling his way along a narrow path, apparently unaware of their presence, was the badger. Slowly, Johnny pulled Eve down to crouch behind some saplings, his face alive with excitement and happiness, and they watched the badger out of sight.

Eve had turned to her companion. 'Well! How lucky was that? Oh, Johnny, he was so beautiful, and he looked so happy going about his everyday business, undisturbed by anyone or anything.'

Johnny had nodded, placing a finger to his lips. They had started to make their way back to the stream when he stopped and bent down to pluck something from underneath a fallen log. Straightening, he twiddled whatever it was he had found round and round between his figures before lifting it to his nose and gingerly smelling it.

Eve had pulled a face. 'What are you doing, Johnny Durrell? I hope that's nothing disgusting, what with you sticking it in your face like that!'

He had held up a large tuft of grey-black hair. 'Badger fur!' he said triumphantly. He offered it to Eve, and she took it between her fingers.

'Today was definitely our day for badgers,' she had said, laughing. 'Oh, Johnny, you are clever! Fancy you noticing that.'

Now, Eve smiled at the memory as she lay in her cosy little bed. What were the odds, she wondered, of seeing the badger the very first time they went on an expedition together and the very last time too? It was as if she and Johnny were the real caretakers of the badgers; as though the badgers would only ever show themselves to the two of them. She knew it was nonsense, of course, but it made her feel as though she and Johnny shared a special bond.

She snuggled further down between the bedclothes. Spring was not far off, but the nights were still chilly. Closing her eyes, she let her thoughts return to Johnny's last night at Drake's Farm.

Once Johnny thought they were far enough from the sett they had congratulated themselves again on their good fortune.

'I think he must've sensed it was your last night, so he came to say his goodbyes,' Eve had said as they made their way back to the lane. 'He was probably thanking us for keeping him and his family safe all this time, and wishing you well in your posting.'

Johnny had grinned, and given Eve a nudge with his elbow. 'You're daft, you are, Eve Armstrong, but there ain't a bad bone in your body.'

Eve had returned his grin. 'I won't half miss you when you've gone, Johnny. Not just because you're such a help around the farm, but you're good company too.'

Johnny had placed an arm round her shoulders. 'I promise I'll come and visit whenever I have leave. I know I won't be able to fly planes for a long time because I'm not old enough, but for now I'm just happy to do whatever I can to help send those bloomin' Nazis back to where they came from.' He looked down at Eve and raised his brows. 'You know, if the war really is coming to an end as quickly as they think it is, it won't be long before you and Chrissie leave Drake's Farm too.'

Eve had stopped short. 'Well, it depends when

Mummy and Daddy are demobilised – is that the word? – but I suppose you're right.' She looked appealingly into Johnny's sparkling blue eyes. 'Johnny, I've realised I don't want to go back to London, or anywhere else for that matter. Drake's Farm is my home, and Chrissie's.' She paused. 'We're not city people any more, we're country folk, and Mummy won't understand how we feel as she's city through and through.' She'll expect me to be like her and get a job in an office sitting behind a desk all day, at the beck and call of some boss or other! Making him cups of tea and arranging his diary and typing his letters.' She shook her head in frustration. 'Oh, Johnny, I can't! It's just not me. I'd go bonkers, sitting indoors all day . . .'

Johnny had smiled down at her and smoothed a hand reassuringly over her wavy locks. 'Eve Armstrong, you're worrying over nothing. Even if the war ends tomorrow, it'll be a long time before your father is discharged from the Navy, and from what you've told me I think your mother may choose to continue working too, which would mean you'd have to stay at Drake's Farm for a good while yet.' He slid his hand into hers. 'You and Chrissie have plenty of time ahead of you, because I'm sure Auntie Bess isn't in any rush to see you leave. From what she said tonight she's not looking forward to the thought of having no children at Drake's Farm, so don't you go worrying about what hasn't happened yet.'

Looking into her companion's freckled face, Eve felt sure that he was right. Smiling up at him, she had nodded. 'Thanks, Johnny,' she said. 'I feel a lot better now, and I know you'll be true to your word and come back to see us whenever you can.'

Now, lying in her bed, Eve felt a small tear trickle down her cheek. Gosh, how she missed Johnny. They had all gone to the station to see him off, Auntie Bess, the land girls and Eve all dabbing their eyes with hankies, Uncle Reg and the farmhands admiring the locomotive and Chrissie chattering in excited tones to the engine driver.

Connie had joined the farewell party, although Eve wished she hadn't when the other girl barely managed to raise a hand in farewell as Johnny's train puffed its way out of the station, before eventually disappearing round the bend with only its trail of smoke still visible. She had met Eve's reproachful look with one of contempt.

'One down and one to go,' she had said in a sharp tone. 'Johnny's the lucky one, getting out of this dump.' She brushed what Eve felt sure was an imaginary speck of dirt off her jumper. 'Still, fingers crossed it won't be long before I'm on a train heading for dear old Liverpool.'

Chrissie had shot Connie a look of disdain. 'There won't be many tears shed the day you say goodbye, Connie Hale. They'll put that much bunting out people'll think the King's comin' to visit.'

'Christopher Armstrong!' Auntie Bess's voice had boomed along the platform. 'There's no need for that.' She turned to Connie. 'He's just upset, dear – we all are.'

Eve had looked into Connie's face and was surprised to see a look of hurt in the other girl's eyes. In all the time Eve had known Connie she had not once seen her get tearful over anything. Normally she would spin into a rage with whoever had offended her, but not today. Unexpectedly touched, Eve put a hand on her arm. 'We're all going to miss Johnny, but he'll be okay, you know.'

The hurt look had vanished as Connie's eyes narrowed. 'I couldn't care less,' she had said disdainfully. 'I just wish I was on my way home.' She gave Eve a condescending smile. 'I'm like your mum, Eve, I'm city through and through. Mud and animals just aren't my cup of tea. In fact, I bet if anyone saw us together they'd think I was your mother's daughter and that you were a Faversham.'

At that point they had heard Uncle Reg calling them and begun to make their way to the hay wain, which Uncle Reg referred to as 'the bus', but Connie hadn't finished. 'I've found it pretty awful living here,' she went on. 'You, Chrissie and Johnny all love life on the farm, looking after the animals and helping with the harvest, but I don't. I love shopping in the city, going to the cinema and eating out at restaurants.' She looked down her nose at Eve. 'We're completely different people.'

As Eve remembered this conversation, her sorrow was replaced with annoyance. Connie, who couldn't give two hoots about Johnny, had received several letters from him, yet Eve hadn't received so much as a note. She sat up in bed and gave her pillow a good thumping. Boys! They just couldn't see what was right under their noses. Eve would have bent over backwards to make Johnny happy, yet it seemed that as far as he was concerned she might never have existed.

Chapter Thirteen

August 1945

Lily had promised herself that when peace was declared and she was free, to a certain extent anyway, to do as she liked, she would return to Drake's Farm. Despite all the promises the government had made, however, it seemed as though the young men coming back to the jobs they had once occupied no longer wished to become, as one man put it, 'ploughboys' once more. They needed jobs in order to keep themselves and their families, but during their absence they had learned a lot. Living in the cities had more to offer, in terms of both money to be earned and opportunity to exercise the skills they had acquired as members of the armed forces. Men who had followed the plough uncomplainingly, when offered their old jobs back, pointed out that they were mechanics, or engineers, or even aircrew. And in the meantime the country could not function without the land girls. It was all very well for Waafs, Wrens and ATS; they could stay or go as they pleased, but people had to be fed, and with many men unwilling to return to their former agricultural occupations it seemed to Lily that there was small chance of being demobbed just yet. Oh, it had started; the day would come when her name would be called and she would be expected to leave the countryside and become a shop girl, or a factory hand, or take some other job until she found a husband, but that day was not yet.

Lily had tightened her lips at the thought. She had talked it over with Mr Parker, who professed himself not just willing but eager to keep Lily on as one of his workers. His cowman had been killed in action over the Ruhr, and Mr Parker had no desire to start another man from scratch.

'Of course there's no saying how long you'd be a land girl,' he had said slowly. 'I don't know what we'd call you. Cowgirl sounds a bit too like the movies, but I suppose the title doesn't matter. It's the job that counts, and I don't mind telling you that it's not every-one me and the missus would want to take on board now that peace is here at last.' He had pulled a wry face. 'I dunno as I should have guessed what would happen, but after six years of war it never occurred to me that fellers who'd flown planes or driven tanks wouldn't take kindly to herding sheep or milking cows.'

He had looked quizzically at Lily. 'You're a grand lass, and you don't need me to tell you that you could have your pick of the young men round these parts. Suppose you fell for one of them? It's idle to pretend that you could cope with the job when the babbies came along. Don't tell me you don't want a family of your own, because I'm sure you do. I've seen you with kids; on VE Day you were in your element, playing games with the little 'uns.

'And what if you suddenly decide to light off on me? They aren't just British lads a-knockin' on our back door and askin' if you're ready to go to the dance. There's a Frenchie who's very particular in his attentions, and a fair number of Yanks who come a-callin' whenever they've got free time. They get short shrift from the missus, I can tell you. Half of them seem to think you live here.' He had looked hard at Lily. 'Someone told me that most of the doughboys have already been either sent home or promised a speedy release, and some of 'em have just about convinced their sweethearts that they own big ranches – which is what they call their farms – when the only ranch their family possesses is four square feet of earth in a window box in New York City!' He had cocked a shrewd eye at Lily. 'Suppose one of yours is speakin' the truth; how about that, eh?'

'I've no fancy to leave England,' Lily assured him. 'Come to that I've never met the man who could lure me away from farm work. But before I start as your official cowgirl I need to take some leave. I'll arrange it for whenever you can manage without me, but I promised myself that when peace came I'd go back to Devonshire and thank the Favershams for all they did for me. What do you say to that?'

'I say that's fair and square and would suit me just fine.'

*   *   *

300

'Hank Ruskin! You and I are supposed to be good friends; in fact I'd go one further and say you're my best friend. You know as well as I do that once you're off to America we may never meet again, so why, for heaven's sake, won't you come with me to Drake's Farm? I've told you how hospitable the Favershams are and you said yourself you'd like to see young Eve again, so why not come with me? Honest to God, you'd be as welcome as the flowers in May. I'd even buy your ticket if you'd agree to come.'

The two of them were in the Kendals' kitchen, Lily making sandwiches for her journey and Hank preparing a flask of coffee which he would presently add to the basket of goodies. It was very early in the morning and no one else in the house was up, Mr and Mrs Kendal having bidden their daughter farewell the previous evening, when Lily had told them very firmly that she had no intention of dragging them from their bads when Hank had already offered to come round first thing and see her off.

'Yes, we're good friends,' Hank said now, screwing the top on to the coffee flask, 'but if I came with you to Drake's Farm it would give rise to talk.'

Lily sniffed. 'I don't care what people say; you're my best friend and we're going to be parted soon enough by thousands of miles of sea. And I've told you so much about Drake's Farm that surely you must want to see it for yourself? If I were in your position I know I'd long to meet the Favershams and young Johnny, to say nothing of everyone else.'

Hank had pulled a face. 'No matter who I'd meet it

wouldn't be this Johnny Durrell,' he pointed out. 'Didn't you tell me he'd joined the RAF? And I'm pretty sure Eve said in one of her letters that he would be amongst the last to be demobbed, so I doubt whether I shall ever meet him.' He looked at Lily under his white lashes. 'I've not told you, but there's a liner sailing for the United States in a couple of weeks and I shall almost certainly be aboard.'

For one moment the kitchen was so still, so silent, that it was as though a magical spell had been cast upon it. Then Lily realised that Hank's last remark had hit her like a hammer blow in the stomach, so that she had to make a conscious effort to breathe normally again. For a moment she could only stare at him, trying to take it in. Life without Hank seemed suddenly impossible to imagine. The summer was almost over, he had had his discharge papers weeks and weeks ago, yet he was still here and she had come, insensibly, to believe that he always would be. Yet he had spoken quite calmly, as though she must have known that parting was imminent. Lily looked away from him, towards the neatly packed rucksack, and spoke as lightly as she could.

'As soon as that? How long have you known? You might have told me before, Hank. I don't believe I'd be spending my leave in Devonshire if I'd known you were going so soon.' She gave him the travesty of a smile and held out the rucksack. 'Oh well, if you've made up your mind at last there isn't much I can do about it. Do Mother and Father know you're leaving so soon? I don't think they can, because they haven't said a word. Indeed, I believe my mother has been looking round for some sort of job for you. I mean, I'm sure she never thought you intended to stay for ever, just that you might need something to do whilst you were still here. When did you say the ship sailed?'

'I didn't, not exactly,' Hank said. 'But I've heard from several people that she'll be setting sail, heavily laden with GI brides, around the time you come back from Drake's Farm.' He grinned uncertainly. 'Thinking of becoming a GI bride yourself? I bet you've had plenty of opportunities.'

Lily felt a flush creep up her neck and into her cheeks. 'The man I wanted never asked,' she said stiffly. 'And the others can go to Putney on a pig.'

Hank laughed and raised his eyebrows. 'That's one British expression I've never heard,' he said. 'In the States we say someone can go to hell on a handcart. Well, they say we're two countries divided by a common language, and how true that is. I've only just got used to saying pavement when I mean sidewalk, and tarmac when I mean blacktop, and now I've got to unlearn everything you've driven into my head over the past few years.'

'Oh, I shouldn't bother if I were you,' Lily said; her tone was cool. She glanced up at the clock above the kitchen mantel. 'Help me on with my rucksack, would you, and let's get going. The journey to Drake's Farm is quite complicated enough without missing the first train.'

Hank followed the direction of her eyes and gave a surprised whistle. 'Doesn't time fly?' he said. 'We'll have to step out, babe, or you really will miss your train.' He walked across the kitchen and opened the door. 'Are you ready?'

'I've been ready for the past half hour, only you would keep on chattering,' Lily snapped. 'You might remember that I walk faster than you. And don't call me babe; it's an expression I simply cannot stand.' She stalked past him, head in the air, and did not see him put out a hand as though he could not bear to let her go, but then they were walking down the path and Hank was assuring her that he could easily outpace her though he seldom bothered to do so. Consequently it became a sort of race to see which of them could reach the station first, and this restored Lily's good humour so that she tried very hard to extract a promise from him not to leave England without a proper farewell. Hank, however, would make no promises, so when they reached the station platform it took a good deal of chaffing to restore good relations. When the train arrived Lily climbed aboard, slung her rucksack up on the string rack overhead and went to lean out of the window so that she and Hank might see the last of one another. Presently the guard waved his little green flag and the train began to move very slowly along the track. Lily leaned out as far as she dared in order to remind her old friend that she could easily leave Drake's Farm a couple of days before she had planned to do so.

'I simply won't let you sneak off to the States without a word of farewell to me,' she shrieked. 'I might even come over to America to make sure you don't forget all about us Brits.'

The train began to gather speed and Lily turned away from the window. She was alone in the compartment, and knowing herself to be unobserved she produced a handkerchief and blew her nose resoundingly. Even as she returned the hankie to her pocket the door slid open and she glanced up to see who had entered. For a moment she could not believe her eyes.

'Hank!' she gasped. 'Oh, Hank, whatever are you doing here? When the train pulled out you were still on the platform, I know you were. How . . . oh, Hank, the next station is miles away, and you've been and gone and got on the train by mistake! Whatever will you do now? I suppose we could pull the communication cord; that will stop the train all right.' She reached up to grasp the red cord but Hank shot out a hand and seized her fingers.

'It's all right, don't get in a state,' he said rather sheepishly. 'I – I've changed my mind. I'm coming to Drake's Farm with you.'

Lily opened her mouth, but it was a few moments before any coherent speech emerged. Hank watched her with the glimmer of a smile, which broadened as she struggled to find her tongue.

'Hank Ruskin, you don't have a single possession with you, let alone a change of clothing or a ticket,' she gabbled at last. 'I know I said the Favershams were hospitable people, but they take paying guests and since you didn't tell anyone you intended to come with me there may not be a spare bedroom to let and the farm is miles from anywhere, so what are you going to do?'

Hank sank into the seat opposite to her own; he did not seem at all fazed by the question. 'I shall borrow anything I need from the nearest USAAF base; the chaps will all rally round when they hear why I'm there,' he said complacently. 'I'll sleep on the base if the Favershams can't put me up. As for clothing – old clothing, I mean – there'll be plenty of that lying around the place.' He grinned at her again. 'I thought you *wanted* me to come with you,' he said in a rather hurt voice. 'I'm only doing what you asked me to, after all. And I've plenty of money – pounds, shillings and pence, not dollars – so I can pay my way. Any more objections, Miss Kendal?'

'Ration book?' Lily said rapidly. Her heart was singing. If he wasn't interested in her romantically – and he said he wasn't – then why would he jump on to the train at the last moment, having already said a conventional goodbye? He had constantly declared that they were nothing but friends and he had no desire for a closer relationship, and when she had occasionally indicated that she would not be unwilling to take things further he had pushed her back, metaphorically if not literally. Was it really because he wanted nothing more than friendship from her, or could it be that he considered himself, for whatever reason, incapable of earning her love? The fact that he had already done so seemed, to Lily, to be beside the point. She had never revealed that she loved him. How could she? Lily was a nicely brought up young lady and nicely brought up young ladies did not propose marriage to young American flyers, especially to one who showed no inclination to reveal anything stronger than liking for herself. But now she had a whole fortnight, a full two weeks, to attempt to discover his true feelings, and one sign that they were not as cool as he pretended was the very fact that he had jumped aboard the train without so much as a platform ticket, and had made it plain that he intended to go with her all the way to her destination.

Hank was a good man, kind and polite to everyone and fiercely protective of his crew, behaving like a father to them despite the fact that a good many of them were older than he. He knew they called him Plug (short for plug-ugly) and Lily resented this on his behalf but Hank did not.

'What does it matter?' he asked reasonably. 'It isn't looks that take the Lib into the air and bring her back safely. They can call me the Hunchback of Notre Dame for all I care.'

'But you aren't a hunchback,' Lily had pointed out, and wondered why Hank roared with laughter.

'See what I mean?' he had asked when he could speak again. 'No, I'm not a hunchback, but you never said I wasn't plug-ugly.'

Lily had started to protest, but realised she had fallen into her own trap and laughed with him. She had been hopeful, then, that he would begin to behave in the way so many of his compatriots did; would in fact fall in love with her and ask her to be his wife. People laughed about GI brides but Lily thought them romantic, and was sad when Hank disclosed that the tales told to these wide-eyed wondering English girls were quite often nothing like the truth which awaited them.

But when they find out – if they find out – they'll make the best of it, Lily told herself. Some of them have made enquiries and backed out; well, maybe they're right, but I'd just think of it as a new start in a new country, a long way from rationing, hard work and promises of better times to come which may never be kept. If I were a GI bride I'd take the rough with the smooth, and if I could no longer believe every word my husband said at least I'd be secure in the knowledge that he'd wanted me badly enough to go to any lengths to get me. And if those girls love their GIs, that's all that really matters.

But now here they were sitting opposite one another on the train, making their way to Drake's Farm. Once I see how he behaves when I have all my friends around me I shall know whether he's truly indifferent or only pretending to be, and if he is I shall back away so fast that my heels will smoke, she told herself. But until then I shall live in hope, because if there's one thing that's absolutely certain, it is that I love Hank Ruskin and want to spend the rest of my life with him. And if, at the end of the fortnight, I still don't know his true feelings then I'm not the girl I think I am.

Having made up her mind, Lily decided to do her best to enjoy the rest of her journey. She had sufficient faith in the Favershams' hospitality to know that if they did not have a room free for Hank they would find him accommodation elsewhere. Everything was in turmoil still, but she knew that Spindlebush Farm was as large and commodious as Drake's Farm itself, knew that somewhere or other Hank would be a welcome guest. The fact that he came without so much as a toothbrush was easily explained. They would tell their prospective hosts that his neatly packed bags had been left back at the USAAF base in Norfolk, for what was the point, if he truly intended to lug them half a world away, in carting them all the way to Devon and back beforehand?

As Lily had thought, the Favershams took the unexpected guest in their stride. Auntie Bess said easily that Hank could have the bedroom once occupied by Johnny, and Chrissie could move back into the attic with Eve, Lily and Miranda for the time being, Connie having left practically as soon as her aunt had begun to pack her bags. She would, the Favershams declared, be far happier in the city of her birth even though the devastation wrought by the Luftwaffe had, she had once confessed, made that once proud port almost unrecognisable. In the back of the hay wain, as it trundled along the country lanes, Hank leaned closer to Eve.

'And how are you enjoying the peace?' he asked. 'Don't forget you are the only person in this . . . vehicle' – he pronounced it 'vee-hicle' – 'apart from Lily who knows me from Adam. Mrs Faversham tried to introduce me to everyone and sort out who was which but I'm afraid I've still got muddled. Which one is Connie? Her name used to appear quite often in your letters.' He dropped his voice still further, casting a quick glance around the passengers behind them. 'I somehow got the feeling that Connie was not your favourite person. Even Lily, who likes everyone,

309

seemed a little doubtful whether she was on the side of the angels, so to speak.'

Eve giggled. 'That's putting it mildly,' she said. 'Connie came as an evacuee but I don't think she liked the countryside particularly. She was what they call a one for the fellers, and when the boys started to leave she grew more and more unhappy with her lot. In fact she abandoned ship, as my father would say, the minute her parents could have her back.'

'Aha,' Hank said, rather obscurely. 'What was she like to look at? It sounds a silly question, but if a girl's got "it" looks don't always matter.'

Eve wrinkled her forehead in thought. 'She was certainly very pretty,' she admitted. 'And I've heard other people talk about a girl's having "it", but I'm really not at all sure how one would recognise it. Would it help if I said that when we were all at school together there was always a certain amount of jostling amongst the boys to sit next to Connie.' She turned round rather astonished eyes on Hank's face. 'I wish I was better at descriptions, but all I can truthfully say about Connie is that she was pretty, and there were occasions when she was really quite nice. Usually to boys, I admit, but I do remember one occasion at least when she took my side and needn't have done so. It was when I skied a tennis ball about a hundred feet in the air and it got wedged in an old chimney. Johnny – he was my particular friend – got hurt and blamed me . . . oh, but that's all in the past. I don't suppose anyone else remembers the incident, so let's talk about something else.'

'Ah, that's another name I recognise,' Hank said, once more glancing around the crowded vehicle. 'Johnny Durrell, wasn't it? But he was older than you and didn't hang around when he had a chance to join the forces. Have I got that right?'

'Not quite,' Eve said. 'Johnny was keen to join the RAF, only at first they turned him down. He took Uncle Reg's advice, though, and tried again, and on his next attempt they accepted him.'

'I see,' Hank said slowly. 'So where's your best pal now? Is he keen on engines? I guess like most fellers he'd like to be aircrew in one capacity or another, but now that the war is over he'd do better to go for a trade which he can use in the peace.'

'I don't know what he intends to do,' Eve said rather frostily. 'He and Connie . . . oh, well, they don't seem to have wasted any time once they got away. They've been going about together and I believe Connie has taken Johnny to meet her parents. But I'm getting over it.' She grinned ruefully. 'Someone told me the other day that people change, and I do believe it's true. The Johnny I knew was just a boy; he was a very nice one, but the Johnny Connie knows is quite different, because he's a young man. And now please can we talk about something else?'

Hank loved Drake's Farm and made no secret of the fact. Although Lily no longer worked for the Faver-shams they raised no objection when she insisted on doing more than her fair share of the chores, but they were certainly surprised when their American visitor insisted on helping too. Even Lily, who knew that Hank had been born and brought up on his parents' farm, raised her eyebrows the first time Hank strode into the milking parlour and sat down on one of the stools.

'Milking's an art,' she said, almost reproachfully. 'You can't just come in here and start tugging on the nearest teats. You might get a few squirts of milk out, but the cow would soon realise that a stranger was at the helm, so to speak, and kick you and your bucket to kingdom come.'

Hank gave a scornful snort. 'I was milking cows when you were in your pram,' he informed her. 'Your trouble is you don't listen, Miss Ever-so-clever Kendal. I've told you many a time that I'm a farmer at heart, but did you believe me? Not you! Now let's get on – we don't want to keep the milk lorry waiting.'

That had been on the second day, and from that moment on Hank was accepted not just as a friend of the family but as a part of it. Auntie Bess dug out an old pair of dungarees for him and he soon proved himself to be an excellent worker. It seemed to Lily that the first week whizzed by and she enjoyed every moment. Halfway through the second week, Hank suggested taking her for a run to one of the neighbouring farms where they were advertising cream teas.

'But why should we bother?' Lily asked. 'Auntie Bess's cream teas are famous, and she won't charge us some exorbitant price.'

Hank laughed, but shook his head. 'I'm only human; I like to have you all to myself sometimes,' he said. 'My plan is to take you out for a bought cream tea and possibly a strawberry ice. Then I thought we could go for a trip to the coast. I've loved being on the farm with you, Lily, but we haven't had so much as five minutes alone together. And in three days' time I shall thank the Favershams for their incredible generosity, and making me feel like one of the family, then head back to the base and quite possibly never see you again.' He tweaked her nose. 'So all I'm asking is just one trip into the country unaccompanied by anyone but you. Is that too much to ask?

Lily reached across the short distance that separated them and rumpled his bright red hair. 'If only you'd see sense . . .' she began, but Hank put his hand across her lips.

'I know what you're going to say, so you can just button your lip,' he said severely. 'That subject is taboo. All right?'

Lily opened her mouth then caught Hank's eye and closed it again. But that evening, to Eve's distress, she lay in the darkness of the attic room and cried herself to sleep. Eve wondered whether she should get out of her own warm little bed and try to comfort her friend, but a new maturity made her stay where she was. She thought she understood the cause of Lily's sadness, and remembered her own feelings when Connie had written – rather spitefully, Eve had thought – to tell her that Johnny had visited the Hales in Liverpool. She wasn't sure she believed it, but still . . .

So Lily isn't the only one who's crying for what might have been, Eve told herself. Didn't someone once say that those were the saddest 'of all sad words of tongue or pen'? Well, it was time she realised the truth of that quotation and stopped dreaming of a future with Johnny. He had only written to her once since the war ended and that had been a pretty brief note simply explaining that he was at the other end of the country and would not be in Devon again for the foreseeable future.

Eve sat up on one elbow and rubbed at her suddenly tear-filled eyes. She was being ridiculous, mooning over a young man who was not interested in her. She should bend her thoughts to the books which she studied every evening, after the farm work was done, for she was now determined, when the Armstrongs returned to London, to apply for a place at the grammar school and even, if she passed her Higher School Certificate, to go to university. The Favershams were wonderful, helping her in every way they could, and sometimes Eve suspected that they knew how much she missed Johnny. But it doesn't matter really, she told herself, lying down again. I should be thinking about my future instead of letting my thoughts wander to the past. Yet even as the thought entered her mind the pictures began to form, and she thought of the pleasures she and Johnny had shared before Connie decided to join in the fun: rides on the hay wain, moonlight walks . . . Eve opened her eyes and glanced up at the great silver moon gazing down at her. All this had come to the surface because of Lily's unreciprocated feelings for Hank. Eve sighed. It was none of her business, and if she didn't get to sleep soon she wouldn't wake when the alarm went off. She snuggled her face into her pillow. If only Hank loved Lily the way she knew Lily loved him! If only . . . if only . . .

Eve slept.

Johnny had said many times that his whole object in life was to join the Royal Air Force and learn to fly a plane. But now that he was actually in uniform he was beginning to wonder if he had made a mistake. He had arrived at the training centre with an excellent school report and a glowing reference from Mr Faversham, and though he had never voiced the thought that these things might set him apart from the usual run of candidates he did hope that he was bound for something other than what someone had described as square-bashing. When he said so to the fellow whose bed was next to his in the Nissen hut, however, he was told in no uncertain terms that if there was one thing the RAF did do, it was treat everybody alike, particularly new entrants.

'It don't matter if you've got a university degree or left school at fourteen, you'll still get given a number and allocated a bed and if you've got any sense you'll keep your head below the parapet, as they used to say in the last little lot.' Jim pointed a scornful finger at Johnny's papers. 'That lot won't take you far,' he added. 'In fact the powers that be will probably put you down as a bighead, if not worse.' He punched Johnny lightly on the shoulder. 'Everyone has the initial training for six weeks; it don't matter if you're a prince of industry or the lowest of the low, you just have to live through it, do your best not to stand out from the crowd and pray for it to be over.'

This conversation took place on Johnny's first day as a member of the Royal Air Force, and though he was dismayed, he hoped his pal was wrong. However, he soon realised that Jim had spoken no more than the truth. Once, he'd have thought standing out as someone worth watching, with a view to a speedy promotion, was something to be commended, but now he knew differently. The corporals and sergeants who took the courses for the new intakes liked nothing more than reducing a brand new recruit to a quivering wreck. Pointing out that he intended to go on to greater things only earned him jeers and extra duties, and when he asked about leave, explaining untruthfully that his mother had been ill and he wanted to make sure her health was improving, he faced guffaws of amusement, not only from the sergeant in charge but also from his fellow entrants.

'Didn't you read all that guff HQ sent you, giving you details of when and where we were to go?' Jim asked, his eyebrows climbing. 'No leave for the first six weeks, not even if your whole family is dead as dodos and you want to attend the funerals. And don't think that's just for the first six weeks, because if you blot your copybook the way you seem determined to do they can shut you up for ever and a day without ever having to give you a reason.' He sighed. 'Don't you understand, you silly little man?' he said, imitating the sergeant's favourite phrase. 'They won't let us out whatever the reason, because they know damned well they'd have the devil's own job to get us back.' He eyed Johnny curiously. 'What do you want leave for, anyway? Got some popsie into trouble? If so, you'd be better off hiding out here for six weeks.'

Johnny shook his head. 'No, nothing like that,' he assured his new friend. He grinned sheepishly. 'How come you're so well genned up? From the way you talk I should have thought you'd been in the RAF for at least ten years.'

'Because I'm one of five brothers,' his new friend told him. 'I've got two sisters as well; one of them's a land girl and the other's a Waaf. Sometimes I feel I know more about the forces than any other living soul, so if you'll take my advice . . .' he laughed, 'if you take my advice you'll take my advice. You follow in the footsteps of AC Jim Williams and you won't go far wrong.'

A few days before the end of their visit, Lily informed Hank that she was going down to the village to say goodbye to her friends there. 'Because I truly meant to see them all while I was here, but the time's gone by so quickly . . . Will you be all right if I leave you?'

Hank smiled. 'I guess I can just about bear your absence for one afternoon,' he said gravely, then turned to grin at Eve. 'That is, if young Eve here will take me for a last walk around the place when she's finished her chores. What do you say, ma' am?'

Eve, who had almost despaired of finding time for a private talk with Hank before he left the farm, said quickly, 'Oh, yes, I'd like that. Chrissie can stay here with Auntie Bess, so we can go for a really long one.

Which way do you think? Up on to the moors or down into the valley?'

'I fancy a stroll along the stream path until we reach the source,' Hank said after some thought. 'I've never been, and you tell me it's real pretty down there. Okay?'

'All right,' Eve agreed. 'Give me half an hour and I'll be ready.'

True to her word, thirty minutes later Eve was strolling down the lane at Hank's side, looking as innocently as she could up into his face as he said severely, 'Now, young Eve, you were mighty quick to jump at the chance of getting me on my own. Do I spot the signs of someone who wants to pump me but didn't like to do so with her little brother's ears flapping? What do you want to know?'

'Well, there is something,' she said frankly. 'I can't help wondering, Hank, whether you've ever considered staying in England now the war's over? I'm sure you could find some sort of work which you'd enjoy. In fact some of the smaller farms are considering joining together to make what they're calling cooperatives.' She smiled coaxingly at him. 'You'd enjoy that, because although you call your parents' farm small I expect it's a good deal bigger than anything we've got around here. Uncle Reg will be able to tell you more about it – I'm sure no one would mind if you stayed on longer than you first intended.' She looked hopefully up at her companion, but Hank was shaking his head.

'No can do,' he assured her. 'I've already outstayed several ships bound for the good old US of A; my parents will think I'm deserting them, which wouldn't do at all.'

'Oh, but Lily's always trying to persuade you to stay on for a bit longer,' Eve pointed out. 'And now comes my really big question, the one I guess you know is coming. Only before I ask it will you promise not to wriggle out of it, or pretend to misunderstand the way you've done in the past when anyone asks you something you don't want to answer?'

Hank laughed. 'I can guess what you're going to say,' he said. 'The really big question which quite frankly is nobody's business but mine. You're going to ask me why I'm not madly in love with Lily like half the men in the neighbourhood and all the men on the USAAF base.'

Eve chuckled. 'You've taken the wind out of my sails, as my father would say,' she said rucfully. 'It isn't as though you and Lily don't know each other well, or you have some secret passion for someone else . . . like me, for instance. I tell you, Hank, if I were five years older or you were five years younger I'd grab you and cart you off to live in London until we could afford to buy a farm of our own. But we're not, so answer my question, please.'

Hank laughed. 'Is there a prize if I get it right?'

Eve smiled. 'Tell you what, I found a goose egg when I went into the orchard earlier. If you tell me the honest truth – honest, mind you – then you can have it, scrambled, on toast for your tea. Is that a fair offer? I call it generous.'

The two continued to stroll amicably in the direction

319

of the stream and Eve was just beginning to think that her question had been too intimate and would not be answered when Hank reached out a square sunburned hand and rumpled her hair.

'It's not just me involved,' he said quietly. 'If you must have the truth, only don't you breathe it to a soul, I've been in love with Lily from the very first day she walked into her bedroom and found me sprawling on her bed. Satisfied?'

'Of course I am, but if you love her why haven't you whisked her up in your arms and told her so? Why haven't you booked an extra berth on that ship? We'd miss her, of course, but you and she were made for each other, so whichever country you decided to settle in would be the right one. Oh, Hank, once you get aboard that ship you may never come within a thousand miles of Lily again, let alone good old England.'

Hank shrugged. 'It takes two to make a successful marriage. Lily could have anyone; why would she want me? Why do my crew call me Plug, as if you didn't know? If I did as you suggest and whisked Lily back to my father's farm, who can say whether she might not hate it, or her love wouldn't simply die, and there she'd be, in a strange country with no friends or kind mom to advise her. She would be far too polite – far too nice – to admit she had made a mistake, so she'd be landed, wouldn't she? Hiding her unhappiness and pretending everything was fine for my sake.' He pulled Eve to a halt, took hold of her shoulders and gave her a gentle shake. 'My dear girl, don't you think I've longed to do just that? But I've told myself a hundred times that such an act would be unfair for all sorts of reasons, reasons a kid like you would never understand.' He smiled down at her. 'Well, now I've told you more than I've told anyone else, so you must just accept that I'm not going to change my mind. I love Lily more than I ever thought I'd love any woman, so I don't intend to ruin her life, okay?'

'Okay, I suppose,' Eve said grudgingly. 'But if you ask me you're being a complete twerp and ruining two people's lives just because you're afraid Lily might change her mind, which I'm sure she wouldn't. She's not a changeable girl, you see. But I won't nag you, if you've honestly told me the truth.'

Hank looked at her solemnly. 'I've told you the truth. Now, where's this deep pool you've told me about?'

Chapter Fourteen

The day before Lily and Hank were due to leave Drake's Farm everyone sat down to breakfast together, for it was a Wednesday and Auntie Bess always made bacon and eggs on a Wednesday as it was market day and lunch would be later than usual.

The only vacant chair was Chrissie's, and just as Auntie Bess began to say it wasn't like him to miss bacon and eggs the back door burst open and he entered the room, clutching a pile of post.

'I put the new young bull in the small meadow by the old byre, like you told me, Auntie Bess,' he said, smiling blindingly at his hostess as she took a very full plate from the Aga where it had been keeping warm and put it down in front of him. 'Nothing for us, Evie, but there's one for Lily and the rest are for Uncle Reg,' he went on cheerfully, handing out the letters. Lily's was from her mother, who had a lively and interesting style and knew what would most interest Lily and her friends, and Eve knew she would be given it to read later. Uncle Reg's post included a copy of the *Farmer's Weekly*, and he had just opened his mouth to comment on a piece about Hereford cattle when there was a brief knock at the door and Freddie, the telegram boy, came into the kitchen, smiling broadly at everyone.

'Morning, Mrs Faversham,' he said, then nodded his head in Uncle Reg's direction. 'Mr Faversham.' He looked down at the envelope he was holding in his hand. 'I've got a telegram for a Hank Ruskin.' He peered around the assembled company and smiled at Hank, who had got to his feet, hand held out to receive the envelope.

'Well dang me!' he exclaimed when he had read the message it contained. He turned to Lily. 'Remember me telling you about my friend Billy Treble? He's a doughboy, and not only is he in England, he's stationed not far from here. I sent a telegram to his base asking if we could meet before I left Devonshire and he says he can. How about that?'

'Oh, that's wonderful, Hank,' Lily said, beaming. 'Where are you meeting him?'

'He's suggesting somewhere in town called the Cosy Café. It'll be grand to see him.' He turned to Uncle Reg. 'Do you think I could borrow the old truck? Only as you know I'll be sailing for the States in a couple of days' time and may not see Billy again for years.'

Uncle Reg agreed, of course, and Lily said that she did not wish to horn in on the meeting of such old friends but would love to meet someone who had known Hank from childhood. Auntie Bess, however, shook her head. 'The lad doesn't want to spend his time introducing this Billy to strangers,' she said reprovingly. 'You should know that, Lily my dear. And when is this meeting to take place?'

323

Hank looked down at the telegram in his hand and then up at the clock on the wall. 'Mrs F, you're a genius,' he said. 'Ten o'clock! I'd better hurry.' He got to his feet and smiled at Lily. 'I'd love you to meet my old pal, honey,' he said gently. 'But this is a fellers' get-together and pretty damned brief at that. I'd rather it was just the two of us, if you don't mind.'

'Of course I don't mind – I quite understand,' said Lily gaily, but Eve, watching her face, thought that she did mind, and felt sad for her. She rushed into speech.

'Are you going to change, Hank? You've probably got time, so Lily and I will clean the old truck up a bit so you don't meet this Billy with straw in your hair and cow muck on your boots.' She turned to grin at the telegram boy. 'Thanks, Freddie, but it doesn't look as though you need to wait for a reply. Hank will get there before the message does at this rate.'

'That's right,' said Auntie Bess, slipping one of her fruitless scones into Freddie's hand. 'Here, take that for the journey back to the village. It'll give you energy.'

Freddie smiled gratefully. 'Ta, Mrs F,' he said, taking a large bite out of the scone and waving a cheery good-bye at the rest of the folk gathered in the kitchen.

When the door had closed behind him, Chrissie started to pout. 'I want to go with Hank,' he said. 'If it's a boy thing then they ought to want me there.' He ran to the foot of the stairs. 'Hank!' he bellowed. 'Can I come? I won't be any trouble, honest to God, but it just so happens that I'm Superman this week and it would be a feather in my cap to meet a real American doughboy.'

Hank reappeared at the top of the stairs. 'Well you can't come. I forbid it,' he said. And then, as Chrissie began to protest, 'That's the end of it. If you pester me to change my mind you'll be sorry.'

Chrissie stomped up the stairs, feeling aggrieved. Hank had told him a few stories of the adventures he and his pal Billy had had as children, and when Hank mentioned that his buddy had appeared in the crowd scenes of a couple of cowboy films his fascination with the famous Billy Treble had been complete. They had done all the things that he most wanted to emulate, with Billy usually the leader, and now his chance had come to meet his hero, or at least to catch a glimpse of him. Yet he had been told in no uncertain terms that this was not to be.

Of course, he could understand the girls not being wanted, for so far as he could recall, no girls had ever been involved in the pair's exciting exploits. In the past twelve months or so he and his best friend, Alex Ryder, had led a gang of would-be adventurers. Taking it in turns to be Superman, wearing an old blanket from Uncle Reg's truck which passengers spread across their knees in wintry weather, they engaged in all sorts of imaginary derring-do, and enjoyed themselves very much in the process. To be sure, Eve did not always approve of their games, so they did their best to see that she knew as little as possible about Superman and his exploits.

Reaching the attic, Chrissie pulled the rudest face he could conjure up and sank down on the foot of his bed.

Today he knew he would not be seeing Alex, because during the holidays Wednesday was the day Alex helped his father by tidying up the Sunday school corner of the church, mowing the grass and doing any necessary cleaning of the sunken gravestones which marked the death, mostly many years ago, of members of the rector's flock.

'Damn, damn, and bloody hell,' he said loudly, secure in the knowledge that the rest of the household, with the exception of Hank, were still downstairs. 'And it was my turn to be Superman, too! If only Alex was free we might think of some way to get a peep at Billy Treble, but of course it's out of the question since today is Wednesday. Oh, damn, damn, damn, and I can't even go and try to persuade him to let the rector do his own dirty work because he made me promise not to plan anything for Wednesdays and I always keep my word even if horrible Hank doesn't care.'

Presently, however, Chrissie's natural good temper reasserted itself. He swirled an imaginary cloak across his shoulders, pulled a face at himself in the piece of mirror over the washstand and set off down the stairs once more. He knew better than to try to change Hank's mind, but surely there must be some way of solving this dilemma. Perhaps if he spoke to Hank, begged for just a glimpse, explained about the Superman game and his own urgent desire to meet the legendary Billy Treble, then he might be allowed to shake the man's hand and tell him how much he was admired – and imitated – by two British boys who, since the advent of Hank, adored all things American.

* * *

Half an hour later Chrissie was curled up under Superman's cloak in the back of Uncle Reg's old truck. Hank had got behind the wheel without so much as glancing into the back and Chrissie thought, triumphantly, that the first hurdle was cleared.

He had heard Uncle Reg telling Hank that driving the truck demanded all one's attention. 'If you're careful and stick to the rules of the road you'll be all right. But if you try any fancy tricks or go faster downhill than thirty miles an hour you'll end up in the rector's churchyard, so don't you forget that, my boy. It's a bit different from a Liberator, I dare say, so it's best to be prepared.'

So now, with the wind of their going even penetrating the rug, Chrissie waited rather apprehensively for the steep descent where the road turned sharply in front of the church. He hoped that Hank would not be so excited that he forgot Uncle Reg's advice, but this did not prove to be the case, and quite soon, by raising his head the tiniest bit and peering about him, Chrissie could see the suburbs beginning to appear and hugged himself gleefully. They had reached the point of no return, where it would be quicker to go on than to turn back. It seemed the success of his venture was assured.

When the truck came to a juddering halt and Chrissie heard voices he thought for one awful moment that he had been spotted, but no avenging hand swept the rug aside. Squinting from his blanket nest he could see that they had come to a halt outside the café and Hank, without a glance into the back, was standing on the pavement consulting his watch. Then, to his dismay, he heard him murmur to himself that he might as well go along to Bibby's Animal Feed to see if there was anything waiting for the Favershams. If so, he might as well pick it up as not.

Hank set off down the street, and Chrissie, knowing that discovery was inevitable if he was still in the truck when Hank returned with a couple of sacks of meal, did not hesitate. He jumped out of the truck, crossed the pavement in two strides and nipped through the café's open door to dive beneath the only cover he could see, which was one of the chequered tablecloths with which the Cosy Café's tables were covered. More by luck than judgement he had chosen a table with an unusually long cloth, and he realised with some relief that it actually touched the ground and would hide him completely from prying eyes.

Breathing more easily, he crouched in the semi-darkness of his refuge and began to consider his next move. He had no intention of emerging from beneath the cloth like a child playing a children's game. He meant to stroll into the café, greet Hank in a man to man fashion, shake hands with Billy Treble and then take himself off to walk back to Drake's Farm. He needed to go back outside and find a spot where he would not be seen by Hank when he returned from Bibby's, then wait there until he saw the two Americans enter the café.

He was about to put this plan into action when he recognised the voices of Mrs Carstairs, the owner of the Cosy Café, and her helper Cathy. Cathy was a great favourite with everyone on Drake's Farm because on market days she brought homemade fudge into the café and sold it in tiny bags to her favourite customers. There was some murmuring about the sugar ration from those who were not offered the chance to buy, but Cathy was generally so well liked that no one made any serious complaint. Now, however, thoughts of fudge were far from Chrissie's mind. If they discovered him, what could he say? Could he pretend to be a customer who had, perhaps, dropped something on the floor and was searching for it? Chrissie gnawed his lip. The last thing he wanted was to make a fool of himself in front of Hank and Billy, and the thought of crawling out from his hiding place under the startled gaze of the two men made him cringe. If he could just get away before they entered the café . . .

The bell by the entrance tinged and Mrs Carstairs, a friendly soul, greeted these early morning customers with her usual good nature.

'Morning, fellers; come in for a nice hot cup of coffee and one of me new-baked scones?' she suggested. 'They'm so hot the butter on 'em melts straight through on to your plate, what about that, eh?' She chuckled. 'You'll be used to a well-buttered scone staying with the Favershams the way you are, but your pal here may not be so lucky.'

For several moments the talk was all of food; Billy was explaining that the American troops were fed by their own countrymen since Britain was hard pressed enough without having to feed their overseas visitors. Then Billy asked about various British customs and Mrs Carstairs and Cathy talked of pictures they had seen at the Odeon in town and film stars they admired. They were most impressed when Hank told them that Billy had had bit parts in a couple of Westerns, and promised to look out for him the next time they went to the cinema. As they talked the café began to fill up and the two Americans, who by great good fortune had sat down at the very table under which Chrissie crouched, lowered their voices so that he had to strain hard to hear what they were saying.

There was a rustling from the table over Chrissie's head and he realised that they were showing each other photographs. He heard Hank's voice.

'The one halfway up the apple tree is Lily; I expect I mentioned her in most of my letters. What do you think?'

Billy gave a long, low whistle. 'What a smasher! Wish you'd brought her with you.' He chuckled. 'Bet she'd fall for my manly charms even if yours have left her cold.'

More rustling. 'Here, this is a better one; she's smiling straight into the camera.' There was a pause, then another rustle and Chrissie guessed Hank was returning the photographs to his wallet and his wallet to its usual place in his pocket. 'They call the girls in these parts English roses, but I prefer to call them lilies myself. Now, if you want to take a look around the town we'd better pay our shot and get going. There's a very good pub up the road where we can have an excellent meal for a few shillings. My treat, of course.'

The two men began squabbling light-heartedly as they went over to the kitchen door to pay their bill.

Billy began sorting through a handful of change, but he finally gave up and held out his hand to Cathy so that she could pick out the required coins. Then he turned to his friend.

'Don't tell me you've lived in the same house as that Lily and not tried to fix her interest,' he remarked. 'I'm your oldest buddy, Hank, and I saw the look in your eyes when you showed me the photos. But I won't press you; maybe she's all looks and no character, and you've always been a feller who likes his girls to have brains as well as beauty.' As he spoke they were heading for the door, and Chrissie only just caught the words which Hank murmured in reply.

'She deserves more than I can give her,' he said quietly. 'A girl like Lily shouldn't have to be content with half a man.'

Half a man? What on earth did that mean? Was it anything to do with 'bit part', another expression strange to Chrissie? But before he could give much thought to either phrase the men were thanking the café owner and her assistant and leaving the premises.

It was the perfect moment. Customers were heading for the only empty table and Chrissie was able to stand up in the most natural manner, as though he had indeed dropped money on the floor, and pull out a chair so that a very large woman, who was panting and wheezing, could sit down and recover herself whilst her three companions followed suit. She thanked Chrissie profusely and then turned to her friends whilst Chrissie slipped unobtrusively out of the Cosy Café.

He looked cautiously around, and saw that Hank

and Billy had already reached the end of the street and were about to turn out of sight. For a moment he considered breaking into a run and pretending he had begged a lift from someone in order to get Billy Treble's autograph, but then it occurred to him that Hank would almost certainly put two and two together and accuse him of ignoring his commands.

Chrissie sighed, but turned away. He had had phenomenal luck so far; why risk being discovered? He would have liked Billy's autograph, but at least he had seen him – and in the circumstances that could be made into a thrilling tale. Chrissie grinned to himself, imagining Alex's reaction when he heard of his pal's exploit. And not only Alex would be impressed; the rest of the gang would think him 'one helluva guy' as Hank would probably put it. Whistling merrily at the thought of the praise to come, Chrissie speeded up. He was longing to tell them all about his adventure, and as he walked and whistled he went over his story several times, embroidering it until it bore, in truth, little resemblance to what had actually happened.

And Chrissie was in luck. Just as he was beginning to think he would have a bit of a rest an old van drew up beside him with a cheerful pip pip of its horn and Mr Spindlebush leaned across the passenger seat and grinned at Chrissie.

'You're about bright and early,' he said approvingly. 'Want a lift? Or would you prefer to continue walking?'

'Oh, Mr Spindlebush, you're a lifesaver. I was just thinking about having a sit down when you stopped.' He was scrambling into the passenger seat as he spoke and expected Mr Spindlebush to start asking questions, so began hastily to invent a reason for his expedition into town. But as it turned out, this was not necessary. Mr Spindlebush was even less at ease behind the wheel than Uncle Reg, and he maintained a stolid silence until he dropped Chrissie off, unchallenged, at the top of the lane.

Because it was a Wednesday Chrissie could not unburden himself to Alex until his friend's chores at the rectory were done, but as soon as he had bolted his lunch he rushed to the old graveyard.

Alex was deeply envious of Chrissie's thrilling adventure and asked a thousand questions, or so it seemed to Chrissie, which he took great pleasure in answering. In fact there was only one question to which he could think of no satisfactory answer; what had Hank meant when he said that Lily deserved more than half a man? So far as Chrissie could see – and Alex agreed with him – there was no such thing as half a man, so it must be some American expression which neither boy had heard before.

It didn't particularly worry Alex, but his brother was a film buff and so he was able to explain that a 'bit part' simply meant that an actor was on the screen for seconds rather than minutes. 'So I suppose half a man simply means the man is on the screen for a bit longer than a bit part, but not long enough to count as a film star,' he said after some thought.

Chrissie sighed. 'It's not important,' he said. 'I just wondered . . .'

A voice from inside the rectory called that tea and biscuits were being served to the Women's Institute and if the boys would give a hand Mrs Ryder would be much obliged. Without having to consult each other, both boys slid off the gravestone and headed for the kitchen. Mrs Ryder's shortbread was famous, and Chrissie knew that if they helped they would be rewarded with a couple of biscuits each and probably a drink of milk into the bargain. Just as they were about to enter the house Chrissie caught Alex's arm.

'We could ask Jez if he knows what half a man means,' he suggested. 'Your brother seems to know everything about film stars, especially the ones who've been making war stories. Can you ask him?'

Alex, clearly less interested in the phrase than his friend, shrugged, but said he would try to remember to ask him as soon as he came home. Jez, who was at agricultural college and was greatly admired by both his youngest brother and that brother's friend, came home most weekends. The two boys entered the kitchen, seized the prepared trays and began to circulate amongst the WI members.

It was later that evening when it occurred to Chrissie that his sister, so much older than himself, might be able to solve the mystery of the phrase 'half a man'. And having decided to ask her, he put it out of his mind.

'Wakey, wakey.'

Eve groaned and sat up. 'What on earth . . .' she began, glancing at the pale light of dawn which filled the room, and then she remembered. Of course, today was the day that Hank was leaving them, and Lily too, though she was only going as far as Norwich. Eve rolled out of bed, shoved her feet into her worn old slippers and went across to the washstand.

'Chrissie's already up and dressed, so if you don't mind using my washing water it's all yours. I went down earlier and got some hot, so it's still at least luke-warm, I imagine,' Lily said. 'Home today, then one day in the Close before I wave Hank goodbye.' She smiled at Eve. 'We've got plenty of time, but Auntie Bess said the trains are still in a bit of a muddle so it would be best to get to the station earlier rather than later.'

Eve could hear from the tone of Lily's voice that she was trying to be cheerful, eager to give the impression that though she might miss Hank when he went home to America it was not the end of the world. Eve thought she was being very brave, because when Lily was off her guard the expression in her eyes when she looked at Hank gave her away. Eve told herself that Lily was bound to meet another man who would catch her fancy, but she didn't really believe it. Her friend had met dozens and dozens of attractive unattached males, and as far as Eve could make out had never wavered in her affection for the American flyer.

Washed and dressed, Eve sat on the end of her bed and watched as Lily packed her bag. She was wearing her land girl uniform and would don her wellington boots as she left the house, so her haversack contained a cotton dress, a woolly cardigan knitted for her by Auntie Bess, a pair of dancing pumps, and little else apart from a sponge bag which contained her washing things and a tablet of wild rose soap which she kept amongst her underwear so that its scent penetrated her clothing. Eve had asked her, when she saw her taking it out of the drawer, why Lily kept it there instead of using it.

Lily had giggled. 'Who knows when I'll get another?' she had answered gaily. 'It's nice to smell of flowers, wouldn't you agree? Colin always said the first thing he noticed about a girl was her perfume, and I do think he had a point. We used to know a girl called Violet who wore some horrible perfume her boyfriend had brought back from France, and Colin said it was enough to put most men off. Not that I care for his opinion, mind you, but even now I like my undies to smell of roses rather than manure.' As she spoke she was fastening the straps on her haversack, then she glanced almost wistfully around the attic. 'It's been fun, a real break from routine, to be back at the old farm,' she said quietly. And then, as Eve began to protest that you could scarcely call moving from one farm to another much of a change, she laughed. 'Oh well, you know what I mean. I know the work was much the same here as at Parker's Place, but it made all the difference having Hank working beside me.' She picked up the haversack and slid her arms into the straps. 'I take it you're coming to the station to see us off? Oh, Eve, I shall miss you and Drake's Farm most dreadfully. I suppose I should have realised that coming here would make the parting worse, but all I thought of was spending an extra couple of weeks with Hank.' As she spoke she opened the attic door and gestured Eve to go ahead of her down the steep stairs. Eve obeyed, but halfway down she turned and barred Lily's path. 'Have you told Hank how you feel about him?' she asked urgently. 'That you'd like to marry him? I know it's usually the boy who asks the girl, but perhaps it's different in America. I've often seen him giving you soppy looks; he can't be so thick that he doesn't realise you love him.'

'Oh, shut up; save your breath to cool your porridge,' Lily said, pushing her way past Eve and galloping down the remaining stairs. 'I have mentioned marriage but he just laughs, or says he has a wife in every state and doesn't need another. Now come along do, or we'll miss breakfast.'

Although it was still very early, for Chrissie with his nose pressed to the passenger window saw the cattle in the fields standing in early morning mist, the station was quite busy. Chrissie was wondering why and asking his sister whether all these people had come to bid Hank farewell when he remembered that today was market day in a neighbouring town, so he bit off his enquiry and asked Eve whether she thought Hank and Lily would manage to get seats when the train came in.

'I don't know,' Eve said. 'But they won't be on this train for long; their first change is only two stops along the line.' She smiled at Chrissie. 'Everyone has got used to standing, or sitting on their luggage, though there's normally a man willing to give up his seat for Lily. And of course folk are still so grateful to the Yanks that Hank would probably be offered a seat as well.

Not that he'd take it, of course. But in any case there's no point in worrying about a seat when you're only on the train for a couple of stops.'

Chrissie nodded wisely. 'Course, I was forgetting.' He looked around him and made for the row of vending machines, as he did every time he visited the station. Once, the machines had been full of bars of chocolate, and though every child present knew that this was no longer the case they could not resist just making sure that it was still so. After all, the war was over and you never knew; some railway official might have refilled the old machines. Chrissie produced his penny and pushed it into the slot. Then he pulled the long metal lever and waited for the clunk which would indicate that a bar of chocolate had descended into the little metal container. It didn't come and he was turning away, not exactly disappointed because he had known in his heart that no chocolate bar would descend, when a voice he knew well assailed his ears. He spun round and stared with delight into the grinning face under the familiar fore and aft.

'Johnny!' he squeaked. 'Whatever are you doing here? Are you on your way to Drake's Farm? Only there's nobody at home – we've all come to see Lily off on the train back to Norwich.'

'Where's your sister?' Johnny asked. 'I thought as I was so near the farm I might pop up and say hello, but they told me at the post office that everyone's down here.' He had swung away from the dispensing machine and was scanning the crowd, but it was impossible to pick out one person in the crush.

'Why do you want Eve?' Chrissie asked as Johnny turned back to him. 'I think she's rather cross with you. You were her best friend but you hardly ever wrote to her after you joined the RAF. She says you wrote to horrible Connie instead, and even went to see her in Liverpool.'

At that moment the train everyone was waiting for drew up alongside the platform and there was a con-certed rush for the luggage van, since there would obviously be no room to spare in the carriages. Instead of answering, Johnny was looking along the platform again, and suddenly he said, 'Ah, I can see Lily – she's getting into that carriage, with a Yank, I think. Is that the Hank that Eve told us about? I'm afraid I shall have to be very rude and push through these market trad-ers, or I shan't have a chance to say hello. Coming?'

Hurrying to keep up, Chrissie had a wonderful idea. Johnny was in the air force – surely he would be able to answer the question which had nagged at Chrissie's mind for nearly twenty-four hours now. But they had reached the train and Lily had spotted Johnny and was leaning forward to tell him that Eve had gone to put her haversack in the luggage van; the train was ready to leave and the guard was walking briskly down the platform, slamming each door as he passed it. Chrissie saw that if he did not seize this opportunity to discover the meaning of the mysterious phrase he might never get a better chance.

He grabbed the sleeve of Johnny's battledress. 'Johnny,' he said urgently. 'I heard something yesterday – it's probably an American expression – which I didn't understand. I've asked around a bit but nobody seems to know what it means, and I thought, what with you being in the air force, you probably hear all sorts and might be able to explain . . .'

'You'll have to shout; that bloody engine is making enough row to wake the dead. Go on, Chrissie, what's this unknown expression? I hope it's not a rude one; if it is you'd better whisper it in my ear.' He bent his head towards Chrissie, but the younger boy was not taking any chances; this could be his only opportunity to find out just what Hank had meant, so he took a deep breath and bawled the question at the top of his shrill young voice.

'Someone said Lily doesn't deserve to go through life with only half a man. What does that *mean*, Johnny? If you were only half a man you'd be dead!'

Chrissie was watching Johnny's face as he spoke, but he realised that everyone within earshot had suddenly stopped talking and instead of answering Johnny merely looked embarrassed; and out of the corner of his eye he saw that Hank, standing just inside the carriage door, had gone brick red. Without a word of apology the American pushed open the door which the porter had only just slammed shut and seized Chrissie in an uncomfortably tight grip.

'*What* did you say?' he demanded grimly. 'Who did you say said such a thing? How *dare* you repeat something which was not meant for your ears?' He shook Chrissie as a terrier shakes a rat. 'Tell me which lying toad said those words!'

'It were you; you said it to your friend Billy when

340

you were in the Cosy Café. I'm awful sorry if it's made you cross, Hank, and I know I shouldn't have listened,' Chrissie said wildly. 'Is it a rude saying? I can see it's made you very angry . . . but what *does* it mean? Is it a joke?'

But at this point Lily alighted from the train and gave Hank a slap across the cheek which sounded, to Chrissie, louder than the noise of the engine. She caught hold of Hank by the front of his tunic and shook him hard and Chrissie saw that her face was wet with tears and that Hank, too, had tears in his eyes, and it was all Chrissie's fault. If he'd kept his big mouth shut . . . and then he saw with complete astonishment that Lily and Hank were clasped in each other's arms and so far as he could see they were both crying.

This time, Chrissie had no option but to hear what was being said.

'I've loved you since the day we met,' Hank was murmuring. 'But how could I tell you that marriage with me would be a mockery? No babies, not ever. Maybe no proper loving . . . oh, Lily, my darling, you need a real man, a whole man who can give you what you deserve.'

Lily raised her tear-wet face from Hank's shoulder. 'A girl doesn't marry the man she loves to get babies,' she said scornfully. 'She marries him so they can be together for always. Now look me in the eye, Hank Ruskin, and tell me we weren't made for each other!'

Hank gave a shaken laugh. 'I guess every person in this station now knows I love you and want you to marry me, babies or no babies,' he said, and hustled her aboard the train just as the guard came along to slam the door again and wave his green flag. Hank opened the window and grinned down at Chrissie, who was still standing on the platform. 'Thank you,' he said quietly as the train started to pull slowly forward. 'Thank you very much. One day I'll ask you just how you came to hear what I said, but . . .'

His words were swallowed up by the whistle as the train drew out of the station and began to pick up speed.

Eve was running up the platform waving and shouting her goodbyes when she spied Johnny for the first time.

'Johnny!' she exclaimed. 'Whatever are you doing here? I thought the air force had sent you way up north somewhere. Were you hoping to catch this train? Because if so you've missed it.'

Johnny raised his eyes to heaven. 'You haven't changed; no hello Johnny, how wonderful to see you, just "What are you doing here?"' he grumbled. 'The air force are sending me to Germany as part of the army of occupation and they've given me a fortnight to get my affairs in order. I've been home and cleared up that end of things and thought I'd pay a flying visit to Drake's Farm before leaving the country for heaven knows how long.' He grinned at her warily. 'Are you mad at me for not writing? A feller can't be everywhere and I knew Connie would pass any news on. And incidentally, I know we were a bit doubtful about the truth of some of Connie's statements, but her family really do own a large shop just off the Scotland Road. Connie invited me to spend a few days with them – did she tell you? Liverpool is in a dreadful state – the Luftwaffe concentrated on smashing the ports, as you know – but it was a grand city once and will be so again. Most of the public buildings were in ruins . . .'

He rambled on as Eve followed him out of the station, describing the damage the Luftwaffe had caused to Liverpool, but Eve did not hear a word. So he *had* visited Connie's home! No wonder he had not written to her, since he had known very well that the two girls were anything but friends, despite what he had just said about their being in touch. But Johnny was asking Chrissie over his shoulder to explain to the Favershams that he would be bringing Eve home later.

Eve had been feeling quite numb, but at these words a tide of rage engulfed her. How dare he assume she wanted to spend time with him? How dare he walk into her life, become her best friend, and then casually admit that he had been seeing somebody else and that somebody a girl Eve positively disliked!

'Don't bother, Chrissie,' she said airily. 'I came with you and I shall go home with you.' She turned to Johnny, her fingers firmly crossed behind her back. 'And if you want me to write to you I'll do my best to fit you into my schedule, but in a few weeks Chrissie and I will be joining our parents in London and I shall be working towards getting a university place. So this, Johnny Durrell, is goodbye.' She held out a hand but Johnny ignored it and seized her by the shoulders. He was grinning, though guiltily.

'My word, you are in a bate,' he said. 'I was going to ask Auntie Bess if I could stay at the farm for a couple of days before I have to go.'

'Do as you like,' Eve said at once. 'Are you and Connie engaged? Not that it's any of my business, of course.'

Johnny grinned again but Eve could see he looked uneasy. 'We've not gone as far as that; we're still just pals,' he told her. 'Look, I've got a lot to do before I leave England and I don't mean to spend my time arguing with you, so let's say goodbye here and now and remain friends. But first you can tell me what all the fuss was about on the station. I gather gorgeous Lily is going to marry that ugly Yank . . .'

He got no further. Eve slapped his face as hard as she could. 'Hank's worth a dozen of you,' she shouted. 'Don't bother to write because I shan't write back. You're a nasty piece of work, Johnny Durrell, and I should think you and Connie were made for each other.' She grabbed Chrissie's shoulder and pushed him back towards the station. 'Tell Uncle Reg I shan't be a moment.' She turned back to Johnny. 'You and Connie are well suited,' she said formally and realised suddenly that she was looking at him through a blur of tears. She regretted what she had said but could not unsay it, and found she could not bear the thought of seeing him back at Drake's Farm. She opened her mouth to say so but Johnny was ahead of her.

'I'm sorry you're so bitter,' he said quietly, putting a hand to his reddened cheek. 'I won't come back to the farm since it seems my mere presence would upset you.' He watched Chrissie talking to the Favershams and then looked back to Eve. He began to speak, then stopped short and seized her in his arms. 'We had some good times together,' he said gruffly. 'Real friendship never dies; in a way I'll always love you, but not in the way you want. Can you understand that?'

And then, before she could reply, he was kissing her, at first gently, and then almost feverishly. 'Johnny . . .' she began, but he had flung away from her to climb into the driver's seat of a battered old car and she saw that the contingent from Drake's Farm was approaching. Johnny waved to them but started the engine, put the vehicle into first gear and jerked unevenly forward. 'If you change your mind and want my address Connie's got it!' he shouted over his shoulder. 'Sorry I can't wait, Auntie Bess; Eve will explain. Love to all, and as soon as I'm settled I'll write.'

Chapter Fifteen

That night, as Eve made her way up the attic stairs, she saw once again the scene at the station and the happiness which had shone from Hank's and Lily's faces. But whilst not for a moment envying the American and the golden Lily their love, Eve felt the pain of Johnny's departure and the fact that she had probably said goodbye to him for ever like a knife in her breast. If he was really friends with Connie she knew the other girl would make sure that the rift between herself and Johnny was given no chance to heal.

And now, as she began to undress, she realised that in all their time together at Drake's Farm, in all their ploys and exploits, she and Johnny had never kissed. Kisses were a polite peck on the cheek when parents came visiting. Kisses were a comfort to a small child who had run too fast, tripped over its own feet, and grazed both knees on the lane's uneven surface. Kisses were given and received on birthdays and at Christmas, but no kiss that Eve knew, could imagine, was like the kisses she had seen exchanged by Hank and Lily. Those kisses had all the passion and pent-up emotion of two people deeply in love, and resembled in no way the kiss which she herself had received from Johnny. There had been anger in his kiss, a desire to punish, yet it had also held another message. Johnny wanted her to remember him when he was far away, to remember the feel of his mouth on hers and the moment of closeness when he had held her in his arms. For maybe a whole second he had held her tight, then thrust her away, muttered something she could not catch and jumped into the old car.

Johnny's kiss, she thought now, had been a sort of apology, telling Eve that her friend wanted to make up in some way for what had gone before. She had wanted to respond, to explain that she wanted to be his friend even if they could never be lovers, but her own words had made that impossible, so she had hurried to the Favershams' old truck, squeezed into the bit of seat they had left for her, and told Mr Faversham gaily to set off.

'Johnny's been posted abroad,' she had shouted above the wind of their going. 'He's doing a round of goodbyes.'

Auntie Bess had turned to stare at her. 'So I take it what we saw just now was a goodbye kiss? Funniest goodbye kiss I've ever seen in all my born days, but then I suppose if he's goin' to live abroad with the air force he'll mebbe not get another chance.' She had put her hand out across the distance which separated them and pinched Eve's cheek. 'Don't go readin' too much into that kiss,' she had said gently. 'Kisses are casual things these days, not like when your uncle and I were young. Then you only kissed the feller you meant to marry, but it's different today. Are you going to write to him?'

Eve had hardly had to consider her answer; her mind was already made up. 'I can't,' she said briefly. 'Well, not until he writes to me, at any rate. I don't have an address for him.' She smiled at the older woman. 'Not unless I write to Connie and ask her for it, and I shan't be doing that. Can we change the subject? What's for lunch? I'm hungry as a hunter.'

Oxford, 2002

Eve looked at her wristwatch. She was over an hour early for her rendezvous, having finished her shopping a lot faster than she had expected. She was just wondering what to do next when a voice hailed her.

'Eve! Eve Armstrong! Well, of all the extraordinary coincidences!' The speaker had run across the road, narrowly avoiding a passing motorist whose hooter blared out an indignant protest. 'My God, it must be sixty years since we last set eyes on each other.'

Eve stared incredulously at the speaker. They were both tall women in their seventies, but there the resemblance ended. After a moment Eve gasped. 'Connie Hale,' she said disbelievingly. 'How amazing to see you! And you haven't changed.' She laughed. 'In fact if I were to be put to the question I'd say I look like a woman in her seventies, which is what I am, and you look like someone in her fifties; how *do* you do it?'

If someone had told Eve she looked twenty years younger than her age she would have been surprised

348

and delighted, but Connie – for it was she – looked slightly affronted.

'I've been mistaken for someone in her forties,' she said rather accusingly. 'Mind you, I suppose that was a year or two ago, and I have had restorative treatment on my facial skin . . .'

She means a facelift, Eve thought, and felt not only a rush of admiration for Connie's courage but also astonishment that anyone of their age could care enough about their appearance to go beneath the surgeon's knife. However, Connie was staring at her, kohl-rimmed eyes widening.

'Didn't you recognise me straight away?' she asked. 'I knew you the moment I clapped eyes on you.'

'Of course I did; recognise you, I mean,' Eve said, allowing impatience to enter her tone. 'You were a pretty thing then and you're a pretty thing now,' she added, crossing her fingers behind her back. She smiled at the other woman. 'Look, Connie, it's lovely to see you after all these years but we can't stand on the pavement getting in everyone's way. I've got some time to kill so why don't we go into the café across the road and have a chinwag over a nice hot cup of coffee? But not if you have other plans for the rest of the morning – if we're going to tell each other our life histories since we last met it's going to take more than ten or fifteen minutes to catch up.'

Connie shot out her hand and consulted a large gold wristwatch. 'Ten or fifteen minutes? My dear Eve, you must have led a very dreary life! By the way, did you ever marry? Don't say you really are still Eve

Armstrong? I've been married three times . . . but look, as you say, we can't talk here, and I've plenty of time.' She patted her pocket significantly. 'I've got my mobile phone and the chauffeur will pick me up at any time, anywhere, as soon as I telephone him. Do you have a mobile phone? But everyone does, I suppose, though I doubt everyone has a chauffeur. Isn't there somewhere a bit smarter where I can buy you a decent lunch?' She fluttered her eyelashes and gave Eve what she no doubt believed to be a provocative smile. 'Husband number three – Jethro Armardi – gave me the chauffeur as a birthday gift when we came back from the States. I'd had a tiny, tiny accident in his Roller and he felt the strain of driving first on the left and then on the right and then on the left again was too much for his wife to have to cope with.' She fluttered her eyelashes again and Eve had to turn away to hide a smile as one of them came half off, giving Connie a very odd appearance indeed, but the other woman was still staring at her, waiting for an answer.

Eve chuckled. 'Thank you, but I'm meeting someone at twelve. Come on, or we shan't get a table. It's a very popular café; what you might call cheap and cheerful.'

Connie looked sulky. 'I told Ed to get himself a pub lunch, because I wanted to explore the town and take some photographs to impress the folk back home.'

'Back home?' Eve said tentatively. 'Is home America now?' she added as they crossed the road and headed for the café.

Connie nodded. 'Yes. I'm an American citizen,' she admitted, 'but Jethro's got properties all over the place – he's a property developer, in fact – so at the moment we're living in Britain. I'm Jethro's second wife and he has a son at college over here. I thought I'd pop over to say hello, but he's not in his rooms, as they call them, so I decided to do some shopping and then try him again this evening. So I've plenty of time on my hands.'

They entered the café as she spoke and made a bee-line for a table for two at the back of the large and airy room, which was already filling up fast.

Eve sat down at the table and indicated that Connie should follow suit. 'You may have plenty of time but I've got to go quite soon,' she said, consulting her own watch.

The other woman frowned, and Eve realised that this was still the same old Connie. She had always wanted to get her own way. When they had ordered their coffee – cappuccino for Eve, something called a 'skinny latte' for Connie – Eve turned to Connie once more.

'Since you've led a much more interesting life than mine, you'd better start,' she said.

Connie smirked. 'My first husband was a theatrical impresario . . . he gave me a part in one of his shows and I don't mind telling you that within three months they put a star on my dressing room door. After that, of course, the parts became more important . . .'

Eve listened with only half her attention, amazed to find that in this respect at any rate Connie had not changed at all. She simply could not resist embellishing every word she spoke, and by the time Eve had finished her coffee she was thoroughly sick of Connie's life history and could not wait to get away. Apologising, she interrupted the story of the house on Long Island, its swimming pool, the servants needed to keep it clean and tidy, and the long garden that was miraculously green and beautiful all year round.

'It all sounds wonderful,' she said brightly, 'but I'm afraid I'm going to have to leave you. I don't have a mobile phone and I mustn't keep my friend waiting.'

Connie leaned across the table and took Eve's hand in hers. 'Don't go yet,' she pleaded. 'Why don't we get your friend to join us? If she's a friend of yours she's bound to be nice and I expect she'd like to hear all about America. Besides, you haven't told me anything about yourself yet and I'm longing to hear what happened to you after us evacuees went our separate ways.'

Eve opened her mouth to respond, but was cut off before she could get the words out.

'Talking of evacuees, I had a bit of a flutter with one of the chaps who'd been at Spindlebush and came to Drake's Farm when that land girl left – what was her name? You must remember him – Johnny something or other – you were keen on him too.' Connie laughed. 'Goodness knows why, he was such a plain-looking chap, with squinty blue eyes and a million freckles.' She grimaced. 'He was nothing special, but I suppose beggars can't be choosers, and he was the only thing Drake's Farm had to offer.'

Eve gasped and opened her mouth to speak, but Connie cut across her again. 'Anyway, I bumped into his mate Robbo a few years back and he said he'd lost touch with Johnny but thought that he'd been badly wounded – or was it taken prisoner? – in Korea.' She shrugged. 'I wonder if he ever got married?' She gave a silvery laugh. 'You'd have to be pretty desperate to marry someone like him.' She leaned forward to pick up her coffee cup and took a delicate sip.

Eve rose to her feet. 'It's been lovely meeting you after all these years, Connie,' she said rather coldly. 'We must do it again sometime . . .'

Interrupting her without apology, Connie said, 'Fancy not having a mobile phone.'

Eve sighed. 'Look, I'm longing to hear the rest of your story, but I really must be going.'

Connie sank back in her chair again, and took out her own phone. 'Oh Eve, just stay with me until the car gets here! I'm sure Ed'll be along in a few minutes. Can't you wait? Be a pal; after all, we've not met for absolutely ages . . .'

But she was too late. There were two entrances to the café and she had not been quick enough to see through which Eve had escaped.

As soon as she saw Connie get into her chauffeur-driven car Eve left her hiding place and headed for Bumble's, glancing at her wristwatch as she walked. She would still be too early, but at least she'd managed to escape the dreadful Connie.

My God, she thought to herself. Of all the people she might have imagined bumping into, Connie Hale was not one. Eve conjured up a picture of Connie as she used to be: pouting, provocative, boastful. No difference there, Eve thought to herself. The other girl had almost never walked along the track by the stream, worried that she might get some mud on her shoes, whereas Eve and Johnny preferred that walk to any other. Smiling, Eve continued on her way to her rendezvous, enjoying the thought that on this occasion she would have some unexpected gossip to impart. Miranda would be fascinated!

*

Eve used a nearby branch to pull herself creakingly up from the log which she had been using as a seat. Smoothing down her skirt, she glanced at her wristwatch. It was a quarter to three. She had no desire, nor indeed the time, to go up to Drake's Farm, but she did have time to go to the place just over the ford where she and Johnny Durrell had had their first proper meeting.

As she began to cross the bridge she placed a hand on the smooth iron railing and closed her eyes, letting her palm slide along as she moved forward until she felt the bridge even out under her tread. Then she opened her eyes, turned, and looked down into the crystal clear water beneath her. She let out a short gasp. So lost was she in her memories that the reflection looking back at her came as a shock, for it was not that of the young Eve Armstrong, with wavy hair in plaits and a smooth young face, but that of an old woman, with short white hair, and a face which bore the lines of a full life's journey.

Time, she considered, was cruel. It took your vitality, your youth, your stamina; yet your character, your personality, your very being remained the same. The reflection looking back at her might have been that of an old woman, but the Eve who looked into that reflection felt like the girl she had been at fourteen. A tear dropped into the water below her and was carried away on a journey of its own.

Eve thought back to that last encounter with Connie – more than a decade ago now – and, not for the first time, questioned whether it had been unfair not to put Connie straight on a few matters. The other woman's information on Johnny had been half right. He had been wounded in Korea and he had got married – Eve smiled and wiped away another tear before it could fall – but not to someone desperate for a partner, or at least Eve did not think of herself in that way. It had been on the tip of her tongue to tell Connie that she and Johnny had recently celebrated their golden wedding anniversary, but the other woman had only been interested in her own affairs.

Eve's smile faded as memory caught up with her. It had been five days after Eve's unexpected meeting with Connie when Johnny had collapsed at home and been rushed into hospital. The doctors had examined him and informed Eve that the next forty-eight hours were going to be crucial. She hadn't slept until the third day.

After that Johnny had made steady progress, and on the morning of the sixth day the doctors had told him and Eve that he might return home, provided he took things easy and went back to his doctor for regular checkups.

Eve was sitting next to Johnny's bed. 'You might as well stay where you are whilst we wait for your medication to arrive,' she said. 'You could be here for a while yet; you know what hospitals are like.' She had produced a punnet of strawberries from her bag and handed them to her husband.

Johnny had dipped into the punnet and taken out the biggest, reddest and juiciest strawberry he could find. He sank his teeth into the tip and munched thoughtfully. 'You know, having this scare has made me do a bit of thinking,' he said, and took another bite. 'We've been meaning to go back to Drake's Farm for years, but we've never got round to it. Once I'm fit enough, what say you and me go for a look?'

Eve had smiled at him. 'I think it's a fabulous idea. It must be over fifty years since I last saw that place. What made you think of it?'

Johnny indicated the strawberry he was eating, and proffered the punnet to Eve. She took a couple, removed the stalk from one and popped it into her mouth.

'The strawberries,' he said, when he had swallowed. 'Do you remember the wild ones we used to pick on the lane going to and from school?' Eve nodded. 'These aren't as sweet as those ones – Auntie Bess always vowed and declared that wild strawberries were better than the cultivated kind – but they reminded me of them just the same.'

Eve shrugged her shoulders. 'Well, we'll leave it a

month or so, until you can walk a fair distance comfortably again, and if we get the all clear from Dr Yates we'll plan our trip down memory lane.'

She reached for another strawberry, but stopped short as the fruit suddenly cascaded across the floor. 'Johnny!' she said with some annoyance. 'For goodness' sake, be a bit more careful . . .' She had risen from her seat to collect the fallen berries when she noticed that Johnny had slumped forward, the strawberry he had just chosen crushed in his hand, smudging the clean crisp bedlinen.

'Johnny! Johnny, wake up!' Eve's voice was desperate. She shook his shoulders violently, sobs rising in her throat as she frantically pressed the emergency button above his bed. 'Johnny, please, please . . .' She held his hand to her cheek. 'Don't leave me . . .' The last words came out in a whisper.

Eve continued to stare into the water beneath her, her tears not even breaking the surface as they fell. She had been determined not to dwell on Johnny's death, only to think of the good times they had had here. She turned, and walked on towards the spot where Johnny had first dropped down from a tree behind her all those years ago.

When at last she reached it, she started to crane her neck to see if she could glimpse the farmhouse from where she stood, then shook her head chidingly. No, no, no. She knew that the house would look different. She had received a letter from Auntie Bess, many years ago now, saying that since she and Uncle Reg had moved into the village the farm had changed hands several times, with the newest couple applying for planning permission to convert the shippon into a bungalow.

You'd not recognise the place, Eve dear. Not a farm at all any more, but a vineyard, would you believe . . .

Eve turned and started to make her way back to the road, fishing around in her handbag for her mobile phone. She grimaced. Five missed calls. She was going to get an earful when her daughter caught up with her, but no matter. Eve knew there'd have been a fearful row if Lily had known she was in Devonshire walking down an old sunken lane, but it was her life and she must live it as she saw fit. However, she stopped, scrolled through to her daughter's name and sent a text.

Sorry, won't be long, got caught up in one or two things. I'll be home later on today and I promise I'll ring first thing tomorrow! Love to you all, Mum xxx

She then rang the taxi and asked the driver if he could meet her where he had dropped her off. Slipping her phone back into her bag, she continued on her way.

When she reached the bottom of the lane she saw that the man who had driven her here earlier was holding the back door of his cab open so that she might get in.

'Hello again,' he said, as she plonked herself into the back seat. He closed her door and hurried round to get in the driver's side. Glancing at Eve over his shoulder, he chuckled. 'I thought you'd been and gone off with the fairy folk.'

Eve raised her brows. 'Fairy folk indeed!' This time it was her turn to chuckle. 'I'm afraid I've not been anywhere as exciting as that.'

Bert started the engine and glanced sheepishly at his passenger in his rear-view mirror. 'Do you mind me askin' where you have been? Only it seemed like a road to nowhere. Tell me to mind my own business if I've overstepped the mark.'

Eve smiled, but it seemed to Bert, watching her, that the smile was not directed at him.

'I've been to the best place someone of my age can go,' she said mysteriously.

Bert raised his eyebrows. 'Where's that, then?' he asked.

Eve smiled again as she looked back at the sunken lane. 'I've been for a trip into the past.'